REBELLION'S
FURY

REBELLION'S FURY

FLAMES OF REBELLION BOOK 2

JAY ALLAN

HARPER Voyager
An Imprint of HarperCollinsPublishers

HarperCollins books may be purchased for educational, business, or sales promotional use. For information, please email the Special Markets Department at SPsales@harpercollins.com.

Harper Voyager and design are trademarks of HarperCollins Publishers LLC.

FIRST EDITION

Designed by Paula Russell Szafranski

Map copyright © MMXVII Springer Cartographics LLC

Title page art © DeltaOFF/Shutterstock, Inc.

Library of Congress Cataloging-in-Publication Data has been applied for.

ISBN 978-0-06-256684-3

18 19 20 21 22 LSC 10 9 8 7 6 5 4 3 2 1

CONTENTS

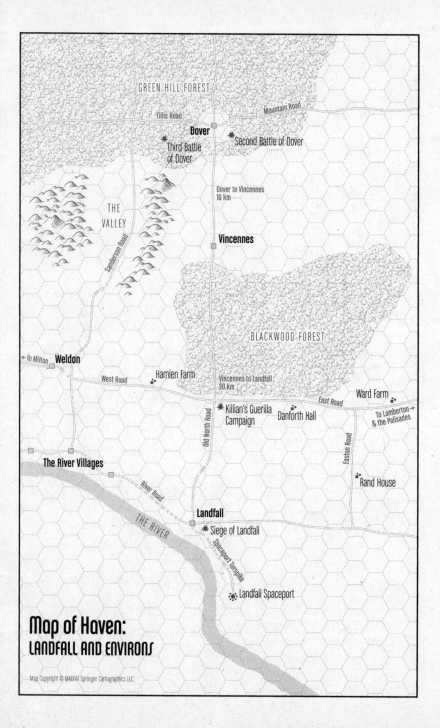

Map of Haven:
LANDFALL AND ENVIRONS

REBELLION'S FURY

CHAPTER 1

"I'm sorry, Alex."

Damian Ward knelt down on the soft grass, feeling the morning dew soak through to his knees. It had been a year to the day since Alexandra Thornton had died on the battlefield outside Dover.

Died because she spared my life . . . killed by my own troops as she tried to escape.

The small graveyard seemed like an odd place to Damian. Burying the dead was an old Earth custom, but one rarely practiced anymore on a crowded, polluted, and largely impoverished planet. A hundred million people had died during the Second Civil War, and whatever traditions interfered with expediency in the disposal of the dead had quickly fallen away amid the apocalyptic hell of that conflict's final years. But the attitudes prevailing on the colony worlds were surprisingly different from those of the home world. Bodies were burned or recycled back in Federal America, but burial had experienced somewhat of a revival on the colonies, perhaps just an effort to differentiate themselves from their so-called lords.

Damian sucked in a deep breath. He wanted to feel like he was fighting to hold back tears. Alex deserved tears. But he had none for her. He mourned her loss, and he felt terrible guilt that she had died because of him. But the rebellion was his mistress now, leaving little feeling for anything, or anyone, else. The infighting, the struggle to keep the army together despite shortages of everything, it all wore him down. And the endless battle to hold off the belief that after almost a year without any hint of federal retribution, the rebellion was already won. Damian knew better than that, but his certainty hadn't prevented his soldiers from leaving en masse when their enlistments expired. Or deserting outright, returning to families they had left and farms that needed tending.

And while he didn't blame them, it still left him preparing for a fight he knew was coming. But how do you make people not used to the realities of war understand the time and distance involved in interstellar conflict? The federals *were* coming, and Haven was far from ready.

The worst thing was that this was a war he had tried his hardest to prevent. But when it came down to it, he knew the Havenites, his people now, hadn't had a choice. Federal America would destroy Haven or, at the very least, change it into a place those who had sacrificed and worked and bled to build the colony wouldn't even recognize. Damian remembered his youth—the terrible conditions, the deprivation, the fear he'd felt when he saw the government security forces moving down the street. And he thought about his life since he'd come here. Life on Haven was completely different from the oppression and squalor most of Earth's population endured. And he would fight to preserve that difference.

Those realizations, though—of what the Havenites had to do, of what Federal America truly was—had cost Damian dearly. He had served in the federal army, fought in the war against the Union and the Hegemony. Indeed, it was his federal service that had changed his life, given him confidence. Even his presence on Haven was something he owed to the army. He had mustered out and settled on the colony world and gained a farm and a real chance at a life, one he'd never have had if he'd remained back on Earth, picking through the garbage in the slum where he'd been born.

He'd joined the army out of desperation, not any particular loyalty to Federal America or desire to serve it. He'd sought only an escape from the poverty and misery, the only one available to someone from his background. Yet he'd found something more. His service had always been a source of pride, something upon which he'd built his own self-worth.

Now that had been stripped from him. He'd seen the brutality of a creature like Robert Semmes. He'd toured the confinement camp in Landfall City, where Semmes had imprisoned the families of those suspected of rebel sympathies. Now the thought of his former service, of fighting for the flag of Federal America, sickened him.

And this is far from over . . .

Because the federals *would* be back. And while the seizure of the orbital platform with its defensive systems intact had protected the planet against any piecemeal invasions the government might launch, when the feds came, they would come in strength. They would destroy or retake the platform, and they would land troops.

Thousands and thousands of troops.

And those soldiers won't be glorified police or internal security bullies in uniforms. They will be regulars. Veterans. Men and women who served in the war. Who served at my side.

Who know how to kill with brutal efficiency.

Against that deadly force, he would be leading a brand-new army. He had been training his rebels for months now, ever since the federals had withdrawn. The victory in the final battle had gained him widespread acclaim, and Havenites had flocked to the banners, enlisting in the nascent army and swelling its ranks. He'd organized the legions of new recruits, and he'd spread his veterans out across the newly formed units, making most of them into officers.

He'd done his best to train his mostly raw soldiers, to prepare them for battle, but what did he know about running an army? He'd been a private when he'd begun his service, and he'd risen gradually to wear a sergeant's stripes, before a moment of battlefield heroism earned him a decoration and a pair of lieutenant's bars. His military career had been successful, distinguished even, but it hardly qualified him for the general's insignia he now wore. And the fact that everyone else seemed to feel he was perfectly capable of pulling it off only made things worse.

Damian had been dreading the return of the federals, almost since the moment the last of them had boarded ship and left nearly a year before. But now time had become an even worse threat than the troops he knew would one day land to try to reconquer Haven. His volunteers were eager, and he'd managed to turn them into something resembling actual soldiers. But they were still farmers and miners and factory workers at heart. As the months passed without any federal threat materializing, they began to lose their fervor, to slip away, to wander back to those farms and jobs.

The provisional congress had passed laws extending the service terms of all Havenite soldiers—and Cal Jacen and the radicals had been screaming from the rafters for him to make examples of those they called deserters—but he'd resisted. He knew his unwillingness to implement harsh measures threatened his army's existence, but he simply wasn't ready to put a bunch of his fellow Havenites against a wall and have them shot, even when they ignored his orders and left the ranks. Some might consider that his weakness, but frankly, he didn't care. He would do anything to win—anything but become what he was fighting against.

"I've been looking all over for you." John Danforth had walked up and stopped a few meters away, standing on the small gravel path that wound its way through the cemetery. "I should have guessed you'd be here. My God, it's been a year already, hasn't it?"

"Already?" Damian rose slowly, turning toward his friend and ally. "It seems an eternity to me, John. I wish the federals would just come. That seems like an odd thing to want, but we're growing weaker now, every month that goes by sapping the readiness of the people. They were fired up after the federals withdrew, but now they think they've won already, and they're starting to argue among themselves about what the future is going to look like, as if the present isn't still happening."

"You're worried about Cal and his Reds, aren't you?"

"I'm worried about a lot of things, John. But yeah, Jacen and his people have got me concerned." Damian had disliked Jacen from the start, but he'd tried to get along with the lawyer and revolutionary firebrand. Jacen and Danforth had worked together for years, and the latter seemed to trust the former. Damian had learned enough politics in this short time to know any internal disputes among the revolutionaries could only lead to disaster if the federals came back, so he held his peace.

But with the man's brazen opportunism, it was getting harder and harder.

Danforth moved his feet, kicking up a few stones from the path. "Cal put as much work into making the rebellion a reality as I did, Damian. I know he can be . . . strident. But he is a true rebel, and he's as devoted to winning Haven's freedom as anyone I've ever met."

Damian exhaled hard. "I don't doubt he's a rebel. But he's a little crazy, too. I'll tell you, John, if he'd been the head of the Guardians and not you, I wouldn't be here. That's a cold fact. And I'm not the only one who feels that way. He's cut from the same cloth as Semmes, and the fact that he's supposedly on our side doesn't change that." Damian looked down at the ground. He wondered if he'd gone too far.

"Cal just gets carried away, Damian. He's not a butcher like Semmes."

Damian just nodded. There was no point in arguing with Danforth. They would never agree on Jacen. He understood Danforth's loyalty to a man who had worked at his side all the years they had planned in the shadows, who had shared the dangers with him. But he trusted his own judgment, and he had little doubt that Jacen would become a problem. If he wasn't *already* a problem. Time would ultimately tell which of them was correct.

"Any progress on recruiting efforts?" Damian asked, changing the subject. "Have the new spots begun airing yet?"

"This morning. On all channels." Danforth was more than one of Haven's rebel leaders. He was one of the planet's wealthiest men, the owner of its largest communications network. He'd used his company cautiously for years, seeking to spread the rebels' message without provoking a federal response. Now, with the feds gone, and with Haven a self-declared independent republic, he'd been far more aggressive in using the network to support the cause.

"Too early to tell if it has had any effect, I guess." Damian shook his head. "Lofty speeches and impassioned pleas don't have the same impact when people aren't scared."

"It's good they aren't scared, though, right?"

"Yes, during peace. But right now they *should* be scared. They should be scared to death."

"That's human nature, my friend," Danforth said, reaching out and putting his hand on Damian's shoulder. "People do everything they can to convince themselves there's nothing to be scared of, and then latch on to that. Sometimes it makes sense, and sometimes it's delusional. But I guarantee you one thing: they *are* scared. It's just not about the feds coming back. It's about whether the crop is going to come in. Whether the child will be healthy. Whether the factory will pay overtime."

"Mundane nonsense."

"*Life*, Damian. They want to live. War—being ready for war—isn't about living. So it's easier for them to just ignore it. Think there are more important things. The key is, at least you and I know better." He looked around. "And consider this: you've accomplished a miracle over the past year. Other than your veterans, our people were a mob when they faced the federals. As much effort as I put into building the Guardians, I didn't have the skill to turn them into soldiers. You did."

"I am proud of them, John. You know that. But I wouldn't call them soldiers—not yet. Fewer than 20 percent of them have seen action. The original Guardians, the men and women who fought at Vincennes and Dover, they're ready. *Maybe*. The training added to their combat experience makes them a capable force. But the others are still raw. For all the drills and the instruction, some of them will throw their weapons down and run when the first shot is fired." Damian frowned, looking down at his feet. He sighed softly.

Danforth looked over at his friend. "I get the feeling that's not what's really troubling you, is it?"

"It's part of it. But I'm also concerned at the rate we're losing them. However good they are—or aren't—they're not career soldiers, John. They're going home. We're losing trained troopers faster than we're recruiting new ones. And too many of them aren't even waiting for their enlistments to run out. They're just going."

"I know." Danforth shook his head. "Cal Jacen was raging about that a couple days ago. He thinks—"

"I know what he thinks. But if you want to take action like that, the first thing you're going to need is a new general." There was a flash of anger in Damian's voice, and a scowl at the renewed mention of Jacen. "I may not be able to ban his Red Flaggers from participating in the new government, but they will never run this army. *Ever*. Not while I'm in command."

"Relax, Damian. I agree with you. I would never suggest you start shooting soldiers, not for missing their families or worrying about their farms. But we do have to find a way to reduce the rate of loss. The troops may convince themselves the fight is over, but as I said, we both know better. And we need them all under arms when the feds come back."

A small wave of frustration hit Damian. "There's something

else, John. And I'm not sure you understand it fully. We don't know what is coming, but I suspect we will be seeing regular line units. Not glorified security guards, not government thugs used to terrorizing helpless mobs. These are battle-hardened soldiers. Veterans of the last war." He paused, looking up and locking his eyes on Danforth's.

"You know I was there, John. The battles of that war were brutal. I still can't get the visions out of my mind. Those troops are career fighters. At Vincennes and Dover, the federals were barely more trained than our forces. It won't be that way this time. They will be vastly superior, both in doctrine and supply. We won't be able to hold Landfall. Not a chance. We won't be able to win a pitched battle. Our only chance will be to fight a guerilla war—a long, brutal conflict. We won't be able to protect civilians, not many of them, at least. Thousands of Havenites, perhaps most of the population, will live in occupied areas, most likely under martial law. What will our soldiers do when they are cut off from their families? What if the federal commander is no different than Semmes? What if it *is* Semmes again?"

Damian took a breath, holding his gaze on his friend for a few seconds before continuing. "I know you had the best intentions when you worked so hard toward this goal, John . . . but I wonder if you really considered all that would happen." He paused again. "I wonder if we're truly ready for the conflict you started."

CHAPTER 2

Senator Alistair Semmes sat behind his palatial desk, staring coldly at the younger man sitting across from him. His visitor was a disgraced soldier, an arrogant fool, a liability. Anyone who'd dealt with Semmes before would have been virtually certain the senator would send the imbecile away, never to be seen again, without so much as a second thought. And they would have been right, save for one inconvenient fact. The man staring back nervously across the desk was Senator Semmes's son.

Senator Semmes had a public reputation as a magnanimous man, a champion of worthy causes and a guardian of the people, but that was all a carefully constructed fiction, one that had served his purposes admirably for decades. The scenes of the dedicated public servant—delivering food packages to needy constituents, roaring with righteous indignation at one injustice or another, cutting ribbons at small business openings—were carefully choreographed, simply one of the less pleasant requirements of the job. But now the doors were closed, the cameras nowhere near—and the real Semmes scowled out of hard eyes, in every measure the arrogant, corrupt, cold-blooded autocrat who had clawed his way to the highest levels of political power.

"It is time, Robert, for your redemption. For too long you have been the shame of this family, your failures casting shadows on the achievements of your brothers . . . and even upon me. Now you shall have your chance to put such regrettable incidents behind you. The preparations have been long, but soon you will leave for Alpha-2. You will crush the rebellion, my son, whatever it takes."

Robert Semmes sat quietly, nodding respectfully. He knew better than to offer his father anything but the gravest respect. The elder Semmes wanted his children to be successful, functioning cogs in the family's political machine. But he was fairly certain the senator would prefer a noble corpse to a live son who disgraced the family and damaged his own extensive interests. He'd been given many chances, but he was clearly at the bottom of that well now, and he had no doubt that the opportunity he was being handed was very likely the last one he would see.

"Yes, sir. I am ready."

"This is the second time I have cleaned up one of your messes, Robert." The senator's voice was cold, and Robert could hear the constrained anger behind it. "And this time was *far* more costly than the first. Obtaining this command for you was very expensive, both in currency and in political capital. You are my son, and you are a Semmes, but there are limits to my reach . . . and my patience." There was no emotion, no fatherly love in the older man's words, just a relentless coldness. He might as easily have been discussing an overdue debt with a business associate. "Do not fail again."

Robert stared back across the desk, struggling to stay calm, to hold his father's gaze. He was angry, consumed with rage, but he dared not let it show. He'd taken much of the blame for the debacle on Alpha-2, but in his mind *he* had been the wronged party. He'd been sent to the colony world in command of troops, but under the authority of the federal observer. And Asha Stanton had stymied him at every turn. She and that damnable Wells. He and Stanton had been sent to undo the damage the governor's weakness had caused, but she had allowed Wells to influence her decisions again and again, holding him back from taking the actions he'd deemed necessary.

If I had been the last word there, the rebellion would have been stillborn . . . drowned in blood . . .

"Do you hear me, Robert?"

"Yes, sir. I understand completely." His voice shifted, becoming colder. "I will not fail, Father. I will destroy the rebel army, and I will restore a respect for law and order in the colonists." There were images in his head as he spoke, scenes of devastation, of mass executions. The Havenites, as they had the audacity to call themselves, had compelled him to crawl before the father he despised. He would make them pay for that. He owed himself that much.

"I'm sorry, Everett, but there is nothing I can do. Old Alistair Semmes put all his weight behind the appointment of his son to command the expeditionary force. I'm afraid this has gone well beyond my level of influence. I have done all I can to help you, for old friendship, but I dare go no further. Not in the current environment." Johannes Gravis sat on one end of a plush leather couch, his eyes fixed on the crackling fire in the hearth, as much to avoid Wells's gaze as anything else.

The office was luxurious, as befitted a senator, though it didn't match the obscene opulence possessed by a power broker like Semmes. Any senator enjoyed a lifestyle that was comfortable beyond the wildest dreams of the normal citizens of Federal America, but even among such a lofty group, there was stratification. Gravis was a junior member of the august body, and his opportunities for personal enrichment and abuse of power hadn't come close to those of men many years his senior.

Wells had helped a young Gravis get his start in politics, giving him his first appointment years before. The protégé had long since eclipsed his mentor, though—having shaken the touch of idealism that held Wells back in the process—while still retaining some level of appreciation for what the man had done for him.

"Johannes, Robert Semmes is a . . ." Wells let his words trail off. He was horrified at the thought of what an unrestrained General Semmes would do on Alpha-2, but Gravis had been a good friend to him since he'd returned from his failure as the colony's governor—just about the only one he'd had left. Because even though Everett Wells had helped a number of his peers early in their careers, Gravis was the only one who'd shown something resembling gratitude.

The others couldn't run quickly enough.

He knew he was political poison. Even Gravis hadn't dared do more than appoint him chief of staff of internal operations, declaring Wells's thoughts of another independent political appointment "quite impossible."

Wells didn't know if he'd be able to rehabilitate his career . . . and he didn't know if he cared. He hadn't enriched himself as aggressively as most would have in his previous positions, but he had a bit socked away. That plus his pay as a member of Gravis's staff ensured him a comfortable living, far beyond what anyone in Federal America—outside government—could hope for. He knew he should be grateful, that he should just keep his head down and stay out of trouble. And he would, if it wasn't for Haven.

Are you that concerned about the people there? Or is it Violetta?

Wells's only daughter had sympathized with the rebels, and when he'd returned to Earth, she'd refused to go with him, instead openly joining the revolutionary forces. It was a public embarrassment to him, of course, just one more weight stacked upon the perception that his softness had allowed things to go as far as they had. None of that mattered to him, not really. But the thought of his only daughter, who'd grown up sheltered and privileged, alone on that world amid the disorder and chaos of rebellion, ate at him. There were no communications between Alpha-2 and Earth, and he had heard nothing from her since the two had embraced a final time in the light morning rain at the spaceport the day he'd left. What would happen to her when Semmes's soldiers landed? When they crushed the rebellion and punished the people, as Wells was certain Semmes would do with brutal finality?

"Everett, I know you are troubled by all that happened on Alpha-2 . . ." Gravis hesitated. "And I can't imagine how upsetting it is to think of Violetta there," he continued as if reading Wells's thoughts. "But she *is* an adult, and she made her choice. I realize a father can never escape from such emotions, but you have to look to your own situation now. If you persist in attempting to interfere in the Alpha-2 pacification operations, you will make it impossible for me to protect you." He paused again, clearly uncomfortable at being so blunt with an old friend. "No one is going to listen to you now, Everett, and especially not about Alpha-2. Do you want to end up with nothing? Or worse? Take my advice, old friend. Lay low. Don't get involved in any of this. You're not going to change anything. You'll just get yourself hurt."

Wells nodded, a somber look on his face. "I know, Johannes, but you know what is going to happen. Semmes is a psychopath. Thousands are going to die."

"I sympathize as well, Everett. But the colonists did nothing to aid those on Earth advocating for restraint. Their unwillingness to work with you led directly to the assignment of the federal observer. Then, as soon as they gained temporary hegemony over the planet, they declared independence. There was a faction in the senate still pushing for negotiations, but the declaration gutted it. Everyone ran for cover. No one in the senate—*no one*—will speak out against military action now, and most are advocating for quick retribution, which Robert Semmes *will* ensure. The Alphans made their beds, Everett. You can't change that, but you *can* refrain from utterly destroying yourself."

Wells sat for a moment, silent. Then he turned and looked over at his friend. "You're right, Johannes. I know you're right. And I am grateful for all you have done for me."

He nodded, and even forced something of a smile. But beneath the facade, he was as restless as ever.

Everett Wells walked into the room and closed the door behind him. It was dark, just a hint of light coming through the heavily tinted windows. The hotel offered lodging, but even more important, it sold discretion, which was a rare and expensive commodity in Federal America. It catered primarily to those fairly highly placed who needed somewhere to bring their more junior associates . . . or any others who caught their fancy.

It was an odd place for a meeting, at least one with no amorous intent, and especially a tête-à-tête with someone he'd generally considered his adversary. But when he'd gotten Asha Stanton's message, it had piqued his curiosity enough to come and see what she wanted to say. Stanton wasn't someone he admired or agreed with on very much, but she wasn't an irredeemable monster like Semmes, either.

Besides, he had few enough prospects, and the fact that anyone actually wanted to see him was refreshing. He even suspected Gravis, as steadfast as he'd been, would be just as happy if he disappeared.

"Thank you for coming, Mr. Wells." Stanton was seated in a chair in the far corner, mostly obscured by shadows. She'd used the correct form of address, though Wells winced at it anyway. A governor's title was given for life, and the individual holding it was so addressed, even after his or her term had ended. But Wells had the distinction of having been formally removed for cause, and the designation as a governor was one of the things that had cost him. It didn't mean anything, not really, and yet it meant everything.

Because I'm an old fool.

"Observer Stanton," he replied, trying to hide the resentment he felt that she had, at least, kept *her* title after arriving back on Earth. Stanton had also returned in failure, and she'd had the unenviable task of explaining to the assembled senate just how the rebels on Alpha-2 had managed to seize the orbital platform and compel her to accept a shameful truce, one the senators wasted no time in repudiating. Still, she had managed to come out of the whole thing in marginally better shape than Wells. *I wonder how much of her family's money that took?*

"Please, Mr. Wells, I know we haven't agreed on everything, but I believe we have common interests now." She paused. "If you will recall, I urged you to work with me on Alpha-2, yet you resisted. I did not come there to cause your disgrace, and I made that clear from the start."

"You did make such overtures, Observer. All you required was that I go back on all I believe in. Those colonists are people. Human beings, first and foremost. They deserved better treatment than you gave them."

"People? What does that mean? Have you seen how the average citizen in Federal America lives? Not up close, I'd wager, because you've never lived that way. Have you gone hungry, Mr. Wells? Have you worked a twelve-hour shift only to come home to your hovel and eat a few moldy pieces of bread before you collapsed from exhaustion and hoped you'd be able to wake up tomorrow just to do it all over again? The world is what it is, and unless you have some master plan to change it, I suggest you come down off your high horse. If you had worked with me, you might have done a few things you didn't want to do, sure, but perhaps we could have stopped the rebellion in its tracks. Now what will happen? Semmes will return, with real troops, and he will crush those people like none of them have ever imagined, not in their worst fears. So consider *that* before you salve your own conscience by labeling me a soulless martinet."

Wells just stood where he was, silent. He wanted to lash back, to

accuse her of unfeeling ruthlessness, but he realized much of what
she said was right. For all his efforts to find a peaceful solution to
the unrest on Alpha-2, things were worse now than he'd thought
possible. And he had no doubt what she said about Semmes would
prove to be true.

"Enough of this nonsense," Stanton finally said. "Sit." She gestured toward a chair near the one she occupied. "Please, Mr. Wells.
Sit."

Wells walked across the room and glided into the plush arm-
chair. "There may be a bit of truth to some of what you say." It
wasn't a sweeping overture, but it was as far as he could force himself to go.

"That is a start." She leaned forward slightly. "I didn't ask you
to come here so we could exchange recriminations. Nor do I have
any brilliant strategy to prevent the nightmare about to overwhelm
Alpha-2." She took a deep breath, clearly hesitating. Then she said,
"But I believe we may be able to intervene in certain ways, to aid
the colonists."

Wells hadn't known what to expect when he'd gotten Stanton's
invitation, but the words that had just come out of her mouth had
never crossed his mind.

"*Help* the rebels?" he asked, his voice reflexively dropping in
volume as he looked around the room. He felt a wave of panic, a
sudden fear that Stanton was setting him up somehow.

"You needn't worry, Mr. Wells. I swept the room thoroughly
when I first arrived. No one is listening to us."

"That is fine . . . assuming I'm willing to believe you." He glared
at Stanton.

"I have no reason to attempt to entrap you, Mr. Wells. My family was able to spend enough to salvage at least a portion of my
career, though I'm not sure there is enough bribe money to get
me to the senate now. For whatever it is worth to you in terms of
shared disgrace, I am the great disappointment of my family. We

are wealthy, sure, but what is wealth in Federal America without
political power? I was the one who was supposed to push us forward
into those hallowed halls. Now, at best, I can hope for a middling
career, one unimportant job after another . . . and the Stantons are
already looking to the next generation for our great step forward."

"My sympathies, Observer." The thought had begun almost sar-
castic in tone, but then he quickly realized he *did* empathize with
her, at least a bit. Stanton was corrupt and power-hungry, but she
was restrained, at least as Federal America's enforcers were concerned. And she was right. For all his efforts to find a peaceful
solution, the colonists had refused to meet him halfway. It would
have been better had he never been sent there at all.

She was waving her hand as if dismissing his last remark. "I did
not ask you to come here so we could trade insincere—or quasi-
sincere—reassurances. I am what I am, and you are what you are.
Yet I think we have more in common than you allow for. I have
thought that from the beginning, but you were too focused on rev-
eling in your own sense of moral superiority. Well, enough of that.
We find ourselves in considerable danger, Mr. Wells, and that is
something we share. Robert Semmes is no friend to either of us. In
fact, he has loudly and aggressively blamed both of us for preventing him from quelling the rebellion on Alpha-2."

"You won't get any argument from me about Semmes. He is one
of the vilest human beings I have ever met."

"Have you considered that he feels the same way about you?
And have you thought about what will happen if he is successful on
Alpha-2? If he returns in victory, with military glory to add to his
family's already substantial power base? He is a vengeful man, one
who does not forget grudges."

"Are you worried about your career again, Observer?"

"I will not defend my desire to salvage something of my position,
Mr. Wells. You may embrace squalid martyrdom, but I do not. Yet
this all goes far beyond that, I am afraid. If Semmes returns trium-

phant, he might manage to generate enough support in the senate to charge you with treason for your part in allowing the rebellion to escalate. The cost of the expedition to pacify Alpha-2 is already astronomical—meaning less money lining their own pockets. They will be amenable to finding scapegoats."

"And your proposal is that I actually commit treason to prevent being accused of it?"

"Treason is defined by those who win, Mr. Wells. I suspect you know enough of the actual history of the last Civil War to realize the truth of that. I don't care about Alpha-2, and while there are some moral limits to what measures I myself would employ to pacify the planet, I would be perfectly content to walk away and allow things to take their course . . . if such a result did not create an enemy too powerful to defeat: a psychopath like Robert Semmes returning as a hero." She glared at Wells. "And you, for all your lectures and your moralizing, if you have the chance to intervene, to prevent the holocaust you know Semmes will inflict, will you take it? Or are your words as empty as your prospects?"

Wells just stared back at her silently. He wanted to argue, to disagree, but she'd hit the mark with her words. Thousands would die on Alpha-2, and they wouldn't all be rebels. Semmes's violence would know no restraint, and innocent blood would flood the streets. And more important . . .

Violetta is there.

"Very well," Wells said, fatigue and resignation in his tone. "How can we affect events on Alpha-2?"

CHAPTER 3

"I'm afraid *Vagabond* is a bit inadequate as an ambassador's transport, Your Excellency. Unfortunately, there is nowhere more comfortable where you can strap in for the jump." Sasha Nerov sat in the captain's chair on *Vagabond*'s cramped bridge, her upper body twisted, looking behind her at her unexpected guest. She'd been back and forth from Haven to Earth three times, taking advantage of the withdrawal of Federal America's fleet from the Epsilon Eridani system to run weapons back to the rebel forces. She'd been shocked this last time, when the agents of the Eurasian Union had approached her with the idea of carrying their representative to meet with the rebel leadership.

"Not at all, Captain Nerov. You have been a most gracious hostess, and I must say, an impressive captain. I feel as though I am in very good hands on this journey." Andrei Kutusov was strapped into one of *Vagabond*'s bridge stations, staring intently in her direction.

Nerov suppressed a laugh. The Eurasian diplomat clearly considered himself quite charming, and he wasn't trying very hard to hide his interest in her. He'd been flirting, or something close to it, almost from the moment he'd boarded the ship. She didn't return the sentiment—not really, at least. The last thing she needed was a foreign diplomat twenty years her senior in her bed. But she also realized the potential utility of getting at least moderately closer to him. He'd already commented twice on the tight leather pants she wore on board, and she couldn't see any compelling reason to explain to him that she wore them because they fit neatly under her survival suit. *Let him think I'm trying to entice him.*

Besides, I do look great in them.

"I am grateful for your forbearance, Your Excellency. I was quite taken by surprise when your government approached me about providing transport to Haven."

"Your associates have performed well to date, Captain Nerov, and we decided it was time to extend some diplomatic feelers. To be clear, I do not want to overstate the meaning of my visit. We will, of course, continue to provide you with supplies and armaments as long as you are able to transport them, but direct intervention is not something I am authorized to offer at this time."

"Certainly, Your Excellency. I wouldn't expect anything more. As I said, I was surprised that the overture occurred at all. I think you will find Haven a very interesting place . . . and I am sure President Danforth and General Ward will be delighted to meet you."

"I look forward to comparing the men to their reputations—"

"Captain, we're getting scanner readings. Multiple contacts, moving toward the jump point." Griff Daniels was Nerov's first officer, and one of the three members of *Vagabond*'s crew on the bridge. "They're about two hundred thousand kilometers behind us."

Nerov's body tensed. Her last two trips had been without event, with not a sign of a federal ship, neither in the Sol system nor in Epsilon Eridani. Now she felt like she had in her smuggling days when the scanners picked up a contact, only worse. She'd never doubted the federals would invade Haven again, and right then, somehow, she knew that nightmare was about to begin.

Two hundred thousand kilometers wasn't that far away, not in terms of space travel. *Vagabond* should have picked them up farther out. Which meant they had been employing stealth technology. And if they decided they wanted to be seen, that wasn't a good sign.

It meant they thought they had nothing to fear.

"Let's kick up the thrusters, Griff. Hiding isn't going do us any good this time. If they're heading to Haven, we've got to get there first."

"Yes, Captain."

Nerov turned back toward Kutusov. "I'm sorry, Your Excellency, but we're going to have to increase our acceleration beyond the abilities of our dampeners to compensate. As I said, I'm afraid *Vagabond* isn't outfitted for comfort."

"Please don't worry, Captain Nerov. I assure you I will be fine. Do what you must to safeguard the ship."

"Thank you, Your Excellency." Nerov turned back quickly, before the smile she was holding back burst past her control and onto her lips. She'd suspected the ambassador's infatuation would have its uses, and that was proving to be the case. She further suspected he'd be a whining, spoiled pain in the ass, complaining about everything . . . *if* he wasn't trying to impress her with his toughness and charm.

Though if you're really trying to lure me in, you have to do a better job of keeping the fear out of your voice.

Let's see how impressed I am after we get out of this jam.

"Full thrust now, Griff. Let's get out far enough to jump."

"Engaging now, Captain."

Nerov took a deep breath, exhaling hard as the g forces slammed into her chest. *Vagabond* was accelerating at a little over 6g, though the dampeners made it feel more like 3g. Still, feeling three times your body weight pressing down on you was no picnic.

"Lock in jump coordinates, Griff. Calculate earliest jump point exceeding base safety parameters." The density of particulate matter in space dramatically increased the chance of catastrophic jump failure, the primary reason why ships traveled to the outer reaches of a solar system via regular thrust before making a jump to their destination. This time, though, they had to risk it.

"Jump locked in, Captain. Time to baseline, one minute, ten seconds, assuming current acceleration level is maintained."

"Very well. Hold acceleration." She took another look at the scanner. There were nine ships there now, all apparently broadcasting jamming signals with impressive strength. Which only confirmed her thinking.

Military.

Nerov knew the terms of the treaty that had ended the last war between the superpowers. No discharge of weapons within the Sol system, not without first obtaining clearance from both of the other governments. But a treaty provision was one thing, reassuring but far less than an absolute guarantee. Nerov didn't intend to stick around long enough to find out just how far the federals would push it, especially since they *had* to know she'd been running guns to the Havenites.

"Ready for jump in thirty seconds." Daniels's voice was low-pitched, gravelly.

"Just lean back, Your Excellency. Relax. You might feel some strange sensations when we transition out of normal space, but that's nothing to worry about. Time will pass . . . oddly. It will only seem like a few moments before we reemerge into Epsilon Eridani, though several days will have elapsed in normal space."

"I understand, Captain." The diplomat was clearly still trying to hide his fear, but with no greater success than he had before.

"Commencing jump . . . now!"

"**Status update?**" **Josh** Garabrant walked across the control room, balancing a large cup of coffee and a pastry in one hand, a tablet and a stack of data chips in the other. He looked like he was about to tumble over, but he managed to keep his balance and glide right into one of the workstation chairs.

"Update? You've asked me that on every shift change for six months, Josh. And what have I said every time? No contacts. You know why there are no contacts? Because there are never any contacts. No ship has come to this system in almost a year, except for *Vagabond* twice. And neither of those times was on my shift." Kip Claren stood up, gathering his personal items into a small satchel. "And do you know what you will report to your relief? No contacts."

"I think you've been up here too long, my friend." Garabrant flashed a smile at his comrade. "Somebody has to keep watch. One of these days something *will* show up on that scanner."

"Do you think? I've been hearing about the federals coming back for a year now. Where are they? When are we going to accept the fact that we're free, and we're on our own, cut off from Earth, from the other colonies? We wanted freedom, and that's just what we got. We're alone. All by ourselves in the universe."

Garabrant could hear a touch of resentment in the other man's voice. He'd long suspected Claren's support of the rebellion was at best lukewarm, at least in regard to the idea of total independence. He'd almost suggested a transfer for Claren to the base commander, but there weren't a dozen people on all of Haven who knew how to operate the orbital station's scanners. Claren was a malcontent, a complainer, sure, but Garabrant doubted he was a true federal loyalist.

"Still, we have to keep an eye out. Just in—"

Garabrant's head snapped around as the alarm bells suddenly sounded. He reached out to his controls, his arm pushing the precariously perched cup off the workstation, splashing black coffee all over the deck. Claren jumped, escaping all but a few drops of the coffee. He looked over at Garabrant, clearly unnerved by the alarm.

"Command, this is scanner control. We've got something coming into the system."

"Acknowledged, scanner control. Start your track."

Two lamps on the outer wall snapped on, casting a yellowish glow across the room as the station went to alert status.

"Commencing track, Command. We're getting something. Single contact, course directly toward Haven."

"Acknowledged, scanner control. Report mass and energy output data when available."

"Command . . ." Garabrant stared at the screen on his workstation. "Hold," he added as he focused on the data streaming in. "It's *Vagabond*, Command. We just picked up her beacon."

"Very well, scanner control. I'll cancel the alert."

"Attention, Haven base. Attention, Haven base." Nerov's voice blasted out of every comm unit.

"We read you, *Vagabond*. This is Lieutenant Garabrant in scanner control. Welcome home."

He leaned back, his eyes darting to the floor as his foot slid on the spilled coffee. It would take almost twenty seconds for his message to reach *Vagabond*, and as long for a signal to return. There was nothing to do in the interim but wait.

Forty seconds later, "Haven base, listen carefully, and retransmit everything I say to General Ward. We have just jumped from Sol. There is a fleet forming there, federal forces organizing for some kind of operation. It can only be the invasion we've been expecting. I don't know if they'll be here in two hours or two days, but it looks like they're coming, and I'd bet they're here sooner rather than later."

Garabrant snapped from his slouched position, suddenly feeling the tension in every muscle in his body. Even after his lectures to Claren, his admonishments about not taking the threat seriously, as he'd sat at his station every shift, he had never actually expected to detect any hostile forces. Now the reality of it closed in on him. He was scared shitless.

"Lieutenant, forward that entire communiqué to army headquarters on the planet and to President Danforth. And send an acknowledgment to Captain Nerov." The duty officer's voice left little doubt that she, too, was shaken by Nerov's words.

"Acknowledged." He reached out and sent the transmission as he'd been directed. Then he looked around the small room and saw Claren's silent, motionless form standing against the wall. There were just the two of them, and suddenly he felt very alone.

"Looks like the yellow alert is still on," Claren said, gesturing toward the blinking lamp.

"My guess is it'll go red long before we see green again." He reached out to the controls, flipping on the comm unit. "Captain Nerov, this is Haven base acknowledging receipt of your transmission. Your report has been forwarded to the appropriate authorities as requested."

He paused for a few seconds, taking a deep breath and swallowing hard. Then he added, "Thanks for the warning, *Vagabond*."

Nerov sat quietly in her chair on the bridge, deep in thought. She gave a silent thanks to whatever gods watched over spacers that Kutusov had been shaken up enough by the transit that he finally left the bridge and retired to his bed.

Her bed. Though not the way she suspected the diplomat had hoped. She'd given him her quarters for the trip. *Vagabond* wasn't exactly outfitted to carry guests, and certainly not diplomats with inflated opinions of their importance. But she knew any help the Union might provide to a Haven Republic struggling to maintain its independence could be the difference between survival and the almost unimaginably unpleasant—for her and the other rebel leaders, at least—alternative. Her quarters were the only remotely comfortable lodgings on the ship, and she figured it wouldn't kill her to bunk with the boys for the trip back from Earth. Bonding with the crew was always a worthwhile exercise, and she suspected she'd been more aloof than usual since revolution had broken out. Her people had all stayed with her when she'd signed on to support the rebellion, despite the fact that they'd joined *Vagabond*'s crew as smugglers, dedicated to personal gain and not to fighting for a cause.

Hopefully, Kutusov found her cabin pleasant, and if he worked himself into a better mood fantasizing that there was more to the offer of her quarters than simple courtesy, so much the better. She wasn't above a little harmless flirting if it helped the cause. But that's all it was ever going to be, and the pompous Russian was going to spend his time in there alone.

She watched as Haven grew on her display. The planet had moved from a tiny dot to a sphere perhaps a centimeter across. She'd jumped about as far in-system as she dared, but it was still more than a day to the planet.

It didn't matter, not really. She'd already sent the warning, and she knew Danforth and Ward would do what had to be done. Assuming anything *could* be done. Nerov was a realist, perhaps even verging on the pessimistic. She'd often wondered if the Havenites had any real chance to win this struggle, and her doubts had only grown one evening after she and Damian had talked long into the night. The commander of the army of Haven had succumbed to fatigue, to familiarity—and perhaps to one brandy too many—and he'd told her what he really thought. It had been sobering, to say the least, to hear that the man in charge of the defense—the war hero almost universally worshipped as the planet's great hope—expected to lose.

He would try, though. Fight like hell. But his concerns only reinforced her realization that her adopted planet faced a grim trial. And even if the Havenites won, Nerov knew not all of her comrades would see the end. Defeat would be disaster, utter and complete, but even victory would claim its blood price.

She allowed herself a brief thought, verging on a hope, that she might live to see a free and prosperous Haven . . . and if that was not to be, she'd already decided on one thing.

She had no wish to survive defeat.

CHAPTER 4

"Still nothing. It has been three days since *Vagabond* landed, almost four since the original transmission of the warning. Are you certain you saw an invasion fleet? Perhaps it was something else. Is it possible you were mistaken, Captain?"

Damian watched nervously as Nerov glared back at Cal Jacen. *Vagabond*'s captain didn't like the radical revolutionary. She disliked him even more than Damian himself did. Indeed, she'd told Damian straight out that, back in her days as a paid smuggler bringing in arms, she'd have put a bullet in the bastard's head if John Danforth hadn't intervened. He didn't doubt her for a second, and part of him wished she'd done it. Jacen was trouble, and Damian was sure it would get worse before things were done.

"Yes, Mr. Jacen, I am sure. You can believe me or not. Or you can go out back and—"

"Captain Nerov is sure," Damian said firmly, interrupting whatever, no doubt more pointed, comment the former smuggler had been ready to hurl back. "I have total confidence in her report, and we will act accordingly." He stared over at Jacen, his eyes almost daring the hotheaded rebel to challenge him. Jacen was a member of the Haven Congress, and he'd acted more than once like that gave him the right to tell Damian what to do. The commander of the rebel—or, by the premature proclamation of the congress, *Haven*—army had a less volatile personality than Nerov, but in his own way, he'd been crystal clear what he thought of any effort by Jacen to order him around. Jacen tended to give him leeway, probably out of fear of the famous warrior, though Damian was fairly certain Nerov was the likelier of the two to shove a blade between the loudmouth lawyer's ribs.

"There is no time for arguments here. I have made myself clear for the past year. The federals have always been coming, and for all the premature celebrations and proclamations, *this* is when we endure our true trial. What has come before, the fighting at Vincennes and Dover, the detainment camps, the executions . . . all of that was just the beginning. The federals will never let us go, especially not now that we've given them no alternative save to fight or accept full independence. If we want that freedom that was so proudly declared, we're going to have to fight for it. And we're going to have to fight harder than any of you have imagined."

The room was silent, everyone present looking at Damian. Even Jacen was still, his eyes focused on Ward.

Damian turned toward Danforth. "John, can you arrange a planetwide broadcast for me tomorrow morning?"

"Of course, Damian. It will go out on all entertainment and news channels, and on the information networks, as well. I think we can get you in front of 90 percent of the population."

"Good. Let's set it for 10:00 A.M."

"What are you going to say?"

Damian paused, stifling a sigh. "I'm going to try to rally the population. I'm going to see how many of our trained personnel I can persuade to leave their farms and families once more and come back to the colors."

"You're going to beg deserters to return? How can we let those who abandoned the cause come back to their positions? They showed themselves to be disloyal, and we should punish them as an example to others."

Danforth was squirming in his chair, looking like he was about to say something to Jacen. But Damian replied first.

"Shut up, Jacen," the general snapped. "I've listened to about as much of your nonsense as I'm going to take. Do you know what is coming here? Have you ever faced a federal soldier, a real front-line trooper, equipped with exos that quadruple normal strength, connected to the command net by a communications network you couldn't even imagine?"

He panned his gaze around the room before landing it once again on Jacen. "Have you ever seen a tank? Not in a museum or a display, but coming at you through the mud, laser-targeted autocannons blazing away as it advances? Have you ever fought in a *war*, Jacen? Not a few pitched battles against glorified riot cops, but actual, full-on war? Or do you believe radical speeches and endless talk can win our freedom?"

Damian shook his head, an angry scowl on his face. "I didn't want to be part of this rebellion. I told anyone who would listen that this was going to be a cataclysm the likes of which none of you are prepared to face. But no one listened, and now we find ourselves exactly where I said we'd be. I'm not here to say I told you so—what's done is done. And what's more, we *will* fight, and we *will* resist the federals with the last of our strength. I will do everything I can to see our forces through this battle. But let me make this clear. We need every man and every woman we can get. Trained, untrained, experienced, inexperienced. If we are to prevail, it will take everything we have, and the sacrifices of thousands of Havenites. Including those who returned home without leave."

He turned and stared again at Jacen. "There will be no harassment of *any* Havenite. We cannot use the tactics of those we overthrew. If we do, why would anyone fight for our cause, much less die for it?" He paused, his eyes still boring into Jacen's. "If I find you interfering with my soldiers in any way, I promise you, you have never been as sorry as you will be then. Do you understand me?"

Jacen shied back, clearly intimidated at Damian's uncharacteristically hostile words, but he rallied enough courage to respond. Barely. "I am a member of the Haven Congress, General. You cannot threaten me."

Damian moved closer, his face perhaps ten centimeters from Jacen's. "Do . . . you . . . un . . . der . . . stand . . . me?" he said slowly, emphasizing each syllable in turn.

Jacen's face was pale, and the revolutionary seemed indignant. But then he answered simply, meekly, "Yes. I understand."

Damian turned around and walked back toward his chair. He was unhappy with himself for allowing so much anger to show. Jacen was trouble, he reminded himself, a dangerous enemy. Scaring him now would buy some time, but in the end, it only increased the chance of problems down the road. He had no doubt the revolutionary was a petty man, one who would harbor a grudge. But right now he didn't care.

One step at a time. One day at a time. You have a hundred problems to deal with before Jacen.

Damian sat at his desk, enjoying the warmth of the fire in the hearth, at least for a few moments. He smiled, at the crackling flames, at all of the half-dozen small comforts he'd found waiting for him when he got home. Ben Withers had resumed his place as a soldier a year past, when Damian had reluctantly joined the fight and taken command of the rebel forces. Withers had served since then as his chief's loyal aide, reprising, after a fashion, the role he'd held six years before, during the war against the Eurasians and the Hegemony. But when he saw that Damian had come back to the farm, he'd donned his other hat, that of a civilian manager and valet of sorts, and among other things, he'd seen that the fire was lit and the library's brandy decanter was filled.

Damian was grateful for the fire, and he leaned back, allowing the waves of heat to radiate into his back. There was a knot there, partially from exertion, but mostly from stress, and the dry heat from the native cedar was almost like a magic tonic. His eyes caught the crystal decanter full of amber liquid, but he left it where it was. He'd never been much of a drinker before, and he suspected it would be a long time indeed before he allowed anything to interfere with his judgment.

He'd been staying in Landfall, in the room he'd had set up near headquarters, but something had called him back to the farm tonight. It was inconvenient, and perhaps it didn't make much sense. It had been late by the time he'd arrived, and he had to leave early to make his address. But the calling hadn't been one born of logic. This farm, the house he'd designed and built himself, was his home, the only real one he'd ever known, and though he'd lived there for just five years, he'd realized it had grown on him immensely in that time.

It was the place he'd come to retire from war, yet war had found him again. He would have been happy to spend the rest of his life there, monitoring crop yields and spending quiet nights reading in front of the fire. But that wasn't to be, at least not now. He knew it might be a long time before he saw the farm again, if he ever did, and one last night there didn't seem like too much to ask.

He knew things would happen quickly when the federals arrived. They would take, or destroy, the orbital platform, and Damian somehow had to make sure it was the latter. Providing the federals with an intact station would only add to his problems.

Then the government forces would land and, unless he was very wrong, they would take the capital, almost without a fight. His troopers had no real chance in a battle in the open, and commit-

ting to a house-to-house defense of the capital would not only reduce Haven's largest city to rubble, it would tie the bulk of his army
to a single win-or-lose proposition—and there was little doubt they
would lose such a battle. Whatever chance his people had was
based not on quick victories, but on surviving. There was no easy
path to success that he could see. If he could drag it out, though,
fight a protracted, bloody, agonizing conflict, perhaps—just perhaps—he could wear the federal authorities down. The war would
cost them a hundred times what it did Haven. Five hundred.
Every soldier, every weapon, every round of ammunition, had to
be shipped from Earth. To that end, the path was clear: the chance
for victory lay not in *defeating* the federal armies, but in avoiding
the destruction of his own forces for long enough that it made the
war untenable. Federal America could not sustain a large force in
action forever. As long as he had an army in the field, the rebellion
would survive.

He looked over at the corner of his desk, at a small cube of high-
density plastic. He reached over, grabbed it, and pulled it close to
his face. He sat quietly, staring at the platinum medallion inside. It
was a lump of metal in the shape of a starburst, attached to a blue
silk strip of fabric, nothing more. But it represented a moment in his
life, one that had, until recently, been the proudest.

He still couldn't remember exactly what had gone through his
head, what had driven him to lead his shattered platoon forward, to
seize the crucial spot on the battlefield, and to hold it for six hours,
against everything the enemy could throw at his people. He would
never forget the soldiers who'd served with him that day, nor the
ones he left behind there, the half of his platoon that died on that
ridge.

He still had the nightmares. That was something he knew he'd
take to his grave. He remembered the cold dead faces staring back
at him. He knew he'd always carry the scars of his service with him,
but he'd never imagined that the pride, the sense of accomplish-

ment he'd brought with him into retirement, would be stripped from him. Now he looked at his decoration, and he wondered what he had fought for. His comrades, of course, but what else? What had any of them really achieved? Furthering the interests of a corrupt, oppressive government, fighting rivals that were just as bad as it was?

He felt a wave of anger, resentment at the rebellion, for stripping him of the simple pride that had been so important to him. Or was he grateful for the clarity, to be saved from the lies he'd believed for far too long? He suspected it was some of each, even though they seemed to be opposites.

No one ever said man was a rational beast.

"Are you hungry, sir? I didn't know you were coming until an hour ago, but I stocked the kitchen as well as I could." Withers stood at the doorway, looking toward the desk.

"No, thank you, Ben. I'm not hungry. I'm just sitting here and enjoying the fire. And thinking." He paused a few seconds, but when Withers looked like he was going to slip out the door, he said, "Come on in, Ben. Sit with me."

Withers stepped into the room and walked across the stained wood floor. The old noncom's posture was as rigidly perfect as ever, and he sat down bolt upright in one of the chairs facing the desk.

"You know what's coming, Ben. You know as well as I do."

"Yes, sir."

Damian almost told Withers to stop calling him "sir." But it had been six years since they'd been discharged together, and he'd never managed it before, so it hardly seemed likely now.

"Tell me what you think, Ben. Have we done enough? Have we prepared them for what they will face?" Damian's tone suggested he had significant doubts. "And, Ben . . . give it to me straight. I want your real opinion."

"Always, sir. Truth is, we won't know, not until it's over. But I think they can do it."

Damian looked back, the surprise certainly obvious on his face. Withers was a cold realist, and he'd expected the aide to deliver an ominous response, not one with rays of hope shining through.

"We're going to be facing regulars, Ben."

"I know that, sir. But strength comes in different forms." Withers hesitated, as if uncertain he should continue. Then he said, "You and I, sir, we came from nothing. We had no homes, none worthy of the word, at least." He paused again before continuing, his usual firm voice betraying rare emotion. "I used to steal food. For my mother. She was sick . . . she was sick for a long time. My father was dead. There was no one else."

Damian sat silently, listening attentively. He had known Withers for ten years, and this was the first time his friend had talked about his life before the military.

"It was hard seeing her like that, but it gave me a purpose, too. She needed me, and anything I could find—some extra food or an old blanket—helped make her more comfortable. It was miserable, living in such deprivation, but she kept me going, even amid the despair of the Chicago slums. When she died, that was all gone. I didn't care about anything. I was fortunate to end up in the army, and to find meaning in serving with my comrades. It saved my life, sir, as I suspect it saved yours. The army was an escape for us, but that's all it was. We fought because we became professionals, because we bonded with the men and women around us. And that gave us something we were missing. But I'm not sure it was a true replacement for what we'd lost . . . or never had. I still remember the look in my mother's eyes when I brought back some tattered old coat, something that could help keep her warm when the heat went out. The feeling that gave me, to help her—in my mind back then, to save her—I've never had that feeling since."

Withers looked across the desk, and for the first time Damian had ever seen, the old veteran's eyes were moist. "These people have something we've never known, sir. They have houses and families. Mothers and fathers, brothers and sisters. They have husbands and wives and children. Homes, sir. They have homes here. Real homes, the kind you and I never had. Until we came to Haven. They may not have the training we do, and they may not have the experience crawling across the battlefield, facing Union and Hegemony troops, but they have a lot to fight for. More than we ever did. We were professionals, sir, but they are defending their homes and families. Don't underestimate them."

Damian considered Withers's words. He realized he'd been almost entirely pessimistic, and for all the effort he'd put into training his army, he hadn't really ever believed they could win. A pall had followed him through every exercise, through each day that the force grew, and more so since it had begun to shrink. He tended to discount the encouragements of others. He'd seen too many times how easily people convinced themselves to believe whatever they wanted to believe. But Ben Withers had been to hell and back with him. His aide, his friend, was a man whose opinion Damian always took seriously.

"All right, my friend. You have made your point. Perhaps we do have a chance. But the truth is, I'm not just concerned about our soldiers. They may be undertrained and inexperienced, but their general is worse. I have no place commanding an army, Ben. I know that, and I suspect you do, too. How can they not?"

"I know no such thing, sir. A leader is more than a list of battles or a benchmark of years served. I followed you into battle when you wore stripes on your arms, and after you exchanged those for shiny new lieutenant's bars. And I followed you here into civilian life. You are the kind of leader people follow, Damian, and the fact that you can't see it only makes it more real." Withers paused. "We will fight for you, sir. Me, the old veterans, the new recruits. We will follow you into battle, into hell itself, if you will lead us there. It lies with you now, General Ward. Will you embrace your destiny?"

Damian took a deep breath, trying hard to ignore the ache in his stomach. He wasn't sure he thought Withers's confidence was as well placed as the sergeant—*no, major now*—seemed to think. But he knew what he had to do, and to have any chance at success, he had to let himself believe, at least a little.

"I will give all I have, Ben. I will fight with every scrap of strength I can muster."

And by God, I hope that is enough.

CHAPTER 5

"There's definitely something there, Command. Energy readings are off the scale. My guess is, we're looking at a minimum of a dozen ships, possibly more." Josh Garabrant had been working twelve-hour shifts for days, ever since *Vagabond* had returned with a warning of approaching federal forces. He heard a quiver in his own voice that he hoped came across as exhaustion, and not the gut-wrenching fear he was feeling.

"Very well, scanner control, maintain your track."

"Yes, Command." He held back a snort of derision at the officious tone of the officer on the other end of the comm.

Here we are, playing at being soldiers. Is even one of us ready for what is coming?

Garabrant was an engineer by training. He'd come to Haven ten years before, and he'd worked most of that time at Danforth Communications, where the worst crisis he'd faced was making sure the nightly entertainment lineup was broadcast on time. Now there were ships coming. Coming to kill him.

He was scared—all-out, unfiltered, 100 percent scared to death. And despite the rank they'd pinned on him and the arrogance in his tone, he suspected Captain Evans in the command center was just as terrified.

He looked back at the screens. He didn't *know* the readings were federal ships transiting into the system, not yet. It was a sliver of doubt and not much more, but it sustained him, at least for another few minutes. Then even that was gone.

"Command, we have confirmation. Fourteen contacts. At least four identified as federal frigates. Inbound directly toward Haven."

"Acknowledged, Lieutenant. Maintain tracking and report additional data as it comes in."

He sounds like he's reading straight out of some kind of manual. But somewhere under the officer-speak, he also sounds about ready to shit himself.

"Yes, Captain." His eyes darted back to the display as another flurry of readings came in. "Sir, we've now got eight confirmed frigates . . . and four larger contacts." Garabrant had never seen a federal battlecruiser, not even an image of one. The navy's heavy ships were classified, kept as secret as possible, deployed in crises only, and otherwise docked at clandestine bases. But he'd *heard* of them—rumors of them, at least. On-screen now, though, the behemoths were far beyond anything he had imagined. Far beyond anything needed to maintain internal order. They existed for one reason only, for wars against the other powers.

And now, to crush a rebellious colony.

"Additional contacts, Captain." He'd been staring right at the screen when another cluster of ships appeared. They were farther back, slower moving.

Transports.

"Acknowledged, Lieutenant."

Garabrant took a deep breath, watching as the federal fleet slipped into something that was beginning to look like a combat formation.

Not that you'd know a combat formation if it fell on you . . .

He'd done his job. There was nothing to do but wait. Wait to see if the enemy landed troops to retake the orbital platform.

Or if they just blasted it to atoms the instant they came into range.

"Damian, we're getting reports from the station." Danforth paused. He'd come close to trying to keep the report from Damian, at least until the rebellion's military leader and he had finished their address to the population. Damian's performance was crucial here. Danforth was, in many ways, the father of Haven's revolution, but he knew Damian was its war hero, the planet's favorite son. He didn't like the idea of dumping the news on his colleague right before such an important speech. He hated lying to his friend more.

"The federals?"

"Yes . . . it appears to be a substantial force." Danforth knew exactly how many ships had entered the system. But feigning less complete knowledge than he had wasn't lying. Not quite.

"Perhaps we should have moved more quickly. The station won't hold for an hour against a major naval task force. How far out are they?"

"Estimates are they will enter firing range in seventy-four hours."

"Three days. A few hours after that, they can be landing troops." Damian stood for a moment, silent. Then he said calmly, "Well, let's do this. We're already late."

Danforth nodded. "Everything is ready."

Damian turned and walked toward the small stage, Danforth right behind him. Damian stopped just short of the center of the stage, and the communications mogul moved up to the microphone.

"We're ready," Danforth said, looking over toward the control station at the side of the platform.

"In five, sir . . . four, three, two, one . . . now."

"Good morning, my fellow Havenites. I come to you today on a matter of the gravest importance. Almost one year ago, our great planet declared its independence from Federal America. As a people, we staked our claim to a future, one of liberty and light not darkened by the shadow of oppression. We knew then that we would have to be prepared to defend that future, to fight for it once again. And now that day has come." He paused, taking a quick breath as he allowed his words to hang in the air for a moment. "Today our scanners have detected a federal fleet approaching Haven. The war we have feared, that many of us expected, is upon us." Danforth stood silently, staring at the camera, and by extension, at the hundreds of thousands watching.

"I urge all of you to be strong, to remember the feelings you felt when you first heard of our world's freedom. We face a difficult time, I will not lie to any of you about that. But if we stay committed, if we stand together, I truly believe we can emerge from our struggle more resilient and more united than we have ever been."

He turned and motioned for Damian to come to the podium. "Without any further delay, I will step aside for General Damian Ward, the commander of Haven's armed forces . . . and the hero of the rebellion."

Damian stepped to the podium, and Danforth could see the frown Haven's general was holding back. He'd known Damian would hate the "hero" remark, but it was what the people needed to hear now, and he suspected his friend realized that, too. Deep down, at least.

"Thank you, Mr. President." Damian's voice was soft, almost as if he was speaking to a friend alone in his study rather than addressing the entire planet.

"As most of you know, I served in the war against the Union and the Hegemony. I know war. I have felt the sting of battle and the pain of loss. I will not give you a flowery speech now, filled with soaring references to freedom. I will not give you empty encouragements, tell you we will surge to victory because our cause is righteous. The justice of our cause has no weight on the battlefield, only the metal of our guns and the mettle of our resolve."

Danforth tried not to show any concern, but his stomach was twisting into knots. He had no idea what Damian was doing. The two had written a speech together, and the words streamed across the screen on the podium. But Damian was ignoring it. He was ignoring every word.

"I will promise you this. I will lead your armies. I will fight the enemy. And never forget, the federals are our enemies now. I may face soldiers I've served with, men and women who fought at my side in our previous battles. I do not relish opposing them now—killing them—but that die is already cast. When I look across the field and see them, they are my enemies. I will do all I can to destroy them."

Damian's voice was gradually increasing in volume, and the cool calmness was slowly giving way to a hard edge. To anger.

"That may sound harsh, it may sound cold. But all of you must understand what we face, and what it will take to see us through, to give us the victory so many speak of with such ease."

Danforth wanted to talk to his friend, to somehow get him back on the program. But there was nothing he could do. And as the general continued, he began to understand a bit of what Damian was trying to accomplish.

"It is one thing to talk about sacrifice, to attend rallies and shout slogans. It is quite another to face brutal combat, to see friends and loved ones killed on the battlefield, mutilated and burned and crying for their mothers. To watch our homes burned to the ground, to flee when we must so we can fight another day. Yet *that* is *exactly* what we must endure, my fellow Havenites, if we are to survive. Only through our perseverance, through our grim, unyielding determination, can we achieve the victory—the freedom—we all crave."

He paused, staring straight at the camera as he stood stone still. "I ask this of every able-bodied man and woman . . . we need you to join us, to fight with us. To all the soldiers who joined our army and then went home when your enlistments expired—and also to those who left before your terms were served—I ask you to come back to us, for the battle you trained to fight is upon us. I don't care how you departed or why. There will be no penalties, no recriminations. Just rally back to the ranks and help us win Haven's freedom, now and for all time. For you are no safer in your homes, waiting help-lessly for the federal forces to reach you."

He started to turn to walk away, but then he stopped. He stood for a moment, silent, looking back at the camera. Then he said, "You have adopted me, Havenites. You have welcomed me to this extraordinary world, though I was not born among you. I was re-luctant to join this revolution, that is no secret. I served Federal America, was one of her soldiers, and I fought in her wars. I disap-proved of the oppression, but I told myself that wasn't my concern. I was a soldier, and all I had to do was follow my orders. At least, that is what I always believed. And when I retired, I took pride with me, pride in the service I had given. But the events of last year, the rebellion and the painful choices many of us had to make, were a reckoning for me. I lost something I had held dear, the idea that I had been a part of something worthwhile. That my service had meant something. Now that is gone, and there is only one way for me to regain it. Victory here. The birth of a strong and free Haven. And I will give every measure of my strength to see that happen." He paused again. "And for those who heed my call, who come to help me in this sacred duty, I offer my devotion and my eternal loyalty. I cannot promise victory, but I can assure every one of you that I will not survive defeat."

He stood for a moment, looking straight ahead. The studio was silent, every man and woman present staring in rapt attention at the man who would lead their army.

Then he turned abruptly, almost as if on parade, and he walked off the stage.

Violetta Wellr rat in her small room, legs curled up under her body on the bed, and stared at the small screen, her eyes fixed on Damian as he spoke. She knew the general, though *knew*, she suspected, was a strong word. Her father had *known* Damian, and she had met him a few times.

Violetta had listened to revolutionary firebrands since the day she'd arrived with her father four years earlier. Haven was unsettled even then, though things had only gotten progressively worse despite Governor Wells's best efforts. She had believed in her father when they'd first arrived, and to some extent she had maintained that faith, save for one thing. Her father was a good man, but he served an evil government. She couldn't understand how he had forced himself to do that, justified his career. How he'd been able to live with himself.

She'd been naïve, too, she realized now. She understood that, listening to Damian's words and remembering some of her father's. It was easy to protest, to thrust your fist into the air and shout out against all manner of outrages, perceived or otherwise. But actions had consequences. She knew that now in ways she hadn't when she'd gone to her father and told him she was staying behind and joining the rebellion.

Only now she realized how much she had hurt him, how she had plunged a knife into him when he was at his lowest, returning home in disgrace, his career in ruins. He'd needed her, and she hadn't even considered that when she'd made her decision. Hers had been an emotional choice, one fueled by the baseless idealism of youth.

She still believed in the revolution, but there was more than that in her mind now, shaping her views. A realization of just how terrible a price her adopted world might be compelled to pay . . .

and guilt for abandoning her father, an open sore on her conscience that the self-righteous young girl of a year earlier couldn't have imagined.

She looked around the ramshackle room, still listening to Damian's words. Her father had left her as much money as he'd been able to, but as governor on a colony world, he hadn't needed much currency. And all electronic transfers from Earth were cut off. Violetta came to realize very quickly how sheltered a life she had led. She'd had to leave the governor's house, of course. Her father and the rest of the federals were departing in defeat, and the mood of the people was restive. Out in the street at least, she was another woman, not a symbol of the hated federals. She could blend in, avoid conflict. If she'd declared some right to remain in the official quarters, she would only have whipped the people into a frothy outrage, a dangerous anger that could easily have turned to violence toward the deposed governor's spoiled daughter.

She'd reached out to various rebel groups as well, anxious to become a true part of the cause. It had been a more difficult experience than she'd imagined, especially when her revolutionary cohorts found out who she was. She'd been ostracized by some, and more than once, she'd feared for her safety. Others had sought to use her identity to further their ends. Violetta was ready to roll up her sleeves and work for the rebellion, even fight for it, but she had no intention of using her name for propaganda.

Finally, she found a place with the Society of the Red Flag. A number of others had warned her that the Society was a dangerous, radical organization, but whatever their reputation, they at least had embraced her fervor and put her right to work. She had protested with them, gone to meetings. She had found a home. For a while, at least.

Now she was worried that the warnings she'd ignored had been correct, that she'd twice succumbed to foolish naivety. The Society was agitating constantly to root out and persecute loyalists . . .

or even those Havenites whose revolutionary zeal wasn't up to the standards they expected. Violetta was still committed to the revolution, but she'd become increasingly uncomfortable with the violent rhetoric of Cal Jacen and the other leaders of the Society. She'd heard rumors of people being beaten, even killed, and while she had no idea what to believe, it all seemed so plausible based on the rhetoric. She would fight the federals, though the thought of actual combat scared her to death, but she wasn't so sure about violence against other Havenites. She understood that the loyalists were against the cause, against Haven's freedom. But the idea of attacking them made her queasy.

She'd been confused, uncertain what to do, but now, looking at Damian Ward on the screen, she suddenly understood. It all made perfect sense. The commander of Haven's army was calling for volunteers to swell the ranks. She didn't have a doubt in her mind that Ward was an honest man, one who would do all he could to preserve Haven's independence. She remembered enough from his visits to her father to bolster her loyalty and confidence.

She looked at the screen, nodding her head. Yes, that was exactly what she would do. She would join the army. She would fight for Haven.

CHAPTER 6

"Jamie . . ." Katia stood at the door leading from the bedroom out into the modest structure's main area. The farmhouse was small, and it had been hastily built, but the past eight months she'd lived there had been the happiest of her life. She had waited years for Jamie to be freed, and as soon as he was, the two of them were plunged into the rebellion. Finally, with Damian's help, they had a home together, and it had been all she'd hoped for those many years.

And now she could feel it slipping away.

"Don't be afraid, Katia. We have a trial ahead of us, but it's not the first we've faced. We will do what we must, and when it's over, we'll spend the rest of our lives together here." Jamie Grant had lived almost all of his adult life in the hellish federal mines, a prisoner exiled from Earth for a series of petty crimes. Katia knew he had suffered terribly, and that if it hadn't been for the intervention of Damian Ward, Grant would almost certainly have died in the mines, instead of gaining a new chance at a life. With her.

"But I *am* afraid, Jamie. For you, for me. For Damian. Why can't they just leave us in peace?" She paused, but only for an instant. She didn't expect a response. Her question required an hours-long answer, or none at all. And she was as qualified to give it as anyone else.

Finally she said, "It's just . . . what we went through a year ago, so many people killed, so much destruction. Now it feels like that was just the start." Katia wasn't a military tactician, but she knew Damian well, and she'd seen the worry in his eyes, the trepidation he thought he hid from everyone. She loved Damian Ward like the big brother he'd become to her—and to Jamie—and she couldn't imagine the load he was bearing now.

"Katia, we made it through the fighting last year, and we'll get through this. We just have to stay strong. You're leaving here, too. We both have our duties. And we will both have to find a way to handle the worry we feel for each other."

She nodded. She was in uniform now, as he was, or at least what passed for a uniform in the fledgling Haven army. Her kit bag was packed and lying against the wall. She felt out of place as a soldier, and a bit ridiculous with the shiny new lieutenant's bars on her shoulder. It felt strange being in the army at all, much less as an officer.

Still, for all of Jamie's reassurances, she knew the two of them would face far different challenges. Katia had worked at her father's side since she was a little girl, and she'd become an accomplished engineer in her own right. Her posting would be with Damian, at army headquarters, helping to keep at least some level of communications going in the face of the federal jamming and other interdictive efforts that would almost certainly accompany invasion.

Jamie, on the other hand, would be leading troops in battle. For the most part, she knew he could take care of himself, that twelve years in a prison where few survived half that long had toughened him in ways she still couldn't truly understand. What was more difficult to accept was what lengths he might go to in order *to* take care of himself.

This last year had been wonderful, yet she hadn't managed to completely come to terms with the monster he became in combat, how the man who was so kind and gentle with her and with his friends could become so terrifying and alien in a fight. He held a powerful rage—an anger forged by the fury of the years of his life stolen and of the mother he'd been forced to leave behind, alone in one of Earth's worst slums—that he kept submerged. Jamie Grant despised the federals with an intensity that scared her, the woman who loved him, to her core. And she feared what path that hatred might lead him down.

"Just promise me you'll be careful, Jamie. I know there will be fighting, and I know you have your duty and responsibilities. But take care of yourself. For me, if not for you."

He turned back and smiled at her. "I will, Katia. For you . . . and for me, too. I've never had a real life, except for these past months with you. I don't want to lose that. But it is also something worth fighting for. Do you think we can have the life we want if the feds retake Haven? Would they allow us to live here, to build that life? I can't imagine what the future would hold under federal rule. If there would even be a future. We can't let that happen, no matter what it takes."

She returned his smile, but it took most of what she had to do it. She knew Jamie, perhaps better than anyone else, and she understood how completely he was committed to the cause. It was admirable, part of what made him the man he was, but it scared her, as well.

Don't do anything foolish, my love.

Please . . . come home to me.

"I have to confess, Jamie, I approved your plan, but I didn't really think you'd pull it off." Damian looked at the ragged group of soldiers—soldiers more or less, at least—lined up in the field behind the two men. *Not that you've pulled it off yet, but you've done better than I thought possible.*

"Thank you, Damian . . . I mean, General."

Damian smiled. He didn't expect his friend to transition easily to the formality of military life, not after over a decade in the prison mines. He almost told Jamie to call him Damian, but he stopped himself. If his people were to have any chance in the fight to come, they had to be as professional as the soldiers they would face. They had to be as much an army, in every sense of the word, as the forces they would be battling against.

"Captain," Damian said, following his own internal advice, "I know you did your share of fighting last year. No one can say you don't know how to take care of yourself, but leading others is something different entirely. And you have an even more complicated situation here, with your . . . soldiers."

Damian's first reaction to Grant's plan had been skeptical in the extreme. Forming a military unit from escaped prisoners seemed like asking for trouble. He'd already been struggling with efforts to separate the real criminals from the political prisoners—and trying to decide what to do with those who remained dangerous. Newly independent Haven didn't have any kind of legal system, let alone courts or jails, save the infamous facilities left behind by the federals. Grant's idea, crazy as it was, provided a solution of sorts.

"I understand these people, General. For most of my life, I was one of them. I can handle them."

As part of Jamie's scheme, every prisoner who fought for the rebellion would receive a pardon for any past crimes, and be accepted as a citizen of the new republic. It sounded great in theory, but he suspected his friend had more than one unreformed sociopath under his command. Combat was difficult and stressful enough without worrying about the men and women behind you . . . and whose side they were on.

That, at least, should work in our favor. Not a man or woman from that mine has anything but searing hatred for Federal America.

Which was why he'd ultimately approved it.

"Just be careful," he said. "Not everyone who was in that mine is like you. Some of them deserved to be there. Even a corrupt government like Federal America will send real criminals to prison."

Grant smiled . . . almost. "Don't worry. I know how to handle *them*, too. If I didn't, I'd have ended up facedown in that mine years ago. I was one of the longest-serving prisoners there, and that creates a kind of jailhouse respect." He paused, and his voice shifted to the darker tone, that of the Jamie Grant who took hold in battle. "Any one of them who tries anything *will* end up facedown . . . in some ditch along the way. And he will serve by being an example to the others."

Damian just nodded. He was still not used to the way Grant's entire personality seemed to change almost instantly in battle, or even when he was talking about combat. The ferociousness was something that just might help Grant stay alive, but Damian still found it a little unnerving, and having seen what he'd seen, that was saying something.

Grant looked back at Damian. Then he said, his voice back to normal, "They've come along well. They're operating as a unit. There's even some camaraderie. Whatever demons run wild in their heads, we all shared a common experience." He paused. "I'm not sure anyone who wasn't there could know what years and years in that place is like."

"I'm sure they couldn't, Jamie. I certainly don't. I hope it works for you. God knows, we're going to need every bit of strength we can muster, and probably more. And your people have one of the most dangerous jobs."

That was another part of the plan that Damian agreed about—that Grant's ex-prisoners be trained in irregular tactics, taking Killian's rangers as their role models. Colonel Killian had even assisted Jamie in getting his people ready, which both reassured and worried Damian even more. Either he had one hundred sixty die-hard fighters, ready to kill federals any way they could, with guns, knives, even their bare hands if necessary, or he had one hundred sixty head cases, men and women just as likely to turn on their own allies and officers over the slightest insult, real or perceived. And he wouldn't know which it was—or if it was both—until battle was joined.

And when things hit the fan, his best friend would be at the head of this unsavory crew.

"General, don't worry. I can handle myself. You've got enough to worry about. I'll make sure this group does what we need them to do. Every one of them faces likely summary execution if the federals win. That's a strong motivator."

"Yes, Jamie, it is." Damian paused. "But watch your back anyway."

"Always. And you, too, Damian. But also, don't forget, you're not in this alone. We're all here to help you. Let us. Share the burden."

Damian nodded. Jamie's friendship was important to him, but he'd taken one lesson to heart as he'd accepted the general's stars and command of the army. All the senior officers he'd respected in his days as a sergeant and a lieutenant had borne the weight of their positions alone. He would do the same. He would put the skills of those under him to work, demand the very best from each of them. But in the end, the ultimate responsibility was his. Victory or defeat, it all hung on his actions, on whether he, a jumped-up junior officer promoted far beyond his experience, could adjust to army command. He was scared to death, not of the enemy, but of himself, of failing to live up to what the rebellion needed from him. Of letting his brave soldiers and fellow Havenites down. As much as he dreaded the responsibilities and feared he would not prove up to the task, he knew there was no one else better qualified.

"You'll do it, Damian," Grant said, almost as though he was reading his friend's mind. "We all have faith in you. Haven is lucky to have you."

"Thank you, Jamie." Damian saw Grant begin to salute, but he leaned in and hugged his friend instead. A moment's lapse of discipline wasn't going to do any undue damage to the army.

"Now go, Captain. Lead your people out."

Grant stepped back and saluted. "Take care of yourself, General Ward."

"And you, Captain." Damian returned the salute, and then he watched Grant walk crisply away. His friend had been nothing but sincere with his words, but they had only increased the pressure on the general. His friends, supporters, the army, hundreds of thousands of Havenites, all depending on his skills. And for all they made of his supposed skills, he'd never led more than sixty soldiers in battle before the previous year. Even then, he'd been in direct command of only his small group of veterans.

How the hell are you going to command ten thousand soldiers, and lead them to victory?

Victory against a real army, one you once served. Against old comrades, friends. Veterans.

CHAPTER 7

"Well, Admiral Taggart? Is the fleet ready to proceed?" Semmes was sitting on *Oceania*'s flag bridge, at a spare workstation. The federal flagship was approaching Alpha-2, nearly within combat range of the orbital fortress the rebels had seized a year before. That act, as outrageously daring and seemingly impossible as it had been, was the one that had destroyed the chances to defeat the rebellion in its early stages.

"Yes, General Semmes. We must decide if we will attempt to retake the orbital facility or if we . . ."

"Destroy it, Admiral." Semmes's voice dripped with arrogance and frigid hatred. Normally the chain of command between an admiral and a general would be tenuous, confused. A question such as the one Taggart had asked would be answered through an exchange of pros and cons and a joint decision, or it would lead to a vicious argument that could threaten an entire operation. But Robert Semmes was also military governor, and the mandate he carried from the senate made him the effective dictator of the entire Epsilon Eridani system . . . the Alpha-2 colony, the station, and everything else, right down to the six uninhabited planets and every last comet, asteroid, and meteor drifting through the cold dark. His decisions were final, and he had the power of life and death over every man, woman, and child on the rebel planet.

"Are you sure, General? We very likely can capture it at an acceptable cost. It would be useful for a number of support purposes. And the cost to ultimately replace it will likely exceed the repair—"

"Destroy it, Admiral. As soon as your ships are in range. It is well past time we send a message to these traitors, one they won't soon forget. We will not parley with them. We will not accept their piteous attempts at surrender. Those who have betrayed their nation, raised their arms in rebellion against their rightful government . . . they must be wiped away without hesitation."

Semmes had raged against his lack of authority on his previous mission, repeatedly blaming Stanton and Wells for its failure. He'd started such declarations in a panicked effort to deflect blame from himself, but now he'd repeated it so many times, he believed it fully. He was in control at last, and no one could stop him. He would crush the rebellion, and he would hunt down every last revolutionary, wherever they tried to hide.

By the time I am done, no one will even be sure this rebellion ever existed . . .

"Yes, General." Taggart's tone didn't entirely hide his disapproval, but Semmes didn't care. The admiral had his orders, and that was all that mattered. He knew the spacers of the fleet, and the regular soldiers under his command, considered themselves professionals, that they bristled at being placed under him. There was significant discontent about being deployed against citizens of Federal America as well, both among the officers and the rank and file. But they *would* follow their orders. Semmes would make sure of that. And he would stand every one of them who didn't up against a wall . . .

"We will be in firing range in three minutes, General. We may utilize some high-g maneuvers in battle, sir." The naval officer paused. "Perhaps you would be more comfortable in your quarters."

Semmes glared back at the admiral. He knew Taggart didn't think of him as a real military officer, no more than the unit commanders in his army contingents did. He was well aware that the combat effectiveness of the regular units in his expeditionary force was vastly higher than that of the security units. But he resented the veterans, despite his own scandal-plagued history as one of them. He detested what he perceived as their arrogance, and he preferred the internal security forces, men and women who'd been expressly trained to control unruly mobs. Like the rebel army. Having these career military men look down their noses at him . . .

Soon they will learn what it means to oppose me.

"No, Admiral. I will be fine here." Semmes's face wore a determined scowl, though beneath it he was a little leery of the rough ride he suspected lay ahead.

"Very well, sir." The admiral snapped his head around. "Commander Samuels, bring all units to battle stations."

"Yes, Admiral."

"Lock attack plan three into the nav systems, and prepare for execution in two minutes, fifteen seconds."

"Yes, sir."

Semmes watched, and as he did he could feel a bit of fear push its way past his anger. The orbital platform was powerful, designed to defend Alpha-2 against an invasion such as this one. He couldn't allow himself to believe the rebels had managed to crew it properly, or that they would put up more than a token defense before they panicked and tried to surrender, but he still felt the tension in his chest as *Oceania* hurtled toward the fight he'd just ordered.

"Entering range in one minute, Admiral. All units report weapons stations on alert and at maximum readiness."

"All units are authorized to fire as they enter range. Target critical systems. We are attacking to destroy, not to disable." Taggart's voice was cool, professional. "Repeat, all units are to shoot to destroy."

"Shoot to destroy. Yes, sir." Samuels turned toward his station and relayed the command. Then he turned back toward Taggart. "Thirty seconds, Admiral."

Semmes reached behind him, grabbing the harness attached to his seat and buckling himself in. His stomach was doing flops, and the coldness of fear gripped his insides.

Fear, but also excitement.

Payback at last.

"Prepare to commence combat maneuvers, Commander. All vessels initiate thrust in ten seconds . . ."

Garabrant sat in his chair, pitched forward, his eyes locked on the targeting display. His official job was to run the station's scanning suite, but the new government of Haven lacked the resources to properly staff the orbital platform. The crew were all wearing multiple hats, and Garabrant's made sense, as weapons targeting relied heavily on the station's scanners. Still, the engineer had never fired so much as a handgun, much less the missile salvos and laser batteries of the massive fortress.

"Federal ships entering weapons range, Captain. Should I fire?"

Captain Evans didn't answer Garabrant. Instead, he sent another transmission to the approaching fleet. "Federal vessels, this is your final warning. You are ordered to decelerate at once and turn about. This is the space of the Haven Republic, and your presence here is an act of war."

Garabrant listened to the captain's voice on the comm unit. Evans didn't sound much better than he had. If the captain's intent was to intimidate a federal fleet commander, it would have to be the reality of the situation and not his tone that did the job.

There was no response, just a touch of static on the otherwise silent comm. No refusal, no threats hurled back in turn. Nothing. It was ominous, and if the federals were trying to rattle the defenders, it was working. At least, it was working on Garabrant.

He waited for the authorization. The station's weapons were

heavier than the mobile ordnance carried by the federal warships, their range greater. And every second that passed ceded some of the advantage the defenders held. But Garabrant understood. He would simply be following orders, but someone had to make the initial decision to open fire on the federal navy.

And accept responsibility for what followed.

The time passed, slowly, each second stretching out into agonizing torment. The AI was engaged, the targeting solutions locked in and ready. All Garabrant—and Claren and the others lined up at their stations—needed was to open fire.

Then it came.

"All weapons stations, fire. All weapons stations, fire."

Garabrant reached out, his fingers moving across a long row of switches. He flipped each of them in turn, his thoughts focused, with only a marginal realization of the megatons of destructive power he was engaging as he armed each missile.

He preferred not to think too much about it. He was as strident a rebel as any, but words and parades were one thing, and killing men and women with nuclear fire quite another. He'd just flipped the last arming switch and was about to hit the launch button when he noticed Claren sitting next to him, doing nothing.

"Kip! We're under attack—fire, dammit." He turned back to his own workstation for a few seconds, hitting the launch control and sending the station's missiles toward their targets. Then he spun around, back toward his comrade. Claren was still frozen in place, staring at the screen.

"Kip, what the hell? You've got to activate those laser batteries!"

"That's the federal navy out there," Claren stammered. "We can't shoot at the navy."

"Kip, pull yourself together."

"We can't . . . don't you understand? We can't . . ."

"Fire those weapons, Kip." Garabrant stood up, his hand dropping to his side, to the pistol hanging there.

Claren didn't respond. He didn't move.

"Now, Kip." Garabrant pulled the gun out and pointed it at Claren. "I'm serious, Kip. Do it."

Garabrant's mind was running wild. The idea of shooting his comrade seemed insane. But he knew the station would be hard-pressed enough, without half its laser batteries out of action. He was scared, too, and hesitant to unleash death himself, but he had no doubts about what would happen to them if the feds regained control—if it even got that far for the people on this station. But if there was a slightest chance his actions could keep him alive—or, worst case, his new country—he had to ensure he did what he could.

Even if it meant shooting Claren for dereliction.

"Get out of there. I'll do it myself." He stepped forward and reached out, pushing Claren away from the workstation. But the other man reacted now, holding on to his chair, resisting Garabrant's efforts to remove him.

"Dammit, Claren. Don't make me kill you." Garabrant stepped back a meter or so from the chair and re-aimed the pistol, pointing it right at the other man's head. The two other engineers in the room looked on in stunned horror.

"Focus on your jobs!" Garabrant barked at them, and they went back to activating the platform's defenses. He turned back to Claren, but the man still hadn't responded. He didn't attempt to attack Garabrant. He didn't do anything. He just stayed where he was.

"I'm not messing with you, Claren. I *will* shoot you." He hoped he sounded convincing, because he was far from sure he could pull the trigger.

His eyes darted down to the screen on his workstation. The missiles he had launched were halfway to the incoming fleet. The federals had picked off perhaps a third of them so far. He knew they would intercept far more of the deadly weapons, but with luck, a few would get through. Yet without the station's heavy lasers opening fire and taking full advantage of their longer range, he knew there wasn't a chance to defeat the fleet. He *had* to fire those lasers, and if that meant he had to kill Claren, so be it.

He stared at the other man, his eyes pleading for an alternative. But Claren didn't even look at him. He just sat where he was, unmoving.

Garabrant's finger tightened slowly. He felt as though he was lifting a great load rather than simply pulling a trigger. The sweat was pooling around his neck, and each breath felt like a thunderclap. He struggled to maintain his aim, but his hands were shaking.

You've got to do this . . .

He resolved to fire, and he squeezed the trigger . . . and then he stopped. He couldn't do it. He wasn't a soldier, not really. He suspected he might be able to shoot an enemy approaching him, one firing back. But he didn't have what it took to shoot the man next to him, even if that comrade's inaction jeopardized the entire battle.

"What the hell is going on in here?" Garabrant jumped back, startled by the figure suddenly bursting into the room. "Why aren't those lasers firing?" Jacob North was one of Pat Killian's rangers, assigned to the station.

And just as certifiably insane as his chief.

North was second-in-command of the defense forces tasked with facing any boarders, but right now he was clearly more concerned about the lack of laser fire.

"Captain—" Garabrant began. He paused for a second, but before he could continue, North roared again.

"Claren, fire those guns right now, or I shit you not, I will blow your fucking brains out and do it myself."

Claren didn't move. He didn't even respond.

"Captain, he's out of it. Something snapped inside him. He needs help."

"He needs to fire those lasers." North pulled the gun from his side. It was a pistol, but it was at least twice the size of the small sidearm Garabrant carried.

"Sir, please . . ."

"Get him out of that chair and fire those lasers, Lieutenant." North stared at Garabrant, his voice like ice. "Or I will."

"C'mon, Kip . . ." He leaned in, but the instant he touched Claren's shoulder the other man swung his arm wildly around, his fist catching Garabrant in the side of the head. He stumbled back toward his own chair.

"We don't have any time for this shit," he heard North say.

"No, sir, no . . ."

Crack.

"No!"

Garabrant's mind was still trying to process what had happened when he felt something warm against his face. He was confused for a moment, but then horror set in as he wiped his cheek and stared down at his hands, covered with blood. Claren's blood.

The workstation was spattered with red, and with small gray chunks his rational mind told him were bits of brain, even as every other part of him rebelled against the knowledge. He retched, trying to hold back the vomit, but failing, at least somewhat. He leaned forward and spit out the acidy bile, struggling to keep what remained in his stomach where it was.

"Garabrant, get the hell over here and fire these lasers." North was standing behind the chair, grabbing the fabric of Claren's coat and pulling the dead man off the seat and down to the floor.

Garabrant stood back up, but he found it difficult to move. He was stunned, staring around him only half-aware of what was happening.

"Doesn't anybody understand we're under attack?" North reached out and grabbed Garabrant by the collar, pulling him hard and shoving him into the chair.

Garabrant didn't respond, but he reached out robotically and flipped the switches, activating the lasers. Then he engaged the AI targeting system.

"Good," North growled. "Now make sure we're firing every-thing we've got at these fed bastards." He turned and walked briskly back out into the corridor.

Garabrant sat where he was, not moving, not exchanging a glance with any of his other comrades. He was just trying not to think about the feeling underneath him, the warm wetness soaking through his pants from the seat.

CHAPTER 8

"Sasha, are you sure you can pull this off?" Damian stood on the open concrete of Landfall's spaceport, under the looming shadow of *Vagabond*'s form rising above. The raider wasn't large as ships went, but it seemed massive to two people standing on the ground next to it.

"I'm sure I've got to try, Damian. Those are our people up there. The battle is hopeless. It's only a matter of time before the station is gone. How can we just leave them up there?"

Damian had watched the reports coming in as the fight above Haven progressed. He wasn't an expert in naval fighting, but he'd never really believed the station and its crew could beat back the fleet the federals had sent. Still, the early reports had spawned some ill-conceived hope around headquarters, and on the station itself.

The platform had been supported by two captured federal frigates, manned with volunteer skeleton crews. With those combined weapons, the initial missile barrage had destroyed three federal ships, and severely damaged two others. It was a morale boost, but an empty one, a short-lived victory having more to do with the greater range of the platform's fixed weapons than any real prospects of ultimate success.

As soon as the federal fleet moved into its own firing range, its ships opened up as well, and it quickly became apparent they had no intention to board the station and attempt to retake it. As hit after hit slammed into the great structure, targeting one vital system after another, little doubt remained that the federals were going to pound the thing to dust.

Damian was surprised. He'd thought the enemy would want to seize the platform, to use it as an orbital headquarters for their attempted reconquest. *He* would have seized it in their position, even at a greater cost in time and casualties. It seemed like a mistake to him, one he couldn't quite figure out.

The federals' choice meant one thing, though. He had sent soldiers to the station for no reason, men and women who were there to repel boarders, who were almost certain to die now . . . unless Nerov could save some.

The lack of the orbital station would hamper the federal operations on the ground. Damian felt pain for the people he was losing, but also a spark of excitement. His enemy was definitely making a tactical error.

He'd issued his own orders to take full advantage of that mistake. He had directed the string of satellites around the planet be linked to the platform, so that its destruction would begin a chain reaction that would take out every eye and ear in Haven orbit. It was a desperate tactic, one that would set the planet's development back years—even decades—after the war was over, but none of that mattered if the federals crushed the rebellion.

"But if you can't get up there in time," he said to Nerov after a long pause, "you'll just risk losing *Vagabond*, too. And all your people."

"It's no greater risk that we asked those crews up there to take, is it?"

Damian shook his head. He couldn't argue with Nerov, not too aggressively, at least. He'd have gone, had he been in her shoes. Indeed, he hated the fact that his position as military commander prevented him from joining her, because every fiber of his being wanted to climb into the airlock right after her.

But he *had* been chosen as the leader, and had in turn chosen to accept, and he'd just have to live with all that entailed. He could only hope she'd still be alive after *her* choice.

"All right, Sasha. Go. But nothing stupid. Save anyone you can, but make sure you make it back. You've got to be clear before the station goes, or before the feds get close enough to target *Vagabond* directly."

"I've been in tight spots before, Damian. I'll make it through this one." It was clear with every word that she was completely ignoring most of what he had just told her. Just like he probably would. It almost made him smile.

"Good luck, Sasha." It was grossly inadequate, but it was also all he could think to say. He stood and watched her snap off something he guessed was supposed to be a salute. Then she climbed up the ladder into the ship.

He stood another moment, but then he turned and hurried to the side, behind a large blast shield, clearing the area under *Vagabond*'s engines.

"Good luck," he whispered again as he ducked down, waiting for Nerov to fire her ship's thrusters and make a mad dash to orbit. "Save our people . . ."

"**Maintain fire, all** ships. And reload missile tubes. I want another spread launched as soon as possible." Taggart's body was rigid, his posture bolt upright as he sat in his chair and directed the actions of the fleet.

"Yes, sir. Projected missile launch one minute. All ships maintaining laser fire." Samuels wasn't quite a match for the admiral in calm and poise, but he still comported himself well under fire. All the staff on *Oceania*'s flag bridge did.

Semmes watched the naval officers go about their duties, seemingly immune to fear, even as ships of the fleet succumbed to the deadly fire from the platform. He'd been certain the rebels would put up at best a token resistance before trying to surrender, and then dying in their places as he denied them quarter. But the station's weapons fired relentlessly, the deadly missiles and high-powered lasers ripping into the naval vessels, slicing through their armored hulls and causing catastrophic damage. The platform had been built to defend Alpha-2 against just this kind of attack, and it was doing exactly what it was designed to do.

Semmes had insisted the attack proceed immediately, a direct assault. Taggart had proposed some alternatives, more elegant plans to cut down on the losses a frontal assault would inevitably entail, but Semmes had shot all of the options down, certain in his assertion that the rebels didn't have a solid fight in them.

He'd had doubts, thoughts in the back of his mind, recollections of the fighting the year before. But every argument his subconscious made was shot down by the arrogant assurance that drove him. The rebels were lucky before, and now he had underestimated only the hardware that had been left behind, the massive fort the rebels had stolen in a surprise attack.

Oceania shook hard, the third hit she had taken. Any excitement he'd initially felt was completely gone, and at the moment, the main thing Semmes focused on was that he didn't understand why Taggart had his flagship so far forward. The fleet had other ships to take the lead positions, and putting both the overall commander and the senior naval officer in danger seemed foolish. He'd almost ordered *Oceania* to retire to the rear of the formation, out of range of the station's weapons, but in the end, fear of humiliation in front of his people won out over fear of the enemy. *Oceania* was a big ship, one of Federal America's massive battlecruisers. It would take more than a few shots from the fortress's lasers to pose a serious threat.

"Admiral, I cannot emphasize how greatly time is of the essence. We need that station destroyed, and we need that done now."

"We are closing, General." The disrespect in the admiral's voice grated at Semmes, enraging him. But now wasn't the time, so he ignored it. "As I explained previously, the fixed weapons mounted on the station outrange our mobile turrets. There is no way to directly assault the fortress without first enduring its fire. If you had allowed us to position for a multidirectional appro—"

"I understand, Admiral. Just get on with it."

Oceania shook again, more gently this time, as she flushed the latest salvo from her missile launchers, and a cluster of warheads streaked out toward the station.

"This last missile attack will likely finish them, General Semmes. We've seriously degraded their interdictive array, and at least a few of these warheads will get through."

"See that they do, Admiral." Even Semmes thought that was a stupid thing to say, but he was so scared, he could barely think straight.

He wanted to get to the ground as soon as possible. He didn't much like interplanetary travel, and war in space was even worse. He wanted to throw up for at least half a dozen discernible reasons, spacesickness and stark terror being just two of them. But he struggled to control himself, to stare out from his position to the side of the bridge with an expression he hoped communicated anything but the gut-wrenching fear he felt.

"Let's go, Garabrant. It's over. *Vagabond*'s on her way up, and she's the only ride outta here. You miss this trip, it's over."

Garabrant looked up from his station, back toward the door. Of all people, it was North standing there, his bulk leaning through the open hatch. He felt a rush of anger, an urge to pull out his pistol and shoot the murderous bastard. But he couldn't make himself do anything, not get up and rush toward the door, not shoot North. Nothing. All he could do was stare at Claren's body, still lying on the floor, not a meter from Garabrant, a pool of slowly congealing blood all around the ruins North had left of the man's head.

"Now, Garabrant," North yelled. "You don't have a gun left hot enough to light a candle, so why throw your life away?"

He looked around. He was the only one left in weapons control. Jorgen had been killed by a falling structural support, and Wertz had just jumped out of his chair a few minutes earlier and run without a word. But Garabrant had remained at his post, working the weapons array as long as he had a weapon left that was able to fire.

"What the hell, Garabrant?" North said, his eyes darting from the body on the floor to the recalcitrant engineer. He sighed. "He was a fed sympathizer, you know that. He had a chance to do his duty." North slammed his fist against the door frame. "It's up to you, if you want to die because you're pissed I shot a traitor. But it would be a damn shame. The rebellion needs men like you, Garabrant." North looked across the room, his cold stare softening. "Now let's get the hell out of here."

The station shook hard, another hit. The federal ships were close now, their lasers slicing through the huge structure. One entire section was already gone, the victim of a nearby nuclear detonation. Garabrant knew there was no time and yet, for some reason, North was trying to save his life. But he was frozen, unable to make himself respond. All he could see was the same image again and again—Claren's head exploding in a spray of gore. And North standing there, pistol in his hand and no more emotion on his face than if he'd taken out the trash.

North lunged across the room, leaping over Claren's body. Garabrant was surprised, and he didn't have time to react. He reached for his gun, scared now that an enraged North was going to kill him, too, but before he could do anything, the ranger's huge fist slammed into the side of his head.

He felt the impact and pain, yes, but more a fuzziness. He

wasn't knocked out, not quite, but he couldn't do anything, either, not even think straight.

Then, something else, North's massive arm, reaching under him, pulling him out of the chair. He was afraid, confused, but then his eyes focused on the floor as he moved across the room and out into the corridor. North wasn't attacking him, he was carrying him, slung over his shoulder. Saving him.

He had an urge to fight, to try to wrest his way free, but the cloudiness in his head was getting thicker, more intense. The floor wasn't there anymore, at least not as a clear image. Just a cloudy grayness. And then he slipped into blackness.

"Griff, stay at the controls. Hold her steady." Sasha Nerov leapt out of her seat and rushed through the small hatch that led toward *Vagabond*'s cargo hold.

"I'll try, Captain, but you know as well as I do, we're out of time. If we don't get out of here in the next minute or two, we never will."

Sasha heard her first officer's words, and she knew they were nothing save for the hard truth. But there were still survivors on the station, and any who didn't get on board her ship were going to die.

"Do your best, Griff." A short pause, just a second or so. "You handle her as well as I do . . . that's the dirty little secret I've never told you." She nodded to her longtime comrade and ducked into the corridor, racing toward the hold.

She knew encouraging words weren't going to get the job done, not now, but it couldn't hurt. Still, the problem wasn't flying *Vagabond*—it was staying docked to a station that was falling apart. The docking port attached to her ship was swinging back and forth, its connection to the orbital platform tenuous at best. There were gaping holes in the fortress's hull and severed structural members dangling by tattered connections or floating freely in space, deadly obstacles, any one of which could slam into *Vagabond* with devastating effect.

The ship shook, whipsawed again as a whole section of the station twisted, snapping the great girders that had supported it. Without the near weightlessness of its orbital position, the giant structure would have collapsed completely by now. But even the slight gravitational pull from the planet, combined with the kinetic energy from various parts of the station blown out of place and slamming into other sections, was enough to tear the whole thing slowly to shreds.

She raced into the inner hold, her head snapping back and forth, noting the nearly two dozen men and women who'd already been rescued. They were crammed together, too many people in too little space. At least five or six were badly wounded, and her eyes rested for an instant on one who looked dead.

She reached up and snapped down her helmet's visor, activating her survival suit as she slipped into the airlock between the inner and outer hulls. The readout was clear about the conditions in the room beyond. Vacuum.

Some of the escapees had made it to *Vagabond* before the entire section of the station lost atmospheric integrity, but now, everyone on the station without working survival gear was dead.

She heard the whooshing sound as the small chamber vacated the air, and the outer door opened. She stared out at a nightmare.

Most of her crew was there, wearing their own survival suits, and trying to help the fleeing members of the station's complement. There were bodies everywhere, floating around the bay, and drifting out into space itself. The docking portal was gone, completely, a good three meters of open space yawning between *Vagabond* and the station. Her people had opened the rear cargo doors, and they were waving for the cluster of men and women still on the station to leap across the growing gulf.

She moved cautiously toward the rear of the hold and added her own gestures to those of the crew. "C'mon," she said, under her breath to herself. *It's your only chance . . .*

She knew *Vagabond* couldn't stay where it was. Griff was performing a minor miracle holding the ship as steadily as he was, but it wouldn't last. And neither would the station. In a matter of moments, seconds perhaps, the platform to which *Vagabond* was so tenuously clinging wouldn't be there anymore, at least nothing of it save floating debris.

And if Vagabond isn't out of here by then, we'll be debris, too.

She looked out on the utter chaos. The station crew were soldiers, technically at least, but they weren't professionals. She tried to imagine the fear they were feeling, and she wondered how many that panic would kill who might otherwise have survived. She had her own memories, dark ones that reached back even before her smuggling days.

Too many.

That's what the butcher bill was going to be for this little operation.

She reached out and grabbed hold of one of the handrails, and she worked her way back, toward the gaping maw of *Vagabond*'s open hatch. She held tightly, but she didn't have a safety line attached. She'd have excoriated one of her people for doing the same thing. Leadership had its own form of well-meaning hypocrisy.

She flipped on the comm line, but it connected her only to the *Vagabond* crew members in the hold. Her ship had been tied into the station's main channel, yet communications were down all across the dying platform now. Which meant, in the soundless vacuum of *Vagabond*'s hold, the most effective way to communicate with the terrified people she was trying to rescue was by waving her arms, just as her crew had been doing.

"Cap, this is Griff. We've got to blast. Now."

"Not yet, Griff." Her eyes darted to the three or four figures floating through space toward the hold . . . and the twenty or more still clinging to the wreckage of the docking portal. "We've got more people here."

"Sasha, we don't have time. The station's coming apart. I've got internal explosions on the scanners, and we've got federal ships coming around. We'll be in their firing arcs in less than a minute." A pause, a second, perhaps two before Daniels continued, his voice tenser, darker. "If we wait, we're going to lose them anyway, and we're all going to die, too."

Sasha felt Daniels's words like a hard punch to the gut. She couldn't imagine leaving those people behind, pulling away and abandoning them to die. She tended to think she could push things further than most people thought was possible, but she'd never put Daniels in that group. Her first officer was as coldly realistic as she was. If he said they had less than a minute, she knew damned well there wasn't a second more to spare.

She waved her arms wildly. "Jump!" she screamed inside her helmet, aware it was a useless gesture even as she continued. "Now! Jump!"

Another crew member stepped off the twisted metal at the edge of the station, toward *Vagabond*. Sasha watched the figure moving slowly toward her, cursing under her breath as she did, aching to scream to the figures clinging to the shattered docking tube to push off hard. A rough landing was the least of their concerns now. A broken bone would heal. She was ignoring Daniels's warning herself, but there were really only seconds left and she couldn't continue to disregard what he'd told her. She *had* to give the order, and she had to do it now.

"We've got to get out of here," she said softly on the ship's channel. "Get ready to close the hatch. Griff, as soon as we're secure, get us out of here."

"Now, Captain . . . not another second." The edge in Daniels's voice was real. She'd heard her second-in-command when they were running from federal cutters and hiding in dust clouds, praying for enough cover to evade the scanners of the ships hunting *Vagabond*. But she'd never heard him as tense as he sounded now.

She saw the figure that she'd watched push off. Whoever it was had aimed poorly and hit hard on the edge of the hatch. Two of her people reached out and pulled the fortunate crew member inside. But Sasha knew that was the last person they could save. She had a dozen of her own crew, and almost forty Havenites aboard. It would be a miracle if she and Griff could get her overloaded ship down at all, but if she waited another ten seconds, they'd never get that chance.

"Captain, we have two federal frigates firing at us."

That was it. There was no more time.

"Close the hatch," she said, her voice like ice.

"Captain . . ."

"Close it. Now!" She stared out at the two figures floating through space toward the large opening that was even now closing. She tried to imagine the stark terror as they saw their salvation slamming shut, and then, seconds later, she heard the sickening thuds as they hit the closed doors. They would have slipped off, she knew, and they were now floating in space, their meager life support dwindling with each passing second.

She looked through the clear window on the back of the hatch. The fear moving through the crowd of stranded refugees was visible, a ripple of frenetic motion as those she'd failed to save came quickly to terms with their dark fate.

She had to get back to the bridge, to help Daniels bring the ship down. But she hesitated, unable to take her eyes off the desperate and panicked people huddled on the docking portal, even as *Vagabond* fired her thrusters, and they shrank back into the distance until she couldn't see them anymore.

"Is it true, Cal?" Zig Welch stepped out of the shadows, leaning in and whispering into Jacen's ear. The Waymeet was home turf to the Society, generally safe ground for any conversation, but the return of the federals meant the revolution was entering its crucial stage. There was nothing to be gained by taking chances.

"Yes. The station is gone, destroyed, just as we predicted." Jacen looked around quickly and gestured toward a table in the back of the small room. *Inn* was a strong word to describe the Waymeet, despite the technical qualification bestowed by the three meager rooms for rent on the second floor. The place was barely a small tavern, a spot on the Old North Road, just south of Blackwood Forest, where Havenites traveling back and forth between Landfall and the farms and settlements to the north could stop for a quick bite. There were half a dozen people there as Jacen and Welch spoke, and four of them were Society members.

Welch could see Jacen wasn't completely satisfied. "What is it, Cal? We'd counted on the federals blasting the station. This will scare everyone into action."

"Yes, but our losses were considerably lower than we'd anticipated. I was counting on a groundswell of anger at the killing of every man and woman on that station . . . but Captain Nerov and her people ran a rescue mission. They pulled at least forty people off the platform before it was destroyed."

"Still, that means over fifty were killed in action, or left up there to die when the station was destroyed. Surely that will enrage the people."

"It will be useful, Zig, but it's not as impactful when there are heroic survivors. We don't need a war here, my friend. We don't need resistance. We need a brutal, no-holds-barred fight to the finish. A crusade. We not only need to defeat the government troops, we have to root out every federal sympathizer hiding on this planet. Every Havenite who fails to rise to his planet's call." Jacen paused. "A crew completely wiped out would have been more helpful in that undertaking than forty-odd survivors." Jacen's voice had a sour tone. He despised Sasha Nerov. The ex-smuggler had her uses, but she was definitely on his list of those who had to go before the revolution could truly prevail.

Zig nodded slowly. "Still, we can enjoy great gains from the entire mess. The federals *did* attack the station without delay and without even calling for a surrender." Welch stopped speaking as the bartender came over and placed two mugs on the table. Hal Dawson was a Society member, but Welch still felt the same caution. This was not the time for carelessness.

"Have we been able to determine if the rumors were true?" Welch continued after Dawson walked back to the bar.

"No, not yet." Jacen shook his head. "But our man on Earth seemed to think it was reliable."

"We can only hope. Robert Semmes is a fool. It would be a gift to us if he is in command of the expeditionary force instead of a regular army general." Welch paused. "Still, I wonder. Semmes isn't a great tactician, I will agree with that. But he is willing to do whatever he must to win. He will not be . . . restrained . . . as Governor Wells was."

"And we will encourage him to do exactly that, Zig. Not openly, of course, but we will prod him. We will use his temper against him. And with each innocent Havenite he kills, the rebellion grows."

Welch didn't show any emotion, but on the inside, he shied away just a little. Jacen had spent years pursuing revolution, first on Earth, and then, after his exile, on Haven. It had been his life, and he was unlikely to let anything interfere now that his dream was so close to fruition. If the new order must be paid for in blood, Welch had no doubt Jacen would spill as much as it required. But it was one thing to eliminate federals and their sympathizers, another to watch civilians sacrificed en masse to further the cause—so much so that it tested even his own fanatical devotion. Cautiously he tried to convey that.

"And yet, too many innocents could mean there's no one *to* join the rebellion. And it may break the will of the people. We must be ready, Cal, to do our own duty, even as General Ward leads the army into battle."

Jacen frowned at the mention of Damian's name, but then he nodded. "Yes, General Ward will be very useful. I daresay he is the only one on Haven capable of forging an army that can defeat federal regulars." He paused, making a face again. "But we must watch the general closely as well, Zig. He is committed to Haven's freedom, I am certain of that. But he is not one of us. His devotion to the revolution is far from complete. He has repeatedly shown that he does not have the strength, the resolve, to do what must be done, at least off the battlefield."

Welch nodded. "He *has* interfered repeatedly in our efforts to root out the loyalist element of the population. A great chance was lost to eliminate federal sympathizers before the government forces returned. Now we must beware of fifth columnists even as our forces fight in the field."

"Exactly. He considers individual lives of greater importance than the creation of a new Haven, one that will last for thousands of years." Jacen paused, and he looked around the tavern again.

Then he leaned forward and whispered, "If General Ward leads our armies to victory, he will be extremely popular, with the people *and* with his soldiers. That would make him dangerous—perhaps *too* dangerous."

Welch stared back, swallowing back a hint of fear. "Cal, a move against the general at this time? I agree with your concerns, but—"

"You are right," Jacen interrupted. "Of course we cannot take any action *now*. We need Ward's tactical ability and his renown as a war hero. And if he is victorious, we can never be connected in any way to his . . . elimination." Jacen hesitated, flashing a glance behind him yet again. "But imagine the service the general could offer the revolution as a martyr, lost to federal treachery in the closing moments of the rebellion. Perhaps a victim of a loyalist assassination plot. The people would rise up in the streets like a force of nature. They would demand with righteous fury that we purge the disloyal elements from Haven. The revolution will be victorious, and with blood and fire, we will remake this world."

Jacen sat and stared at his comrade. His hands were clenched into fists under the table, his usual control faltering, his rage clearly on display.

The thought of moving against Damian Ward was a difficult one, even for the second-in-command of the Society, but Welch reluctantly agreed. The danger of leaving someone so uncommitted to the greater ideals of the revolution alive was not an option. "Perhaps you are right, Cal. But we must be careful. The act can never be connected back to us. That would be disastrous."

Welch tried to imagine the fury of Haven in such a situation. Damian Ward was already the planet's favorite son. Leading her armies to victory, making her independence a reality, would make him the most popular Havenite by a large margin.

"We will be careful, Zig. We are *always* careful. And for now, that's the least of our concerns. First we must help the general win, for there can be no revolutionary Haven without victory in the field."

"Which is why so many of our members are with the army. They will fight, obviously, and help to win the war. And they will also be in a strong position to watch the general."

"Yes, our brothers and sisters in uniform will do their share for the cause, both in battle . . . and in keeping us close to the general. Yet the Society must do more even. There are traitors in our midst, those who would work against us, seek to aid the federals in enslaving this world." There was anger growing in Jacen's voice.

"The loyalists. Of course. General Ward has protected them, prevented most of our efforts to root them out for the past year. But now he will be . . ."

"He will be busy. He will be in the field. There is little doubt our forces will be driven from Landfall. The enemy will target the capital and the other cities, because they believe if they control those population centers, we will break. They do not know us at all. But we have tentacles everywhere, and we can go places the army cannot. When the federals take control of Landfall, the traitors will come flooding out into the open. They will feel safe, protected. Many will even seek to aid the federal army. And we will be in the shadows, waiting to strike." Jacen paused, clearly realizing the volume of his voice had been rising. He leaned forward and continued softly, "We will cleanse this world of traitors, Zig, and we will set an example for all of Haven of what happens to those who fail the revolution."

Welch looked back across the table, nodding. "It is time . . . time at last to cleanse our world. Let it begin, my friend. Let it begin now."

"They're finally here."

Jerome Steves crouched forward, his nearly two-meter frame not even coming close to fitting under the low rafters above the building's rough basement. The house was one of the oldest ones in Landfall, hastily constructed in the days before the colonists had heavy equipment and imported building materials. It was in the old section of town, of course, on a narrow, winding street, dead center in a small cluster of neglected blocks that were gradually deteriorating into Landfall's first real slum.

The building's original use had long been supplanted by newer structures along the broad avenues of the more modern sections of town. But even in obsolescence, there was utility, and its abandoned status on an almost forgotten stretch of road made it an ideal place for clandestine meetings.

"I confess, I'd almost lost hope." Elizabeth Mullen was considerably shorter than Steves, and even she just barely fit without leaning forward. Her hair had caught a few times on the rough, splintered boards just above her head, but she was standing straight, looking a lot more comfortable than her companion. "I have been afraid, not so much for myself, but for my parents, and my grandmother. Things have gotten so bad, they've been afraid to leave the house."

"If it hadn't been for General Ward's intervention, I fear many of us would have been murdered in the street." Steves moved to the side, banging his head on a low-hanging support for the third or fourth time. He grunted softly, reaching up and rubbing the spot.

"Even with the general's meager efforts to enforce some semblance of control over the Society and the other elements of the mob, we have been harassed. Some of us have been beaten, and we have all lived in fear." Ray Isaacson was the third person in the cellar. There was an element of anger in his words that made his voice more caustic than those of his comrades. "Now it is time for us to strike back. The federal troops could be here any day. We must spread the word. Now is the time for any man or woman who is loyal to his government, who does not wish to live under the fervor of revolutionary zealots, to come forward. We must support the federal forces in any way we can, for as long as it takes to defeat the rebellion."

"We don't dare come forward while the rebels control Landfall and even less so if the army marches out but the federals do not yet occupy." Still crouching, Steves turned, first toward Mullen, then back facing Isaacson. "No doubt, the Society will try to take advantage of such an absence to attack any of us who expose ourselves."

"Damn the foul Society to hell, I say," Isaacson snapped. "If the army is gone, if the illegal government flees, let us face the Society head-on. In the street, yes, but also in their homes, as they would invade ours. As they threaten us, let us do to them. As they would injure us, so shall we injure them. And if they would kill our people, we will kill theirs."

Mullen looked shocked. "Ray, if we do as you ask, the streets will run red with blood."

"Then they shall run red, and the blood shall be that of traitors." Isaacson hesitated for a moment before continuing. "I understand your concerns, Beth, and your commendable wish for a less drastic solution. But is there one? As long as people like Cal Jacen and the Society exist, we'll never be safe. We must strike at every opportunity, even before the federals move in and fill the vacuum. I guarantee the Society is not planning to sit idle, and nor, my friends, should we. Would you be sheep, waiting to be slaughtered by your enemies? Or would you stand up, your fist in the air, and meet the enemy on his own field of battle?"

Steves sighed. "I don't like it, Ray," he said softly. Isaacson could be as aggressive in his own right as Cal Jacen or any member of the Society, and he and Jerome often butted heads about the best course of action. But that didn't mean he was wrong now. He sighed. "Still, you may be right. We could wish for peace and ask to be left alone, but we all know that's going to fall on deaf ears. These people mean to *kill* us, not reason with us, so why pretend otherwise? Besides—they *are* traitors." He paused. "I am with you, Ray. I do not relish the thought of violence, but sometimes there is no alternative."

Isaacson smiled, and he reached out and shook Steves's hand.

Then he turned toward Mullen. "Well, Beth? I know you don't like violence, but they will come for you whether you fight or not. Are you with us?"

Mullen stood for a moment, her eyes darting between her two comrades. There was pain in her expression, agony at the terrible choice that lay before her. Finally, though, she closed her eyes and nodded, just barely, but it was enough assent for the words she couldn't compel her mouth to speak.

"Then we are agreed. Let us spread the word. We must be ready to strike if the rebel army leaves Landfall."

CHAPTER 10

"We'll never hold Landfall, General. Unless everything we've discussed has been very mistaken, you know what they're bringing down. Even if they weren't able to transport heavy weapons, what they can put in the field is going to be more than we can handle."

Colonel Luci Morgan sat at the table with the rest of the army of Haven's senior officers. She was one of Damian's old comrades, another ex-federal officer who'd taken a farm on Haven as a mustering-out bonus.

Damian had called Morgan and the others in for a final strategy session. The fall of the orbital platform meant the federals could be landing troops planetside at any time now.

"So we need a way to ensure we aren't pinned down, that we don't give them the chance to trap us and destroy the army." Morgan was spirited. She'd been known for her calm and pleasant personality as a farmer, but now that she was back in uniform, she had reverted to the aggressive—sometimes abrasive—demeanor those around the table who'd served with her before remembered.

"No," responded Tucker Jones, another veteran, his own voice rising in volume in lockstep with Morgan's. "It's not just what kinds of troops they have, but how those troops are supported. We all know they have superior logistical systems, and that means they will have more transports and mobile capability than us. Running around won't solve anything—we can't win a war of maneuver. We can only win a war of attrition. And fighting in the cities, fortifying every building, every developed area, is the way to tie them down. City fighting is an equalizer. It will reduce the effect of their superiority. We can inflict maximum casualties, force them to expend more ammunition and equipment."

"At the cost of the utter destruction of Landfall, and every other city on the planet," Morgan said. "Do you have any idea of the civilian casualties that would result? We would turn Haven into a graveyard."

"Colonel Morgan," Jones snapped back, "that may be our only choice. Can you imagine what it's going to be like if the planet is reconquered? The restrictions they would impose? And the punishments they would mete out, not only to our soldiers, but to any Havenite who has shown the slightest support for the rebellion—which, at this point, is the majority of the population? Would you put it past the federals to virtually depopulate this world to set an example to the other colonies?"

"So we should beat them to it—"

"Please," Damian said, cutting off the argument between his two officers. "You are both right. We are not in a situation that offers us ideal choices. Whatever we do will come at a cost." He moved his head, panning his view to each of those present, one by one. Then he sighed softly.

"But Colonel Jones is right, too." He held up a hand to stave off Morgan's interruption. "No—he *is* right: we cannot simply abandon Landfall. It's Haven's capital, and by far its largest population center. Those people deserve protection. And more, we must consider what kind of message we send out if we retreat without putting up any sort of resistance. Not just to the federals, but our own people. This is going to be a hard war, and without their support, without a steady stream of volunteers swelling our ranks—and resistance groups striking at the federals behind the lines—we don't stand a chance. We can't change that reality. The federals can draw on the resources they need. They can order their soldiers anywhere. We have nothing . . . nothing save the people.

"So yes, Colonel Jones's analysis is correct. We cannot hope to defeat the federals in the field, not in open battle. We will be hemmed in by whatever airpower they are able to transport to Haven, and that will greatly restrict our mobility. We must take advantage of every force multiplier we can obtain. And urban warfare is just such a multiplier. This *will* be a war of attrition, and we're starting with a massive disadvantage in terms of skill and matériel. We don't have soldiers on Earth, and have no means to threaten any federal possessions. As such, we can only win our freedom by compelling the federals to give up the effort to subjugate us."

"So what does that mean?" Morgan asked.

"It means we must defend Landfall, at least to some extent. I can't think of anything more disastrous for morale than simply fleeing and leaving the capital open to the enemy. Yet," he said, looking at Jones, "Colonel Morgan was *also* correct in much of her assessment. Our victory, if it comes, will be the result of raids, of lightning strikes, of hiding from the enemy's major forces and hitting them when and where we can gain temporary advantage. And we must continue this until we have worn them down. We cannot allow ourselves to be penned in any one spot, however important that place may be. If they can surround us, if they can hem us in, the rebellion is over. Even in the face of catastrophic casualties, the federals will never withdraw if they feel they have us cornered and on the verge of defeat."

"It sounds like you have a plan, General. What do we do?" asked Devlin Kerr, another ex-veteran and now a colonel for the rebellion.

Damian had an idea of what he was going to order, but the truth was, he was still uncertain. He wanted to hurt the federals at Landfall, to blood them badly in what he was sure would be their first attack. But he was leery of committing a major portion of the army. Some of the recruits had a fair amount of training, but he was far from confident his army could handle complex maneuvers under stress. If he committed the whole force to the defense of Landfall, and they were forced to retreat, he knew it could be a disaster. If his people were caught out in the open, exhausted and demoralized after a bloody fight for the capital, the federals could crush the entire force. And yet if he left too few as part of the defense, they'd be easily overrun after, perhaps, inflicting a few wounds into the federals' cause. It felt like a lose-lose proposition.

He looked across to the far end of the table, and wondered if perhaps there was a third option. Patrick Killian hadn't uttered a word during the meeting. He'd just sat there, listening attentively to all that was said. Killian had a reputation as a hothead, and the exploits of his rangers were still spoken of in many quarters with fear and revulsion—talk still persisted that Killian's people had scalped their federal victims at Vincennes—but he was an effective officer, and right now, that's what mattered the most.

Sure, Damian suspected there was more to the rumors than pure fiction, but he'd also decided he didn't want to know. He needed Killian. The man was the best all-around fighter he'd ever seen, and though a lot of mystery surrounded his dishonorable discharge from the army, Damian knew Killian had been set up to take the fall for someone else: Robert Semmes. It had driven Killian almost to the breaking point when Damian had allowed Semmes to leave with the retreating federals the year before, but the man had stayed on. And that meant he was still willing to fight.

Kerr wasn't quite correct—he didn't exactly have a plan.

But one was forming.

"I want to thank you all for coming," Damian said abruptly. "Go now, and get your commands organized. The enemy may commence their landing at any moment. I will have orders to each of you by the end of the day.

"Dismissed."

He sat and watched as his officers stood up, one or two of them hovering for a moment, as if they wanted to say something. But finally they all filed out. All except for Killian.

Of course he stayed. He knows this is a situation for his rangers.

"I want to discuss our options."

"Yes, General."

"We're all out of our depth, Patrick. A bunch of noncoms and junior officers playing at being colonels and generals." He meant no insult to any of his people, and he certainly included himself at the top of his list of those promoted well beyond their experience levels.

"That's true, sir. Yet this has often been the case in war, hasn't it? Is a senior officer with thirty years of experience in peacetime ready to lead troops in war? We have seen ourselves escalated in rank, but we have experienced battle, you and I, right? As have most of those who were in this room. I have confidence in our officers, sir, and in you most of all."

"Thank you, Patrick. Nevertheless, I find myself pulled in two directions. We must bleed them. And Colonel Jones is correct that Landfall is an ideal place for that. But if we commit fully, if we are trapped there—"

"You don't need to convince me, sir. If you've got an idea, just tell me. Give me my orders, and I'll see them done."

Damian smiled ruefully. His procrastination had clearly been showing, and he appreciated Killian's blunt nature in getting to the point.

"I want you to remain in Landfall. You will have your own forces, of course, but reinforced with several battalions. I am sorry to give you this duty. There's not a high level of tactical success to be gained, I fear. But it's crucial for the overall effort, and you are the most suited to the kind of fighting this battle will involve." He paused. "And you are my best independent commander."

"You don't need to explain to me, General. You're in charge, and I'm going to follow you. You can count on that, and you can count on me. And all of my people."

"I know I can, Patrick." Damian sat silently for a time. Then he said, "I know I don't owe you any explanations, but I do want to be clear that I don't consider this a suicide mission. You are to remain in Landfall only as long as you can mount an effective defense. Then you are to break out, however you can, and disperse your forces. I want your people in the enemy rear after you leave the city, ready to operate against their supply lines and logistical bases. I want you to run a guerilla war. Draw in the population any way you can, but feel free to take chances."

"You want me to hit their forces, ambush smaller columns?"

"To a point, Colonel. Inflict as many losses on the federals as you can, but damage to matériel is even more important. Every vehicle you destroy, every crate of supplies you deprive them of, brings us closer to victory."

Killian stared intently. "You really think wrecking their equipment will be enough to make a difference?"

"You remember our time in the service. What was the thing that we were always bitching about—other than just wanting to get the hell out of there? Supplies. Ammo. Better food. Yes, going after matériel is going to be key. Supply will be their weakness, Colonel. They have to bring everything they need from Earth, weapons, ammunition, food. The cost is, literally, astronomical. We will not win this war on the battlefield, at least not *only* on the battlefield. We must hit at them where it is most costly. We must drive them to the end of their economic resources. Only then can we win our freedom."

"That's not really what I do best, sir. You know my people are better suited to, well, *wetter* work. We can take out some weapons and force them to send a few more ships, but so what? They'll just send the ships."

"There's going to be plenty of chances to get your hands bloody,

Colonel. Because I'm not talking about 'some' weapons. I'm saying we target their heaviest ordnance, we infiltrate their bases, and we destroy their transport and their armored vehicles, then we go well beyond 'a few more ships.' The goal is to compel them to send ship after ship, one load of replacement equipment after another, until the economy back on Earth approaches total collapse. Then we'll see how determined they are. For all the wealth at the top, you and I know Federal America's economy is not strong. They can only endure so much expense fighting us before it falls completely apart. And the senate will give up before they allow that to happen."

Killian still didn't look convinced. "You know more about all that than I do, sir, but how much damage can we inflict with just raids?"

"A lot, Patrick," Damian said, reverting back to the ranger's name rather than his rank. "The last war between Earth's powers didn't end in victory, as the propaganda says. It didn't end in defeat, either. Exhaustion was the peacemaker there. Economic exhaustion, of all the powers. The combatants simply made peace because none of them could afford to continue the war. That was only five years ago. I am no economist, but I joined the army because of my own poverty. So did most of the people in my unit—as I'm sure you did, as well. That poverty didn't end after the war, and I'd wager Federal America's resources are still heavily strained.

"Think about it this way: Do you know what it costs to transport an armored vehicle from Earth to Haven? Probably ten times what it costs to build the thing, and perhaps more. Every one of those your raiding parties can destroy costs the federals a fortune. And as much as they probably hate the loss of face of having a colony rebel, they hate the loss of revenue from that colony even more. I don't know the exact mathematical tipping point, but if we can make that cost-benefit ratio outrageous enough, they'll swallow their pride, blame the loss on a scapegoat, and leave us the hell alone.

"At least, that's what I hope." He looked at his officer, his eyes cold with resolve. "Because it's the *only* way we can win that I can see, Patrick. You're an old vet like me. What do you think about our chances against the federals heads-up?"

Killian nodded slowly. "There is no chance. You're right, General." He sighed softly. "I still don't understand the economic stuff like you do, but I trust your assessment." Another hesitation as Killian looked right at Damian. "Don't you worry, sir. We'll bleed them dry in Landfall, and then we will make sure they can't move so much as a transport full of field rations without a huge escorting force."

Damian nodded. "That's what I was hoping you'd say, Colonel Killian." He stood up, waiting as the ranger followed suit. Then he extended his hand, grasping Killian's and shaking it firmly. "Take your rangers and command of the first and second regiments. They are the best-trained and equipped of our forces. Dig yourselves into Landfall . . . and wait. The enemy will be here soon."

"Yes, sir." Killian stepped back and gave Damian a heartfelt if sloppy salute. Then he turned and started toward the door.

"And, Colonel?"

Killian stopped and spun back around. "Yes, General?"

"Try to keep civilian casualties in Landfall to a minimum." Damian's voice deepened, a dark cloud seeming to pass in front of him. "But the battle is your primary concern. And victory will not come without cost." Damian shuddered to think of what the fearsome warrior would do, what measures he might take to defend Haven's capital. But he simply couldn't throw someone into such a maelstrom with his hands tied.

And he was sure he'd end up doing a lot of things he didn't like before the fight for Haven was through.

"Dismissed."

CHAPTER 11

"General, I've got my people in place. We're ready." Luci Morgan was crouched down in a foxhole on the outskirts of Haven's only spaceport. The spaceport was the natural place for the enemy to attack first, and one of the best to defend. The federals needed the port to bring in larger numbers of troops, as well as supplies and equipment, and that meant they couldn't soften Morgan's positions with orbital bombardment, not without chopping up the landing areas they needed to bring down their heavy cargo shuttles.

"Good. We're tracking landing sleds inbound. We can't confirm they're heading for your location, but everything checks so far."

"We'll be here if they head for the spaceport, General."

"Luci, if they want a beachhead badly enough, we can't stop them. So do as much damage as you can, but pull your people out of there before you get trapped or overwhelmed."

"Understood, sir." Morgan still wasn't sure how quickly she was planning to obey that order. Her military experiences had been coming back to her since a year before—memories, habits, the feeling of being a soldier. And her hatred of running. Luci Morgan despised paying twice for real estate, and she knew she'd never have a greater advantage against the federals than she would while they were landing.

"Good luck, Colonel. Ward out."

The line went dead, the silence lasting perhaps thirty seconds before her own people started chiming in with sightings on their own short-range scanners.

"Enemy craft heading this way."

"At least a dozen federal ships, Colonel."

"Colonel, we've got two attack waves coming in."

She flipped on her unitwide comm. "All units, we have enemy forces approaching. You all know what to do, so I'm not going to go over it again. Let's just get it done."

She had two regiments, about sixteen hundred troops, most of them Guardians of Liberty or early recruits. At least a quarter of them had fought at Vincennes and Dover, and they were the closest thing to veterans she had, beyond the dozen or so ex-federal soldiers commanding her companies.

They were dug in all around the spaceport, facing both directions. She couldn't be sure if the federals would try to land right on top of the port, or if they'd come down along the outside perimeter and move in, so she was ready for either eventuality.

She didn't have much heavy equipment, but the six big rocket launchers her force possessed were spread out, and she'd scraped up anyone she could find with any experience to crew them. They were shorter-range than fixed defensive installations would have been, but with some luck her people might still take out a lander or two. Any federals they shot down were that many they wouldn't have to face on the ground.

She pulled a small tablet from her belt, squinting as she stared at the tiny display. She watched as the first wave of enemy ships moved into range. There was no question now. They were definitely heading toward her positions. And in a few seconds, they'd be in range of her defenses.

She tapped the side of her helmet, activating the comm unit

and connecting with the rocket batteries. "All positions, commence firing. Concentrate on lead ships."

A wave of acknowledgments came back, and then she saw a long white smoke trail rising up, a few kilometers to the east. Then another, and another, until six weapons were in the air, heading up toward the not-yet-visible enemy landing sleds. About twenty seconds later, another wave of missiles streaked up through the blue morning sky.

She glanced down at her screen, watching the weapons moving toward the landers. The enemy craft began evasive maneuvers, moving jerkily through the sky. The assault sleds were designed to get troops to the ground in the teeth of opposition, and she knew her inadequate defenses didn't have a chance of defeating the attack. The best she could hope for was inflicting some losses on the enemy while she had the chance. Because once they got down in enough force, her troops would never hold. That was a difficult fact for her to accept, but it was a fact nevertheless. Damian had been clear. She was there to inflict as many losses as she could, while preserving her own force intact. She recognized the tactical sense in the general's orders, but that didn't make them any easier to accept.

She looked back down at the scanner, swiping her finger across, changing the display to a schematic of her ground positions. Her people were dug in, mostly occupying a series of partially interconnected foxholes designed to face an attack from either direction. It was a relatively complicated series of works, one that Damian had ordered constructed months before. There was room for debate on many aspects of federal strategy, but there hadn't been any doubt on one issue: the enemy had to take the spaceport first.

A flash in the sky caught her attention, and her head snapped up. There was a billowing cloud above, glints of reddish-yellow fire showing through in places. She felt a rush of excitement and moved her finger across the screen again, confirming what her eyes had already told her. One of the rockets had taken down a federal lander.

Her hands tightened into celebratory fists, and she nodded hard to herself. But there was something else, too. She had images in her head of men and women she'd served with in the last war, and she wondered for an instant if she'd just killed any of them.

She was still struggling with her mixed feelings when another explosion, this one closer, erupted in the sky above. There was no time for soul-searching. If the landers coming down were the T-9s the army had used when she'd served, her people had just killed eighty federals. It was war, and the time for worrying about whom she was fighting was well past.

"All right, people," she shouted into the comm, "here they come." The first wave of twelve landers—now ten—were seconds from reaching the ground. Her people were about to have their hands full, even with their numerical advantage.

Temporary numerical advantage . . . because this is surely only the first wave.

"General, Colonel Morgan reports her forces are engaged. The federals landed outside her perimeter, and they are attacking the eastern section of her line." Ben Withers sat at a cramped workstation in the corner of the underground bunker. Damian didn't think the federals would bombard Landfall, but he wasn't sure enough to risk his army's command and control center, especially not when Danforth Communications had a secure subbasement normally used for data storage. It wasn't exactly a hardened military facility, but it was a lot better than nothing.

"Very well, Major. Advise Colonel Kerr to have his forces on alert and ready to cover Colonel Morgan's retreat." *Assuming she pulls back like I told her to . . .*

"Yes, sir." A few seconds later. "Colonel Kerr acknowledges. His forces are in position, waiting for your orders."

Damian felt the urge to send Kerr's troops in right away, but that would only escalate the battle at the spaceport, and he didn't want to get drawn into a costly fight there. Not when he couldn't win in the end. Morgan was there for one purpose: to attrit the enemy while they were landing and disorganized. Once the federals had enough troops on the ground to launch a coordinated advance, he wanted her out of there. The day would come for a full-scale fight to the finish, but it was not today.

"Has Captain Nerov reported in yet?"

"Not since *Vagabond* lifted off, sir."

Damian had thought Nerov was crazy when she'd told him her idea. He was no expert on piloting spacecraft, but he'd have thought what she suggested was impossible. The ship captain had a way of explaining things, a strange concoction that mixed confidence and a little performance art to make the insane seem plausible, if not downright routine.

In the end, though, he'd given her the go-ahead. He wondered if she was really as confident as she'd seemed, or if she had just been desperate to find an alternative to scuttling her beloved ship, but he had to admit, the idea of hiding *Vagabond*, of maintaining even the hope of a tenuous link with anything beyond Haven's surface, had its appeal.

He'd never thought about hiding a spaceship in the ocean but, of course, *Vagabond* was proofed against the vacuum of space and the pressures of liftoff, so a hundred or so meters of water shouldn't be any real problem.

"General, we're picking up more landing craft. Two more waves."

Another eight hundred federals.

Damian hated sitting in an underground hideout while his people were fighting. It took everything he had to keep himself from running through the door and rushing down to the space-port. If the fight there had been his only responsibility, he'd have been in the line already. But he had troops stationed throughout the capital and all around it, and his place was here, coordinating everything.

"Get me Colonel Morgan, Major," he said, struggling to hide the tension in his voice. "Now."

"It's confirmed, General: they're regulars. Full exos and everything. These guys are picking off anything that even pokes its head out, so I'm guessing it's a crack outfit."

Morgan was crouched low, looking out from the foxhole. She'd moved forward, much farther than Damian had intended for her to go. But her people were hard-pressed, and they needed her. She'd lost track of her losses, but at least fifty of her people were down, and maybe double that.

"We've got two more waves coming in, Colonel. I want you to begin your withdrawal."

"Sir, my position is good. We can hold. Request permiss—"

"Denied, Colonel. You are to pull back now." He paused. "Luci, we've got at least eight hundred more federals coming down. You said it yourself, these are veteran regulars, and you're about to lose the advantage of numbers. Get out of there. *Now*."

"Yes, sir," she said. Damian was right, but she hated to give ground. Her people had inflicted heavy losses on the federals, so far giving out worse than they'd gotten. That had more to do with the fact that her forces were defending from cover while the feds were landing and launching attacks across a killing ground her people had prepared in advance than anything else. But that wasn't nothing, either, and she felt confident she could cause even more damage. Yet the federals were still gaining ground, pushing her troops from their forward positions, and the cost was getting higher and higher. When they were reinforced, they would slice through her lines, and if she didn't get her people out, there was a good chance they'd be trapped.

Shit.

She reached up to the comm controls on her helmet, switching to her forcewide channel. "Third regiment, fall back by odds and evens. Fourth regiment, hold your position."

Her commanders already knew where to go. She'd gone over the retreat plan three times, pounding it into their heads until she was sure they could recite it back to her. She'd seen what confusion could do to forces on the battlefield, and she was determined to avoid paying that blood price.

She looked around her current position. She was in a foxhole with a platoon of the third regiment, men and women she'd just ordered to pull back. "All right, you all heard the order. Odds, hold your positions and maintain fire. Evens, withdraw to the next line."

She moved toward the front of the trench, informally nominating herself as an "odd." She peered out at the enemy positions in the distance, a line of roughly dug pits. The cover wasn't a match for her troopers' more extensive works, but it was enough to turn the ongoing firefight into an exercise in keeping heads down.

The federals had made one attack already, but it had been hastily launched, and her people had beaten it back. She suspected whoever was in command over there had underestimated her troops, expecting them to flee at the approach of federal line soldiers. She suspected, too, that was a mistake he wouldn't make again. The next assault would be better coordinated and executed, and if she pulled this off, none of her people would even be there.

She slid her rifle from her back and stepped up to the firing line along the lip of the trench. Her fire wasn't needed, not yet at least, but she was sending a message.

She turned and looked back, seeing that the evens were almost in place. "Odds, let's move. Fall back, past the evens, to the next position." She leaned forward and took a few shots, and then she turned and followed the platoon over the top of the trench's rear wall and out into the field beyond.

She moved quickly, crouching forward, staying low. She'd reminded her troopers to keep down, but some of them stood up to run, and more than one fell, the victims of federal fire.

She didn't have the communications network to keep close track of her losses, but they could only be increasing. Even the part of her that resented Damian's orders to withdraw now saw the wisdom in pulling back.

"Colonel, the federals are advancing again."

She stopped and went prone, snapping her head around to look across the field. It was no surprise. It made perfect sense for the enemy to move forward and take the trenches she'd abandoned.

She watched the federals coming on, their formation tightly organized, their speed impressive, even as they utilized every shell hole and ripple in the ground for cover. Her thoughts pulled at her, trying to drift back to her days as a federal soldier.

God, their precision . . .

"Keep moving," she shouted into her comm. "Evens, get ready to move as soon as the odds are in position."

She looked back for a few more seconds. Then she spun around and continued toward the waiting trench line ahead.

One step at a time.

CHAPTER 12

Violetta marched down the street, trying to stay close to the man in front of her. She'd been a soldier of the revolution for less than a week, and she was already in the field, getting ready to face the federal forces when they attacked.

She'd known nothing about being a soldier when she'd joined, and her knowledge had grown only marginally since then. She'd had no idea what to expect when she had walked into the make-shift recruiting office, but she'd envisioned some kind of training program, weeks of boot camp and instruction on all manner of skills. Instead, she'd gotten a uniform of sorts—no more than a coarse brown shirt and pants that more or less matched those of her comrades—and a rifle with a bag of ammunition cartridges. Even the weapons were irregular. She'd seen at least three different kinds of assault rifles just in her platoon. She'd had few thoughts in her life about military logistics, but she imagined the variety of weapons would make supplying ammunition a challenge.

As far as training was concerned, three days was all she got, a hurried, disorganized affair during which she'd fired her weapon a grand total of eleven times. She'd been on two runs as well, the longer of which had left her doubled over and vomiting in a ditch. A quick lesson in loading and maintaining her rifle and a review of rank insignia rounded out her training. Her graduation had been an order to grab her pack and jump on a waiting transport.

She was regretting her decision already, especially the fact that she'd signed the new enlistment papers, which set her term of service as the duration of the war. The fervor she had felt for the revolution, the emotional response that had driven her to reject her father's entreaties and remain on Haven, was still there, if a little shakier than it had once been. But the reality felt quite different than the romantic notions she'd nursed before.

She tried to keep up with the troops in front of her, but she struggled with her pack, and she kept falling behind. The sergeant had yelled at her half a dozen times, and she could see him looking her way again, but it didn't make her legs move any faster. She'd expected to be assigned to a unit of new recruits like her, at least, but Colonel Morgan's battered regiments had streamed into the city just as she'd completed her brief training program, and she'd ended up assigned to help replace losses. So instead of serving alongside comrades as raw as herself, she was surrounded by the closest thing the Haven army had to hardened veterans.

The buildings all around were ramshackle structures, run-down and filthy. She'd never been to the Spacer's District before. It wasn't the kind of place the governor's daughter tended to frequent, but she hadn't expected it to be *this* bad.

Most of the . . . establishments . . . were closed, some of them shuttered with metal screens or boarded up. No one knew what General Ward planned to do to counter the federals massing at the spaceport, at least no one in her current circles, but it was clear the local business owners wanted no part of it.

Neither did she.

"Halt. Fall out . . . ten-minute break." The lieutenant's voice was music to her ears, and she stumbled a few meters to the front of the nearest building, sitting hard on one of the steps. She slid the pack off her shoulder, and she rolled her neck around, wincing at the soreness.

She shivered as she sat there, feeling the fall chill more harshly now that she'd stopped moving and struggling with the heavy kit. She wondered where her father was, how he had dealt with the repercussions of all that had happened. She missed him, and though she hated herself for the weakness, part of her wished she had gone back with him. She still supported the rebels, but now she felt lost, and so alone. Her days had become one misery after another, and she remembered her old life, the comfort, when all she'd had to do if she wanted something was to call for it.

You are weak, Vi. Pathetic. All your education, the opportunities open to you, and you are nothing but a wealthy man's spoiled daughter.

The thoughts came from within her, from some deep place she hadn't known before. She saw herself, reflected in her own mind, and she didn't like the image. She had taken a stand, finally done something meaningful with her life, and now she was proving too weak to see it through.

No, I am not weak. I will not be.

She felt a burst of determination, a stubbornness that hadn't been there before. She could do this. She could be something more than a politician's privileged offspring.

"All right, up, up, up. Time to get moving."

The lieutenant's words cut through her thoughts, and the reality of resuming the march slammed into her new enthusiasm. Her legs were cold now, stiff, the pain of the march wracking her entire body. She wanted to stay still, to run off down one of the alleys and hide until the platoon had gone. But even as she thought about wanting to flee, she began to pull herself to her feet. She reached down and grabbed her kit, hauling it with a moan over her shoulders. She felt a sharp pain as the straps moved against the bruises they had caused earlier, but she ignored it, shuffling forward, one small step after another, until she was back in line.

"Platoon . . . forward."

She stood for a few seconds as the column started to move from the head. Then she followed the man in front of her, her feet moving almost on their own, without conscious thought.

She wanted to cry at the pain, the fatigue, but she didn't. She just took one step and then another, keeping pace, ignoring the stiffness in her aching legs and back.

She wasn't ready to give up. Not yet, at least. And that was a victory of sorts.

"Let's go. You've all got your lists. We've got a couple hours maximum. Then the patrol changes, and our people are off duty." Zig Welch stood in front of a dozen men and four women, Society members all. They'd come by different routes, sneaking through the quiet late-night streets of Landfall. They were here for one reason. The federals had been landing shuttles for over a week, and the entire area around the spaceport had turned into one giant armed camp. The fight for Landfall would begin any day. And before it did, they had unfinished business to complete.

"What you do tonight must be done. We cannot leave loyalists in our midst, traitors lurking in the shadows behind our brave soldiers, waiting to strike. Tonight, we cleanse Landfall." Jacen had been standing in the darkness next to Welch, but now he stepped forward and looked over at his people. They were all loyal Society members, and he'd handpicked them for the operation. It was one thing to protest, to shout and chant and slam fists on tables, and quite another to act. And the sixteen people standing in front of him would do what they had come to do. He was sure of it.

There was a voice calling softly from the street. Jacen turned and walked over, one hand behind his back, gripping the small pistol shoved in his belt.

"It's me, sir," the voice called again, a hushed whisper he barely heard.

"What is it?" Jacen snapped back, the annoyance in his voice clear. "You are supposed to be patrolling the streets."

"I am. But I needed to reach you. There are units moving through the streets all over the city. I didn't hear about it earlier, or I would have gotten word to you."

"Units? What units? Where are they going?"

"I don't know. Whole regiments, marching through. It looks like they're leaving the city and heading north."

"*Leaving* the city?" Jacen couldn't understand. The fight for Landfall was about to begin. Why would units be leaving?

"Yes, Mr. Jacen. They're heading up the Old North Road."

Welch came up behind Jacen. "Maybe we should call off tonight's operation. If there are troops moving around, it might be too dangerous."

"We're not calling anything off, Zig. I don't know what General Ward is up to, but we've got to deal with these loyalists while we can, and we're almost out of time. If we leave them, the feds will arm them and they will raise battalions."

He turned back toward the sentry. "Return to your position. Don't do anything to draw any attention to yourself."

The soldier nodded and turned abruptly, walking briskly down the street.

"Are you sure about this, Cal?"

"No choice, Zig. If we wait until the fighting starts, it will be too late." He paused. "We have to go tonight."

He walked back down the alley, and he waved to his people. "Okay, let's go. All of you. You know what to do. And keep an eye out for army patrols. Just get where you're going, and do what you have to do. Don't hesitate. These are our enemies, as much or more than any federal soldier."

He watched as they all moved forward, each pair pausing at

the end of the alley to check and confirm that the street was clear. Then they disappeared into the darkness.

Jerome Steves couldn't sleep. He turned over on his side, trying without success to get comfortable. He could see the silhouette next to him, the tuft of red hair sticking out from the covers.

It was a mistake, he knew, to let things go so far. He and Elizabeth Mullen were allies, dedicated to seeing Alpha-2 returned to its rightful place as a colony of Federal America. That promised, in every way he could imagine, to be a dangerous endeavor, one that required prudent thought and caution. Sex would only complicate things, not to mention anything else that was going on between the two of them. He told himself he'd just given in to normal lust, but he had to admit he'd been lonely in the six years since his wife had died. He enjoyed Elizabeth's company, and it felt good to have someone there, next to him. But he was still worried.

He heard something. He was a nervous sort by nature, but now he froze, not moving, not making a sound. He listened, trying to disregard Mullen's loud breathing. There it was again. A scratching sound.

Someone is outside the house . . .

He'd been called paranoid before, and he'd roused himself more than once for a false alarm. But he knew Alpha-2 had become a dangerous place, especially for those who considered themselves loyal citizens of Federal America. General Ward had enforced a policy of tolerance, his army maintaining order and keeping the rebel and loyalist elements of the population from coming to open war. But now the federals had landed, and the soldiers were busy. By all accounts, Ward's army had lost over two hundred men and women in the fighting at the spaceport. Steves knew such things could breed resentment. He wondered if the soldiers would still restrain the radical rebel elements, or if they would look the other way when acts of violence were perpetrated against loyalists.

Or if they would join in.

He moved slowly to the side of the bed, careful not to wake Elizabeth. He turned and reached over to the nightstand, slid open the drawer, and pulled out a small pistol. He'd kept it there since the federals had withdrawn, sure he'd need it one day. He'd never shot at anyone before. He'd never even fired the weapon, but he was sure he could pull the trigger if someone was trying to harm him.

He stood up and walked slowly toward the door, the floor cold under his bare feet. He stopped suddenly. Another noise, louder this time. The others had been outside, but this one sounded like it was *in* the house.

He tensed up, his hand tightening around the gun. He took a deep breath, frozen in place for a moment. Finally he pushed on, continuing toward the door. His heart was beating rapidly, so loud he was sure anyone else in the house would hear it. He paused at the door, gripped again by fear, but then he got ahold of himself and walked out into the hall.

The house was a two-story building, with two bedrooms upstairs and a living area on the first floor. He crept to the small staircase and peered down. There was a small rug at the bottom of the stairs. It was twisted, rolled over into a crumpled ball.

His body tightened, and a wave of near-panic came on him. Steves was a fastidious man. He'd never have left the rug like that. There *was* someone in the house!

He stood at the top of the stairs, unable to will himself to go down. He held the gun out in front of him, waiting. He heard footsteps now, someone trying to be quiet but not quite managing it. Then he saw a shadow in the moonlight streaming through the window. Someone was moving toward the stairs.

He felt like he was going to vomit, but he held himself in place, nailed to the top of the staircase. He waited, his arm fully extended, gun pointing down the stairs.

He realized later the whole thing couldn't have taken more

than a few seconds. But standing there, scared, waiting, it seemed like an eternity.

He watched as the shadow grew larger, the partially muffled footsteps louder. He could feel beads of sweat forming around his hairline, beginning to drip down his face, his neck.

Keep it together, Steves . . .

He felt a sudden pang of concern. What if this wasn't some crazed rebel come to kill him? What if he shot someone else?

No, nobody else would have broken into your house. If you wait, if you give this person time, he will kill you. Then he will kill Elizabeth.

The thought stirred an anger from deeper within, one that pushed back against the fear. He disliked the rebels for what they had done, for the havoc they had wreaked on his world. He considered them traitors, but he'd never broken into any of their houses or tried to kill one of them. He'd argued ceaselessly with Isaacson, urging his comrade to refrain from the violent actions he proposed again and again. But now, his home invaded and his life in danger, Steves began to understand that way of thinking.

An enemy is an enemy. If I don't kill this person, he will kill me. Maybe Ray is right. If I'd acted sooner . . .

Suddenly, he saw the figure at the base of the stairs. Not a shadow, not the sound of a distant footstep, but a man clad all in black clothes, standing, looking up in his direction. Steves felt he was frozen, as though he'd hesitated for a long time. But then the shot rang out, his gun firing even before his enemy fully realized he was there.

He caught the shock in the rebel's face, the instant of realization that came just as his gun fired.

It was the first shot the loyalist had ever fired, and it found its mark. The man fell back, dropping his weapon and falling hard to the floor.

The next few seconds were almost a blur. He heard Elizabeth

scream, awakened by the gunshot. And something else, downstairs. No, not something. Some*one*.

He didn't think. He didn't call back to reassure Elizabeth. He just acted. It was pure instinct driving him, the will to survive.

He raced down the stairs, knowing on some primal level that whoever else was in the house was warned now. There would be no repeat of what had happened, no would-be assassin walking blindly into his field of fire.

He heard the footsteps downstairs now, louder. All efforts of either combatant to hide had been abandoned. He spun around the bottom of the stairs, his pistol out in front of him. Then a loud crack. But it wasn't his gun.

He heard the sound, and he felt the force of the shot hitting him. But the pain didn't come immediately, not until later. He felt his balance slipping away. And as he started to drop, his eyes focused on his foe, standing about three meters away, aiming, about to fire again.

He whipped his own arm around, pulling his feet from the floor. He fired, one shot, without time to aim, an act of pure desperation, and as he fell he saw the other man standing there, a look of disbelief on his stricken face as the top of his head exploded in a spray of blood.

Steves landed hard, the gun slipping from his grasp as he hit the floor. He gasped for air, shouting loudly as the pain finally hit, a wave of agony like he'd never felt. He was scared, and now it came out, panic he could barely control. He wanted the pain to stop, but instead it just got worse, burning like fire.

Then a shadow over him. Was there another enemy, a third killer in the house? Was he about to die?

"Jerome . . ." The voice was familiar.

He looked up, trying to focus, the fear subsiding, just a little. "Elizabeth?"

"Yes, Jerome, it's me. How badly are you hurt?"

He'd thought he was mortally wounded. Nothing else could hurt so much! But now he realized the projectile had hit him in the shoulder. He was bleeding—and my God, the pain was like nothing he'd experienced before—but he began to realize he would survive.

"I'll be . . . okay." He was regaining some of his senses. Were both of his assailants dead? Were there more? "Get . . . my gun. Make sure . . . no one else . . ."

He watched Elizabeth scrambling toward the pistol, grabbing it, glancing around the room. He could see her staring at each man in turn, and then she looked back at him. "They're both dead," she said softly. She knelt next to him for a moment, her cheeks wet with tears, but a determined scowl on her face. She held out the gun, ready for anyone else to come. But no one did.

"I don't think there was anyone else." She reached over to the sofa and grabbed her shirt from where she had discarded it earlier that evening. She wadded it up and pressed it against Steves's wound.

He winced at the pressure, and the fresh wave of pain it caused.

"I'm going to call an ambulance." She turned and started to get up.

"No."

"What do you mean, 'no'?" She had been fairly calm at first, but now Steves could see she was starting to lose it.

"We don't know what is going on out there." The pain was still bad, but either it had subsided some or he'd gotten used to it. "Were these Society thugs, acting on their own? Or did the threat of the federal army drive the rebel forces to harsher measures? No, we can't take any needless risks now. Call Ray. Tell him to get Doc Marek and bring him over here."

She looked like she might argue for a few seconds, but then she nodded, and she got up and ran into the other room, to the communications unit.

Fear had filled Steves's mind, and pain, distress. But now there was something else. Anger. He'd been a moderate, a voice against the loyalist elements arguing for more active resistance. He had urged his fellow loyalists to refrain from escalation, to hold back from violence. He had argued that General Ward was a reasonable man, that he would protect the rights of those still loyal to Federal America.

But no more.

He was with Isaacson and his allies now. All the way. It was time to see this destructive rebellion end, to return Alpha-2 to its proper and legal place as a colony of Federal America.

Whatever it took.

CHAPTER 13

"Colonel Killian, I want you to find Cal Jacen right now. If he resists, if he so much as looks at you with an expression you don't like, shoot him."

Damian Ward was angry. No, more than angry. For the first time in his life he was quivering with uncontrolled rage.

"No, Colonel. Don't even bring him here. Just find him and shoot him."

"Yes, sir." Killian looked rattled staring back at Damian—and for someone with his reputation, that was a surprising reaction. When the colonel spoke, his usual unshakable tone seemed tentative. "Are you certain you don't want me to arrest him? I'm not sure how shooting him down in the street will be received. We've got a lot of Society members in the army, sir."

"If they don't like it, I'll find a brick wall for them, too." Damian had spent most of the last year trying to maintain order in Landfall, to prevent rebel and loyalist forces from tearing each other apart, and to hold together a coalition that had elements that mistrusted each other as much as they did the federals. Now, perhaps hours before the federal attack they all knew was coming, he had to deal with the entire city in an uproar. Thirty-one murders, in the middle of the night, over a period of three hours. Thirty-one loyalists killed in their homes. But that wasn't the end of it. The enraged federal sympathizers had struck back, just before dawn. At least a dozen rebels were dead, including two Society members who'd been found burned alive, their charred bodies thrown in the street. The rapidity of the response told Damian that the loyalists were better organized than he'd thought. And that was the last thing he needed right now.

"Damian, wait." John Danforth came rushing into the room. "We don't know Cal was behind this."

Damian turned abruptly to face his friend. "We don't? Who has been trying to move against the loyalists all year? Who heads the biggest pack of bloodthirsty lunatics on Haven?"

"Damian—"

"No, John. No. You've convinced me more than once to let that psychopath off the hook, but he's just pushed me too far." He turned back toward Killian. "Why are you still here, Colonel? You have your orders."

"Yes, sir," the ranger replied, but he still stood where he was.

"Damian," Danforth said, a hint of pleading in his voice. "Please don't do this. Not this way. You don't have the authority to order a summary execution of a member of the Haven Congress. It would be murder, pure and simple."

"Authority? Of course I have the authority. This is a war zone, and I'm the commanding officer. Do you realize what has happened? We're going to be attacked here any day, and now we've got every loyalist in the city out screaming for blood. We can't hold Landfall, you know that, and if angry mobs in the street interfere with our withdrawal, your revolution could end right here."

He slammed his hand down hard on the table he was standing next to, so hard he felt pain radiating up his arm. "Cal Jacen is dangerous. I know you let him slide because he was there in the early days, when you formed the Guardians, but he is not one of the good guys, John. Tonight proves that. How much has he already set back our defenses? He's going to cause worse trouble than this. A bullet in his head now will save a lot of lives down the road." Even as he said the last part, the intensity of anger in his voice waned slightly. He was still incensed, but his rationality was coming back, slowly reestablishing its usual control.

"Damian, you're not the kind of man who acts against someone without proof. Cal Jacen is more radical than you, or me for that matter, but we don't *know* he was behind this. We just suspect it."

Damian shook his head. Danforth, for all his intelligence and his devotion to the cause, had a naïve streak in him, at least where Cal Jacen was concerned. His friend viewed the leader of the Society as someone who pushed too far sometimes, perhaps, a well-meaning zealot, or something of the sort.

His friend was wrong.

They would all be sorry if Damian didn't kill Jacen now. But he'd gained control over the fury that had taken him, and he realized he just couldn't. He *knew* Jacen was responsible, but he didn't have any real evidence. And if the fight against Federal America was supposed to have true meaning, Haven's congress—even its army commander—had to conduct themselves according to the ideals they claimed to represent. Otherwise, he'd be no better than Robert Semmes or Asha Stanton.

"John," he said, his voice deadly serious. "I want you to find Jacen yourself." He stared right at Danforth, his eyes boring into his friend's with a relentless intensity. "Tell him when the rebellion is over, if he was involved in this, I will see that he is prosecuted for his crimes, and that he hangs for them. And if he does anything further, if his people cause any trouble or harm to more civilians, I will hunt him down myself, and I will put a bullet in his brain, Haven Congress and its laws be damned. He'd better stay out of trouble, and he better damned well tell me if anyone else is planning anything, because if there is another incident, I'm going to blame him, and the hell with evidence or due process. Do you understand me?"

"I understand you." It was impossible not to—Damian's tone left no room to doubt his words. None. Danforth nodded slowly. "I will find him, and I will keep him out of trouble. Whatever I have to do."

Damian just nodded. It was a waste of Danforth's time, but Damian wasn't going to succumb to savagery if he could help it. Then he turned back toward Killian. "Colonel, you can focus on getting your people ready. I'm going to order the withdrawal as soon as we detect enemy forces approaching. With any luck, they will assume the entire army has fled. Then your people will strike from their hiding places."

"Understood, General." Damian caught a glint of anticipation in the ranger's eyes and was reminded how much Killian enjoyed his work.

"Remember, Colonel, you're just here to attrit the enemy, to cause as much damage to their equipment and supplies as you can. This is not a fight to the death, and your people are *not* expendable. I don't question your courage or your will to fight, but I want you to look me in the eye right now and swear to me you will withdraw once the federals regain their balance. The mission is to inflict casualties and damage equipment. If you stay too long, you won't win the battle, you'll just give back what we gain in the early stages. And I do *not* want to see Landfall reduced to rubble."

"I understand completely, General." Killian looked right back at Damian. "You have my word, sir. We will inflict as much damage as we can, and then we will slip away."

Damian nodded. "Very well, Colonel. We will probably lose contact with you after the army withdraws. I don't know what jamming capability the enemy has without the orbital platform, but they'll almost certainly block comm in and out of Landfall, especially when they realize they've got an entrenched force to deal with." He paused for a few seconds. "You know what to do, Colonel. Good luck." Damian extended his hand.

"Thank you, sir. We won't let you down." Killian reached out and took the general's hand. "We'll make them *pay*, sir, and then we'll get out and take position in the woods around the city."

Damian nodded. Killian was a capable officer, probably the best fighter he had. He trusted the ranger to do his best, but something about his tone when he said "pay" gave Damian a shiver.

What you did was not only brutal and criminal, it was stupid. What the hell are you trying to do? We've got thousands of federal troops ten kilometers away, and you choose now to kick up a firestorm in Landfall?" Danforth was mad, perhaps not as murderously enraged as Damian had been, but still angry. It had taken him hours to find Jacen, and when he did the Society's leader had admitted at once to being behind the events of the previous night. Danforth wasn't surprised, not really, but he'd been trying to convince himself his suspicions were wrong, that Jacen was aggressive and dedicated to the revolution, but not someone who would do something like this.

"John, you and I have been in this since the beginning. Do you remember those days? How many people have we lost? How many good freedom fighters died in the mines? Or on the scaffold? We nursed this rebellion from its tentative birth, and we fed it with the blood of true patriots, often because someone ratted us out. How do you stand there, with hundreds dead in battle a year ago and more almost certain to die now, and tell me we should leave traitors in our midst, waiting until they stab us in the back?"

Danforth was repulsed by what his ally had done, but there was sincerity in the man's hard voice. Jacen clearly believed what he had done was right, and as much as Danforth's emotional response was negative, he couldn't argue that his colleague had not acted as he thought best for the rebellion.

Still, it didn't make it right.

Did it?

Jacen wasn't finished, though. "John, you saw what happened a year ago. Loyalist groups were forming military units of their own to support the federal forces. The seizure of the orbital station ended the fighting before they saw any action, but do you think the federals will be so easily driven away this time? Because unless you do, these loyalists, these *innocent* civilians, will end up in the field, killing our soldiers. Killing your Guardians."

"Cal, I understand your anger. Your desire for revenge. And I am also aware that many of those killed last night were dangerous to the cause." He paused for a moment, his tone turning even more serious as he continued. "But this can never happen again. Never." He had some loyalty to Jacen, driven by memories of the tough spots they'd been in together, and the dangerous work they'd shared for so long. But as convincing as the man could be, Danforth wasn't as blind to his cohort's radical tendencies as Damian believed he was. He'd always considered Jacen's extreme views to be a concern, and this last incident had him worried . . . more so than he'd admitted to Damian. Still, he wasn't ready to give up on his old friend, especially when the rebellion needed every able man and woman if it was to survive.

Jacen just stood silently for a moment. Then he said, "John, you know there is no one more dedicated to Haven's freedom. I did what I thought was necessary, what General Ward wouldn't do. You know as well as I do the harm those people could have caused, especially when we leave Landfall."

Danforth shifted his feet uncomfortably. "That's not the point. You're right—many of those loyalists would have been key organizers of support for the federals. But there are simply things we can't do . . . and extremes to which we cannot allow ourselves to resort."

"How many have died? Are the men and women from last night more dead than the hundreds killed in last year's fighting? Or those who went to the scaffold before the rebellion even began? We both lost friends, John, men and women who worked with us, and who paid the ultimate price. With so much death, so many brave allies gone, are the deaths of a few dozen traitors to the cause really of such concern?"

Danforth understood the point his comrade was making, but it *was* different, at least to his view, and definitely to Damian's. The problem was, Jacen didn't see it that way . . . and almost certainly never would. And while he wanted to condemn the revolutionary, he couldn't get the thought out of his mind that the absence of so many loyalist leaders would probably save the lives of Haven soldiers.

"Just don't do anything like that again, Cal. Please. There are other things to consider, and we need to keep our own coalition together."

"Damian Ward." There was a hint of distaste in Jacen's voice.

"No. Or, at least, not *only* Damian. *Many* of our people disapprove of what was done last night. Including me." The last two words came out with less conviction than he'd hoped. But at least he'd said it.

Jacen didn't look convinced, but after a few seconds he nodded and said, "Very well, John. No more secret operations." The patronizing tone set Danforth's teeth on edge.

"I mean it, Cal. Damian was enraged. I barely managed to convince him not to have you arrested." *Shot, actually.* "You may not get along with him, but the army needs Damian Ward, and if we lose him we will lose half our support and strength. He is one of the most popular people on Haven, if not the most. A confrontation between the two of you can only do irreparable harm to the cause we all serve."

Jacen nodded again. "I understand, John. I won't cause any trouble."

Danforth just stood quietly for a moment, looking at his old ally.

Jacen's words were what he wanted to hear, but something in the tone still gnawed at him.

I have to keep an eye on him. If I don't . . . Damian will kill him next time.

And that's if Jacen doesn't get us all killed first.

CHAPTER 14

"General Semmes, the rebels are retreating from the city!" The staff officer came running into the large room Semmes had commandeered as his office. It was plain, and the desk was a makeshift affair, a board thrown across two large crates. Landfall's spaceport was a sparse facility, light on the kind of luxury to which Semmes had become accustomed as a senator's son. He was anxious to get into Landfall. Alpha-2's capital was provincial in the extreme, especially to his Washington-dulled sensibilities, but it would be a massive improvement over his current situation.

At least I'm off that godforsaken ship . . .

"Excellent, Lieutenant. I knew the rebels didn't have the stomach for a real fight."

"Yes, sir." It wasn't clear the aide shared Semmes's opinion, but the general didn't care.

"Get me Colonel Granz."

"Yes, sir." The aide walked out of the room. A few seconds later, the comm unit on Semmes's desk buzzed.

"Colonel Granz, sir." The aide's voice cut out, replaced by Granz's.

"Yes, General?" Granz was regular army, a veteran of the last war, and, Semmes believed, a man who had shown insufficient deference to his new commander-in-chief.

"Colonel, the rebels are fleeing the city. I want you to increase your timetable. Advance at full speed into Landfall. With enough effort, we may be able to catch some of the rebel forces as they're running."

"General . . . the reports I've received suggest that the rebels are not 'running,' but rather exercising a very orderly and apparently well-planned retreat. It looks too much like something they had rehearsed and ready to go. We have no idea what they left in the city, if there are forces remaining, or if they have mined any areas or booby-trapped buildings. I strongly suggest that we exert more caution, not less . . ."

Everything Granz said made sense . . . and that infuriated Semmes. He hated being looked down on by these veteran officers, and detested having his orders dissected and analyzed and dismissed so easily by them. They were supposed to be the great soldiers—let them figure out how to handle the situation if things got hot.

"Colonel, your concerns are noted, but I think you give these rebels too much credit. They are an armed mob, nothing more. We must not allow ourselves to view them as more than they are. You are to advance directly into the city, General, in force and without delay. You are to attempt to engage any retreating rebel units you can catch. To crush this rebellion, we must destroy their forces in the field, and I see no reason for further delay. With some effort, we might be able to end this rebellion here and now."

"Yes, sir," the colonel replied, sounding unconvinced.

Semmes felt a surge of anger—as much for Granz questioning him as for his rash decision. But what was done was done, and the men underneath him had to know who was in charge. His last time here, he had been questioned, and that's how the planet was lost. Maybe deep down he knew that was a partial lie, but it was also the partial truth. So he wouldn't let it happen this time. *We have the weapons and we have the soldiers. And we have what Stanton and Wells never did: a decisive leader.*

Alpha-2 will *be ours again.*

His eyes dropped to the large tablet on his desk. Its surface displayed a map of Landfall and the surrounding area, and doubt hit him once more.

What are you up to, Ward?

He detested the rebel army commander, considering him twice a traitor, as he did all the other army retirees who had ignored his summons to return to duty. Almost to a man, the veterans had gone over to the rebels, and Semmes had sworn to himself he'd see every one of them dead, in the field or on the scaffold. He didn't deceive himself for an instant. He knew full well it was that small corps of experienced soldiers who had turned the tide and sent him home in disgrace. He would have his vengeance.

"It looks quiet up there. I guess the civvies are hiding indoors." The soldier was a dark shadow in the growing dusk, the bulk of his exos and equipment making him look twice the size of a normal man. "I don't see any signs of a defensive line. Or any troops at all, really." Sergeant Otto Coblenz was the Third Assault Regiment's chief scout. He and his two dozen subordinates were a few kilometers in front of the advancing army. Normally he'd have expected to have a day or more to scout the approaches to the city, but for reasons he couldn't understand, Colonel Granz had ordered the regiment to follow up right on his heels.

"Roger that, Sergeant. You are authorized to send a squad forward. Probe the city limits, and confirm there are no hostiles."

"Understood, Lieutenant."

Coblenz was crouched low, about three hundred meters from the outskirts of Landfall. He'd seen what passed for cities on a number of colonies, those of Federal America and its rival powers, and

Alpha-2's capital was typical, if somewhat larger than average. Colonial cities were different than their Earth equivalents, not only smaller, but also lacking the belts of suburban sprawl that tended to surround terrestrial metropolises. Even the oldest and most built-up colonies had an almost comical abundance of land relative to populations, and the result was a scattered cluster of cities, their developed areas ending abruptly and transitioning in a matter of meters to farmland and the estates of the wealthy.

"Corporal Wright, take your team and move into the city. Penetrate three hundred meters and report back."

"Yes, Sergeant." Wright's reply was sharp, professional. The corporal had served under Granz since the last war, as had nearly half his people. The Third was one of Federal America's most elite formations, and the regiment had been spared the postwar force reductions that had sapped the combat readiness of so many other units.

Coblenz held his position, looking through the small scope in his hands as six of his people crept out of the sparse cover and moved through the waist-high grass toward the line of buildings. Though heavily armored, the scouts' exos were lighter than those of the line troopers.

They were exposed, though—the ground right around the city limits dead flat, with no depressions or hills, not even a tree to hide behind—and that worried him. Any capable adversary, or even a bunch of amateurs with guns, could have cut them down in a few seconds. But nothing happened.

Coblenz continued to watch as his people reached the first buildings, following the road until they were out of sight behind the row of mostly two-level structures.

His stomach was tight, and he half expected to hear the distant sounds of gunfire as his people were ambushed by waiting defenders. But there was nothing but silence for a moment more. Then his comm crackled.

"Sergeant, we're about a hundred meters in. No hostile contacts. It's quiet, not a soul on the street, though there are some indications that there are people in several of the buildings. They look like residential blocks. Best guess, some of the locals are still here, hiding in their apartments. No indication of snipers or other combat forces."

Not that you'd know until they want you to . . .

"Very well, Corporal." He hesitated, his mind racing for a few seconds. Colonel Granz had been clear. His people were to scout quickly. The regiment advancing behind them would not halt, nor even slow its advance. Coblenz still didn't understand what was going on. He'd served under Granz since the colonel had been a captain, and his company commander. He'd never known Granz to be reckless. In fact, if anything, his commanding officer had always been cautious, meticulous. Coblenz didn't know what was happening, but he was sure the urgency hadn't originated with Colonel Granz.

None of his speculations mattered. He had his orders. But still, he was going to be as careful as he could without outright disobeying.

"Wright, pick out two or three of the buildings, and check them out. Try not to start anything with the civvies, but make sure we don't have any armed personnel holed up anywhere. I'll bring the rest of the platoon up in support."

"Yes, sir. And if we encounter any armed personnel?"

Coblenz struggled to hold back a sigh. "You know the orders in that case, Corporal." He didn't like it any more than Wright did, or any of his other troopers, for that matter. But the command had come down from the top, from the military governor himself. Armed personnel were to be killed on sight, whether military forces or civilians. No surrenders were to be accepted, and any prisoners who fell into federal hands were to be summarily executed at once. He hoped any rebels his people encountered would fight, at least.

The idea of shooting down men and women as they tried to surrender sickened him. In truth, he didn't know how he'd react if and when he encountered that situation, whether he would follow orders or not. He didn't know much about the governor, but what he did know suggested that insubordination would not be treated lightly.

He flipped his comm to the unit channel. "We're moving forward. First and third squads, take point. Second squad, one hundred meters back, ready to provide covering fire."

"Yes, Sergeant."

"Understood, sir."

"Yes, sir."

His three squad leaders replied in rapid succession, and he watched as two thirds of his troopers moved out from the sparse brush they'd been using as surprisingly effective cover. He moved forward himself, pulling the rifle from the clip that held it to his body armor.

He felt edgy. Despite the fact that his advance party had already covered the ground to the city, he was uncomfortable being out in the open (as any soldier worth his armor would be), and he half expected fire to break out, to sweep the field and annihilate his small force. Memories of previous battles crept into his thoughts, engagements where a platoon advancing across a grassy field would have been wiped out in seconds.

His people had gone most of the way toward the nearest row of buildings when he heard a distant shot. He crouched down instinctively, as did every soldier on the line. His eyes scanned the buildings, looking for movement, for any sign of enemy combatants. But there was nothing.

"Corporal Wright, report!" He held his rifle out with one hand as he worked the comm controls on the side of his helmet.

"It was a civilian, Sergeant." He could hear the emotion in the corporal's voice. "An old man. He had a weapon, an ancient rifle.

I think he was just scared, trying to protect his house. But Hojack thought he was going to shoot . . ."

Coblenz shook his head slowly. Collateral damage was a feature of war, as inescapable as it was painful. And the man had been armed. He was certain Private Hojack had reacted to the perceived threat, and he wondered how well any of his people would have handled just shooting the man down because he possessed a weapon.

"All right, let's keep moving. No one told any of you to stop." Then, a few seconds later, "Wright, hold your position. Wait for the rest of the platoon."

"Yes, Sergeant."

Coblenz moved forward, tenser even than he had been. There was no sign of real resistance, but his sixth sense was still wild with concern. Something was wrong, he was sure of it. He didn't know what he dreaded more: running into a real urban fight here, or just watching as his soldiers gunned down civilians who had armed themselves only to defend their families.

These are our own people, citizens of Federal America. How many of them will die before this is over?

More important, how many will I kill?

"They're moving in, Colonel. One scouting party moved up directly from the spaceport and into the Spacer's District. The other marched around and came in from the east, pushing mostly through residential neighborhoods."

"Very well, Lieutenant." Killian was sitting on a crate against the wall of the warehouse that was serving as his makeshift headquarters. With Ward and the rest of the Haven forces gone, he'd had his pick of places—army headquarters, one of the hotels, even the Danforth Communications offices. But the dusty, almost abandoned storehouse somehow felt right to him. Let the federals move to army HQ and find it deserted. Let them ransack the center of town, search all the commercial buildings and any other place they'd expect to find resistance. His people were hidden, whole platoons packed into underground storage areas and sewers, hiding in equipment yards and shuttered factories. And they would stay that way, at least until the main body of federal soldiers had entered Landfall.

He did not intend to disappoint Damian. He knew his orders, and he relished the opportunities they afforded him. His best guess was that there were already seven to eight thousand federal troops in the city, with more still at the spaceport.

They were about to find out what motivated men and women could do.

Of course, once he unleashed his people, the federals would tear the city apart hunting them down. Which was why he would shift his forces around, keep them on the move constantly, striking and running, striking and running. He was confident he and his troops could manage that. What had him worried was the withdrawal. He had no idea how he would extricate his forces and get them deep enough into the woods to evade pursuit. They'd just have to find opportunities when they presented themselves. He had no intention of being killed or captured, and he knew the city *much* better than the federals.

"Lieutenant, send the word down the chain. No more comm use. We can't take the chance of being detected. From now on, we rely solely on runners, at least until I give the evac order. Is that clear?"

"Yes, sir." Lieutenant Desmond Black was one of Killian's rangers, and his most trusted aide.

"We start tonight, Des. Make sure all the platoon commanders are notified. They all have their orders and their designated targets."

"Yes, Colonel." Black nodded, the closest thing to a salute any of the irregulars bothered with, and then he turned and ran down the stairs to carry out Killian's orders.

"Tonight," the colonel repeated to himself. *And if we manage to execute the plan, these federals will think the fight at the spaceport was a picnic on a sunny day.*

CHAPTER 15

"Ambassador Kutusov, I apologize again for the inconvenience we have put you through. I realize that you are accustomed to rather different conditions." Damian had just walked into the tent. It was fairly large, and as plush as he'd been able to manage amid the retreat from Landfall. He'd planned the withdrawal to the slightest detail, but he'd known all along such designs rarely survived implementation. Despite the confusion and the delays moving units on the overburdened roads, however, things had gone well enough. Just. He owed that mostly to Pat Killian and his rear guard. By all reports, the ranger was giving the federals fits, providing the distraction his disorganized columns needed to escape.

"Not at all, General Ward. As I was just telling President Danforth"—the diplomat gestured toward Haven's head of state—"I anticipated somewhat of an adventure on this mission, and it has not disappointed. I will have stories to tell when I return to St. Petersburg." The diplomat's demeanor was surprisingly pleasant considering the situation, but Damian was a little concerned it suggested Kutusov considered his time on Haven to be more of an expedition of sorts, rather than a serious diplomatic effort. He had his own doubts that the Union or the Hegemony could be moved to intervene beyond some clandestine supply efforts. And even if they could, he was still struggling with the fact that a few short years ago they were his deadly enemies, not prospective allies.

Damian nodded, though, a forced little smile on his face. He detested diplomacy, and he liked diplomats even less. He considered 99 percent of what they did a waste of time. But Haven needed that other 1 percent, and without it, the cause was likely a hopeless one. His soldiers couldn't have won the victories they did a year earlier without the weapons Federal America's enemies had supplied. Now the federal blockade had cut off even that tenuous supply line. He'd managed to stockpile a reasonable amount of weapons and ammo before then, but they would be exhausted soon enough.

"Thank you for your understanding, Ambassador." Then, abruptly: "So, what do we have to do to get the Eurasian Union to recognize the Haven Republic? To intervene?"

Kutusov stared back at Damian for a second, a stunned look giving way gradually to an amused one. He glanced over at Danforth and grinned. "You were right, Mr. President. I believed you when you said he was direct, but still I find myself surprised."

"Yes, General Ward does not mince words." Danforth looked a bit uncomfortable at just how quickly Damian had come to the point, but the general didn't care. He didn't have the time to care.

"I am sorry, Ambassador, but I do not know the niceties of the diplomatic arts. I am a soldier and a farmer, and my skills are limited to those trades. I mean no disrespect. Indeed, I seek not to waste your time with pointless nonsense. If the aid we need is not a possibility, there is little reason to prolong ultimately futile negotiations."

Kutusov smiled. "No need to apologize, General Ward. I find your demeanor refreshing, if somewhat . . . blunt. It should come as no surprise that I am a great admirer of your cause. I respect what your people have achieved to date against the federals, and, while I could never express this sentiment at home, I will tell you I have read of your exploits in the last war, and I am very impressed. If the Federal America forces had too many more like you, I daresay the conflict would have ended rather badly for my side.

"But," he said, the grin fading from his lips, "I'm afraid there are many factors that need to be addressed before my government could commit to meaningful support—beyond, of course, the weapons we have already provided through Captain Nerov. My sympathies with your rebellion are not sufficient."

"No doubt, Ambassador, and please do not take my soldier's manner for a lack of appreciation for your own efforts, or what your government has done already."

"Of course, General. I will take your lead, and perhaps be more direct myself than I might have been. It cannot be any great secret that the Union would be glad to see Federal America humiliated and weakened. Yet we are barely more than five years from the last, very costly, war. There is a split among those on the Ruling Council, with perhaps a third of the members hawkish, and ready to openly support your rebellion."

"With two thirds against?"

"No, General. Not against, not most of them, at least. But not ready at this time to make a commitment that could risk a widespread renewal of the general war. I do not believe there is a single member who wouldn't like to see Haven embarrass Federal America. There is just some level of . . ."

"Of?"

"Of concern that your revolution will fail. That we will openly recognize your nascent government only to see it fall. It would create a dangerous crisis, one that could lead to widespread war for a lost cause. It would be one thing to support a rebel-controlled Haven, and quite another to *take* it from the federals. We must know that you are able to sustain this fight as long as necessary. That we will be assisting you, but not fighting the war *for* you."

Damian nodded slowly. "And the fact that we have been chased out of our capital less than a week after the federals landed does not especially build confidence."

Kutusov looked back, a somber expression on his face. "Please understand, General. I follow your tactics, and, as far as my limited knowledge of the military arts extends, I'm inclined to agree they are correct. But, I'm sure you can see how the situation would appear to those already . . . skeptical . . . of your chances. I'm afraid if I returned home now, assuming I could even get there, of course, I would have very little chance of persuading the Ruling Council to take immediate action of the kind you desire. That said, I did have some contacts with the Hegemony government before I left, and I have limited authority to treat with you on their behalf as well. If they agree to join with the Union, I believe it would make a difference with some of our wavering Council members. But the Hegemony is no less cautious."

"What are you getting at?"

"I need *more*, General. More to convince my own government, and possibly that of the Hegemony, to openly assist your rebellion."

Damian nodded. "I understand all you have said, Ambassador. If you will excuse my clumsy soldier's ways again, I would ask you another direct question. *What* do you need? Specifically? What would make a difference?"

"General, your strategy of wearing down the federals is no doubt tactically valid, and the wisest move in your situation. But raids against supply lines and ambushes of small groups of soldiers do not translate well in reports and entreaties to intervene." Kutusov sighed softly. "I need a military success, General. I need your forces to meet the federals in battle and secure a victory. Then perhaps I could convince the skeptical members of the Council that your army is indeed a capable fighting force and your rebellion has sufficient strength to justify the risks of recognition and open support."

Damian just nodded silently at first. He'd known the answer

before the ambassador had spoken, and he'd dreaded it. His entire strategy was based on *avoiding* pitched battles, and he had no idea how his citizen soldiers could openly defeat the more experienced and better trained and equipped federals. But he also knew hit-and-run raids wouldn't be enough to win Haven's independence, at least not for a very long time. He needed the Union's support—and that meant he had to find a way to defeat the federal forces, his old comrades, in a straight-up fight.

"I understand," Damian finally replied, "and I appreciate your own directness and honesty." He stood silently for another moment. "I will get you that victory, Ambassador. We will prove to your government that Haven is a force worthy of their support."

Damian looked over at Danforth and then back at Kutusov. He'd never been one to make promises he wasn't sure he could keep, but the rebellion had led him down more than one untraveled path. "If you will excuse me, gentlemen, I have much work waiting for me."

"Of course, General." Kutusov rose and extended his hand, grasping Damian's. "I believe you will do just as you say. Your people are fortunate to have you to command their army."

"Thank you, Ambassador, though I fear you are too kind. We will speak later, I trust."

"Of course, General. I look forward to it."

Damian flashed a glance at Danforth, who nodded back to him. Then he turned and slipped out of the tent, deep in thought, leaving his comrade to continue working on the ambassador.

He knew what he had to do, but he had no idea how he was going to do it. No idea at all.

The /entry wa/ walking slowly, back and forth across a line of perhaps ten meters in front of the nondescript building. He was a federal regular, fully armed and clad in armor and exos, but it was clear from his posture he wasn't as alert as he should have been.

Jacob North crouched down in the alley, peering cautiously around the edge of one of the buildings across the street. The whole area was deserted. The new military governor had declared martial law and imposed a curfew. Any citizens found on the streets after dark were subject to summary execution. North didn't doubt the brutal edict had enraged the people of Landfall, but it had also served its purpose and driven them from the streets.

He turned and looked behind him. He had ten troopers, all veterans of the previous year's fighting. Each of them had a black cloak covering their coarse brown uniforms. They were good, loyal soldiers of Haven, he knew, but they were out of their element in this kind of warfare. He would do as much of what had to be done as possible, relying on his people mostly as backup in case more federals appeared.

North looked up at the single small floodlight on the edge of the building, casting a tentative illumination right in front of where his soldiers were lined up. It was dark everywhere else, overcast, the thick clouds blocking what scant moonlight might have lit the late night.

He gripped his assault rifle tightly in his hands. The armored soldier would have been a difficult target for a lighter civilian or militia weapon, but North, like most of the rebel—*no, Haven*—army, was armed with leading-edge military weapons, courtesy of Sasha Nerov's desperate smuggling runs of the last few years. The same Sasha Nerov who'd rescued North at the last moment, while the shattered orbital station was falling into its final death throes.

He glanced quickly at the weapon, grateful not only to Nerov and her crew, but also for the limited support of the Union and the Hegemony, both of which were anxious to see Federal America humiliated by its rebellious colony world. He'd once considered himself a citizen of Federal America, but all vestiges of any loyalty he'd felt were gone now. He detested the Washington government, and the fact that the Union and the Hegemony were just as totalitarian didn't matter. They didn't have soldiers here trying to enslave the Havenites. Federal America *did*.

He was tempted to take the shot, to gun down the guard from his hidden position. He had the advantage, and he was a crack shot. But he held his fire. The guard seemed a bit careless, easy pickings, but he couldn't assume there were no other federals nearby. If there were, a gunshot would bring them all running, and worse, it would sound the alarm. North and his people weren't here to get into a firefight they couldn't win. Their job was to blow up the warehouse and destroy the ammunition and supplies the feds had stored there.

Can't risk the noise . . .

He reached down to his belt and pulled out a long knife. It was a nasty-looking thing, the blade more than a quarter meter in length, notched about halfway up from the hilt. North had killed with the thing more than once during the previous year's battles, but it hadn't drawn blood—yet—in this new stage of the conflict. He'd expected to use it on the station, fighting to repel boarders, but the federals had just blasted the fortress to atoms, without the slightest attempt to capture it. Now it was time.

"Stay here until I deal with the guard. Then check down the streets and make sure nothing is coming before you come out and follow me. Understood?" North's voice was a raspy whisper.

The men and women behind him responded with a collection of nods and whispers. They looked tense—he suspected they were scared to death—but they were what he had. At least they had all seen battle before. They knew what to expect, more or less.

He looked back and forth one more time, and then he moved out into the street. His steps were soft, silent, but his body was tense. He didn't think the federals had yet managed to deploy the detection grid throughout the city, but he couldn't be sure. If he was being picked up by some scanning device, even as he killed the guard, dozens of federal soldiers could be on the way to crush his small group.

Nothing to be done about that . . . just have to hope for the best.

He held his breath the last few steps, angling to come up directly behind the soldier. He was a single step away when the man heard him and started to turn.

But it was too late.

He lunged forward, swinging one arm around the man's head and jerking it to the side. He drove the knife hard, into a small opening between the helmet and the shoulder section of the soldier's armor. Patrick Killian had trained his people extensively in every aspect of federal armor. Most Haven soldiers would fight the enemy at longer range, firefights and bombardments of the sort common in modern war. But the rangers fully expected to engage in hand-to-hand combat, and they were as prepared as their remarkable leader could make them.

The soldier shrieked, North doing the best he could to muffle the sound with his hand. It was still louder than he liked, but it was short. The blood poured out of the gaping wound, the wet warmth all over his hand and lower arm. He felt the man's body go limp, and he pushed his body into his enemy's, letting the federal's corpse slide slowly to the ground.

He turned and looked around again. Nothing. No signs of anyone approaching, no sounds of alarm. That wasn't a guarantee, but he'd take it right now. He looked back toward the alley, grabbing with his free hand the small light clipped to his belt. He aimed it toward his troopers and flashed it twice. The signal to advance. Then he reached down and dragged the dead soldier's body to the side of the building, out of sight.

He could hear his people coming up behind him. He shook his head, frustrated at how much noise they were making. But he realized almost immediately they weren't really that loud. For a bunch of farmers turned soldiers turned commandos, they were doing as well as could be expected.

"All right, let's get this done. We're on borrowed time here." He gestured toward the large cargo door. "If we have to blow this thing to get in, we'll have every federal in Landfall here in a minute. So let's see if we can't cut our way in." He waved his arm toward two of his people, who were holding a large device. The plasma torch wasn't ideal for stealth either, but it was a damned sight better than an explosion.

The two soldiers moved forward, taking perhaps a minute to set up the torch. North knew they'd done it quickly and efficiently, but he was still impatient. He stood behind them, looking back and forth down the street, despite the fact that he already had most of his people doing the same.

The plasma torch made some noise, mostly from the power generation unit, but it wasn't too loud. The brightness was another matter. Even with the shielding that blocked most of the intense illumination, it was still hard to look directly at the thing when it was in operation. On the dark street, the torch might as well have been a mini-sun, bringing virtual daylight to a ten-meter semicircle in front of the building. But there was nothing to be done about that. Nothing but to hurry.

"As soon as we're through, you and you"—he pointed to two of his soldiers, both corporals, and the most experienced people he had—"go in first, weapons ready. If there's anybody in there, you shoot to kill. Is that understood?"

"Yes, sir!" The two replies came almost simultaneously.

"Explosives team . . . you're next. We're here to plant the bombs, and get the hell out of here. Get those charges planted and armed as quickly as possible."

Another round of acknowledgments.

"We're in, sir." North's head spun around as the soldier spoke. The torch had cut through a roughly man-sized section of the large metal door.

"Do it," North said, tensing for the noise he knew was coming but couldn't be avoided.

The soldiers both kicked at the section of door, and the metal fell inside, crashing loudly on the concrete floor beyond. "Let's go," North snapped, unnecessarily, as it turned out. The three soldiers with the bombs were already moving, climbing through the opening in the door, careful to avoid the still-glowing edges of the cutout.

North stayed outside, his eyes panning both ways, looking down the street. Nothing yet, but it was only a matter of time. The guard had been careless, a new recruit perhaps, but Federal America's line forces were no joke. They'd have redundancy and someone would almost certainly be coming by soon.

"Status?" he asked, leaning back toward the opening in the door.

"Almost done, sir. Thirty seconds."

North's head snapped around, almost on instinct. He was sure he saw something, a flash of light. But there was nothing.

"You've got twenty. Move your asses." He stared down the street. He had *definitely* seen something. He was sure of it. Then he saw it again. A light of some kind. No, two.

A patrol . . .

"Let's go. Time's up!" He turned for an instant, looking at his people inside before he jerked his head back toward what he was now certain was a group of approaching federals. "Now!" he added as he saw the cluster of soldiers coming into view. They were advancing in battle order, at least twenty, and maybe a lot more. It was not a random patrol. His people had been discovered.

He turned again to repeat the command, but he saw the explosives team climbing out through the opening in the door. "All done, sir."

"Move out. Escape route B." The original planned path was directly toward the approaching soldiers. Even as he spoke, a shot rang out.

Then all hell broke loose.

"Becker, Stahl, with me. Grab some cover. We've got to hold

those federals back for a few seconds, give the team time to pull back."

"Yes, sir." The two men both replied instantly, but Becker's tone was more gung ho. Stahl sounded, perhaps not scared to death, but something close to it.

North ducked to the side of the building himself. There was a small, waist-high concrete barrier. It wouldn't stand up to anything heavy like a rocket launcher, but he was pretty sure it was solid protection against small arms.

He whipped around his assault rifle, taking an instant to aim before opening up, firing three shot bursts. One of the approaching figures dropped, and the others scattered, some flopping down to the ground, others diving for nearby cover. Then they opened fire in earnest, and a storm of projectiles slammed into the wall, sending shards of shattered concrete flying.

North snapped his head around, looking behind him for a second. "Get the hell out of here," he shouted to his troopers, half of whom had paused a few meters from the building. "Now!" He maintained his fire, but there were no more easy targets. His two fellows in the rear guard had both dropped behind the half wall flanking him. They had been behind him, but now they were firing, too.

North turned again, watching as the last of the main force fled down the street. He was just about to let himself believe they'd all gotten away when the last one—Volges, he noted—fell to the ground. North didn't know if he was dead or wounded, and there was nothing he could do about it, not now. He had to hold back the federals, who were already moving forward around the flanks, surging from covered position to covered position, all the while maintaining heavy fire.

Killian was right . . . these soldiers are nothing like the ones we faced last year.

He kept firing anyway. They were good, but bullets killed them just the same. His biggest concern was that he was almost out of time. His eye had caught figures on the rooftops all around the warehouse, more troopers moving to vantage points. In a matter of seconds, his position would be untenable.

"All right, guys, we've got to get out of here."

He turned toward Becker, who nodded and said, "I'm with you, sir."

"Stahl?" he said, looking to his right. The trooper was there, leaning against the wall. He was silent, unmoving. North leaned over and grabbed Stahl's shoulder, and as he did, the man slid down along the wall. There was a perfect round hole in the center of his forehead.

Damn.

"He's dead. Let's go, Becker. Nothing more we can do here." He turned and crouched low, squeezing whatever parting cover he could get from the wall. "And stay low."

He lurched forward, moving as quickly as he could while keeping down. He paused where Volges had fallen, but he, too, was dead. Then he continued on, almost feeling the federal bullets zipping past him as he zigzagged, doing all he could to present a difficult target. Then he turned a corner, escaping the enemy's field of fire . . . just as the explosives went off, a thunderous roar tearing through the night.

He'd lost two of his people, but they'd gotten the job done. *At least that's one batch of ammo the feds won't have to use on us . . .*

But he wondered if all the destruction, if the constant drain on the federal supplies could really make enough difference. It was expensive to transport materials to Haven, but the enemy could keep doing it, as long as they were willing to endure the cost. And he suspected Federal America would go to great lengths to get its wayward colony back in line.

That's fine.

We'll just have to destroy that much more.

CHAPTER 16

"Keep moving. We've got another ten kilometers to go, and we're not stopping until we get to the edge of the woods."

Violetta Wells willed one foot forward, then the other. She felt as if she'd fall at any moment and die by the roadside. But somehow she didn't. Her body was wracked with pain and her legs burned with fatigue, but she was also finding reservoirs of strength she'd never known she had.

Her shoulders were raw. She'd managed to get a look at them the day before—it was a new experience for her to view something as simple as a mirror with such rarity. There were deep channels cut into her shoulders where the straps of her pack had dug into the soft flesh. They were inflamed, and in a couple of places, bloody. She regretted her reckless leap into the army on a regular basis, something like every five minutes or so. But on another level, she knew she was settling in, getting used to her new circumstances, at least a little.

They'd stayed in the encampment at the southern edge of Blackwood Forest for several days, just over fifteen kilometers north of Landfall. For a while, she thought General Ward was going to make a stand there, but then the orders came to move north again.

Apparently the enemy had sent part of their forces out of Landfall. They had followed the Haven army and were no more than three or four kilometers from the south end of the wood. News like that had a way of making its way through an army, especially when virtually every member of that fighting force was scared to death of the heavily armed soldiers pursuing them.

As much as her aching body wanted to stop, she was completely in favor of continuing north. The idea of facing federal soldiers scared her, and although she'd come to grips with it more and more, it still tested her commitment when she had time to really think about it. For no matter what had happened over the last year, she was a daughter of Federal America, and that was really the only government she'd ever known. Growing up in the governor's mansion meant that even though she could see the abuses, she was also instilled with patriotism for Federal America. And now she was being asked to kill its soldiers. She was willing to do that if she had to, because the Havenites were right to want their independence, and even though she was barely an adopted native, she was still willing to fight to make that a reality.

Even if it means killing federal soldiers.

Or being killed by them . . .

So it mostly came back to the dread she felt. She'd managed to get somewhat of a grip on her fear, but it still ate away at her, a weight she carried with every step. The army was fairly safe for the moment, shielded as it was by the cover of the woods from federal air power. But she knew the terrain around Landfall fairly well, and there was a stretch of open ground between the northern border of the Blackwood and the southern edge of the much larger Green Hill Forest to the north. *Fifteen kilometers, at least.*

No, she thought, remembering the map in her father's office. *At least fifteen.*

She didn't know much about war or about air power, but she'd heard the stories everyone else had. General Ward had sent patrols out from the army's initial position, down the West Road toward

Weldon and the East Road toward Lamberton and the Palisades. Both had been attacked by federal gunships, and both had been driven back to the woods with heavy losses. Fifty percent, she'd heard, even more. Some people were saying seventy, and one or two had sworn both patrols had been wiped out entirely. She tended to doubt that, but there didn't seem to be any question that the federal air forces, sparse as they were, put any infantry in the open in terrible jeopardy as soon as it was spotted.

And we've got fifteen kilometers to cross . . .

She trudged forward, trying not to think about the open ground she knew lay ahead. That was tomorrow's problem. Right now, she had another ten kilometers to cross before she could sleep. And tonight's rest was as far ahead as she was prepared to look.

"Colonel Granz, the situation is absolutely intolerable." Robert Semmes sat behind a large desk, one that had been Governor Wells's at one time, and also Asha Stanton's. He'd enjoyed a moment of satisfaction when he'd first sat and claimed it for his own, but since then he'd been inundated with a seemingly endless series of problems.

"General Semmes, we moved on Landfall before we were able to organize our forces at the spaceport. Then you ordered us to send forces after the rebels, a piecemeal approach that has left us strung out and disorganized. We have forces north of the city, with no real tactical plan directing operations. Our supply arrangements in Landfall are a mess, which contributed to giving the partisans operating against us easy targets. And we still have units tied down at the spaceport, at least until we finish fortifying the area."

"Are you finished with your litany of excuses, Colonel?" Semmes did nothing to hide his derision. "Perhaps I should apologize for expecting your vaunted veteran soldiers to be ready to conduct operations at a reasonable pace. If I allowed things to move at the speed you would set, it will be years before we quell this rebellion, if ever."

"General, operations take time. If we hadn't rushed to move our supply nexus to Landfall, we would have had time to centralize and construct proper defenses. Instead, we've got supplies scattered all over the city, in whatever facilities we could find."

"Why did you scatter your logistics, Colonel? It would have made more sense to cordon off an entire area of the city and use that."

"Yes, but we prioritized finding empty or near-empty spaces. The expedited schedule did not allow time to track down civilian owners to move—"

"'Track down civilian owners'? What is this, Colonel? A social event? These people are *rebels*. They have no rights. We do not allow concern for them to interfere with our actions. You are to consolidate all supplies in the most easily defended area, and you are to do it immediately. Confiscate any goods already in those buildings that are useful to us, and destroy the rest. Is that understood?"

"Yes, sir. But you should know there is a considerable loyalist element in Landfall, and by all accounts, many of the local businesspeople are—"

"Did you hear me, Colonel Granz? This planet is in a state of insurrection. Any here who remain loyal will have the opportunity to prove it by joining the support battalions we are forming and fighting their traitorous neighbors. If they lose some of their goods to support the army sent here to do what they should have done themselves, it is the least their nation can ask of them."

Granz shifted back and forth on his heels, looking uncomfortable, as though he might say something else. But he just replied, "Yes, General."

"I want what remains of our forward supplies secured as quickly as possible, and until that is done, you are to triple the guards at each location, and increase them fivefold at the most vulnerable ones."

"Understood, sir."

"Go then." Semmes waved toward the door. He sat and watched as Granz saluted and then turned and left. He stared down at the desk, trying to make sense of his frustration. Landfall wasn't much of a city, not by Earth standards, at least. How could there be so many rebels hiding, sneaking out, striking at his supplies?

They have to have help.

It was the people, the rebel sympathizers among the population. They had to be helping the fighters hide, communicate, move around without being detected. There was no other answer.

His expression hardened. If that's the game the people of Landfall wanted to play, that's what they would get. Granz's people were here for the fight against the rebel army, to crush Damian Ward and his so-called soldiers. But he'd brought his own units, too, specialists. Just for a situation like this.

"Lieutenant . . . Callas." He'd almost forgotten who was on duty outside his office.

"Yes, General?"

"Get me Major Brendel at once."

"Yes, sir."

Brendel had won her commission putting down the New York food riots of half a dozen years before and her major's cluster breaking a Washington-based underground group—and she'd shown no squeamishness in either instance. She was just the officer he needed right now.

And when she is done with the Landfallers, they won't be hiding any more rebels.

However many survive, at least . . .

"**Maybe we should** pull out now, Colonel." Jacob North crouched low under a low beam.

The cellar was far from an ideal place for the effective headquarters of the Landfall resistance operation, but Killian had been adamant about involving as few civilians as possible. News had spread throughout the forces in the capital that the invasion force was commanded by none other than Robert Semmes. Most of the veterans under his command knew something about General Semmes, and just what he was capable of doing, but Killian *truly* understood what a psychopath his forces were dealing with. He had met Semmes before, during the war, and it had cost him his career and, he knew many believed, a good part of his sanity. He had promised himself Robert Semmes would not leave Haven a second time, whatever the cost, and he was almost glad someone saw fit to give him the chance to rip out that bastard's throat with his bare hands . . .

But even his insatiable craving for vengeance took a back seat to the rebellion, and to the men and women under his command. He might throw his own life away for a chance to kill Semmes, but not those of the soldiers he led.

"No, Jacob, not yet."

"Sir, I agree with Lieutenant North." Des Black was shorter than North or Killian, and he was the only one in the cellar who could stand up straight. "The federals have consolidated their supplies and vastly increased the strength of their guarding forces. Casualties have ramped sharply on our most recent operations, and we've had more failures than successes in the last few days. General Ward was clear, sir. He wanted us to withdraw before—"

"They'll lose." Killian's words were hard-edged.

The two officers stared at their chief, questioning looks on their faces.

"If we go now, the rebellion will fail. It's that simple. We've weakened the federals, but not enough. You saw the flame trails in the sky the last few nights. The feds are bringing in more supplies. We've been a thorn in their side, for sure, but as long as they can replenish from the fleet in orbit, we've accomplished nothing. We have to make them send to Earth for more shipments, drive up the costs. What is here is already funded. We need to make Federal America commit more ships, more ordnance and supplies. We've got to buy time, cripple the federals' ability to move against General Ward and the army."

Black and North exchanged glances. Finally North spoke up. "That's all well and good, sir, but what more can we do? There aren't many outlying targets anymore. The enemy has seized every structure near the Federal Complex, and they've built fortifications all around the whole area. The only way to move against them is a full-scale frontal assault on their lines, and those they can reinforce in minutes."

"We have to find a way." Killian had no idea what to do, but he knew there had to be something. Damian was counting on him. The whole army was.

"Colonel Killian . . ."

The instant Killian heard the voice from the top of the stairs, he knew something was wrong. "What is it, Sergeant?"

"Lieutenant Folker sent me, sir. He requests you come to the plaza down the street from the Federal Complex. There is something happening. I think the federals are . . ." The sergeant hesitated, his discomfort clear. "I just think you should come and see for yourself, Colonel."

Killian looked at his two officers, both of whom nodded. "Let's go, gentlemen." He glanced up toward the top of the stairs. "Lead on, Sergeant."

"People of Landfall, hear now what I have to say. Many of you have sheltered traitors, violent killers who have shed the blood of Federal America's soldiers. Those who assist traitors are themselves guilty of treason. And now, by the order of the Governor, His Excellency, General Robert Semmes, such vermin will be dealt with in the manner they so richly deserve."

Avery Brendel stood in front of a company of soldiers, speaking into a microphone as she looked at the crowds gathered outside the perimeter fence. She wore a black uniform, as did all of the troopers behind her, the feared garb of Federal America's elite paramilitary organization. The Federal Peacekeeping Force, or FPF, as it was more commonly called, did not fight in foreign wars. It was tasked solely with maintaining order within the borders of Federal America, and within that mandate, it operated almost without accountability. Once committed, its officers and soldiers were immune from prosecution for any of their actions, save those against certain protected groups, mostly the political classes and their allies among the industrialists.

FPF units had gunned down protestors, broken into homes, and tortured their occupants for needed information. They existed to serve the state, and to ensure its survival and power. Their black uniforms inspired fear, and among the cowed civilians of Federal America Earthside, at least, that terror did half their job for them.

But Haven was a tougher target, its people more defiant. Harsh measures were clearly required.

Brendel stared out at the crowd, watching as more people gathered. They were restive, angry, but she wasn't concerned. Granz's troops were on full alert, and if the mob decided to storm the fence, they would be washed away in a torrent of blood. That might be useful, even. She wanted the crowd. She *needed* it. Executing the traitors was useful in itself, but she was more concerned with preventing future incidents. And for that, she needed to scare these people.

"Captain Lonigan, if you please . . ." She turned briefly to face the commander of the company deployed behind her.

"Yes, Major." Lonigan turned and snapped out orders to his troops. The formation split, the two halves moving to the flanks, revealing a line of civilians standing against a stone wall.

There were three mounted autocannons deployed about a dozen meters in front of the line.

"These citizens have been apprehended for aiding the terrorists. They are traitors, criminals of the worst kind. They deserve only contempt." She paused, pondering, noting the increasing restiveness in the crowd. "And now they will pay the price of their crime."

Her voice was cold, no rage or anger, just an iron strength. There was no mercy, either in her tone or her mind. She believed in order, in people obeying their leaders, and she had been an implement of that demand for obedience her entire adult life.

"This spectacle has been arranged for all of you. It is essentially a service, a last chance to steer you from the destructive path of treason. You will watch, all of you, to learn what happens to those who betray their government. And I sincerely hope you will learn this lesson. Future incidents will be dealt with immediately, and without mercy. Any of you who harbor terrorists, who aid them or hide them—even those who fail to report them—will be denied even the formality of arrest. You will be summarily executed on the spot, along with your families."

She could see the mob surging forward, not exactly storming the fence—not yet, at least—but still seething. *Wait until the shooting starts . . .*

She didn't know if the mob would attack. She hoped it did—it was part of the display she had planned—but there was no way to be sure. She'd done everything she could think of to provoke the crowd, even including several teenagers among the condemned standing against the wall. A demonstration of the futility of resistance would be useful, but it wasn't entirely necessary. The executions alone would send a powerful message.

She turned her head again. "Captain, proceed."

The officer yelled to his black-clad troopers manning the autocannons. Then he looked back to Brendel. She just nodded.

"Fire," the officer yelled. An instant later, the autocannons opened up, firing thirty rounds per second. The men and women lined up against the wall fell, some silently, others screaming in fear and pain. Their bodies were riddled with bullets, and blood sprayed onto the wall. Shards of stone broke off and flew about as the high-velocity projectiles slammed into the masonry. One body—that of a young woman—was practically torn in half.

"Cease fire."

The autocannons stopped, the cacophony of their fire giving way to an eerie silence. Brendel looked out at the mob. There was no shouting, no movement, nothing. Then it started. One scream, angry, loud. Then another. Almost as one, the thousands gathered there roared, their rage and hatred creating a nearly deafening sound.

Brendel watched, her face cold, impassive. Inside she felt a smile wanting to form, and she knew, an instant before it happened, that she had provoked the response she'd hoped for.

She looked out as the mob surged forward, the people throwing themselves at the fence, screaming for blood.

She just stood where she was, and slowly—sickly—the smile emerged on her lips.

CHAPTER 17

Otto Coblenz stood on the roof looking out over the scene below. He'd heard Major Brendel's words, and he'd seen how the executions had affected the mob. He'd dreaded this, since the moment he'd gotten the orders. He'd even appealed to Lieutenant Barrington for another assignment. But his scouts were elite troops, and that's what Brendel had demanded. The best. He'd gotten the impression the lieutenant had sympathized, but Barrington had also rejected his pleas and confirmed the orders. Coblenz had almost argued further, a very uncharacteristic display of defiance to orders, but he'd stopped himself. Barely. He knew Barrington couldn't do anything.

Now, on the rooftop, looking down over the nightmare unfolding below, Coblenz was as close as he'd ever come to disobeying orders. He was a veteran, one who had killed before, more than once. But his victims then had been enemy soldiers, and they'd been armed and trying to kill him. Now his people were expected to kill civilians. They were in rebellion, and threatening to attack the Federal Complex, that was true. But they were shopkeepers and factory workers. *And children.* Coblenz knew the autocannons would not discriminate by age or guilt. When his people opened up, people would die. Adults, children. Hard-core rebels, and those in the crowd out of benign curiosity. Dozens would be killed when his autocannons roared to life. More likely hundreds.

He watched the crowd push forward, and he heard the sound of the portable comm unit buzzing. He ignored it, for just a second or two. He knew what the orders would be, and he didn't yet know if he'd accept them. He wanted to disobey, to do nothing. That would be the end of his career, of course, and even the end of his life if the enraged mob truly managed to take control of the Federal Complex. But he still wasn't sure. Death seemed preferable, in some ways, to moving forward with a burden he wasn't sure he could bear.

In the end, it was his troopers that swayed his mind. He could choose disobedience, disgrace—even death—for himself, but not for his men and women. Some of them had served with him for years. He couldn't throw their lives away, whatever nightmare he had to endure.

He heard the comm unit buzz again, and his stomach tightened. But then the unit was in his hand, against his face. "Coblenz here," he said softly.

"Open fire, Sergeant. All emplacements." There was grim resignation in the voice. It was clear that Lieutenant Barrington was as unhappy as Coblenz about what was happening. *But he is still doing it . . .*

A pause.

Just as I will . . .

"Sergeant!" Barrington's tone was stressed, but Coblenz could hear the understanding in the officer's voice.

"Yes, sir. Understood."

His head snapped around as he heard the distinctive sound of heavy autocannons firing. It was the group posted on the other side of the pavilion. Sergeant Danner, he reminded himself. Danner was a good soldier, even a friend. *And she is following her orders.*

He watched as Danner's autocannons ripped into the dense crowd. People screamed and fell, some torn almost in half by the massive projectiles. The emplaced weapons were designed to deploy massive fire against enemy forces, armored and in cover. Against the unprotected crowd in the open, their effect was almost too terrible to watch.

Panic began almost at once, and the mob seemed to split, perhaps a third still pushing forward while the rest began a terrified flight, devoid now of all control, running, shoving, trampling over those in their way.

He watched, feeling each second pass with agonizing slowness. He could hear Barrington's voice on the comm, repeating his orders, the anger and volume increasing steadily.

There was no point to disobedience now. All he could achieve was to destroy his own life, and those of his people. He would already get a reprimand for being slow to follow orders, no doubt. But if his people didn't open fire at all, the consequences would be far grimmer. For all of them.

He wretched, caught himself and swallowed the acidic bile that had worked its way up his throat. "Fire," he said, his voice grim. "All guns, open fire."

"A hundred dead? Two hundred?" Des Black was pacing, clearly shaken, and that was something Killian had never seen before, even in combat. "Because of *us*, sir. All because of us. We can't let the people of Landfall help us anymore, Colonel. We just can't. We —"

"Sit down, Des. Try to get ahold of yourself. I know it was terrible, but this is war." Killian hated being so cold-sounding, but he could succumb to emotion later. Right now he had to decide what to do, and whatever course he took, there would be a price to pay.

Black sat, dropping hard into the rickety wooden chair. It seemed for an instant as if it would shatter from the impact, but it held. He took a deep breath and looked at Killian. His eyes were still wide, almost glazed over, and his hands were shaking. He didn't say a word.

"I know you want to take up all the blame you can for what happened, Des, but stop that right now. First, everyone who assisted us *wanted* to help. They were volunteers, and they knew the risks." *Even if they may not have understood them.* He looked into his officer's eyes. Black was listening to him, but he knew his words weren't quite sinking in. Causes were all well and good, but the fresh images of a street literally running with blood were more powerful. So he had to push a bit harder.

"And second, helping us is not what got those people killed, whatever you think. It was just the excuse. The reason is that Robert Semmes is insane. There is *nothing* he won't do. The success of our operations pushed him to drastic measures, but be assured, he would have lined up any dozen people he could find against that wall, probably without any provocation. I'd wager no more than half of them actually aided us. The others were just unfortunates, the bodies Semmes needed for his display. And he would have found a way to make that demonstration of force even if we were a thousand kilometers from Landfall."

Black hesitated, his expression displaying something between doubt and agreement. "That may be, sir, but it is also because of us, because we're here. Maybe he would have done it anyway, but even so, it might have been less severe. Or taken him longer."

"Maybe. Maybe not. But does that matter? He *did* do it. And we did what we did. So what do *we* do now—tuck our tails and run away? What alternative is there? General Ward is counting on us to keep the enemy disordered, to prevent them from mounting a full-scale assault on the army as it pulls back and tries to form a defensive position in the north—it's one of General Ward's keys to victory."

"That may be so, sir. But what if they shoot a hundred tomorrow? Or a thousand the next day?"

"With Semmes in charge, that's entirely possible. But what if we leave and they do that anyway?"

"So, it's a devil's choice, sir? Because if General Semmes is as brutal as you say, can we really stay here, focus the nexus of the war on Landfall? Whatever he might do, surely it will be more intense if we continue our campaign. Too, it seems unlikely we will be able to stay under cover for long. What if he starts burning down whole sections of the city to flush us out?"

Truth was, it *had* already started, although not as bad as Black envisioned . . . But whatever that meant, Killian had already lost over one hundred of his people. Perhaps two dozen of those had been killed or wounded during operations, but most had simply been discovered, their hiding places raided by roving bands of federal troops. That drain was only going to get worse.

Yet it didn't matter. His people had done well, better even than he'd expected, but it still wasn't enough. Not yet. If he ordered the withdrawal now, then all those deaths were for nothing. His people could try to harass the federals as they marched north, but the first twelve kilometers passed through open farmland, with nowhere to hide, and the federals had plenty of supplies to keep the war going. He could dispatch small forces to take cover on the local farms and launch raids, but most of his people would have to flee to the woods as quickly as possible, and try to reach the main army before the federals cut them to pieces.

No. We stay. We fight.

We make a madman madder, and see if we can help him lose his head.

His own head spun around at the sound of someone coming down the squeaking wood stairs. His hand tensed and dropped to the pistol at his waist, but an instant later Jacob North appeared around the corner. He was disheveled, his tunic torn and his boots and lower pants legs caked with red mud.

No, Killian realized with a sickening certainty. *That's not mud.*

He knew what he had to do. It was bold, as crazy as his reputation, perhaps. But it was all he could think of.

Semmes was trying to drive a wedge between his troopers and the civilians. The federal commander was trying to clear the capital of insurgents without the protracted effort of a slow house-to-house antiguerilla campaign. It angered Killian that the psychopathic bastard would use such tactics, just to save a little time. Nevertheless, he couldn't argue against the effectiveness, and his rage only increased as he began to realize Semmes's strategy was going to work. He couldn't sustain his force's efforts without the support of the people. And even the staunchest supporters of the rebellion would falter when their homes were invaded, their children and loved ones threatened and killed by Semmes and his black-coated "peacekeepers."

"We can't stay in Landfall much longer. That much is clear." He looked at his two subordinates in turn. "But we can't just pull out, either."

"So what do we do, Colonel?"

Killian was silent for a few seconds. Then: "We hit every target on our list, including the ones within the main security cordon."

"That will take weeks, sir, if we can even penetrate the defenses. Can we last that long?"

Killian shook his head. "No, not weeks. Not even days. We hit everything simultaneously. Tomorrow night."

"*Tomorrow?*" Black and North replied almost as one.

"Sir," North said, "that's impossible."

"Why is it impossible? None of our raids have required more than a day's preparation and planning."

"That was before they consolidated most of their key operations, sir. Also, those were individual hit-and-run missions. Now you're talking about dozens of assaults, with most of those in the same general area. Against heavily defended targets."

"The strength of the targets argues *for* my approach. We have conducted limited, fast ops up to now, small groups sneaking in quickly, quietly. That won't work anymore, not with the defenses the federals have in place. But if we commit everything, all our forces, we can overwhelm the defenders, even at the most highly protected sites."

"Yes, sir. Perhaps for a few moments . . . and then the federals will respond, and probably aggressively. They have vastly more strength in Landfall than we do, and they are much better equipped."

"What is our alternative? Stay, try to hide as the people suffer and begin to resent us more and more? Or just leave? Let General Ward and the army down? And what chance do we have of getting to the cover of the woods if we just slip out? A massive attack, whatever the risks and cost, will create an uproar. It may even give us the diversion we need to evacuate, to get some of our people, at least, to safety."

"But tomorrow? Maybe we should give ourselves a little time . . ."

"For what? For more civilians to be killed as Semmes tries to smoke us out? For the enemy to root out more of our own people? No, time is not our ally. Every day that passes only makes the federals stronger, and us weaker. There is no time to delay." He reached over to the end of the makeshift desk and grabbed a battered tablet with a cracked but still functional screen. He ran his finger across, and it lit up, displaying a map of Landfall. "We need to plan everything. Right now." He looked up at his two subordinates. "Then we have to send out runners, tonight under cover of dark. Everybody needs to be ready and in place by dusk tomorrow."

CHAPTER 18

"I almost didn't come. We can't meet here again. It's too dangerous. If anyone is watching us . . ."

"It has been more than a month since we met. Besides, if anyone is watching us, they'll probably think we're having an affair. Half the midlevel senate staffers have weekly assignations here. That's why I chose this place." Asha Stanton gazed at Wells across the dimly lit room.

"Us? An affair? Who would believe that? Our history is not exactly one of friendship, much less an intimate relationship. I still can't understand why I keep meeting you." Wells shook his head, and then he looked quickly back toward the door. He was nervous, as he'd been the past two times he'd met Stanton. He'd just about convinced himself she wasn't trying to set him up, but he was still uncomfortable. And he was far from certain that neither of them was under surveillance, despite her assurances. "What do you want? I have to get back to the office."

"It is time, Everett. Time to intervene in matters on Alpha-2."

"It has been time since we first met, but I still have no idea what you mean by that. I've tried every avenue still open to me, and all I've managed to get were warnings not to pursue it. There is just no way—"

"Yes, there is." Stanton looked over at Wells. "I have a new contact, and I believe he can assist us."

"A contact?" Stanton was an intelligent woman, but he wasn't at all sure she was thinking rationally about either Semmes. For all he knew, she'd been sharing her plans with an undercover government operative, and they'd both end up on the scaffold if she wasn't as smart as she believed she was. "Who could possibly help us? No senator would dare move against Alistair Semmes, not on this. And no one else is powerful enough to accomplish anything."

"No one in Washington."

"What are you talking about? What do you have, some kind of military contact? What can an officer do without senatorial support?"

"It is not a military officer, Everett."

"Then who?"

"He is a . . . government representative."

"I thought you said it wasn't someone in Washington—"

"He is not a representative of Federal America."

Wells was confused for a few seconds. Then cold realization set in. "Are you insane?" He turned and looked around the room, suddenly positive that they were being watched. "I want no part of this. I disagree with the government's policy on Alpha-2, and I detest Semmes, but I am no traitor."

"Don't be naïve, Everett. Senator Gravis's sense of obligation has kept you out of the abyss, but I assure you he will not be able to stand up to the Semmes clan if the pacification of Alpha-2 is a success, if he even tries. More likely, he will disassociate himself from you altogether—or feed you to Semmes as a way to curry favor."

"But listen to yourself. You're saying treason is my only chance to survive. Well, I'll say it again—I want no part of this." Yet even as Wells's words came out of his mouth, they didn't sound as skeptical as he'd intended.

"Stop with the 'treason,' Everett. It's simplistic and infantile. I do not propose that we sell military technology secrets, or that we aid the Hegemony in taking Alpha-2 for themselves. But stopping Robert Semmes is a necessity, and if the Hegemony can aid us, we must pursue it."

"Who is this contact?"

"He is someone I was able to reach through my family's business contacts in Beijing. He is the son of a member of the Central Committee. I am assured he has the ear of the premier."

"*Assured?* That's a little less concrete than I'd like. Have you even met with this person yet?"

"No. That is why I called you to meet today. He is here in Washington, along with a trade delegation. I wanted the two of us to meet with him before he . . ."

"You are insane. Absolutely crazy. Do you have any idea what would happen to us if we were caught conspiring with a Hegemony agent? Hell, even found *talking* to one? We're both on thin enough ice as it is."

"Nothing worse than what will happen if Semmes gets his way."

Wells was appalled at her suggestion. He was ready to turn and walk out immediately, but something held his feet to the floor. Stanton had been his rival, adversary even, and her relentless efforts to save her political influence in the face of massive human suffering disgusted him. But he'd always known she was smart and capable, and right now, her words carried truth. Semmes *would* come after them both, and he would hurt them any way he could. Wells's choice now went beyond high-minded ideals. The issue at hand was nothing less than survival.

"What exactly are you proposing?" He wasn't convinced yet, but he was still there.

"You know as well as I do that the rebels cannot win, not without some kind of outside assistance. We know they received weapon shipments during your time there, and mine. The guns used against us were military-grade, both Union and Hegemony models. A few crates of such weapons could have been acquired on the black markets, but the numbers we saw employed, and the quantities of ammunition utilized, suggest rather materially that both powers were supplying arms directly."

"Yes, no doubt both the Union and the Hegemony were selling weapons to smugglers, as no doubt we would have done had one of their colonies been rebelling. That is a far cry from active support, however. Selling guns to third parties even provides deniability." Wells shook his head. "And I suspect even this level of aid has been cut off. The fleet sent to support the expeditionary force is substantial. I can't imagine many smugglers' vessels getting through, or even trying."

"True. But there are other factors at play, things that could push the other powers to risk more substantive involvement. For one, Alpha-2 is perhaps the most valuable colony any Earth power has settled. It is fairly well developed, resource-rich, and located along prime trade routes. Federal America's colony network is far superior to that of either the Union or the Hegemony. The loss of Alpha-2 would go a long way toward equalizing the situation. Conversely, looking ahead another twenty years—as long as their infrastructure isn't completely wiped out by Semmes—a more developed Alpha-2 would contribute to making Federal America vastly stronger in space."

Wells nodded. "Do you truly believe the Hegemony and the Union can be persuaded to intervene? That you and I, our positions as weak as they are, can influence them in some way?"

"We have to try. We may face . . . difficulties . . . at home, but we are the last two people to wield legitimate executive authority on Alpha-2. I believe that will carry weight with the Union and Hegemony authorities. As will the influence exerted by Stanton Industries. I have arranged for some . . . inducements . . . to pave the way."

Wells opened his mouth to respond, but he stopped himself. He wanted to argue that bribery wasn't going to help, but he realized that would have been his own pointless idealism talking. Payoffs certainly got things done in Federal America—Stanton's family and the growth of their businesses was proof enough of that. He doubted Earth's other two main powers were any less corrupt. *Still* . . .

"Bribes to win desirable concessions or contracts are one thing. We are talking about actions that could lead to full-scale war. Do you think anyone wants to risk that so soon after the cessation of hostilities? The last war was enormously costly, in lives *and* capital. I wager the economy came closer to total collapse than either of us would care to admit, and the Hegemony and the Union, if anything, are more vulnerable."

"And that's exactly why they might take the risk. Think about it: How will they be served if Federal America wins the colonization race? More and larger worlds equal greater resources. That turns into more ships and troops. Extrapolate that into the future, and you get my point. They may not *want* to risk war right now, but can they actually refuse the chance to create better parity in the interstellar power dynamic?"

Wells disliked Stanton, and he pitied her for the lust for power that drove her, but he couldn't help but be impressed from time to time. She was no fool, he reminded himself. But he didn't know if they could succeed, or even if they should try. He wanted to save himself, of course, but helping to shift the colonial race in favor of Federal America's enemies wasn't close to treason.

It *was* treason.

Yet he glumly asked, "Can we do this? Fencing with Semmes is one thing. I'd like to see that man destroyed. But what we're talking about could damage Federal America's ability as a global—and galactic power—for years to come. I am out of favor, angry even at how I've been treated. But I am no traitor."

"Fine, you're not a traitor. Are you a father?"

Her words hit him like a sledgehammer. He just stared back, his thoughts suddenly light-years away, wondering where Violetta was, whether she was close to any fighting, if she was safe . . .

"Violetta is on Alpha-2, Everett. Semmes is a horrible man, but he is not stupid. He knows she stayed behind. He may not be able to find her amid the ongoing fighting, but what do you think will happen if he is victorious? What way could he hurt you worse than through her? Think about that when you are prioritizing your loyalties. If Semmes is defeated, if he is killed, she will be safe, or at least has a chance at being safe. If he wins . . ."

Wells closed his eyes tightly, knowing she had him.

"Very well," he said. "Set up the meeting. I will go with you." He paused. "But we only give them information pertaining to Alpha-2. No other details about the military, or anything else of the sort. If we are to be traitors, let us be controlled ones. We will limit the damage we do." He hesitated again. "Not that it will matter if we are caught."

"Thank you, Everett. It's the only way to save ourselves and Violetta." A tiny smile slipped onto her lips. "And we won't be caught. We will exert the utmost care." She reached out her hand. "Go back to your office. I will contact you the same way as soon as I have the meeting set. It may take a few days."

Wells held back a sigh and reluctantly extended his hand to grasp hers. "I will wait." He turned and looked around the room nervously one more time, as if he realized he'd forgotten to check something. Then he looked back at Stanton and added, "But whatever you do . . . be *careful*."

"How is this even possible?" Alistair Semmes sat at his palatial desk, his face twisted into a combination of anger and genuine surprise. "How could any product of my genes be so useless? If I hadn't seen his DNA report myself, I'd swear his mother'd had a fling with one of the servants."

"Sir," the aide said tentatively, "the communiqué reports considerable progress. It would appear that his forces have defeated the orbital fortress, landed, and taken both the spaceport and the capital. That is much to be . . ."

"Are you that much of a fool, Barnes?"

"Sir . . ." Barnes's voice tapered off, and his eyes dropped to the desk.

"Don't whimper, Barnes. But don't kiss my ass, either. I'm not an idiot, and I don't like being treated like one, by you or by that simpering fool my wife whelped."

"Sorry, sir. I meant no . . ."

"Enough. Look here. It's plain enough to see, even for someone of your limited abilities. Look at these supply requests. They are enormous. The cost of this operation is already exorbitant, but these new requests could be crippling. I bit the bullet and secured all the funding we needed at one time. The invasion fleet was backed up by two dozen freighters, carrying all the supplies and ordnance needed for the whole campaign. And already that idiot son of mine is asking for more? What did he do with the supplies he had? There is no word of any major battles, nor even of significant resistance. Either he lies to me about the completeness of his victories, or he is selling the stuff on the black market."

Semmes slammed his fist down on the desk, and Barnes jumped. "Damned if I wouldn't prefer that. Basic corruption I could understand, but stupidity I will not tolerate."

"What do you plan to do, Senator? If we are to ask the senate for additional funding, we need to start working on the bill. Based on the debate last time, we will have to make it good."

"And what will that do, Barnes? If you and your band of hacks write the most exquisite proposal in the history of governance, do you think it will matter one bit? The last authorization passed the senate on the strength of anger at the rebels and fear of the message allowing Alpha-2 to secede would send to other colonies. And the almost poetic codicil your people drafted, speaking of Robert's capabilities and experience with Alpha-2 in such soaring terms, did absolutely nothing. My fool son got his posting in dark rooms and in private conversations in the clubhouse, and it was paid for by a considerable chunk of this family's funds, not to mention a number of political favors I cashed in."

"But with General Semmes there and in command, is there any choice but to give him what he needs? He is your son, but also, would not his failure reflect poorly on you?"

"That's why I pay you, Barnes. To state the obvious." He shook his head in disgust. "Listen closely: the problem is one of degree. I have the influence to secure some amount of additional funding, I am sure of that. More, perhaps, if I put everything into it. But even my power is finite. I have to make a decision, and once made, I have to stick to it."

"To support the general?"

"No, Barnes. I must support my *son*, if for no other reason than we are already in this so deeply, and losing Alpha-2 would have severe repercussions on our position in space. No, that decision is made for me." He paused, taking a deep breath. "The decision I have to make is a more difficult one, fraught not only with political ramifications but also with personal embarrassment, even feelings."

He exhaled hard and let his hand drop onto the desk. "I have to decide how far I will go . . . and then at what point I will pull back and abandon that imbecilic son of mine to his own fate."

CHAPTER 19

"Keep moving. Fire a few bursts, and move to a new spot. We're trying to cause casualties, not take them." Grant was crouched down behind a large tree, peering out toward the road, about ten meters from his position. The woods were thick here, the large old-growth trees sturdy enough to provide meaningful cover, even against the high-powered assault rifles both sides were using.

"Jamie . . . I mean Cap . . . Pollack is down." Grant's ex-prisoners were fighting well, but the rest of military conduct and protocol was proving a bit more difficult. For every time one of them called him "captain," there were at least three "Jamies," and even one or two of his old nicknames from his prison days. "Griswold, too. He's dead. The fire is really thick over here."

"Push out to the side, Illich. Don't let them get around your flank or we'll all be lying in holes by nightfall." In the same way discipline was light coming from the ex-prisoners, Grant found himself devolving into his prison persona during combat, abandoning all attempts at military procedure and speaking to his troopers in raw terms.

"We need help over here, Cap'n. There's a lot of these damned feds, and they keep comin'."

"Swing back at an angle and find good cover. Stretch out your line. You can't let them get around, whatever it takes."

Grant shook his head and spit on the ground. He was hot, sweat pouring down his neck. He reached down, grabbed his canteen, and threw back his head as if to take a deep guzzle. But he felt the lightness of the canister, and he pulled back, took a small swig. He was almost out of water, and he had no idea when he'd get a chance to replenish.

His people had been deployed along the army's line of retreat. With Killian's rangers all involved in guerilla operations in Landfall, his pack of freed prisoners was the closest thing the army of Haven had to scouts and commandos.

The first fight had erased many of his concerns. His people had fought savagely, and fortunately only with the enemy, not with each other. He'd had to repeat a few orders, and add a few threats his long history in their minds made credible, but in the end, everyone had done their duty. They had fought three more times along the way, and they'd given as good as they'd gotten, which, considering the disparity between their training and experience and the federals', was pretty good. Still, he'd lost thirty of his troopers. Half of those had been wounded. With any luck, they'd made it to the mobile field hospital, and most would return to service. But sixteen of his one-sixty were dead, their bodies lying along the army's line of retreat—and with them their precious guns and ammo.

Still, that was war, and Grant was just starting to develop some level of comfort in his command position, but now his stomach was tight. This was different than the other fights. There was more power behind the federal advances.

This is a real attack. They're not fencing with our rear guard anymore. They're coming after the whole army.

He pulled his comm to his face. "Rodrigues, get your people

over to the left. Back up Illich and his squad. We've got to hold here, at least long enough to get word to the general."

"Yes, sir. On the way."

The voice was staticky but audible. The federals were trying to jam his communications, but without the orbital platform and its resources, the effect was limited. It might have been enough to black out the Havenite comm network, but their engineer had tinkered with the army's equipment, putting all his weapons design and electronics experience into his efforts. The channel shifters he'd installed in the comm units had rendered them considerably harder to jam, and to date at least, they had preserved communications . . . to a certain extent.

This was clearly not one of the good moments. "General? General, do you read me?" There was nothing but static. Army HQ was five kilometers from Grant's position, too far with the amount of jamming the feds were putting out.

"Wasserman," he shouted, turning his head toward a small group of troopers standing behind him. "Get back to headquarters now. Tell General Ward I believe the enemy is pushing down the Old North Road in force. It is my opinion we are seeing the spearhead of a major attack." He stared at the soldier. "You got that? All of it?"

"Yes, Captain."

"Then go, now. As fast as you can."

The trooper nodded, and he turned and jogged off into the woods.

"Run, dammit!"

Wasserman broke into a sprint and disappeared into the green.

Grant flinched at the sound of gunfire slamming into the tree in front of him. He crouched back into full cover, and he pulled his rifle off his shoulder. The enemy was close now, and judging from the thickness of the fire, they were two hundred strong at least.

He peered around the edge of the tree and fired a burst. He

hadn't sighted any targets, but he was at least going to give the enemy something to think about as they approached.

"All reserves," he said, leaning his head down to where the comm was clipped to his jacket, "forward now. Reinforce the line. Dig in, and get some good cover. We're going to be here for a while." *At least until Wasserman gets through to Damian.*

He eased himself to the edge of the tree trunk, firing once but ducking back as a blast of automatic fire ripped a large chunk of the tree to matchsticks. The enemy knew where he was. Time to move on.

He whipped around and blasted at full auto for a couple of seconds. Then he dropped low and crawled off to the side, looking for a new piece of cover.

"Dr. Holcomb, I know conditions are not ideal for your continued research, but we need every weapon we can find if we are to have a chance." Damian stood at the doorway of the meager tent that was serving as the brilliant scientist's laboratory. He wasn't badgering Holcomb, not exactly, more casting out a line and hoping for some aid from the rebellion's chief researcher.

"No worries, General Ward. Most real research happens in the mind." Holcomb paused. "Our problem isn't research-based anyway." He gestured toward his portable workstation. "I have a number of projects ready for testing and implementation. The problem is the lack of manufacturing capacity. There is little value in a weapons system we can't produce."

Jonas Holcomb had been Federal America's lead weapons designer for decades, until he'd become disillusioned and refused to continue his work. That act of defiance had earned him a trip to the dark and mysterious prison on the far side of Haven, one intended to break him and compel him to resume his work. That plan had backfired badly when rebel forces staged a daring rescue mission and broke Holcomb out of captivity. The scientist had been stunned at first, but he quickly joined the rebel cause, and his efforts had played no small part in the victory that had sent federal forces retreating from the planet.

"I understand. And I don't think we can mass-produce anything, Doctor, not anywhere that wouldn't be discovered by the feds. But perhaps we can set up a modestly sized operation of some sort. Of course, raw materials will also be difficult. Most mines and production facilities are closed now, and any effort to open them en masse is certain to attract the attention of the federals."

"That is exactly it, General. I want nothing more than to contribute to the success of our war against Federal America . . ."

"But you need to actually have the wherewithal to do it," Damian finished for him, and Holcomb nodded. "If I could secure limited production facilities—and I'm not saying I can—what among your inventions would make the most difference in small numbers?"

"The suits, no question."

"Suits?"

"Here . . ." Holcomb slid over and grabbed the portable workstation, shifting it so Damian could see the screen. He tapped a few keys, and an image appeared.

It was manlike, but bulkier, almost like a medieval knight in armor. "What is that?"

"It's what I was working on before I quit. It's a huge jump forward in fighting capability."

"Powered armor? For real?" Damian had heard of similar projects before. The world's militaries had been trying to develop a working design for powered armor for decades.

"Yes, it is very real. I had to re-create the design from memory, since I destroyed my research when I quit the institute. I couldn't develop something like this for Federal America, not knowing how the government would have used it. I'm not sure I reproduced everything exactly, but it is close. It is the nanotechnology, you see. That's what other designs were missing."

"This is amazing, Doctor. I can't imagine how valuable these suits would be in combat. But it must be an enormously complex thing to produce—far beyond our current capability."

"No question, General. Manufacturing these suits would require a purpose-built facility of considerable sophistication."

Damian shook his head. "An impressive piece of work, Doctor, but not one likely to help us now."

"Not in its full form, General. But perhaps we can come halfway."

"Halfway?"

"Yes. I believe I can create a stripped-down design. It would lack the advanced AI control and the full trauma response system. The servos would be considerably less detailed, and consequently, they would not handle as well as the original version."

"But you believe they'd still be effective?"

"I do."

"And you believe we could actually build these? Some kind of version of them?"

"I do, as well. Haven produces considerable quantities of tungsten, and tungsten-carbide would be a suitable material for the armor. I would have to redesign the offensive systems—we'd never be able to produce the energy weapons, or even power them . . ."

"Doctor?" The expression on Holcomb's face had twisted into a frown.

"Power. I'm sorry—I forgot about the power."

"What about it?"

"The power system is another problem. In this design, the suit is powered by a miniaturized fusion reactor. It's highly advanced, something I invented specifically for this project. There is no way we can build them with the resources we have."

Damian felt the scant ray of hope he'd allowed himself to fade. "Powered armor isn't much good without power." He glanced back toward the entrance to the tent. He had tasks piled on top of tasks and no more time to waste discussing impossible weapons systems.

"Do the best you can, Dr. Holcomb. You have already contributed far more than your share." He shifted his foot toward the tent's opening.

"Wait, General." Holcomb looked up at Damian, a glimmer of hope in his eye. "We can't build the *fusion* system right now, but that doesn't mean there isn't a way. I can probably rig up a miniature fission reactor strong enough to power a stripped-down version of the suit. It would be a little primitive—we don't use fission for much since the development of fusion reactors, and what I can put together quickly here will be very basic. But it might just work." A pause.

"What is it now?"

"It might work . . . if you can get me some uranium or plutonium."

Damian was silent for a moment. "That's a pretty tall order, Doctor. But I have to believe we could find a moderate quantity if it was important. Do you really think that could work?"

"It will be less powerful. Since I'm already modifying the suit's design, though, it wouldn't take much more to cut out power-intensive features. I'd have to take out the particle accelerators anyway, and they're one of the biggest energy drains. Fission power should be sufficient to power the suit's movement and basic systems. Yes, I do think it would work. Though . . . there would be some drawbacks, as well."

"Drawbacks?"

"For one, it would be considerably dirtier. The fusion reactor would produce relatively clean energy, and with a well-designed system to cut the reaction if the magnetic bottle is breached, it would be fairly safe. Fission, on the other hand, has a number of negatives. The fuel is considerably more hazardous, especially if its containment is breached. The risk to the wearer would be higher. Radiation poisoning is a distinct possibility. I doubt we will be able to create 100-percent-effective shielding on an expedited schedule. But yes, I do think I can make it work. At least some version of it."

Damian imagined his soldiers in the new armor, enduring the dangers, not only of things like radiation leaks, but also simple malfunctions in the field. If the mechanicals stopped working, it wasn't like a trooper could move himself inside a multiton monster of a suit.

"And you believe it is possible to build a number of these?"

"I do. But, General, you must understand. In normal circumstances, not only would vastly greater resources be available to a project like this, but the testing period would be extensive. I believe we *can* build a simplified version of the suit, but your people would be essentially testing them in battle. I will be as meticulous as possible, but with the expedited schedule and the lack of proper facilities and materials, the risk factor and the chance of malfunction will be enormously increased."

Damian wanted to reject the proposal out of hand. The idea of putting his soldiers into an untested radiation-leaking hunk of metal sickened him. He would have detested some politician who'd put his comrades in that position years before, and his opinion hadn't changed.

But his position had. He would do all he could to lead the army, but they couldn't win without some edge, a surprise he could spring on the federals. He knew his old comrades too well. However much a fool he considered Semmes, the officers and troopers in the field knew what they were doing. They wouldn't be lured into simplistic traps or goaded into foolishness. And if the intel reports were correct, if Colonel Granz was in tactical command, things were even worse. Damian had never met the colonel, but his exploits in the last war were already part of infantry lore. There was no way he was going to trick Granz . . . he had to outfight him. And he had no idea how he could do that.

But if we can actually build these things . . .

"Do it," he said. "You have priority access to any resources. Take what you need, Dr. Holcomb, and whatever personnel, too. Build me these suits, as many as you can."

Damian paused, pushing back the urge to recant all he had just said. Then: "As quickly as possible, Doctor."

"Yes, General. I understand."

Damian was about to say something else, but then Katia Rand came running through the tent flap. "General," she said, her voice cracking.

"What is it, Katia?" Her tone said it all: that something was wrong. Very wrong.

"A runner just came in. Jamie sent . . . I mean Captain Grant sent him. The enemy is attacking from the south."

"Doctor, I have to go." He turned and gestured toward the opening in the tent, following Katia out into the cleared ground just outside. "Did he request reinforcements? Or can his people hold?" The enemy had been probing at his forces for over a week now, and Grant's people and the other scouts had managed to repel them relatively easily.

"General . . . Jamie's people are falling back. He reports enemy forces moving forward in strength. He said"—she hesitated a moment, clearly struggling to continue—"his people will delay the enemy as long as possible, but he warns he thinks this is a major attack."

"Focus, Lieutenant."

She swallowed, but her voice didn't waver. "Yes, sir."

Damian accelerated his pace, moving past Katia, leading her back to the command tent. He considered his options. His initial thought was to withdraw and avoid the enemy. But it was too late for that. His retreat could be only to the north, through kilometers of open country, with enemy airpower attacking from above and the federal troops on his tail. Besides, he knew the enemy still had considerable strength tied down in Landfall, dealing with Killian and his people. So even if this was a major attack in force, it might not be quite the all-out offensive he feared. Perhaps now was the time, the best chance he'd get to secure that early victory he needed. Prove to Kutusov the Haven Republic was legitimate.

"Sir?" Rand asked, awaiting his orders.

"Send word to all battalion commanders, Lieutenant Rand. All units are to go to full alert. The army is to prepare for battle."

CHAPTER 20

Jacob North was bent forward, his back aching from scrambling through the low tunnel. He glanced down at his timer. His people were on schedule. No, actually, they were a few minutes ahead.

"We'll stop for a few minutes, catch our breath." *And stretch out a bit. Before my spine snaps in half.* "When we start up again, we're right into it, so if anybody needs to review your part of the op, now's the time to ask."

North glanced back, his eyes moving as far down the ragged column behind him as he could see in the broken light of the battery-powered torch. Not a word was spoken.

He dropped low and let himself fall back gently, leaning against the wall and stretching out his legs. The ground was cold, the hard concrete unyielding, painful against his bruises. But it felt so good to extend his legs and straighten his back, he hardly noticed. He had only a minute or two, and then his people had to push ahead.

Every Haven soldier in the city was on the move now, the rangers, and the two battalions also under Colonel Killian's command—those who were left after the feds' series of purges, that is. Still, it was a sizable number—thirty teams were moving toward designated targets, all with orders to strike at precisely the same moment. The various forces were positioned to launch attacks at dozens of locations, diversions to sow confusion in the federal ranks. North had been stunned at the scope and meticulous organization of Killian's plan, all the more so since the colonel had put it all together in just a few hours.

If the attacks were successful, the federal army's logistics would be badly damaged, its ability to sustain offensive operations degraded or even crippled. North didn't think total success was likely, but he hoped the teams could cause enough damage to at least disorganize the federals enough to cover their own retreat. Each team and support group had orders to slip out of the city after their operations were complete. With luck, many of them would make it to the cover of the woods in the north before the federals were able to launch an effective pursuit.

Whatever forces were able to make good their withdrawals were to move out on their own, harassing the enemy forces that had been moving north in pursuit of the main army, if opportunities presented themselves.

He closed his eyes for a few seconds. He'd been running constantly for the past forty-eight hours, helping to prep the night's operations. He was exhausted, and all he wanted was to stay there with his legs extended and sleep. But that wasn't an option, and sleep, in any case, was a long way off. Even if he survived his group's mission—and he knew that was a significant "if"—he faced an immediate, desperate flight to the partial and fleeting safety of the forest.

"All right, let's go. Rest time is over." He could hear the groans of his people, but even more, he could *feel* them. They were tired, sore, scared. But they were here with him, and even as he pulled himself up, back into the agonizing crouched-over position to navigate the tunnels, he could hear and see them doing the same. Not one of them hesitated or argued.

He was proud of them. A few were rangers, and all were veterans of the last war, but except for him, none had real military experience before the rebellion broke out. They were amateurs of a sort, but they were dedicated and courageous, and he decided he couldn't ask more from warriors than that.

He pushed on forward, the pain in his back and legs coming back almost immediately. The column continued for nearly another kilometer, moving as quickly as they could in the tight confines. Finally he extended his hand behind him and said, "Okay, halt."

He dropped to the floor again, stretching his legs as he had done before. A glance at the timer on his wrist confirmed what he had already known. His people were early. H-hour wasn't for another eighteen minutes.

"You've got a few minutes. Stretch out, but use the time well. I want everybody to check their weapons, make sure your spare magazines are accessible. Explosive teams, check your gear. You're not going to have time to waste once we go in."

No, we'll be lucky if we can get you in at all. His eyes moved up to the metal hatch along the side of the tunnel, and to the markings next to it identifying the facility beyond as one of the main power transfer stations in the city. If North's people were successful, half of Landfall would lose its power, for hours if not days. His mission was crucial to the success of a dozen others, but that hatch looked pretty strong. He shook his head at the negativity.

We'll get it done.

It wasn't just the hatch that bothered him, though. He stared at the sign next to the small doorway. It was an obvious target, too, and that meant it would be well defended. His people were going to have one hell of a fight on their hands in . . .

He looked down at the timer.

Eleven minutes.

He started checking his own weapons.

"I want these criminals and terrorists hunted down and destroyed, Major Brendel. The loss of supplies has been intolerable for weeks now." Robert Semmes was sitting at his desk, his face an angry scowl as he vented his frustrations to Avery Brendel.

Brendel just listened, nodding occasionally in agreement but not interjecting her thoughts. Mostly because she had none. Brendel's specialty was intimidating civilians, and the guerillas infesting Landfall might not be professional soldiers, exactly, but they weren't shopkeepers and factory workers who could be intimidated by a few executions or some time in an internment camp. They would have to be rooted out one by one and killed, a process that Brendel knew took time. And one that was well under way already, even if slower than the spoiled Semmes wanted to see.

"I want you to take charge of the operation personally, Major." Semmes finally said what she'd expected was coming, and what she'd hoped to avoid. Brendel wasn't squeamish about killing enemy guerillas—she wasn't squeamish about killing *anyone*—but this wasn't a job she wanted. In the first place, she didn't have enough of her Peacekeepers, which meant she'd need to use regular soldiers. And federal frontline troops were squeamish about killing civilians, and also *persuading* captives to rat out their allies. It would be a headache from beginning to end, and Brendel could tell right then that Semmes's impatience was going to make any realistic result inadequate.

There was no way to avoid the assignment, though, so she didn't even try. "Yes, sir. However I can be of the greatest assistance. It does seem that the efforts to date have been somewhat successful, at least the centralization of supply depots. Losses have declined considerably, have they not?"

"Yes, though they are still too high. But better safeguarding of supplies is not the same thing as eliminating the infestation of traitors and terrorists. We 'control' Landfall, and yet our troops are in danger unless they are in large, reinforced patrols. Not a morning passes without the discovery of some guard or messenger murdered. It is intolerable, and I want it stopped." He stared across the desk, his eyes cold. "You have the authority to do anything you feel is necessary, Major."

"Yes, sir." Brendel wondered if Semmes understood what she was coming to realize, that Alpha-2's people were different than the long-oppressed and terrified masses back on Earth. She'd expected her initial display of ferocity, the executions and the massacre of the mob, to go a long way toward breaking the will of the populace. But the typical deluge of tips had not occurred. Even prisoners who were aggressively interrogated provided a substandard flow of intelligence. Whatever Semmes had convinced himself of, she knew the rebel elements of the population were still committed to their cause. She wondered if more brutality would break them, would finally crush their spirit to resist . . . or if it would inflame the rebellion further, creating an endless stream of martyrs and zealots. Mentally she shrugged, because that wasn't her concern. She'd hated the idea of coming to Alpha-2 at all, but orders were orders. As was still the case.

"I want you to start at once, Major. Obviously all of your own people will be available for your operations, but I will assign any other forces you require. Simply let me know what you need. There is no higher priority right now. I want Landfall pacified. At once."

Almost as if in answer, the office shook, and a loud rumbling sound filled the air. Then another one, and a few second later, a whole series of what could only be explosions.

Then the sounds of distant—and not too distant—rifle fire.

And then the lights went out.

Brendel took a deep breath, even as Semmes leapt to his feet in the dim light of the emergency lamps, roaring for his aide to come into the office.

This assignment was going to be a nightmare . . .

"Let's go. Move!" Jacob North stood alongside the shattered section of masonry wall, just about all that remained of the building that had housed the transfer station. He was shouting, his voice as loud as he could manage with his parched throat. His people had brought extra explosives with them, in case any were lost, and he'd ordered them to be emplaced. The explosion had been huge, and he didn't imagine his people could hear any better right now than he could, so he compensated with volume.

He shook his head, an instinctive effort to clear the loud ringing in his ears, but it was no more effective than it had been the other half-dozen times he'd tried it.

He moved toward the edge of the broken brick wall, peering around. There were federal troopers everywhere, but they were disorganized. The explosion had taken out a good number of them, and the others had ducked for whatever cover they could. It wasn't going to last long—in fact, the enemy soldiers were already reordering themselves—but it was the best chance his people would get. What was left of his people, at least.

"Let's go. Across the street and through that alley." He'd had multiple escape routes planned out, but there were too many federals around most of them. The path across the street would have been his last choice, but now it was the only one. "Now!"

It was easier said than done, though. His force had been fighting the federals since they'd emerged from the underground tunnel, and casualties had been heavy. Now there were more soldiers, reinforcements he could see rushing down the street. If his people didn't get moving, they'd be trapped.

He reached out, grabbed hold of the trooper next to him, and pushed hard, out into the street. "Let's go," he shouted again, his voice hard.

One by one, his troopers, their faces stricken, looking almost lost, followed his orders. They trickled across the road, the first five or so making it without any enemy fire. The shooting started, sparse and disorganized at first, then increasing in intensity. A few of his people slowed and brought their own weapons up, returning the fire.

"Keep moving!" He waved his arms toward his troopers in the open, even as he was still pushing others forward. "Don't stop, don't worry about returning fire." There was no chance of winning this fight, only of escaping it. *And every fighter who stops in the middle of the street to shoot is not getting away.*

His thought was confirmed as one of his troopers dropped, followed by another. The others stopped firing and ran, more than one of them actually dropping their rifles. He knew there was a difference between retreating and routing, but right now he didn't care, as long as they kept running.

I'll yell at them about their weapons when we survive.

He turned and looked behind him. All his troopers had moved out across the street. He hadn't counted, not exactly, but he was pretty sure he'd lost more than half his people. Some were dead. Others, he knew, were wounded. The idea of abandoning those too injured to move on their own ate at him. But his orders were clear, and disobeying would serve no purpose.

He looked out one last time. The street was full of federal soldiers, now in something resembling a formation. They were moving forward, and the street was under withering fire.

It's too late. I'll never make it across. He leaned forward, trying to overcome the fear, to make a dash toward escape. But it wasn't fear, he realized, it was analysis. There was no chance of making it across the road, not now. He was too late.

He took one last look, watching as his final few troopers moved down the alley and around the corner. Then he reached to the belt on his chest and pulled off a grenade. He couldn't escape, at least not with his people. But maybe he could do them some good.

He spun around, throwing the grenade as far as he could, and then pulled out his rifle, firing a burst at fully automatic. He lunged back, just in time, as a blast of fire slammed into the wall, sending shards of shattered concrete in every direction.

Then he turned and ran, not after his troops, but back the way they had come. His path led deeper into the city. But at least he was still alive, still fighting. His only other option was surrender . . .

The hell with that.

North wouldn't have given up, even if there had been a possibility of any result except summary execution . . . or worse, what the federals called "aggressive interrogation." No, he'd come this far. He damned sure wasn't going to surrender now.

He raced as quickly as he could, even as the enemy fire zipped past him. For a moment, he felt he might get out of this particular jam, but then he felt the impact of a bullet slamming into the back of his shoulder. He stumbled forward a few steps, but he regained his balance and he pressed on, putting every last bit of strength he had into it.

The tunnel was up ahead. With any luck, the enemy hadn't discovered the route his people had taken to the target, not yet. The underground passage wouldn't lead him out of the city, but it might get him out of immediate danger. And at the moment, that seemed like a pretty good option.

He plunged toward the darkness, as tracer fire illuminated the way behind him.

CHAPTER 21

"Are you sure, Damian? Perhaps we should retreat deeper into the woods. Green Hill Forest stretches at least fifty kilometers to the north." John Danforth rarely interfered with military decisions, but the republic's president looked concerned.

"I agree, sir. If that is a large force of regulars approaching, can we really face them?" Luci Morgan glanced at Danforth and then back toward Damian.

"Am I sure?" Damian almost laughed. "What surety is there in war? What I'm sure of is that our best chance of securing Haven's independence is to convince the Union or the Hegemony, preferably both, to recognize us and intervene. And that's not going to happen unless we can prove our forces are capable of defeating the federals." Damian's words were virtually the opposite of anything he'd proposed previously. His plans had always been based on retreat, on restricting engagements to hit-and-run attacks and avoiding pitched battles. But his talk with Kutusov had affected him deeply, and he'd realized his hopes of wearing down the federals were tenuous at best. Union involvement in the war was a far likelier route to success, and his only chance of gaining that would be to fight a field battle . . . and win.

He was far from certain his people could do it, but now was

the best chance. By all accounts, Killian's people had Landfall in a state of utter chaos. Thousands of troops were still tied down there. If Damian waited, his army would only face greater numbers . . . and his own supply situation would deteriorate. The guns and ammo Nerov's daring journeys had provided were not infinite, and whatever chance he had of securing a win would be completely gone when the ammunition ran out.

After a long silence, he continued, "I don't like committing to battle, but I believe this is the best course of action."

Morgan looked doubtful, but finally she nodded. "We'll do everything we can, General. We'll find a way."

"That's all I can ask. We can't win this by ourselves, and no one's going to help us unless they think we can win. Even a draw, something we can use to show we can face the feds . . ."

"It makes sense, Damian," Danforth said. "You're our leader. If you think it's the right move, the army will be with you. *I'm* with you." Danforth extended his hand, smiling as Damian took it. "We've been through a lot to get this far, my friend, and if you think this is what we need to do, then that's what we do."

Damian nodded. "We stand. We will meet them here. Colonel, I want your forces in the center."

"Yes, sir. I better go and get them ready." Morgan stood at attention for a moment, and then she turned and walked out of the tent.

"John, I know you're probably going to want to stay near the front, but you've got to go north . . . just in case. You're the republic's president, in effect its entire government since Landfall was taken. If you get killed, it will hurt the rebellion worse than almost anything else that could happen."

Danforth looked for a moment like he was going to argue, but then he just nodded. "Good luck, my friend," he said softly, before he followed Morgan out into the muddy main street of the makeshift headquarters camp.

Damian looked over at Withers. "You've been quiet," he said, moving back toward his desk and sitting down.

"What is there to say? You know everything I do. We're not likely to win a pitched battle, but if we're going to try, now is the time. We're just going to get weaker, at least for the foreseeable future." Withers hesitated.

"Say it. There's no time for niceties."

"I understand the gamble, Damian, but we need to hedge. We need to be sure to keep the retreat route open. If the federals win, at least we can pull back into the deep woods, away from any air cover, and over difficult ground they'll have trouble crossing quickly. A long shot to try to grab a victory is one thing, but we can't bet everything on it."

"I couldn't agree more, old friend. That's why I want you to do exactly that for me."

"Sir?"

"I want you to take some of the reserves and pull back. Make sure the path of retreat is clear and ready, in case we need it. And while you're waiting, get ready to drop trees, lay traps . . . everything we can to slow any enemy effort to follow up."

Withers had looked like he might object to being sent away before the battle, but then he said, "Yes, sir. I will do everything I can." The ex-noncom stood up, his eyes still focused on Damian. "I'd better get moving. It looks like the battle is almost here." He walked toward the door, and then stopped and turned back. "Good luck, sir."

"Good luck to you, too, Ben."

"**Send all reserves** forward, now!" Colonel Morgan was crouched down behind a bank of recently disturbed dirt, a makeshift defensive line her people were still struggling to complete.

The battle had been raging for nearly four hours. The rebel forces had held firm, for a while, at least. But their losses had been high, the training and equipment of their adversaries showing. A few of the Havenite units, including Morgan's battalions, were more or less solid formations, consisting of veterans from the prior year's fighting. Much of the rest of the army was filled with troops who'd received at least some level of training, but few had seen battle before. Then, of course, there were the masses of troops who had rallied to the flag in the days following the arrival of the federals. Most of them had gotten no more than a week or two's basic drilling, and they were raw. Those who had been filtered into experienced units had done well enough, but half a dozen green battalions had already thrown down their arms and fled.

Morgan's people were dealing with the repercussions of that right now. They'd stood, and beaten back two federal assaults . . . but then two of Tucker Jones's three raw battalions broke, and Morgan had been forced to spread her veterans out in extended order, desperately attempting to fill in the gap in the line.

Morgan had kept a single company in reserve, a testament to her belief that the side that committed their last reinforcements first had lost the battle. But now she had no choice. Her battered veterans had a dozen gaps in the line, and the next major federal assault would slice through them like a knife through butter. She was far from sure her last company would be enough to stop that, but it was all she had.

We're losing the battle anyway . . .

Morgan was proud of her people, and of the army as a whole. Damian had decided to take the risk, to see if the rebels could win in the field against their enemies. The army had performed, perhaps better than she'd thought possible, but they weren't enough.

Her concerns about facing federal soldiers had been exactly on point, but one thing had surprised her. She'd thought it would be difficult to face her former comrades, to fight against those with whom she had once served. And it had been. But she realized now that there was little motivation more powerful than someone shooting at you. She'd quickly forgotten who they were when their formations advanced, and she'd urged her people on, directing their fire, using all her knowledge to kill as many of her enemies as possible.

No doubt, later she would feel the guilt, the pain. But now, nothing mattered but victory, and if that was not possible, then an orderly retreat with minimal losses.

She stepped up along the small berm, peering cautiously over. There was fire, fairly heavy, and she could see movement in the distance. The woods were moderately dense here, nothing like the deep forest farther north, but reasonable cover nevertheless. Yet cover worked two ways, and she knew the advancing federals would also be protected. She needed an open killing ground, and she didn't have one. Her people would inflict casualties, but not enough to repulse a serious federal advance.

She reached down and grabbed her comm unit. "HQ, this is Colonel Morgan. HQ, do you read?" Nothing but static. The federals were jamming.

She'd been ready to hold back the federals for as long as possible, but now she was thinking she should pull back. The effort to win the battle was futile, and if more of the units around her force fell back or retreated, her veterans were going to be in deep trouble. Damian had wanted to fight, to try to win a victory, but Morgan knew now that wasn't going to happen. The overall federal effort might be disorganized, but the forces leading the attack were crack units. She'd even heard rumors that Colonel Granz was leading the advance. She remembered Ian Granz from the war against the Union and Hegemony. He'd led her unit, the Third Assault Regiment. He'd been echelons above her then, but his reputation as a professional, and as a gifted tactician, had been well known.

I can't pull back, not without Damian's orders. But if I can't reach him . . .

She turned her head abruptly, staring through the trees and underbrush as the intensity of the enemy fire increased. She could hear the distinctive sound of mortar rounds, too, and she knew her concerns about whether to withdraw were moot.

The enemy was coming.

"Captain Grant is to pull his troops back to the extreme left. I want them ready to slip around and deploy to the flanks of the route of retreat." Damian was standing inside the headquarters tent, pacing back and forth nervously. He hated the idea of sending Grant's battered forces right back at the enemy, but he'd just fully realized what was happening. There were more federal forces involved in the battle than he'd expected, and even now those unengaged units were moving around both his flanks. The battle was over, a costly defeat, and all that remained was to save the army. If he even could, at this point.

"Yes, General." Katia Rand's voice was tentative. She had proven to be an outstanding communications officer for Damian, and she'd been tireless in her efforts, putting her engineering skills to use between normal duty shifts, keeping the army's old and worn comm gear functional. But sending orders to thrust Jamie Grant into the heat of what was clearly becoming a disastrous battle was a hard job for her to handle.

She did it, though—Damian listened to her passing on the command to Grant, trying to hold back the emotion, and he wished he'd done it himself rather than through her. His own mind was distracted, by the crisis of the battle, by the need to extricate his army from what was starting to look like a disaster . . . and by the realization that his first major engagement as commander-in-chief of the Haven army was beginning to look a lot like he'd led his soldiers into a trap.

"Ja . . . Captain Grant confirms, sir." A pause. "He reports his forces have lost almost a third of their number."

"Very well, Lieutenant." His voice was soft, as comforting as he could manage amid the stress and tension working its way through his mind. He knew Jamie's losses weren't as bad as his report made them sound. A third sounded terrible, until you realized that some of them were wounded, and not all of those badly. Some were lost, cut off. Some had probably panicked and slipped away. There would be dead, certainly, and badly wounded, but he suspected that, when the final tally came in, it would be less than half as many as the report suggested.

Of course, that's still too many. Far too many. But I'll take whatever positive news I can at this point.

"Get me a line to Colonel Kerr, Lieutenant." The best thing he could do for Katia was to keep her busy, and even if Grant's forces made it to their positions in time, that was only one flank covered. He needed to cover the right, as well.

"I'm sorry, sir. We can't get a signal through. The jamming in that area is very intense."

Damn.

"Try to raise Major Jones." Even as he said it, he wasn't very hopeful. He'd sent Jones's reserve up to the front to try to plug the widening holes in the line. *They're too close to the enemy now. They'll be jammed, too.*

"I'm sorry, sir. Nothing. I will keep trying. Maybe if we can get some extra power packs in here, it will . . ."

"No, Lieutenant. We don't have any battery packs to spare, and it wouldn't work anyway. They're too close to the jamming sources." He sighed. "See if you can get me Colonel Morgan." Contact with Morgan had been spotty, as well, but Damian figured they just might get a brief connection. "Use the reserve power if you have to."

Damian had sent a runner earlier to tell Morgan to pull back. Her people had held in the center against everything the enemy had thrown at them, and when the forces on both of their flanks withdrew, they stretched out their own lines and still held. But they had paid a terrible price, and her two battalions were easily the most shot up in the army. *Which was why I called them back . . . and now I have to cancel that, send them back in.*

"I've got Colonel Morgan, sir."

"Luci . . . it's Damian." The first names just popped out, a tell on just how guilty he felt about the orders he was about to give. "I need you to stop your withdrawal." He paused, finding it hard to even force the words out. "The federals are trying to outflank us . . . I don't think I need to tell you what will happen if they manage to pull it off before we can retreat. I can't reach any of the other forward forces through the jamming." He didn't need to explain, at least not by the standards of military command. But he did anyway.

"Understood, sir. We're on our way."

Not an argument, not even a word of protest or a reminder of how battered her forces were. Morgan couldn't have struck harder at Damian's guilt if she'd tried.

"Thank you," he said. Then: "Good luck, Colonel."

CHAPTER 22

"Are the flanking forces in position yet, Colonel?" Robert Semmes was sitting inside the command vehicle, staring out at his field commander as he spoke. The large ATV had a hard time in the semidense woods, and it was restricted mostly to the road, despite its rough terrain capability. Semmes knew Granz was surprised he'd come up so close to the front. *The pompous fool forgot I, too, was a soldier.*

"Nearly, sir. The main force on the left has run into some unexpected resistance, which has slowed their advance."

"That is unacceptable, Colonel Granz. Those soldiers have the advantage in equipment, training and, I suspect in that sector, at least, numbers. I will not tolerate excuses." Semmes shifted himself, turning to more directly face Granz. *I'd swear this fool is deliberately standing back there, only half in my field of view.*

"Sir, this terrain is extremely difficult. If we had sufficient air support to defoliate these . . ."

"Enough, Colonel." Semmes's patience, what little of it had been there, was gone. He was sick of reasons for failure, of explanations for delays. "If we had more air support, if the woods weren't there, if the other soldiers didn't have guns . . . the litany of causes for failure could go on forever. We have no time. These arrogant rebels have fallen into a trap, and if we can close it in time, we can end this conflict here and now." He paused, staring coldly at the colonel. Ending the rebellion so quickly would undoubtedly save thousands of lives, but Semmes's thoughts were more focused on the impact it would have on all those who doubted him, that shit of a father at the top of the list. The victorious general who crushed the rebellion in a single battle would be a hero, with influence and power from sources other than the auspices of Senator Alistair Semmes. "If that effort fails through cowardice or lack of effort, I assure you, any officers responsible will be severely punished."

Semmes could see the disapproval in Granz's expression, and he imagined the things going through the officer's head, the comments he dared not actually state. He didn't care. Semmes knew the military types looked down on him, considered him a disgrace to the service. They thought he was a fool, just as the rebels did . . . but he would make them all see differently. The flanking maneuvers had been his plan, a masterstroke to not just win a victory, but to destroy the entire rebel army in one fell swoop. He hadn't been at all sure Damian Ward would give him the chance, that the rebels' decorated leader would fall into the trap he'd laid, taken in by the apparent disorganization of the federal forces in pursuit of his army. But Ward had stepped into the snare, and Semmes had no intention of allowing it to fail because the soldiers wouldn't push themselves hard enough to make it work.

"General, the troops are doing the best they can. This is very difficult terrain in which to mount an offensive, and it favors the forces trying to slip away, especially when those forces are more familiar with the terrain. We are already assured of a significant victory, and with any luck, we will cut off a portion of the enemy's forces from retreating."

"See that we do better than a *portion*, Colonel. My plan was flawless, and if it is not entirely successful, I'm going to find out who is to blame, I can assure you of that."

"Yes, sir." The colonel was barely holding back the disgust he clearly felt.

"Go, Colonel. Let us finish this."

"All right, Lieutenant Strong. We've got to retake that hill or these bastards are going to mow us down." Morgan stood next to the officer, not an army veteran like many of her company commanders, but one of the heroes of the past year's fighting. She'd performed well since her commission, but now she looked at the colonel, unable to hide the fear in her face.

"We're all scared, Lieutenant," Morgan said, trying hard to sound supportive and not punitive. Hell, she'd have wagered Strong wasn't any more scared than she was. But there was no time for fear now.

"Yes, Colonel." Morgan wasn't sure how much she'd gotten to her officer, but it seemed to be enough. It had to be—they had to counterattack now, before the battered federal force that had taken the small ridge was reinforced.

"All right," Morgan yelled, looking down at the ragged line of Strong's survivors. There were no more than twenty of them—eighteen, she told herself as her subconscious finished counting, not including Strong or her. "We're going to advance and we're going to take that hill back . . . and we're going to do it right now." She pulled out the assault rifle she had slung around her back, gripping it tightly with two hands. "Follow me," she shouted, lunging forward, out past the line of fallen trees her people had been using as cover, into the semiclear patch of waist-high grass.

She was about halfway to the hill before the enemy opened fire. She was surprised to see federal regulars so lax in their response time. *They don't respect us . . . they're not as sharp as they would be against Union troops.* The thought drifted through her mind, and though her concentration was dominated by fear and by the combat surrounding her, she still had enough attention left to be offended, downright pissed.

She opened fire as she ran the rest of the way, unleashing her rage on the soldiers along the crest of the hill. She caught one out in the open, hitting him at least three times before he crumpled to the ground, but then the others were back in position, and the incoming fire ramped up enormously.

She swung to the side, crouching as she continued forward, trying to present as small a visible target as possible. And finally, she looked behind her, confirming that her people had actually followed. She'd had faith they would, but seeing all of them moving up the hill made her proud.

That pride shattered into despair as one of them dropped as she was looking, and she could tell that at least one other was wounded, but still moving forward, staggering as he did. Morgan shook off any emotion, and turned her attention back to the ridge. She kept up her fire, even as she shouted, "Open up, all of you. Hose down that hillside now!" Her people weren't likely to take down any of the enemy, not as long as they stayed down behind the crest. But if they remained in cover, it would also minimize the incoming fire at her soldiers.

She felt her feet slam into the higher, harder ground of the hill. She popped out a spent cartridge and slammed another in place, not slowing at all as she did. Every second she stayed out in the open was another chance to be hit. The federals were better equipped, more extensively trained than anyone she had, all massive advantages in close combat. But at least in a hand-to-hand fight her soldiers wouldn't be out in the open, facing a protected line.

Her hand moved to her belt, pulled off a grenade. She threw it hard, up and over the crest, even as she raced toward the target area. She could hear the explosion—and now she was close enough to hear the shouts and yells, the sounds of men and women startled or wounded, she couldn't tell which.

It doesn't really matter.

Then she leapt up over the top of the hill, firing her rifle on full auto as she did. The federal troops were clearly surprised, and she took out two of them before they could respond. But the others fell back a few meters, forming a thin line as they did.

Her peripheral vision caught another fed, down, missing one leg and screaming in pain. A *grenade victim*, she thought.

She turned to face a pair of federals about three meters to her side, and as she did, she caught the image of her troopers coming over, perhaps six or seven at first, and then the rest, all firing wildly as they ran forward at full speed.

The federals opened up, taking down two—no, three—of her new arrivals, but then the two lines crashed together. Rifles swung hard, makeshift clubs now, and knives flashed in the partial sunlight. She was startled by the ferocity of her troopers, at how aggressively they had rallied to her call for the attack, to the example she had set. But close combat was a fearsome thing, and the training and body armor of the federals were huge advantages.

She saw more of her people go down, one or two seriously hurt, the others battered by rifle butts or sliced by combat knives. But they were taking down federals, too. She was fighting with one herself, pushing forward with her rifle, shoving the butt into his upper thigh, just below the black breastplate that covered his vitals. The soldier stumbled as his leg gave way, and he dropped to one knee.

Morgan loosened her hands, let the rifle drop as she pulled out her own knife. It was a quarter meter long and razor sharp—she had always seen to its sharpening, even in her peacetime days on the farm. She shifted her body, dropping down and shoving the blade up sharply, plunging it just under the soldier's body armor in the spot she remembered, the one that had always felt vulnerable to her in her army days.

She felt some resistance, the thick protective cloth that extended down below the hyperkev armor. The blade stopped, and for an instant, she thought it might slide off, diverted by the protective gear.

But then she felt it sliding forward, ripping through the material and deep into the man's abdomen.

The soldier she was fighting had grabbed his own knife, but he'd been too slow, and now it slipped from his grasp, falling to the ground with a loud clang. Morgan felt hot blood pouring out of the gaping wound, all over her hand. She pulled hard, removing the knife from the wound before plunging it in again . . . and again. Until her adversary stopped moving, and his body went limp. Then she stepped back and let him fall to the ground.

She wasn't bloodthirsty, and she drew no pleasure from killing a man who once might have been her comrade. But she knew enough of war to realize it was a choice between her and the enemy. If she turned her back, left him alive . . . well, she'd seen too many friends die that way.

She looked all around, making sure she had no enemies right by her. Then she took a second and panned her eyes across the field. It was horrifying, a nightmare she could barely stand to watch. At least half her people were down, and some of those on the ground were wrestling with enemy soldiers, brutal fights to the death with blades, rocks, bare hands. She'd been afraid her people were about to break, that they wouldn't follow her into yet another fight. But now she was stunned at the pure animal rage she saw. They were struggling for the rebellion, against the invaders of their world . . . and they were fighting to avenge the friends they'd lost in today's battle, and in the fighting of the previous year. But most of all, they were fighting for themselves, for each other. They weren't as skilled as their adversaries, and they paid a cost for that in blood, but they had something the federals could never match, a home to defend, a nation and future they dared to believe in. If the rebel forces managed to prevail, if they won freedom for themselves and their families, it wouldn't be training or experience or weapons provided by Federal America's rivals that made it happen. It would be their spirit, their dedication to the idea of a future the downtrodden people on Earth could never imagine.

The spirit being shown now.

The rebel army was full of inexperienced troops, raw would-be soldiers driven to the ranks out of patriotism, fear, anger. But that wasn't her people. They were different now, evolved from what most of their comrades were, from what they had been. Changed in a way she understood deeply.

They were veterans. They were her comrades.

She ran in to help them survive.

CHAPTER 23

"Colonel Morgan is going to be fine, General. We just got an update from the aid station. The doctor tried to get her to stay and rest awhile, but she told him . . ." Katia Rand's voice stopped abruptly.

"Yes, Lieutenant, I can imagine just what Colonel Morgan told him." He'd been worried since he'd gotten the word that Morgan had been wounded, even more concerned, that is, than he already was about the battle, the army, the fact that Robert Semmes had turned out to be a more dangerous tactician than he'd expected. Damian knew Semmes had not been alone, that the precision and organization of the attack was owed to the federal officers and their troops. But that wasn't the whole story. The brutal federal commander had given the impression that his forces were far more disorganized than they actually were.

Semmes had outfoxed him.

He suckered you in. You commanded this army just like a lieutenant jacked up way too far above your capability. How many men and women died today so you could play general?

Damian wasn't being entirely fair to himself—there was no one on Haven any more qualified who could have taken his place—but he was in the mood for self-flagellation, and he had little interest in making excuses for himself.

If it hadn't been for Jamie's people on the left and Morgan's on the right . . .

He knew the flank forces had held off the worst of the potential disaster that could have happened, and though he didn't have complete numbers yet, he also had a pretty good idea of the price they had paid. A price that almost included Luci Morgan. Damian considered Morgan a good friend, one he'd known since his days in the federal service, but more, though he'd never made it official, he looked at her as his number two. *My replacement, if the congress comes to its senses and fires me . . .*

For a terrible few hours, perhaps three, he'd truly thought the war was over, that the rebel army would be surrounded and destroyed. He'd imagined endless firing squads, operating around the clock as Semmes taught Haven—Alpha-2, it would be called again—a lesson that would last at least as long as living memory. But his worst fears subsided, at least temporarily, as the reports streamed in. Grant's and Morgan's forces held, longer than he'd dared to hope, and each moment, each hour they did meant more units of the army streaming up the Old North and Sanderson Roads. Green Hill Forest only grew denser to the north, the scattered clearings around Dover giving way to tangling undergrowth and soaring trees. The terrain would slow any federal pursuit, and probably stop it in its tracks, at least until the enemy could move up more supplies and start clearing support trails.

"Damian, I'm glad to see you're all right." John Danforth walked into the tent, looking disheveled, but not injured in any way. "I was worried . . . we heard that headquarters was in danger of being overrun. If you'd been captured . . ."

"If I'd been captured, what? No doubt you can find somebody else who can lead the army into a trap. It's not highly ranked among military skills."

"Damian . . . you did a magnificent job of pulling out of the battle. My understanding is that three quarters of the army is already out of immediate danger."

"Yes, we did an excellent job of running away."

"Damian, we both knew this would be a difficult and lengthy fight. One lost battle is not the end."

"It nearly was, John. Go talk to Jamie Grant and Luci Morgan and their people—if you can find any still alive and in one piece. They held back the enemy, not me. Whatever credit is to be given for keeping the door open so we could run away, it goes to them."

"Damian . . ."

"No, John. I know you're my friend, but I'm not qualified to do this. I don't know how to command an army, and I was insane to think I could." He paused, sighing softly. "Mr. President, I offer you my resignation as the commander of the republic's army."

"And as president, I categorically reject that offer."

"It's not up to you alone, John. The congress should decide. I've let them all down, and . . ."

"The congress is in session right now in a farmhouse about six kilometers north of here, my friend. I just came from there to bring you the results of the sole resolution it has passed since being driven from Landfall."

Damian looked at his friend and nodded. "I understand, John . . . I would probably have done the same . . ."

"The resolution was a vote of continued confidence in you, Damian . . . and it took place before we even knew that most of the army was going to escape from the trap. No one has given up on you." He put his hand on the general's shoulder. "Damian, no one expected this struggle to be quick or easy, or to be without great cost."

Damian heard his friend's words and felt his hand, and he drew strength from them, though he was pretty sure that there had been plenty ready to give up on him. He was far too aware of the realities of political bodies to think anything but that Danforth had used all his own clout to sustain his position.

"Thank you, John, but . . ." Damian realized that part of him wanted to quit, to run from the responsibility, to escape from being the one who had to send more of his neighbors to their deaths. But as disappointed as he was in his own capabilities, he knew Luci Morgan—or anyone else who took his place—couldn't do any better. The rebellion was always going to be a long and brutal struggle, and he was surprised at how unprepared he was for the reality he'd so long predicted.

I tried to win the war in one battle. And I failed. But we didn't fail, and maybe that's the best we can ask for right now.

"No *buts*, Damian," Danforth said as if agreeing with his thoughts. "Just see to the army. Finish extricating your troops from this fight, and then think to the next. Because there *will* be a next. And one after that . . . until Haven's freedom is undisputed."

Damian liked to think of himself as someone who didn't need any outside support, but he had to admit, Danforth's confidence had energized him, at least a little.

Enough. It will have to be enough.

"John . . . thanks."

"We're all in this together, Damian. And we need you. We need everything you can muster if we're going to win this."

Damian just nodded.

The two stood silently for a few seconds. Then Damian said, "You better get back up north, John."

Danforth extended his hand. "See to your soldiers."

Damian reached out and shook his friend's hand. Then Danforth turned and slipped out the door.

Damian turned toward Katia Rand, who'd been silent during the entire exchange between the two men. "You do a good impersonation of a piece of the furniture, Katia."

"I, ah . . . I just thought President Danforth could tell you what you needed to hear better than I could. The army still supports you, sir. The soldiers still look up to you."

Damian nodded, but he knew her words were at least partially wishful thinking. Many of the soldiers were no doubt still loyal to him, but now they had experienced the true reality of the task they'd taken on. They'd fought two battles the year before, and they'd lost one and won the other. But the casualties they'd taken here, in what Damian guessed would end up being called the Second Battle of Dover, were many times the number that had been lost in the combined fights of the previous year. The village of Dover was a smoking ruin, and at least two thousand of his soldiers were dead or missing. Danforth's support, and Katia's, and that of his officers and whatever soldiers still looked up to him with loyalty and dedication—none of it changed the suffering and destruction that had occurred here, under his command.

He knew human nature well enough to understand his relationship with the troops would never be the same. Even those still totally dedicated would be more distant now, the easy camaraderie gone. Which, he realized, was probably for the best. He was the one who sent them into battle, who spent their lives, and who would again. He had wanted to consider himself their neighbor, but that wasn't what they needed. They needed a leader, which meant the time for sentimentality was over.

I can worry about what they think of me when we win.

And yet, still he wondered if he could really believe there was a chance of victory . . . and then he wondered if there was, would it come at such a grievous cost that it wouldn't matter anymore? Was fighting for freedom worthwhile, if all that remained to be free was a silent wasteland, a graveyard where once a vital and growing world had been?

Violetta Wells stumbled down the path, feeling like she was about to drop, but somehow taking one step after the other, following her comrades as they continued the retreat from Dover.

Her mind felt numb, almost as though she couldn't hold together a structured thought about anything. Her service in the army had pushed her to the limit, the exhaustion, the fear. But now she'd seen battle, in all its brutality, and she feared the cost had been her sanity.

She hadn't been wounded, not really, though she had cuts and scrapes from falling, and her whole body ached beyond anything she'd ever imagined. She didn't know what was keeping her moving, and each tortured step felt like the last.

She still had her rifle, which was something not all of her comrades could say. Her feelings of pride in that fact were forestalled, however, by the fact that she hadn't fired the weapon in the battle. Not once.

She'd stayed in the line, terrified to near insanity, as the veterans of her unit stood and fought off the advancing federals. She wanted to flee, and truth be told, she'd been there praying for her comrades to break, for all of them to do the only thing that seemed remotely sane. Run.

Finally she'd gotten her wish, after what had seemed like an eternity standing there, each second feeling like the one when an enemy shot would find her, when her life would end. She'd managed to stop herself from tucking tail and running, at least before everyone else did, but that was pretty much all she could say for her actions.

Because she hadn't been able to do anything else.

She wasn't sure if it had been unwillingness to harm the federal soldiers—*no*, she thought, they'd been firing at her, and she didn't feel any compunction about killing someone who was trying like hell to kill her. So perhaps just paralyzing fear. Regardless, for those long minutes she'd just stood there, behind the moderate cover of the woods, and held her weapon in front of her, but never pulled the trigger. Pathetically, she had *acted* as though she was shooting. But every round still remained in the clip she'd loaded before the battle.

She knew she'd made a mistake. She'd known it before, but the battle had left no doubt in her mind. She still supported the rebellion, still longed to see Haven freed from the iron grip of Federal

America, but she knew one thing for sure: she would never be a soldier, not a capable one. All she could think of was running, slipping into the woods and . . .

And what? Where could you go? Father is back on Earth. Landfall is occupied by General Semmes. You'd be a deserter to the rebels and a traitor to the federals.

She cursed herself for her folly, for the impetuous actions that had put her in this situation. The idea of another battle scared her out of her wits. Perhaps she'd do better next time. Maybe she'd even fire. But she knew she would never become proficient at combat . . . and, moreover, she had a dread certainty that all that lay ahead for her in her next battle was death.

"All right, let's take a break." The voice was different from the one that had shouted out commands as her company had marched north from Landfall. Lieutenant Quinn had been hit in the battle—she'd heard rumors that he was dead, but there hadn't been any confirmation of that. Sergeant Winger was definitely dead. He'd been standing less than five meters from her when he'd taken a shot in the head. Violetta was half convinced one of the stains on her shirt was from Winger's blood, but she couldn't be sure. Half a dozen troopers had died close enough to her to splatter her with their innards.

She turned and walked off the path—Winger had told her again and again to step off the road during rest periods. Though the Sanderson Road barely qualified as anything more than a pass this far north of the Tillis intersection.

She looked around, images in her mind of someplace to sit, a log or even a large stone, but there was nothing but muddy ground. She might have avoided it if the prospect of standing another second hadn't been so onerous, but before she had another conscious thought, she was sitting in the driest spot, a patch of ground still damp enough to soak the seat of her pants in a second or two.

She sat there for a few minutes, her primary thought revolving around whether the memories she had of comfort and good, warm food were hallucinations brought on by exhaustion.

"Excuse me, are you Violetta Wells . . . yes, you are!" There was a man standing next to her, dressed in rough terrain gear, but not a uniform, or what at least passed for uniforms in the Haven army.

"Mr. Jacen?" She'd met Cal Jacen a number of times at meetings, but she'd hardly said more than a word or two to the Society's founder. She was surprised he even recognized her.

"Yes, Violetta. I had heard you joined the army, but I hardly expected to run into you here."

"I still can't believe I am here, Mr. Jacen." Her exhaustion poured out with her words.

"Please, Violetta, I'm Cal. And I can only imagine the difficulty of army service. I only wish I could have joined you, but the needs of the congress called . . . not to mention the Society."

"Yes, I am sure you are enormously busy . . . Cal." She looked up at him, realizing just how surprised she was to see a man of Jacen's importance here, amid Haven's beaten and retreating soldiers.

"There is nothing more important than our brave troops. I could not stay away, and the more so after I realized the federals had pushed us back." He paused. "I was surprised to see General Ward so easily beaten by Robert Semmes."

"General Ward did his best, Cal. I am sure of that." Violetta remembered Damian from the times he'd come to see her father. She'd found him to be pleasant and charming . . . and something more. He'd clearly struggled with joining the rebellion himself, and his ultimate acceptance of the struggle for independence had, as likely as anything, been the final influence that pushed her to openly support the revolution, and to abandon her life and father and remain on Haven.

"Of course, Violetta," he said reassuringly. "It's just that the general *was* a federal soldier. He *must* have some level of divided sympathies."

Violetta had never considered Damian's past, or how it might affect his judgment now. Was it possible his sympathy for federal soldiers had played some part in the disastrous battle? *No*, she thought, not General Wells. Yet, exhausted as she was, Cal Jacen was making a certain amount of sense, too. Through the fog in her brain, a tiny nub of doubt could be felt.

"I don't know, Cal. The few times I've met General Ward, he always seemed to be an honorable man."

"He is, most certainly. But even admirable men can be pulled in different directions. I support General Ward fully . . . but I also want to be sure to help him however he may need it, whether he asks or not." He paused, and then he said, "Violetta, you seem out of place here in an infantry unit. I don't doubt your courage, but I am sure General Ward would make a place for you at headquarters. There are many ways to serve, you know."

"Leave my unit?" Violetta felt a wave of self-loathing at the prospect of using her status as the ex-governor's daughter to get herself moved from the front line.

But she also knew it wouldn't stop her.

"Why, Cal? Because of who my father is?" She wasn't foolish enough to think Jacen was interested in her by random accident.

"No, Violetta. Your father, noteworthy individual that he is, no longer has any meaningful role in the rebellion. But you do. You are a member of the Society, and we are all brothers and sisters. And your past, your upbringing . . . it is not your fault that you were insulated, that it is harder for you to transition to a soldier's life than it is for a farmer accustomed to physical toil."

She looked back at Jacen, but she still didn't believe him, not completely, at least. But the thought of being in headquarters instead of here, or in the front line of another battle . . . it was intoxicating. "Do you really think I could serve at headquarters?"

"Of course, Violetta. I will ask President Danforth to speak with General Ward. I suspect we can have you transferred by tomorrow."

Violetta turned and looked at her comrades. But she couldn't resist the prospect of staying farther away from enemy fire, of traveling in a vehicle instead of marching endless kilometers on foot. "That would be wonderful, Cal . . . if you are willing to do it for me."

"Of course, Violetta. In fact, I believe it can be of help not only to you, but to me and to the rebellion, as well. I will use my influence to get you assigned to General Ward's staff . . . and as a member of the Society, perhaps you can keep me advised of what is happening."

The fog shifted a bit, and along with the doubt, a bit of suspicion emerged. "You want me to spy on the general?"

"No, of course, not, Violetta. But we both agreed, General Ward is in a difficult situation. The job he has taken on himself is more than any one man can manage. It is our place to help him, to give him the support he needs, to bolster his strength and his will. I would never disrespect the general, and if I tried to help him directly, I'm afraid that is how it would seem to him. But you may be able to help him, and help President Danforth and me to help him, as well."

There was something in Jacen's voice that made her nervous— not exactly hostility toward General Ward, but something that made her vaguely uncomfortable in a way she could not pinpoint. But the prospect of getting out of the field, of escaping the endless marches, she couldn't resist. She respected Jacen. He was one of the fathers of the rebellion, and she'd never heard anyone call him out as anything but the most fervent patriot.

"I will do anything I can to help the Society and the rebellion, and General Ward." She looked back at her comrades, listening as the sergeant who had taken Winger's place belted out the command for the company to re-form and prepare to resume the march. She felt a rush of despair at the prospect, and whatever doubts she might have had about Jacen's offer vanished in a wave of self-justification. "I would be greatly appreciative, Cal. I want to serve the rebellion, but it's obvious I won't do a thing to help secure Haven's freedom on the front line of a battle. I was not cut out to fight, let alone to kill."

"Then it is settled. I will make the arrangements. Your transfer should come through tomorrow, or the next day at the latest." He paused. "You will serve under the general, aid him in his enormous task." He hesitated again. "And you will report to me when you can, help me aid the general, to assist him in avoiding mistakes."

"Thank you, Cal," she said as she stood up and moved slowly back toward the road. "I will do everything I can to help you and the rebellion."

CHAPTER 24

"They've occupied Danforth Hall, Colonel. At least a platoon in the house itself, along with some officers, but I'd say there's a whole company there, counting the outposts and the troops deployed in the outbuildings and on the grounds." Desmond Black had just returned from the scouting mission Colonel Killian had ordered. Killian had intended for him to send a patrol, not lead it himself, but Black was cut from the same ragged cloth as the commander of the rangers. For all Killian had come to depend on his valued aide, Black was no staff officer who could sit behind a desk—or under a tree—taking notes all day.

"It's a damned shame. Those bastards in Danforth Hall. John Danforth is the father of the rebellion. Don't think they don't know that. There are two dozen big houses a lot closer to the action. They could have used any one of those, but that bastard Semmes knows just what he's doing. That's their area HQ, all right. That will be the focal point of their efforts to root us out of these woods. And I'll bet anything when they're done, they'll level the place."

"They'll need more than President Danforth's house to chase us down, sir . . . a lot more. We've got each unit in its own designated area, spread out but in mutually supporting range in case the enemy tries something. And we've still got people making their way out from Landfall. Our numbers are growing every hour."

Killian looked over at his aide, a grim expression on his face. "I'm afraid that trajectory will reverse soon, Lieutenant. Any sign of Major North?"

"No, sir. Not yet." Black looked down at the ground for a few seconds before returning his gaze to Killian. "But that doesn't mean he . . ."

"No, Lieutenant, it doesn't mean he's dead. But his people made it back. Whatever happened to him, he made sure of that. None of them saw him killed or captured, but no one had any idea where he was, either. So it seems there are two possibilities—he went down in the fighting, or he was captured, and no one saw it happen." Killian's tone suggested he thought little of the possibility of North allowing himself to be taken alive. "Or maybe there's a third: he's still in Landfall. Somewhere." Killian wondered if that was possible, ultimately deciding yes, he thought it was, at least for someone like Jacob North. But after the wave of strikes his people had managed to pull off, he had no doubt that the federals would be tearing Landfall apart, looking for anyone responsible—or even those who weren't necessarily responsible, but whom they could blame. He'd bequeathed a nightmare to the residents of the capital, and it pained him, the misery he imagined being unleashed even as he stood there. But there was no place for half measures in war.

"If he is still there, sir . . ."

"Yes." Killian understood exactly what his aide was thinking. "If he is still there, he's going to have his hands full just staying alive." Killian wondered just how many of the people of Landfall would still support a trapped ranger after Semmes got done punishing them for the loss of his supplies.

"I'm afraid Major North is on his own, Lieutenant." *Assuming he is still alive.* "There is nothing we can do for him. We have to keep our eyes forward. If we see him again, it will either be toasting victory or in Hell."

With that note of finality, he turned his attention to the reports he'd been getting. One shining piece of news was that his teams' one-day frenzy in Landfall had left most of Semmes's aircraft inoperable. That had been one of Killian's priorities, and he was heartened to have done damage to one of the feds' biggest assets. There were still a few—enough to make open terrain treacherous—but it meant the rebels had at least a little time to maneuver and regroup.

"Colonel Killian, a scout from the north just arrived." The voice was from one of the rangers, and the second Killian heard it, he knew something was terribly wrong.

"Calm down, Sergeant. What is it?"

The ranger took a deep breath, and he seemed to regain a bit of control. "Sir, the army engaged the federals near Dover." His voice stopped for a few seconds, but Killian understood completely. "They were defeated, Colonel, and driven deeper into the woods north of Dover. Reports suggest casualties were heavy, perhaps as many as three thousand."

All thoughts of his success in Landfall went out the window. Killian hadn't expected *that*. Three thousand was a huge number, especially since the army of Haven had never been more than twelve thousand strong, and that had been before the one-year enlistments had begun to expire.

He'd been trying to keep the sergeant calm, but now he felt his own insides twist into knots. He wasn't surprised the federals had driven Damian's army back . . . in fact, anything else would have been unexpected. But he was stunned at the thought that Damian had allowed his forces to be hit hard enough to lose a quarter of their strength. Assuming, of course, the reports were true. Such things were prone to exaggeration. But he also believed it this time. And in a way, he could use the bad news—it gave him his next move. Because as sure as he was of anything, he had to do something to take the pressure off Damian.

He turned toward Black. "All right, Des . . . General Ward needs us. We've got to cause some trouble, foul up the federal supply lines to the north. I want a dozen operations ready to go by nightfall tonight. We're going to shut down the road, blow up their supply transports. By the time we're done, they're going to think they've got another army on their flanks."

"Yes, sir," Black said with a feral grin.

"It's going to bring heat down on us. I want every trooper we've got left to be on guard every minute. They'll send teams in these woods to hunt us down, but that's exactly what we want. We're going to have to be nimble, but the more they're chasing us, the more those are resources that won't be pursuing Damian and the main army."

"Yes, sir. Don't worry, Colonel. We all understand what is at stake."

"Good. Des, one more thing . . ."

"Sir?"

"While we're hitting these bastards along the road . . . I want a raiding party deployed right here."

"Here, sir?"

"Yes, here. As long as we're going to poke at the federals and bring hellfire down on us, we're damned sure not going to let the federals keep President Danforth's house. We're going to hit it at midnight, just as the other groups attack the logistics trains." He paused and stared at his aide. "And no one gets away, not one. They've got tech on their side, and training. It's time we put something on ours.

"Fear."

Black stared back and smiled, wolfish once more. "Yes, *sir.*"

Jacob North slipped through the dark alley, cautious about making noise or even allowing his shadow to be cast out from any lights he passed. He'd tried to get out of town by three or four different routes, but he'd been blocked on every one. There were federals all around the city, covering the streets, smashing down doors, dragging terrified civilians out of their homes.

Ninety percent of the rangers' attacks had succeeded, plunging Landfall into utter chaos. Millions of credits of food, ammunition, and medicine had been destroyed, and from the looks of things, Robert Semmes had been driven to uncontrolled rage. The capital city had turned into a nightmare, and North could hear the gunshots in the distance . . . and sometimes not so far off. Civilians were being killed, and more would die before Semmes's rage died down.

North felt the urge to intervene, but there was nothing he could do. He'd be lucky enough to avoid the enemy patrols—for an hour, a day, however long it took to find a way out. *Or to empty a gun in my mouth.*

Because he was sure of only one thing: he wasn't going to let himself be taken prisoner. He had too good an idea of what Semmes would do, not only to a captured rebel, but to one on which he could focus the wrath caused by burning airships and obliterated warehouses.

For now, though, he was going to do everything he could to stay alive. He looked all around, and then he moved out again, edging up slowly toward the street and peering out. It was a back road, and it seemed empty. He'd worked himself as far as he could from the areas of the main attacks, and he'd also avoided the heavily built-up zones. He was close to the originally settled area, where the first colonists had built ramshackle structures with little concern for layout or durability. That area had quickly degraded, and all but the poorest residents had long ago moved to better areas. It seemed like the perfect place to hide and decide what to do next.

He was about to rush across the street diagonally, toward another alley tucked between two buildings, but he saw something, a light down at the end of the street. A guard? He paused, sliding back into the shadows.

The figure turned, moving toward him, slowly. Clearly he hadn't seen North yet. He kept coming, and soon he was close enough that North could tell he was a soldier.

Damn.

North wasn't looking for a fight, and leaving a dead federal trooper behind was like marking his trail with paint. But if he stayed where he was and the soldier saw him . . .

He reached down for the pistol shoved under his belt, but he stopped. No, he couldn't risk a gunshot. He had no idea who else was near.

He grabbed the heavy survival knife he'd carried since the invasion. It was twenty-five centimeters long, notched along its length. An ugly weapon for ugly work.

He pressed himself up against the wall, waiting as the fed moved closer. He could hear the footsteps now, and he held his breath, struggling to remain motionless, silent.

Then he saw the faint shadow, cast from the light of the sole functional streetlamp in the area. It wasn't much, but it was enough. He lunged out into the street, and then he angled himself into the trooper's side. His arm swung down, bringing the blade right for his adversary's neck . . . but he missed, slightly. The wound would have been fatal, without question, had the knife not caught on the top of the man's combat armor. The tip was still for an instant, pressing against the hard composite of the armor. Then it slid down, leaving a slight scratch on the protective gear but doing little other damage, even as the uninjured trooper reached for his own weapon.

If the man had possessed a pistol, North knew he'd have been dead. But the soldier's hand reached around, pulling at the rifle slung across his back. It was a slower move, and more cumbersome.

North pulled his knife away, angling for another stabbing motion, but his target was alert now, and he moved aside, struggling to bring the assault rifle to bear.

North had no choice. He let the blade fall to the ground and whipped out his pistol, even as his other hand shoved at the fed, pushing the rifle's barrel away.

He fired as his enemy was moving his own weapon into place. Once, then a second time. The soldier fell backward, his hand tightening on the trigger, letting off a burst of three shots that blasted through the night air, echoing into the distance.

North looked down the street. He couldn't see anything, but as his eyes darted back to his victim, he could hear sounds from farther down the street. The fed was lying on his back, still breathing but clearly badly hurt. North looked more closely. The first shot had glanced off the trooper's armor, but the second one had hit just where he'd intended his knife strike to go. The wound was mortal, if not immediately, and it was clear his enemy wasn't able to threaten him further.

But he can tell them where I went . . .

North looked down at the wounded soldier, and his thought filled with images of friends who'd fought at the spaceport, and in Landfall, some of whom—*many*—were now dead. He felt a short burst of pity, a hesitancy to kill this man in cold blood. But it didn't last.

He's dead anyway. And you didn't come invade their home. They came to yours.

He leaned forward, slipping the pistol back into his belt as he reached down and picked up the knife. He glanced up, staring down the street again. The noises were louder, getting closer, and he could see movement now, at the far end of the road.

He knelt down next to the soldier, his eyes momentarily pausing, fixed on those of the dying man. Then he held the knife next to the fed's throat, slipping it over the lip of armor until he felt the press of soft flesh. The man looked up at him, seeming as if he was going to say something. But he remained silent.

North hesitated for a second, but then he looked up again. There were definitely soldiers coming, at least five or six, and they were getting close. There was no time.

He jerked his hand quickly, the razor-sharp blade slicing the fed's throat. The soldier's eyes widened as he drew a final, gurgling breath.

North leapt to his feet and ducked back into the alley. He had to put some distance behind him and the soldier. The approaching feds would go batshit crazy when they found their dead comrade. He was going to be actively pursued now, a target on his back.

He turned around a corner and raced along the back wall of a decrepit old building. He was running, but he had no direction . . . or idea what he could do next.

"Brocketing force, open fire. Assault teams, get ready to move out." Killian stood and stared across the once-manicured lawns of John Danforth's estate as his three autocannon teams opened up, sending a stream of deadly fire across the open space, shattering the masonry walls of the great house.

"Assault teams . . . move out!"

Killian watched as sixty of his people surged out onto the open hillside, rushing toward the house in columns separated by three carefully placed fields of fire. He had no reason to attack the Danforth property, no purely tactical ones, at least. But he felt it important to teach the enemy the true depth of the war they had come to fight. And here, in his friend's house they were despoiling with their presence, he intended to do just that.

"Keep up that fire. The assault forces know the killing zones." Technically that was true, but Killian was also enough of a veteran to guess that more than one of his people would wander into their own friendly fire before this fight was over. He could only hope now wouldn't be that time.

"Des, you stay here and watch over the gun crews."

"What are you going to do, sir?"

Killian didn't answer. His aide already knew. He pulled the heavy weapon he had slung across his back, more a light autocannon than an assault rifle, and he flashed a single wicked smile at Black. Then he leapt out into the field, following his troopers in.

CHAPTER 25

ABANDONED DOCKSIDE
BALTIMORE
FEDERAL AMERICA
EARTH, SOL III

Everett Wells pulled up the collar of his sweater and shivered against the cold predawn breeze. The cold was so numbing, so biting, it made him forget how terrified he was. For a moment.

He'd spent a significant amount of time with Asha Stanton, more than he'd ever imagined he would have. Whatever else he thought of Stanton, she'd done what she'd promised, and the two were about to meet a representative of the Hegemony . . . to discuss matters the government of Federal America could hardly consider as anything but treason.

"Your Excellencies," a voice came from near where Wells was standing, and a man stepped out from behind a partially collapsed masonry wall.

"That is no longer my title . . ." Wells turned to face the man as he waved for Stanton to come over from where she'd been looking for their contact.

"Ah. I, too, am addressed as 'Your Excellency,' Governor Wells, though I would propose that we all put aside such niceties and speak informally, even as friends. My name is Xi."

"I appreciate the informality, Mr. . . . Xi. But surely you are aware of my current status. My ranks and forms of address have been stripped from me."

"That assumes one acknowledges the actions of Federal America's senate, a pack of gangsters and nothing more. Their disrespect for a man like you was revolting."

Wells felt a shiver move through his body. He wasn't all that pleased with the senate's actions himself, but hearing the foreigner say it made the reality of what he was doing all too plain.

For Violetta . . . this is for Violetta, he reminded himself.

"Xi, welcome. I certainly did not expect you to come here yourself. Please ignore my partner. I'm afraid Governor Wells is a bit edgy about our endeavor."

Edgy . . . I'm disgusted. And scared shitless.

"I understand, of course. Loyalty speaks well of a man's character, even when it is to an entity as undeserving of it as the senate. But perhaps now we should turn aside from politic discussions and get on to specifics. I almost sent a representative to meet with you, but your father's request was quite emphatic."

Wells had known Stanton's family was a significant trading partner with several firms in the Hegemony. That wasn't treasonous, not since the end of the last war and the ratification of the treaty requiring all three of the superpowers to open their markets to one another. But it sounded a little too cozy to be totally legitimate, though he realized Stanton's connections were the only thing that provided a chance to stop Semmes.

Before he crushes the rebels. Before he finds Violetta . . .

"You have my thanks, Xi, and my father's appreciation." She paused and looked over at Wells. "The former governor and I are terribly concerned about the prospects of the federal expeditionary force defeating the rebellion on Alpha-2."

"That is a somewhat surprising position, particularly since the two of you had been charged with just the same thing. Is that not correct?" Then, before either could answer, Xi continued, "I take it your concern is about General Semmes securing the victory where both of you . . . were unable to do so."

"Yes, something like that, Xi." Stanton sounded a bit touchy, but she kept her calm. "But there is more at stake than our pride, or even our rivalry with Semmes. If the federal forces put down the rebellion, it will send a signal to the other colonies, discouraging resistance. Fear is a powerful motivator, and I can assure you that General Semmes will instill fear in those who witness what he does to the defeated rebels. Your government has a choice, Xi, to see Federal America strengthened, its hold on its colonies tightened beyond the prospect of weakening, or to see Alpha-2 slip away, and send a spark of resistance to the other worlds." She stopped, staring at the Hegemony minister as he stood silently. "We all know Federal America is winning the colonization race. That *was* the true cause of the last war, was it not?"

Wells watched, impressed at Stanton's arguments, but also concerned at the aggressiveness of her hostility toward Federal America. Wells himself was uncomfortable even interfering with the rebellion on Alpha-2. The thought of their efforts leading to more uprisings and the weakening of Federal America's lead in space made him nauseated.

"I cannot discuss any specific positions of my government, of course, but I do not believe it is any secret that we would prefer more of a balance of power beyond the solar system. However, that does not mean that we are able—or willing—to intervene, to risk the renewal of the war. An invasion of Alpha-2 by our forces would almost certainly have that result. There is no way your senate could leave the Hegemony, or the Union, in control of their former colony. Certainly not their largest and most valuable. There is little doubt that they would go to war to prevent that."

"I am not suggesting you take Alpha-2, Xi. I am proposing that you assist the rebels in winning their war, in achieving their independence."

The Hegemony representative stood there with a stunned look on his face. "Do you think that is even possible? Our intelligence suggests that there were considerable forces sent to crush the rebellion."

"There were."

"And you believe a makeshift rebel army can defeat them? I'm sorry, Asha, but I just can't see that as reasonable."

"You misunderstand. I do not believe the rebels can win without assistance . . . but I *do* believe they can achieve victory on the ground. With the right support."

"We provided them considerable supplies of guns and ammunition, but with the federal blockade, I'm afraid that conduit is shut down."

"It is the blockade of which I speak when I ask for your aid. If your forces and the Union's were to launch a combined operation, you could drive the federal fleet from the planet, at least temporarily. If the federal supplies are cut off, and reinforcements cannot get through, I believe the rebels could then win their ground war."

Wells had just been watching the exchange, but now he was as incredulous as the Hegemony representative. He knew Stanton had intended to ask for aid, but he had no idea her intention had been to call for Federal America's combined enemies to attack the fleet.

"Asha, I won't be a part of this any further. This is not what we had discussed." Wells had expected her to request ammunition shipments, possibly the commissioning of blockade runners . . . not the outright request for a combined enemy force to attack the naval force at Alpha-2.

"Everett, there is no other way. If Senator Semmes is able to send a continuous stream of supplies and reinforcements to his son, the rebels have no chance. But the senate will rebel against Semmes's pushing Federal America into a resumption of the war. The last treaty was advantageous, and a renewed conflict risks all of that. They will negotiate rather than risk total disaster. They will accept Alpha-2's independence, as long as neither the Hegemony nor the Union controls it."

Wells was going to respond, and he was still trying to think of a nicer way to ask what he was thinking than *Are you insane?* when Xi beat him to it.

"Asha, I'm afraid Everett here"—he looked at Wells—"if I may call you Everett?" Wells nodded. "Everett is correct to be cautious about your plan. What you propose is quite aggressive, and I will go so far as to say brilliant . . . but it is also terribly risky. You ask us to take the chance of restarting the war, to mount a major multinational fleet expedition that would be financially devastating. And our reward? Are we to control the colony once it is wrested from federal control? No. We are not even to have any reliable certainty that Alpha-2 *will* be liberated. If the rebels are unable to defeat the federals—and despite your seeming confidence, I must say I consider this a highly unlikely occurrence—we will at best cause a temporary stalemate, a victorious ground force trapped on the colony they have pacified. In such a circumstance, I think there's a very good chance the senate will mobilize the entire federal navy rather than back down. Then our adventure will not just be enormously expensive and light on rewards. It will be a desperate battle to which we will be forced to commit virtually all our fleet assets. You ask much, Asha. Perhaps too much."

"The loss of Alpha-2 will reduce the differential between your colonial revenues by 64 percent, and the Union's by 58 percent. There is no one action that can make such a dent in federal superiority in colonization, and leave a Union-Hegemony alliance ahead of Federal America for the first time since the first extrasystem travel." Stanton's voice was firm, confident. "I understand the risks of what I am asking, Xi, but let us not try to kid each other about what you have to gain, without so much as one of your soldiers touching down on the planet."

Wells just stood, dumbstruck, even as Xi digested Stanton's words. Eventually the Hegemony contact said, "Very well, Asha. Let us be frank. You know we would do almost anything to see Federal

America humbled in space, perhaps even risk open war. But we would not do so recklessly, and I'm afraid I cannot quite accept your assertion that if reinforcements and supplies are interdicted for a time, the rebels will defeat the federal forces. It seems, honestly, impossible, and even if you could somehow convince me, I can assure you that I would not be able to gain enough support from my colleagues, not without some kind of evidence to bolster the idea that a rabble of revolutionaries can somehow have a decisive victory over federal regulars." He hesitated, taking a deep breath. "Even if there was such evidence, if the rebels are fighting well, even gaining the edge, there is no way to know. The Union sent an ambassador before the federal invasion departed, but now he is trapped on the planet—or worse—and there is no way to get word in or out, not without chasing away the federal fleet, which will require resources we cannot commit without evidence of rebel success on the ground."

Which means we're at a standstill, Wells thought. *They can't help us until they know we can win, and we can't win unless they help us.*

Stanton was silent, too, and for the first time since the meeting began looked dejected. She clearly didn't have an answer. They were close to getting Federal America's two superpower rivals to interfere in the rebellion, but there was no way to close the deal. Wells had doubts about whether the requisite success on the ground was possible, but he also had a lot of faith in Damian Ward . . . so there was some hope. But what there wasn't was a way to get the word out, to even know what was going on. And without that, it didn't matter what victories Damian achieved.

"Will you at least discuss the plan of action with your people?" Asha asked suddenly. "With the idea that any approval would be subject to sufficient evidence of rebel success on the ground?"

Xi paused for a moment. Then he looked back at Stanton. "You are very persuasive, Asha. I will discuss the matter. Perhaps we can even begin some tentative planning in the unlikely event we do intervene." He stared at her intently. "But I can promise you there will be no action—and nothing but outright denial of any involvement by my government—unless we are satisfied the rebels have a real chance at victory."

"Very well . . ."

Wells had been listening to his two companions, but now his head snapped around, almost instinctively. He'd heard something, he was sure of it. But he couldn't see anything.

He turned back toward Stanton, pausing halfway. There it was again! He spun, and even as he did he saw the movement, heard the footsteps on the cracked concrete.

"Run," he said, louder than he'd intended. Stanton and Xi looked up, silent and stunned for a second. Then both took off, racing into the block of shattered buildings, even as the blasts of focused light began to hit the walls and buildings all around.

Wells ran, trying to hold back the terror and move as quickly as he could. He raced forward, watching as his two companions ducked behind a section of three-story-high brick wall. He lunged forward, driving toward the same spot. He was three meters away, then two. One last leap to cover.

Then his body froze, wracked by agony, his muscles spasming under the high-voltage charge. It was a stunner, he guessed, in an ethereal, vague way. He'd never been shot by a stun gun, of course, but it seemed like it would feel this way.

He knew he had to get around the corner, to escape with Asha and Xi, but it was impossible. He felt helpless, his bodily functions slipping from his control. There wasn't pain, at least nothing serious after the initial shock, but he was nauseated, his head woozy. Then he dropped to his knees, teetering with tenuous and fading balance before he fell forward, hard onto the ground, and lost consciousness.

CHAPTER 26

Damian walked through the woods, along the makeshift trail his people had made. It wasn't created by deliberate design, but simply by walking along the most level section of ground for months now. He knew Ben Withers would be apoplectic when he saw that Damian was missing. The aide hated it when his commander went out alone, without so much as a single guard with him. For that matter, so would John Danforth, Luci Morgan . . . even Violetta Wells. They'd all gathered around him like a pack of dogs protecting him. He appreciated the thought behind it all, but that didn't stop it from driving him crazy.

But none of that mattered, not now. He just had to get away, to steal a few moments for himself. If he didn't he'd go insane . . . and then he'd be no use to anyone.

His army had been camped here through the winter, a brutal and bitter one, worse than any other, at least as long as he'd been on Haven, and, according to some of the native-born troopers in the army, the worst in forty years.

Cold weather wasn't something residents of technologically advanced civilizations usually worried too much about, but his people were refugees of such a society now, driven far from their homes, from anything but the untouched, and for three straight months, snow- and ice-covered forest.

Damian had continued his army's retreat after the disastrous Second Battle of Dover, driving his exhausted survivors all the way to the northern reaches of Green Hill Forest. That put them almost a hundred and twenty kilometers from the capital, with the wild rapids of the Far Point River and vast stretches of dense forest between his battered force and Landfall.

Still, he hadn't been able to explain why the enemy hadn't pursued his fragile army. Damian had expected the federals to move north, right on his tail, to finish the rebellion with a final crushing victory. He'd have had no hope of defeating such an assault. None.

But the weeks turned into months, and still no offensive came. He and Luci Morgan and the other veterans used the unexpected time to train their force of Havenites, driving them hard, as often as not through knee-deep snow and subfreezing temperatures. The exhausted troops built shelters and defenses for themselves, using the trees as raw material, and as often as not crude hand tools as construction implements. The rebels were short on everything, and much of the army's scant supply of generators and power plants had been reserved for Jonas Holcomb's secret project. So like an army from centuries before, the troops burned logs to stay warm, or at least something as close to warm as they could get. And every day they rose at dawn, achingly, miserably, to another day of drilling that had to seem merciless to them.

Damian had watched his army waste away even as he trained them, and every day's roll call told of a new pack of deserters, men and women fleeing the terrible weather, the brutal training, the feeling of a lost cause. Damian chafed at seeing his force withering away, and he gave speeches, marched in the snowy clearings with his troops, shared their meager rations. But he didn't punish the deserters, not even when his people caught them. He understood, and didn't blame the soldiers for slipping away. He struggled any way he could to keep them in camp, posting guards at night and patrols along the roads leading off, as much to discourage potential deserters as to actually apprehend those who left anyway. Still, for all he could manage, every idea he had come up with to hold his force together, he'd been unable to halt the flow . . . and unwilling to resort to extreme sanctions, the kind of terror that Cal Jacen and many of his Society allies demanded. The apoplectic rage on Jacen's face was his only solace in the whole bad business. Pissing off the Society leader was something he considered a pleasure, and he told Jacen again and again he would not allow deserters to be executed. Sometimes that came in professional language, the kind of semiformal response one expected from a general—but others, it was blunter, rougher.

There was a bright side, besides annoying Jacen, at least of a sort. The soldiers who remained, the ones who endured everything Damian and his veteran officers—and the weather—could throw at them, they'd become something very much like real veterans and, Damian dared to imagine, even a match for the federals. For all that his year of preparation had been intended to achieve the same thing, in practice, the proximity of the enemy and the urgency of the situation had been the missing elements then. Now his soldiers did what they had to do. They were committed to a fight to the end, and their desperation awoke an inner strength Damian doubted most of them had realized they had.

He owed the achievements that had been made to the troops themselves, the men and women who'd endured relentless agony for months. He owed it to his officers, as well, and to John Danforth, who had somehow kept the Haven government together, despite the fact that every major population center on the planet was controlled by the federals. But he knew on some level that most of all he owed it to Patrick Killian, and however few of his tattered rangers and soldiers were still alive.

Killian had taken it on himself to inflict terror in the hearts of the federal troops near Landfall, and against all odds, he'd done something very much like that. Damian's information was spotty, of course, and always well behind, brought to his camp by stragglers and the occasional hardy scout who slipped south to secure intel for the army, but it was clear. Killian's campaign had started in the autumn, just after the massive string of sabotage attacks in Landfall that preceded the rangers' evacuation from the city. Killian had pulled his people out under the cover of night and confusion. But he hadn't stopped there.

The first attacks after the retreat had been against the enemy supply line on the Old North Road . . . as well as a particularly savage and gruesome assault on John Danforth's house, which had been occupied by federal forces. The rangers had shown no mercy there, and when the feds retook the place, they discovered a true nightmare. Their garrison had been killed to the last man, and not in pretty ways.

Damian often didn't approve of Killian's methods, as he didn't here, but he couldn't argue with the results. The federals went crazy, pouring increasing amounts of their strength into trying to root his raiders out of the woods near Landfall, and to hunt down and destroy the force that had so savagely killed their people. That struggle, which had raged all winter, had been beyond brutal. No quarter was asked for, and none was given. The two forces faced each other in the frigid woods and through raging blizzards, and the rangers held their ground against assault after assault from their more heavily armed enemies.

But eventually, numbers and resources told, and Killian's force dwindled, soldiers dying in combat, on the retreat, the wounded freezing to death in their scant tents. Finally the survivors were driven ever farther north, surrounded and hunted down one man at a time. Damian didn't know how many Killian had left, or even if the ranger commander himself was still alive. But he knew he owed him a debt, one he could never repay.

Killian's raids against the supply lines had done more than in-convenience the federals. They had saved the rebel army. The fed-eral forces who had won the battle at Dover were forced to pull back. Almost cut off from Landfall by the rangers, they had to move back along their lines of communication, clearing them and re-opening the flow of supplies. By the time they had finished that, the rebel army had retired farther to the north and dug in. And the federals had a new focus, the extermination of the guerilla forces hiding in Blackwood Forest, and in every farmstead and barn the cooperative citizens could provide.

"Damian!"

He turned abruptly, startled by the loud yell, but only for an instant. He would recognize Ben Withers's voice anywhere.

"I'm sorry, Ben." He'd been wagering in his head who would track him down first. John Danforth and Luci Morgan had been likely prospects, but his old aide had been the favorite by a large margin. "I know I shouldn't leave the perimeter, but . . ."

"No, General, it's not that." Damian realized Withers was ex-cited about something. "It's Dr. Holcomb, sir. He's been looking all over for you. He has a prototype ready to show you. A suit, Gen-eral . . . he has a suit ready to show you."

Damian felt a rush of surprise. Jonas Holcomb was a genius, not in the way the word was bastardized and thrown around, but in the true, literal sense. Damian had respected Holcomb enough to divert supplies to his project, things that his suffering army des-perately needed elsewhere, but even so, he'd never quite believed that the scientist could build something as sophisticated as he'd proposed, not in a row of hastily built wooden shacks hidden in the woods.

Damian lurched toward Withers and said, "Let's go, Ben." He felt a rush of excitement. He was proud of his soldiers, of what the stalwarts had become. But he knew there weren't enough of them to defeat the federals, not without some kind of edge.

Maybe we've finally got that edge.

It was against his nature to allow optimism to excite him, but now he did it anyway. He considered hope a poor tool of the tactician, but he already believed himself a poor tactician, so he might as well own it.

For some reason, that thought made him feel better than he had in weeks.

"General Ward is a good man, Mr. Jacen. He took me on to his staff when I . . ." Violetta Wells had jumped at the chance to get off the battle line when Jacen had offered it, but she bore the guilt of leaving her comrades for the relative safety of headquarters. She was glad to be where she was, to be away from the relentless exhaustion and fear, and she knew if she'd stayed where she had been, she would have died. But the shame was still there, some days weighing heavily on her.

"Yes, Violetta. And how many times have I asked you to call me Cal?" he said with an oily smile. "Damian Ward is a good man, in many ways. But these are not normal circumstances. When General Ward allows soldiers to flee, for example, to renege on their commitments, to the revolution, and to their comrades, he weakens us all." A pause. "He makes it far likelier the rebellion will fail. Far likelier all of us will end up on the scaffold. This is the kind of area where he needs our aid, Violetta. Too much of the pressure is on him constantly. We must help carry some of the weight."

She was always uncomfortable when Jacen started talking this way about the general. What he said made sense, but it also felt . . . not quite right. Helping the general bear his burdens was one thing, but she felt a vague queasiness listening to Jacen. It wasn't his words so much, more a . . . feeling. Damian Ward had been good to her, yes, but Jacen had been as well, and, as much as the doubts nagged at her, she had to admit she did agree with him, at least on some level. She'd sacrificed everything to remain on Haven, to join the rebellion, and the idea of men and women who had sworn to fight for it sneaking away in the middle of the night, it revolted her. And then thoughts of her own special treatment flowed back into her mind, and her revulsion of others turned to disgust with herself.

"I understand. But the general does what he does out of kindness, out of love for his soldiers, all his soldiers." She stopped for a few seconds, and when she continued, her voice was shaky. "I don't know that I wouldn't have run myself, Cal, if you hadn't helped me get a posting here. I was at my wit's end then, and the winter hadn't even started. How much can I hate people for doing what I can't be sure I myself wouldn't have done?"

"Violetta, it isn't about judging people." Though his voice suggested he had indeed judged the deserters. "There is no room for half measures, no place for weakness. Not now. We have declared independence. We have thrown a challenge directly at Federal America's government, and they do not take such things lightly. Do you have any idea what the federal army does to troopers who desert? We cannot hold our soldiers to lesser standards, not if we are to win this fight."

Jacen stared at her for a moment. Then he said, "I am not asking you to do anything to hurt the general. I just want you to continue to provide me with information on what he does, what he says when he is in conference with his officers. With John Danforth. I'm trying to help the general, Violetta, not to harm him. But I want to do what I must for the rebellion, too. Will you help me?"

She hesitated, still feeling uncomfortable with what she had been doing. She hadn't been privy to any real secrets, and sometimes she even wondered why Jacen cared about the reports she gave him. But he was right. It was going to take more than ideals and compassion if Haven was to win its freedom. More, she'd seen how stretched thin General Ward had been. She admired him—his courage and commitment—but as an organizer, it wasn't hard to see he wasn't necessarily at his best. Cal Jacen, though, had helped organize the whole rebellion, and had juggled the many members of the Society for years. So if he was able to help, why wouldn't she in turn help him? She'd joined the Society because she'd believed that drastic measures were called for, and she still felt that way. More so, in ways, now that her childish naivety had been stripped away.

"Yes, Cal." She felt the guilt even as the words came out, but as she walked away back toward the camp, she told herself she was doing it for the rebellion, even to help General Ward himself.

The thoughts made her feel better, for a moment, but the doubts were quick to creep back out of the shadows.

CHAPTER 27

"My tolerance is at an end, Colonel Granz. For three months, no, nearly four, I have waited and watched as your celebrated veterans have been dragged all through the area around Landfall chasing a band of brigands you do not seem to be able to eradicate. All the while, we have been unable to mount a final attack on the rebels, and even routine supply shipments need massive escorts to get through. Can you explain this to me, Colonel?"

Granz stood at attention, his discipline slammed in place, restraining his more human thoughts about a hundred ways Semmes could get killed near the fighting. *If he ever came near the fighting . . .*

"General, the pacification operation is moving along satisfactorily. The enemy guerillas have been seriously degraded. While I cannot provide a meaningful estimate on their percentage casualties, they are clearly more than 50 percent, and perhaps as high as 80. Escort requirements have dropped considerably, and it is clear the enemy no longer has the capacity to mount major operations. Within a month, two at most, the entire area within fifty kilometers of the capital will be fully secure."

"Another month? Two? That is unacceptable, Colonel. Why are your people so incapable of finishing this?"

Granz bit back his anger again. "Sir, you have to understand.

The people, many of them are on the side of the rebels. We have enemy soldiers moving in groups of three and four, taking shelter in farmhouses, and getting intelligence from the locals. Every time we send out a strong column, the word spreads before we can reach the objective. This is not the kind of operation my men are trained to implement, sir."

"*That* is the problem, Colonel. You are too soft on the locals. You consider it beneath your military dignity to do what you must to neutralize them as a factor. Do you know what it says to me when the locals are still aiding your enemies? It says they *are* the enemy. It says they are *not* scared of you. Perhaps you should do something to change that. I have some other units here in Landfall. They have secured the city entirely. Perhaps they can instruct you in the tactics you require to finish your own mission."

Granz chafed, fully aware Semmes was talking about Major Brendel and her "Peacekeepers." *Butchers.* "General, I don't believe those kinds of tactics are . . . advisable. We have executed over one hundred civilians convicted by military tribunals of aiding the rebels. But we do need to reintegrate this planet into Federal America after this conflict is over, do we not?"

Semmes looked over at Granz, and the expression on his face made the officer's blood run cold. "This *planet* will be just fine, Colonel. As to the people on it, they are expendable, certainly any who have turned traitor and rebelled against their government. Collateral damage is not a concern in our plans here, Colonel. It makes little difference to me if a hundred are killed, or a thousand . . . or a million. As long as this detestable revolution is ended. Is that clear?"

"Yes, sir." Granz tried to hide the disgust in his voice, but he knew he hadn't even come close.

"You do not have to like my orders, Colonel Granz, but you do have to obey them. Unless you, too, wish to face summary execution for mutiny."

Granz bristled at Semmes's words, but he knew enough to take them seriously. The colonel was proud of his career and of the men and women he'd led, but he also knew what Federal America truly was. His own family, both sets of grandparents, had been on the losing side of the civil war, a family secret he'd never dared to allow to become known.

"No, sir, I do not." Granz wasn't sure how he'd gotten the words out civilly. Self-preservation, perhaps.

"Then you will brief Major Brendel on the status of your operations, and you will include her in all planning sessions. You will, of course, as per your rank, retain command of the overall operation. But, Colonel Granz, if the major reports to me that you are holding back, that you are not pushing the pacification effort as aggressively as possible, the fact that I will immediately relieve you of your command will be the least of your concerns. Do you understand me?" Semmes glared at Granz for a moment.

Granz nodded.

"Good. Oh . . . and you will also deploy the new Loyalist battalions, Colonel. Those people have much to prove, cleansing themselves of the traitors who have shamed them. And no doubt, they are much more familiar with the countryside than you and your soldiers."

Granz stood stone still for a moment. He hated knuckling under to a monster like Semmes, but the general could make good on his threats. The only thing that made any of this remotely bearable was Granz could read a quartermaster's report as well as anyone. And while Semmes's family connections were what kept the continuous, and almost unimaginably expensive, flow of supplies coming, there had to be a breaking point, a level of devastating expense that even the senator's legendary political influence couldn't overcome. And when that happened, the younger Semmes would be well and truly screwed. It was alien for Granz to hope for his side to fail in a conflict, but he couldn't deny, some small part of him would enjoy watching Semmes squirm.

"Yes, sir," was all he managed to force from his parched throat.

He stood there holding back his anger, and his shame. Granz had seen hell before, fought in battles so terrible they still tormented his sleep. But he'd never felt as dirty as he did now. He believed his forces could defeat the rebels, that they could bring Alpha-2 back into the fold. But he wasn't sure he'd ever be the same again afterward.

"Your soldiers look good, Jerome . . . or should I say, Captain Steves."

Steves turned toward the voice, smiling as he did. "As do yours, *Captain* Isaacson." Steves had been working his men hard, something all the more impressive because his own military knowledge didn't extend far past the few hours of indoctrination at the hands of Colonel Granz and Major Brendel. But General Semmes had insisted on having Loyalist units ready to support the final campaign to secure the areas outside Landfall, and that had left little time for settling into the reality of military command.

Isaacson and Steves each commanded rump battalions, hurriedly assembled units of roughly three hundred fifty troops each, picked from the best of the Loyalist volunteers. There were some security forces and police in the mix, but most had never even held a weapon. Three weeks of intense training had changed that, however, and while he wouldn't say his people—or, for that matter, he—were ready for combat, they were a lot *more* ready than they'd been less than a month before.

"We're moving out tomorrow. I just got the word." Isaacson sounded anxious. He'd always been a bit rabid, his opposition to the rebels often seeming very much like hatred. But now Steves sounded a lot more like his friend than his previous measured self.

Having an assassin in your house would do that.

Still, he was more scared than anxious about leading his forces into battle.

Steves looked back at his friend. "Ray, do you think we're ready?" His voice was hushed. The last thing he needed was for any of his soldiers to hear his doubts.

"Ready? These bastards tried to kill you, Jerome. They've thrown our world into a nightmare. Whatever happens, things will never be the same because of them."

"I don't mean that. I mean . . . aren't you worried about going into action? Our people haven't had a lot of training, and these rebels in the woods to the north have been fighting off the feds for months now."

"That's only because they know the terrain so well . . . and because traitors up there have been hiding them. But we know this area as well as any rebel scum, and we'll help the federal troops root them out, one at a time if we have to."

Steves nodded. He was as angry as Isaacson. Landfall was badly damaged, whole sections of the city in rubble, from the battles, the rebel raids, the federal punitive expeditions. If the rebellion didn't end soon, the whole planet would be a smoldering ruin.

"You're right, Ray. Captain Isaacson." He felt a little better. Isaacson was right about knowing the ground, and he was sure that's why their units were being ordered up there. They couldn't add much to the overall combat power deployed, but their ability to assist in search-and-destroy missions would be invaluable. And there was more than a little rage in the ranks. He shuddered to think of what would happen when his people met rebels.

Then he wondered if he'd make any effort to stop them.

"Keep moving, all of you." Des Black was running through the woods, shouting orders to what was left of the patrol he commanded. His people had endured the winter, using the time to build hidden shelters and to form alliances with the locals, who provided hiding places and intel on federal movements. They'd suffered losses, heavy losses, but they'd managed to hang on, remaining a thorn in the enemy's side, and taking the heat off the main army. But something had changed.

Suddenly the federals' operations were much better targeted. Caves, well-protected hillsides deep in the woods, all the strongholds that had anchored their operations since they'd abandoned Landfall, it seemed that suddenly they were all under attack by overwhelming federal forces. It had been a mystery for the first few days. Then the rangers captured their first Loyalist.

The federals were finding their way to the most defensible and hidden spots because Havenites were showing them the way. Black bristled at the thought of his countrymen betraying the rebellion. A small smile slipped onto his lips as he remembered what had happened to that Loyalist once he'd been persuaded to share all he knew. That one and the dozen others his people had captured. He'd wondered for a moment if such savagery weakened the rebel cause, if it made him and his soldiers the monsters. But then he thought of the men and women he'd lost, the desperate retreats from strongholds that had protected his people for months, and he decided he just didn't give a shit.

Through all the federal attacks, the freezing winter, the constant effort to endure and survive, Colonel Killian had managed to maintain some frequency of raids and attacks on enemy logistics and communications. But now the entire force, what shattered bits of it remained, was in full-scale retreat. The colonel's initial reaction had been to stay, to fight it out to the bitter end, but then Black and his people had come upon a farmhouse.

Rather, what was left of a farmhouse, and a family that had aided his rangers.

The brutality was astonishing, and Black still couldn't force the image of that butchered family from his mind. It had been the Loyalists, no doubt aided by the Peacekeepers, he was sure of that, and he cursed himself for any regret he'd felt about what his soldiers did when they captured the first Havenite traitor.

It wasn't that first house, nor the second, nor even the greatly ramped-up casualties—Black wasn't even sure exactly what had finally driven him to give up, to issue the orders for all units to head north by whatever paths they could, their only instructions to survive, and try to find their way back to the main army.

He gasped for some air, the early spring morning still chilly, but nothing like the brutal winter deep freeze. His people had been moving all night, but as far as he could tell, they were just ahead of their pursuers. That had been a determination based on gut feeling through most of the night, but just before dawn, a Loyalist platoon had caught up to his rear guard. He'd had six of his people back there, dug in and waiting, protecting the rest of the small column while it retreated. They'd fought well, but they couldn't hold against more than forty Loyalist militia, specially equipped as they were by the federal armory and supported by a team of Peacekeepers. Their fragile position had fallen shortly after daybreak, and the chase continued.

Only two of his people had come back, but the sacrifice of the others had bought time, just enough time to keep his dwindling force ahead of the pursuers who would destroy it.

Barely ahead.

The question was, what would joining with the main army even accomplish, at least in terms of adding strength to the fight? Colonel Killian had conducted a masterful guerilla campaign, keeping the federals tied up around Landfall, and shielding the battered army from a full-scale federal offensive. But now, whether a few of the rangers and their comrades made it back or not, the way was open. General Ward and his soldiers had lost their shield, and the addition of a few ragged and exhausted survivors, however seasoned, wasn't going to tip any scales.

The federals would come now, soon. They would march north, right toward the army's main camp, and General Ward and his people would face a desperate fight for their lives.

One Black was far from sure they could survive.

CHAPTER 28

"It's rough, General." Jonas Holcomb stood in front of the small building that had housed his main lab through the winter. He'd been in there every waking hour, working with such intensity that it worried even Damian as he drove his own soldiers so hard. "It's ugly, not polished at all." A pause. "And it could be dangerous, to the wearer and even those around it. I did my best, but we're limited on effective materials for shielding radiation, and those reactors I managed to cobble together don't exactly meet safety parameters."

"I understand, Doctor. We've discussed this before. No one expects you to produce something up to laboratory specs." *Hell, I didn't really expect you to come up with anything workable at all.*

"Very well, General." Holcomb turned, a nervous look on his face. "Captain Grant, please come around now."

Damian stared in shock, his mind still fixed on the name of his friend. He'd told Holcomb to find any volunteers for his project, but he'd had no idea Grant had gotten involved.

He heard the thing first, a loud, dull clanking sound coming from behind the building. Then it came around the corner.

Holcomb hadn't been kidding. It was ugly, as cumbersome and unfinished as such a thing could look. It was metal, a bit larger than man-sized, covered with rough plasma-weld marks and ridges from poorly matched sections. It was dull gray, with a large protrusion on the back.

"Well, Damian . . . I mean, General Ward . . . what do you think?"

Damian could barely recognize Grant's voice. The speakers were poor quality, with significant distortion. "I think I'm a little surprised. I had no idea you were involved in this project."

"I asked Dr. Holcomb to keep it quiet. I wanted to surprise you. I know this is important, and I thought you should have someone you trust wearing his first suit."

And you knew if you told me I wouldn't have let you do it.

Damian's mind wandered to all the risk factors, radiation and power overloads being just two of the potentially fatal ones. He was fond of Jamie, very fond, and as much as he hated to see any of his soldiers in unnecessary danger, it especially troubled him to think of Grant being slowly poisoned by his reactor or, worse, killed by an overload that seared him to a crisp.

"Well, since you somehow managed to justify 'surprising' your commander with something like this, tell me, what do you think of it?"

"It's uncomfortable as hell, and I'll be damned if every centimeter of my body didn't start itching the instant they sealed it up, but it's pretty amazing." He turned his head. "Doc?"

"Yes, Captain, by all means. Show the general what you've learned to do."

Grant looked back, pausing for an instant before he leapt, jumping over six meters straight up. He landed hard, but his legs held, and he stood and stared right back at Damian before he took off, running at what Damian figured had to be at least one hundred kilometers an hour. It was noisy and clumsy-looking—no one was going to use the suit to sneak up on anyone—but Jamie kept going until he was out of sight, and then a few second later he came racing back.

"The suit has built-in weapons, as well, General," Holcomb said. "As we discussed, there was no way to construct the particle accelerators in the original specifications, not with what was available, but I was able to include a built-in autocannon, constructed to utilize Union ammunition . . . though it will be necessary to take the rounds from the existing cartridges and put them into the suit magazines. That will be tedious, I am afraid."

"Autocannon? Like a squad weapon? Each suit has one?"

"Yes, General, just like the squad automatic weapons the federals use. You know . . . or perhaps you don't . . . that I designed the MV-211s that the federal infantry forces use."

Damian just nodded. He kept forgetting that Holcomb had been the feds' top weapons designer.

"How much ammunition can the suit carry?"

"With the external supplemental magazines I've almost got finished, five thousand."

Damian stared back, stunned. "Did you say five *thousand*? How could a man carry that?"

"I don't think you realize the power magnification of the suit. You just saw Captain Grant run and jump." Holcomb turned toward Grant. "Captain, perhaps you could show the general the strength you possess in the suit."

Grant nodded, a somewhat comical exercise in the cumbersome armor. Then he looked around before his focus settled on a tree, a giant at least fifty meters tall. He turned around to make sure no one was nearby, a clunky effort in the suit. Then he thrust his arms forward, slamming his fists into the tree. Splinters flew all around as his armored hands penetrated deep into the heart of the tree, and then, as Damian watched in stunned surprise, the massive brownwood wobbled two or three times and fell over in a monumental crash that thundered throughout the forest.

"You see, General? It is not the weapons, nor the protection offered by the armor plating that is the suit's greatest strength. It is the power source. Instead of a man, powered by biological chemical reactions and fuel as inefficient as food, the suited warrior has the power of the atom at his fingertips. That was the true breakthrough I had made, the miniaturization of a fully functional fusion plant, bringing the size down to something that could be incorporated into a fighting suit. When we first discussed the project, I was far from sure I could extend the miniaturization process to a fission reactor, but I was able to do it."

"It's amazing."

But instead of accepting the praise, Holcomb frowned. "It is what it is. As I originally surmised, there are certain longer-term hazards to the wearer, which is why I suggest volunteers are chosen for the new corps. The main problem is actually if there are others in the vicinity, and those dangers are likely to manifest only when a suit is damaged."

"Which is quite likely, since we will be sending them into battle." Damian sighed softly. He knew the risks of asking soldiers to fight in Holcomb's suits, but were they really any worse than expecting his outnumbered, outclassed, outsupplied army to go back into the field and face the federals? "I'm sorry, Doctor. I still stand by my earlier praise—what you've achieved here is staggering. And I must confess, I didn't really believe you could do it. Now I understand why the feds wanted you back so badly."

Damian could see the mention of the federals was upsetting to Holcomb, and he immediately regretted saying it. "Truly, we're glad to have you as one of us, Doctor. Perhaps you can help us win this fight, and gain a new home for yourself as well as freedom for all Haven."

"I will do all I can, General. Should Grant show you what else it can do?"

"It can do more?"

"The autocannon is the secondary weapons system. There are also two small X-ray lasers, one attached to each arm. Their purpose is primarily for combat in vacuum and space conditions, and I'm afraid that in atmosphere, their range is severely limited. Still, they should be quite lethal to any lesser-protected target within, say, one hundred meters. They . . ."

"I'm sorry, Doctor, did you say the autocannon was the *secondary* weapon?"

"Yes, well, perhaps I should have said, I hope it will be. There was no hope of building the particle accelerators the original specs called for, but I believe I am on the verge of developing a working electromagnetic force projectile delivery system." Holcomb glanced at his onlookers, every face with a confused expression. "Colloquially, something like a rail gun," he added. "Though much smaller than most similar systems, not exactly what most consider a rail gun, but more of a magnetically charged hypervelocity weapon system."

"A rail gun?" Damian was stunned again. He knew Holcomb was an extraordinary scientist, and he likely wouldn't have doubted anything the man had promised, in a proper lab with real production facilities. But there was something hard to grasp about producing cutting-edge technology, or at least a rough facsimile of it, in a bunch of shacks in the woods. "Doctor, I don't know what to say. I guess I should just ask, can we produce these in any kind of numbers, and if so, what do we need?"

"More uranium, for sure. And the metallic ores for the armor. Items that will likely be difficult to obtain, I realize. Mass production is obviously an impossibility, but if you can find the materials, and you will supply me all your people with any relevant industrial experience, I think we could build a couple hundred of them in a reasonable time, perhaps two months."

Damian nodded. "That would be extraordinary, Doctor." He had no idea where or how he was going to scrape up the materials but he knew who might at least help. John Danforth was vastly wealthy, and he'd smuggled goods to the rebels for years before the revolution even began. If anyone could find what was needed on Haven, it was the republic's new president himself. "Get your people together, Doctor." Damian gestured toward the two figures standing silently behind him. "Major Withers and Sergeant Wells will provide you any assistance you require. You can requisition anyone you think will be helpful."

He stood silently, just staring at Grant and the massive suit he wore. "And since *you* worked your way into this project, Captain, you can head up recruitment and training for the personnel who will wear these things, assuming we're able to build them. I don't know how much time we have before we'll be forced into another fight, but maybe we can have a surprise for the federals when that day finally comes." *We're damned lucky we haven't been engaged already.* "Just make sure we've got someone in those suits besides convicts from the mines, okay?"

Damian didn't wait for an answer. He looked over at Holcomb and said, "Doctor, if we're able to actually produce enough of these things, and they're as incredible as they seem, you may just have saved the rebellion."

Holcomb smiled and nodded. "I will do anything I can, General, as I promised you last year."

Damian returned the smile, and then he turned around. The instant he did, the grin vanished, replaced by a worried frown. He had to go find John Danforth, and he had to find a way to scare up a bunch of stuff that was hard to find. Really hard.

Damned near impossible.

CHAPTER 29

"Mr. Wells, or may I call you Everett? I assure you this will be much easier on you if you cooperate. We know you have had . . . difficulties . . . since your return from Alpha-2, and your past service will certainly be considered in any consideration of leniency *if* you aid us in identifying your accomplices. We know you were not alone, Everett, and if you choose to protect fellow traitors, it will hardly speak well of your repentance."

Wells looked up at the interrogator. The man was meticulously dressed, almost bookish in appearance. Not intimidating at all. Not what one would expect to encounter in the deepest, darkest prison in all of Federal America. But looks could be deceiving, and though Wells had long tried to feign ignorance, to himself as well as others, of the things he knew the government did to maintain order, now that he faced the menace himself, there was no self-delusion.

He'd tried to tell himself they had no evidence, that as long as Asha and Xi had escaped, there was no way to convict him. But he heard the derisive laughter in his own mind, the mockery of his own naivety. Evidence wasn't a requirement to convict him. Such things were merely words, used to placate the masses, to give the veneer of justice to the brutal methods used to sustain the state. Nothing he could do or say would matter. He could cooperate, give names, do anything his captors asked, but when they had gotten all they could from him, he would be convicted of treason anyway. And there was only one punishment for betraying the state in Federal America.

Oddly, the prospect of almost certain death gave Wells a sort of courage. He was still scared, so terrified he'd come close to soiling himself more than once since he'd been brought to Blackstone, but the certain realization that giving up his contacts wouldn't save him made it easier to resist.

Until they push things to the next level . . .

There was no torture in Federal America's prisons—or so the official government position stated, one Wells had been content to believe for years. Now he cursed himself for a fool, and he knew his jailers would do whatever was necessary to break him. They would bribe him, make false promises of leniency, but when all of that failed, they would resort to more forceful measures. Wells was determined to resist—more out of hope that Stanton's scheming might protect Violetta than out of concern for his coconspirators—but he knew he would talk, eventually. He was a man of conviction—at least, he liked to think he was—but he didn't try to fool himself about his endurance for physical abuse. He suspected Blackstone had housed some rough types, men and women who'd withstood almost unimaginable torment before breaking, but he wasn't one of those. He'd been ignoring the interrogator's questions, but now he decided if he responded, he might be able to delay the inevitable enhancement of the questioning.

"You are wrong about what was happening. There was no treason. My . . . circumstances . . . have changed, as you note, and I find myself in need of funds. My meeting was with a band of smugglers. Nothing political. Just an attempt to use what little remained of my influence to prop up my finances." Wells knew his story wasn't going to hold water. Despite the decline in his prospects, he was actually fairly well set financially, something his interrogator could determine with a routine asset check, if he hadn't already. It was actually worse than that, he suspected. Anyone would assume that he'd used his prior positions to generate some level of illicit income. No one would believe the truth, that his idealism had prevented him from using what power he'd had for personal gain. It had all seemed perfectly rational to him at the time, but now he wondered if he was the only honest member of Federal America's government.

Honest until you started conspiring with the Hegemony.

It almost made him smile. But this wasn't a place for smiles.

The interrogator paused for a moment, a vague look of uncertainty passing over his face, just for a second. "That seems very unlikely to me, Everett. You came from some wealth, and you had many long years of government service." The man paused. "I can go and review your finances, to see if they support your story, but I warn you, there is nothing to be gained by lying to me. It will only be worse for you later."

Wells just nodded. "I was involved in a smuggling deal. It was stupid and foolish, and I am ashamed. But that was all."

The interrogator was wrong. There was something to be gained. Time. Time until the drugs and pain and all-night questioning sessions. Time until the misery. Until they broke him.

It wasn't much time, perhaps until the next day. But even a passing instant was better than nothing.

And it was all he had.

"Father, we have to find a way to help Everett." Asha Stanton stood on the plush carpeting of her father's library, looking across the antique desk at the silver-haired patriarch of the family fortune. Trevor Stanton was a hard man, but Asha knew her father had a soft spot for her. He'd spent an enormous amount of money to get her appointed to her position on Alpha-2, and he'd forgiven her for her failure after only a mild tongue-lashing. He'd even agreed to her latest stunt, one that now threatened not only her own future—and her life—but also the continued existence of the Stanton companies.

"Asha, my dear, there is simply no way to rescue someone from Blackstone Prison, and certainly not from the Political Zone, which is where Everett Wells is no doubt being held. No amount of money, no bribes or blackmail, at least none within my reach."

"But if we don't get him out . . ."

"Yes, daughter. I spoiled you when you were younger, far too much. You were always smart, Asha, too smart perhaps. I indulged you, tried to aid your ambitions to a political career. When you returned from Alpha-2, I said to myself, perhaps our aspirations to become a senatorial family would be postponed a generation. Still, I said yes when you came to me, asked for my introduction to our Hegemony contacts. Your latest failure could cost you your life, and with it the future of this family. If we are tied to treasonous activity, we could all end up on the scaffold, and Stanton Industries will be confiscated."

He was angry, something she'd rarely seen from him aimed at her. But his anger was misplaced. There was no *time* to be angry. Their situation was desperate, and sitting around being angry accomplished nothing. For as much as Everett Wells was a good man, an honest man, he was a fool as well. He would try to hold out, but he was hardly the toughest man she'd ever seen. The interrogators at Blackstone would break him, that was a certainty. And when he gave up her name, it was over.

But it didn't have to be.

If only you'll do something, Father!

Yet he wasn't having it. "I have explored the possibility of having him killed, but even that seems impossible. No guard is ever alone with him, and even if one was, there is no way to do the deed and escape." He paused, staring at the fire roaring in the hearth. "All your grandfather started, that I spent my life building . . . we may lose it."

Stanton stared silently at her father. The idea of having someone murder Everett Wells seemed terribly harsh to her. The two of them had never gotten along, not really, but he'd tried to work with her on her plan to thwart Semmes. He was naïve, perhaps, but he was a hard man to completely dislike.

He will suffer in there, and the longer he resists, the more terrible it will be. Then he will die, no matter what he tells them, no matter what anyone does to try to save him.

Unless . . .

"Father, we may not be able to break him out of there, but do you think we could get a message to him? And a small package?"

Trevor Stanton looked up at his daughter, a quizzical expression on his face. "Perhaps that would be possible." He sat and stared at her, silent for a moment. "What do you have in mind, Asha?"

Everett Wells sat on the cold metal bunk in his cell. It was too short for him to lie down, not without bending his knees. And when he did that, it was hard to stay on the narrow platform. It was hard, uncomfortable . . . and on purpose, all part of the gradually increasing coercion he was enduring.

His ruse about needing money had bought him longer than he'd expected, two full days, probably because of his interrogator's workload more than any actual difficulty in investigating his finances. However, when the reckoning came, it brought with it the first round of physical abuse he'd endured. His accountant-looking nemesis stood and scolded him for his lies as a large, unnamed man beat him with a long metal truncheon.

It wasn't bad, he suspected, not by the standards of what went on in the bowels of Blackstone, but it was the most painful, horrible experience of his life, and he was howling in pain, his face soaked with tears by the time they dropped him back in his cell.

He'd had three more beatings since, each one progressively more severe than the last. They hadn't drugged him yet, at least not as far as he knew, nor had they done any permanent damage. But despite the fact that he knew he was still near the beginning of the path, he felt he was close to breaking. He'd almost given them Asha Stanton's name during the last session.

He'd held back only out of the dim and fading hope that Stanton would somehow manage to continue what they had begun together, that she would find a way to defeat Semmes before he pacified Alpha-2. Before he found Violetta.

It was a wild long shot, the most tenuous thread of hope to which he could cling. It had gotten him this far, but it wouldn't take him through much more.

He heard the door rattling. *It's not time yet. I'm not ready!* A wave of panic hit him, and it was only because things hadn't quite progressed that he had the thought that changing the schedule could just be more of the psychological torment his captors would use to make him talk. Then he saw the guard come in with a tray, and he could feel the oxygen return to his body. His dinner. He'd forgotten. Meals were harder to remember when his jailers skipped them half the time. Another way to wear him down.

The guard put the tray down on the floor, as always. Then the man stared at him, his eyes moving to the tray and then back to Wells. He stood there for a moment, definitely longer than usual, and then he turned and left.

That was strange . . .

Wells sat still for a moment, his eyes moving to the tray. Against all odds, the food at Blackstone, when they chose to give him any, was actually pretty good. He felt a spark of defiance, an impulse not to eat what his captors had given him. They could have drugged the food, and even if they hadn't, his hatred for them was growing. It sickened him to take anything from them. But he was hungry. More than hungry. Now that he thought about it, he hadn't eaten since the middle of the day yesterday. *What I think was midday.* He had no window, no way of keeping track of time.

He sat on the bunk for another minute, but then he dropped to the floor and reached down to the tray. It was some kind of stew, with a chunk of surprisingly fresh bread next to it. He grabbed the spoon, the only utensil they had given him. As he picked it up, the paper napkin moved, and underneath there was a small piece of plastic.

He pulled it up, recognizing it for what it was immediately. A message. But from whom? Were his jailers toying with him somehow?

He glanced around nervously, but realized there was nothing for it. Either they were watching him or they weren't—the torture was going to come regardless. So he held it up, close to his face so he could read the tiny lettering. It had no identity on it, but he immediately knew it was from Asha Stanton.

> Everett, I have tried every way to get you out of there, but I am afraid it is just not possible. As you know, the interrogators will break you eventually. I know we are not friends, that you have no loyalty to me, but I offer you this bargain. Under your plate you will find a small tablet. It is a way out for you, one that will spare you at least from the torment that lies ahead.
>
> There is no escape for you anyway, and nothing but pain between now and your eventual death. I know this is a terrible situation, but I give you my word, I will do everything possible to continue our plan, and I will try to save Violetta, or if we fail, I will try to have her smuggled off-world before Semmes can get to her. I am sorry there is no way to save you, but you can still give your daughter a chance.
>
> There is a special coating on this message slip. Your body heat activated it. It will disintegrate in a matter of seconds. You will want to drop it or your hands may be burned.
>
> Goodbye, Everett.

Wells stared at the thing in stunned surprise. He wondered how she'd managed to get even the message to him, much less the poison lying under his bowl. *The Stanton money . . .*

He remembered her words, and he dropped the small sheet of plastic, just as it flared brightly for an instant and disappeared.

He sat there quietly for a moment. The idea of killing himself to save Asha Stanton was far from appealing. She'd gotten him involved in the whole sordid affair to begin with, and now he was the one in Blackstone Prison, and she was worried about keeping him from ratting her out.

But there was more to it than that. It was an escape of sorts. Remaining where he was could only mean more torment, even if he told them all he knew. They'd work him over until *they* were sure he'd broken and revealed all he knew. Then he'd be executed, humiliated as a traitor as he was dragged to the gallows. And if Asha Stanton went down, the last chance of helping Violetta would be gone. He didn't think Asha would really somehow manage to stop Robert Semmes from reconquering Alpha-2—he wondered what he'd even been thinking, how he'd convinced himself such a thing was possible. But rescuing Violetta, getting her off-world before the worst of the retributions began? That seemed like something within reach of the Stanton money.

He slid the bowl aside, his eyes focusing on the small white tablet. It didn't look like much, smaller even than an analgesic one would take for a headache.

How simple . . . to end one's life. Is it quick? Painless? Stanton hadn't described the poison she'd chosen, just identified it for what it was.

Wells felt a burst of fear. He knew he'd decided what he had to do, but now the thought of taking that step almost overwhelmed him. He slid away from the tray, from the deadly little pill sitting there. *No, I can't do this . . .*

But images flooded his mind, mostly of Violetta as a child, back when her mother was still alive. He had to help her, any way he could. Even if it was only a small chance of saving her.

He reached out, struggling against his resistance, and picked up the small pill. He was dead anyway, he told himself. The only difference was the amount of pain, the days of torment that surely lay ahead. It was a mathematical equation, one beyond question, but now he found even a few extra moments of life were precious. It was one thing to contemplate suicide, to plan it, and quite another to actually do it. To say, *Now, this is the moment I will die.*

He longed to wait, but he didn't have time. The guards would be back soon to take his tray. *Or even sooner if they're monitoring me in here.* He wondered whether they could revive him if they found him soon enough, even after he'd taken the pill. Every second he delayed lessened his chances of succeeding. Of escaping the agony.

Of saving his daughter.

He took a deep breath and he shoved the pill in his mouth. He held it there for a few seconds, an acid taste on his tongue as it began to dissolve. He pulled together all his strength, his courage . . . and then he heard sounds outside.

The guards!

He swallowed, a panicked reaction to the noise in the corridor. It was quick, almost merciful in its lack of forethought. It was done. Now all he could do was wait, and see how long Asha's poison took.

He felt a wave of light-headedness, even as he heard the door start to open. *It is quick.* It was painless, too.

He could feel himself floating away, drifting into nothingness, the vague feeling of the guards' hands on his arms, and then nothing at all.

CHAPTER 30

NORTHERN EDGE OF THE GREEN HILL FOREST
118 KILOMETERS NORTHWEST OF LANDFALL
FEDERAL COLONY ALPHA-2, EPSILON ERIDANI II (HAVEN)

"Hold!" The sentry's voice rang out in the crisp, cold morning air. They were challenging the approaching group of ragged-looking fighters, but if Patrick Killian and his small band had been enemies, the guard and his three comrades, all of whom Killian had spotted a hundred meters farther back, would be dead.

"Hold this, you young pup. You go and tell General Ward that Colonel Killian is here and needs to see him. Now."

Killian walked down the center of the path, what passed for the road leading into the army's camp. He was careful to stand in the middle of the open area, no more than a two-meter-wide dirt road, gesturing for his comrades to do the same. He didn't need a nervous guard shooting at him . . . mostly because he didn't want to have to kill the sentries.

"Stop where you are and hold your arms out where we can see them, all of you."

Killian sighed as he stopped, watching as two of the guards rushed forward, guns at the ready. They moved up closer to him, and as they did, he noticed they were sharper than he'd expected, and the two they'd left behind were covering them. This wasn't the army Killian had seen evacuate Landfall, and he suspected it wasn't the force that had been beaten so badly the previous fall.

He and his people had fought—and paid a terrible price—to buy Damian time, and it appeared the rebel general had not wasted that respite.

"Drop your weapons now, sir."

Killian was impressed. The caution of disarming the as-yet-unidentified arrivals, and the care to call him "sir," in case he was who he'd said he was.

"That will not be necessary, Corporal."

Killian recognized the voice at once. He waited while the soldier acknowledged and took a step back. Then he said, "Well, if it isn't Ben Withers. I'm not sure how an old fossil like you made it through this winter."

"If you haven't noticed, the one thing we have in abundance is trees, Pat. And trees burn."

"That they do. I need to see the General." A pause, then, "He's . . ."

"Yes, he's fine. Despite his tendency to wander off without any guards. Come with me. I think he's in the main HQ shelter right now."

Killian walked up toward Withers, giving a quick nod to the guards as he passed. They'd earned it.

"My God, I'm glad to see you, Patrick. I'd just about given up on you two days ago when Des Black walked in here with seven of his people. They're the last ones we've seen, at least until your group walked up the road."

"It's good to see you, too, Damian . . . General."

"Damian's fine. I think military formality can stand aside for a minute when old friends get together."

"How many, Damian?"

Damian looked back as though he was confused, but he knew just what Killian was asking.

"How many of my people made it back?" Damian expected he was ready for bad news, but he wasn't sure *how* bad.

"Ninety-two," he said. "Including you and the eleven who just got here with you."

"Ninety-two?" Killian looked stricken. "That's less than a tenth of what I started with."

"I'm sure there are more, Patrick. Some of them probably ran off in different directions. Maybe some even snuck away and went home." He hoped his tone sounded like he believed that more than he did, but a quick look at Killian suggested neither of them was fooled.

"What do you think of a commander who survives when more than 90 percent of his soldiers died?" Killian's tone was deadpan, almost emotionless, but Damian knew his friend was hurting.

"In this case, I think he's a goddamn hero that saved the rebellion. Patrick, if you hadn't kept the federals so occupied—and I still have no idea how you managed that—they'd have marched north long ago. And if they'd caught us right after the fight at Dover, we'd all be hanging from a gallows, or worse. You did an amazing job, and the soldiers you lost are heroes of the Haven Republic."

"They are, at least."

"Trust me—so are you. Our losses would have been ten times higher if the feds had caught the army when it was retreating from Dover. And we've used the respite well. Our numbers have dwindled, but the soldiers are hardened now and well drilled. I like to think many of them are a match for federal regulars now, or at least close to it."

"The sentries looked sharp, Damian. I noticed that right away." Killian sighed. "Well, I hope you're right, and I hope that these soldiers of ours are ready. Because there's nothing stopping the federals from marching up here now. We're going to have a fight on our hands, and probably sooner rather than later."

Damian turned and exchanged glances with Withers and the other officers present. "I'm counting on that, Patrick," he said a few seconds later. "In fact, I'm wondering how you'd feel about provoking them a bit, jamming a stick into Semmes's ass until he gets pissed enough to come at us."

"I'm not sure I understand, General."

"Oh, you will, Patrick. You will. We've been doing more than training up here, thanks to Dr. Holcomb." Damian smiled. "We've spent enough time hiding."

"Are your people ready?" Damian was walking through the woods, with Jamie Grant next to him. The two were alone, perhaps a hundred meters from the camp perimeter. Even here, Damian could hear the sounds of his people tearing down everything portable. This had been the army's home for almost six months, its refuge. His people had come here disordered, defeated, demoralized, but the brutality of winter, and the effort he and his officers had put into training, had forged that rebel force into a real army. This land—Tucker's Glade, the few locals had told him it was called—would become a sacred place if Haven won its independence. He imagined children, generations distant, coming here, visiting a park and learning of how Haven became a republic. Then he shook the thought from his head. It was a pleasant daydream, but not one he had time for. If it was to become a reality, he still had a tremendous amount to do.

"Define *ready*." Grant laughed. "Yes, they're ready. Do I wish we had more time? Yes, absolutely. It's damned hard to work those suits. But I'm confident we can bring hell to the feds with these things."

"Confidence is good. I'll admit I was far from confident we'd even have the armor—it's a miracle we were able to produce them at all. We can thank John Danforth for that." Haven's president had found all the raw materials needed. Somehow. Damian still didn't quite understand, and the whole effort reminded him just how much support his people had planetwide. Men and women beyond those openly declared for rebellion had taken great risks to send shipments of supplies to the army, uranium and heavy metals and the other hard-to-find items required. Much of the uranium and plutonium was scavenged piecemeal from equipment that used the radioactive decay as a backup power source, and Damian had no doubt more than one vital machine had been torn apart to gain the materials Holcomb had needed. Sacrifice and devotion to the rebellion came in more varieties than just military service.

When it was all done, Holcomb and his team of engineers, technicians, and factory workers had built 302 of the suits. Minus three discarded as defective and two burned out in testing, that meant Jamie Grant would be leading 296 armored soldiers.

Multiply that by the five thousand cartridge magazines the autocannons had, and that was a *lot* of bullets to find federal soldiers.

The two men walked for a moment, silent. Then Grant said, "This is it, isn't it, Damian? I know you want a victory, something to help gain the support of the other powers. But it's more than that. If we don't win *this* fight, it's over. Isn't it."

Damian felt the urge to deny what Jamie had just said, to tell his friend there would be other chances. But Grant deserved the truth. "Yes, Jamie. If we can't defeat them now, after all the drilling and with the suits as a surprise, I don't see how a beaten, weakened army can do any better. Another federal victory will also help eliminate whatever good was done by Killian's raids. The senate won't pull the plug if they think they're on the verge of winning. We need to let them know that despite the trillions of credits they have poured into this war, we're still here, in the field, and able to beat the best they can send. It's all or nothing now."

"That's how I saw it, too." Another stretch of silence, and then Grant stopped and turned to face his companion. "I won't let you down, Damian. You're the best friend I've ever had. You gave me my life. I'd be dead in that mine without you."

"Jamie, you're a good man, one I'm proud to have as a friend. But you gave yourself your life back. You endured a hell most men couldn't imagine, somehow didn't let it destroy you, and pulled yourself out of that mine. All I did was make sure you didn't fall back in again." Damian took a deep breath and put his hand on his friend's shoulder. "I'm proud of you, Jamie. Now go—we're marching at dawn, but that still leaves tonight. You've done all you can to get your soldiers ready. Take these few hours, go see Katia."

Grant nodded. "Thank you, Damian. I would like that." Grant stood there for a moment, and then he turned and walked back toward the camp.

Yes, go see Katia. While you can. Because there's a good chance your friend who saved you from prison is about to send you to your death.

It had been more than a year, considerably more now, and thoughts like that still haunted him. Every decision, every instant of command—they lingered with him and probably always would. How many people—friends, loyal followers—could one man send to their deaths before everything that made him who he was died, as well?

That's assuming, of course, it hadn't died a long time ago.

"The scouts are reporting massive movement up from Landfall."

Damian sat in the headquarters tent, looking out at his officers. They were seated at a makeshift table, really just some boards from packing crates, nailed together and thrown on top of a couple of large barrels.

"It looks like your plan worked, sir." Luci Morgan spoke calmly, but her face couldn't hide her uncertainty. The army had marched all the way down to Dover, the place from which they'd retreated the year before in such haste and disorder. But Damian hadn't left it at that. He'd sent Patrick Killian out with what remained of his rangers, plus another several hundred of his top veterans, to find federal patrols or supply convoys and ambush them. He wasn't leaving anything to chance, in case advancing to within just over forty-five kilometers of the capital wasn't provocation enough to stir Robert Semmes.

He'd felt terrible about sending Killian back out so soon, after all the colonel had been through. But he understood the man—at least, he thought he did—and on some level, it was a mercy to keep Killian busy. His friend was a tortured soul, even before he'd lost more than 90 percent of his forces. At least hunting federals gave him a purpose, and a distraction from the ghosts that haunted him.

"Yes, Colonel. Now we'll see just how wise it was to poke a tiger." Damian was edgy. They all were. He knew luring the federals in, springing Grant's new corps on them by surprise, was the best chance of scoring the victory he needed. But it was far from certain, and even if his forces won, it wouldn't be the end of the rebellion. It would only mean it wasn't the end of the rebels. The true fruits of victory could only be realized by somehow getting Andrei Kutusov back to Earth. Sasha Nerov had given him bold assurances that she'd get the ambassador past the federal blockade . . . somehow. But "somehow" was far from convincing enough to get the Union ambassador to risk his life on what could charitably be described as a coin toss.

That was tomorrow's problem. Today's was securing the victory that even made Kutusov's transit an issue.

He'd planned out the battle carefully, meticulously. No detail had been too small to obsess over. The key was pulling the federals in, even as his army feigned withdrawal. Then Grant's armored troopers would strike from the flank, almost from behind, just as the rest of the army launched a massive counterattack.

It all looked good, on paper at least. It should work, by the science of war, by every maxim of combat planning. The shock of an inexplicable attack, by forces as bizarre and unexplainable as Grant's massive armored soldiers, should break even federal regulars.

But "should" was not "will," and Damian knew that well. A hero officer making a key stand, rallying troops, a wave of contagious bravery, a foul-up among his own troops, the unknowns of Holcomb's new weapons—there were countless ways things could go wrong, and any one of them could turn vital triumph into disastrous defeat.

There was nothing more to be done now save fight. No use for worry and second-guessing. He had done all he could.

The die was cast.

CHAPTER 31

The Third Battle of Dover–The Opening

"Let's go! Those feds are right behind us." Patrick Killian raced along the rough gravel path—the Sanderson Road wasn't paved north of the Tillis intersection—his rifle in his hand. He felt alive, excited, the tension of impending battle driving away the morose feelings that had taken him in his quiet moments.

He'd done all Damian had asked of him, ambushed half a dozen federal parties, and he'd managed to keep his losses to a minimum. Every casualty hurt, but he couldn't help but feel relief that 274 of the 290 troopers he'd led south five days before were returning with him.

He ducked, more instinctively than out of any real belief that it would do any good. The fire wasn't heavy, and it wasn't aimed either, but it only took one lucky shot to do the job.

Killian felt good that he'd come through for Damian, that he'd done what the general had needed of him. He intended to edit his report, though, to leave out some descriptions of just how he'd handled the federal troops he'd encountered—and especially the way he had *disposed* of the squad of Peacekeepers he'd run into. The bastards had still had the booty from the farmhouse they'd raided, and the blood of their victims was still wet on their boots and gloves. At least that group of federal thugs had murdered their last civilians.

Killian turned and looked back. He was near the end of his column, but there were a few stragglers behind. As he was looking, one of them pitched forward, falling to the ground. The soldier next to the stricken man slowed to stop, but Killian shouted, "Keep going! I'll take care of this."

He dropped next to the wounded soldier. His eyes darted to the wound. Thigh. It could be bad, but probably wasn't fatal, not as long as he could get the man back behind the lines.

He's not gonna walk, though, not even leaning on someone.

He looked up toward the standing soldier who still hadn't followed his order to move. "Take this . . . and get the hell back to the lines. Now!" He handed the trooper his rifle, and then he reached down, slipping his arms under the wounded soldier. He took a deep breath and pulled the man up, thrusting his legs hard to get back to his feet. He grunted loudly, and his legs wobbled for an instant before stabilizing.

It's never the small ones . . .

He stumbled back toward the line again, following the other soldier. It wasn't far now, and most likely, the pursuers would break off in a few seconds. Until then, it was dumb luck, and not military skill or courage, that would keep a bullet from slamming into his back.

He could hear shots on both sides of him now, the rebel pickets opening up, providing what covering fire they could. There were shouts, too, encouraging the rushing soldiers to hurry, to get behind the lines to temporary safety.

Killian heard the sound of gunfire from behind him slacken off and stop. He felt relief, and he kept running, or as close to running as he could manage carrying the wounded trooper, and a few seconds later he stepped past the forward sentries and then the main front line.

"Medic," he yelled. "I need a medic."

"Here, sir." The trooper raced up, the only sign that he was a medic the white cross hastily painted on his helmet.

Killian dropped slowly to his knees and set the soldier in his arms down gently. "Leg wound, but a bad bleeder."

The medic leaned over, but a few seconds later a grim expression crossed his face. "The bullet hit the femoral artery. He bled out." He looked up at Killian. "He's dead, sir."

Robert Semmes looked resplendent in his impeccable uniform, his decorations, granted for his father's wealth and power instead of the dedication to bravery they usually signified, polished to a sparkling sheen. The damned fool had decided to go north with the army, much to Granz's chagrin, to be there, as he put it, "when the rebellion meets its end in blood and fire."

Pompous ass.

Granz had come of age in the first war with the Union, and he'd commanded a battalion in the recent conflict that had seen the other two powers allied against Federal America. He'd witnessed horrors he still couldn't get out of his mind, but he'd never wanted anything quite as badly as to get the hell away from General Robert Semmes.

"You may launch the attack, Colonel. There is little to be gained by waiting."

Granz knew Semmes was right. He somehow found it frustrating that, for as much as the general was a simpering blowhard, his tactical abilities were genuine. Semmes had been as responsible as Granz himself for the previous victory in these woods, and his orders for the current operation were sound. The federal army was in position, and nothing was to be gained by waiting. It was already after dawn, and he wanted as much daylight as possible. He had actually come to respect the rebel fighters, but his duty was clear, and he was determined to end this destructive conflict here and now.

"Yes, sir." Granz could follow his orders, but he just wished Semmes had stayed behind in Landfall, safely in his headquarters and out of the way.

"With your permission, General . . ."

Semmes nodded. "Go. There is no time to waste." Semmes stared at him for a moment, until he spun around and moved forward, toward the advanced positions. Then the general, who'd clearly put on some weight over the long winter, turned around himself and strode toward the massive mobile HQ vehicle he'd brought forward, deploying two dozen troops just to widen the cleared area around the road to force it up through the woods.

Granz looked to the left and the right as he walked down the gravelly road. His forces were in position, three waves of troops, one supporting the next. When he gave the order, eight thousand federal regulars would move forward.

Granz was confident, to a point. There was just one thing bothering him. From what he knew of Damian Ward, the rebel commander was no fool. He hadn't met Ward during the war, but he had heard of him, and nothing he'd learned since could explain to him why Ward, outclassed and outnumbered, would advance and provoke a battle he likely couldn't win.

He told himself there were a number of possibilities. The rebel army was demoralized, its strength slipping away. Perhaps supplies were dwindling. A desperate gamble was better than no chance. It all sounded reasonable, and yet he still felt unsettled.

We're missing something . . .

"Major Harrigan, status report."

Harrigan spun around abruptly. Granz had surprised him. The officer had likely expected his orders over the comm, but Granz intended to direct the battle from the front. If Damian Ward had some kind of trick up his sleeve, Granz wanted to be ready to counter it.

Harrigan recovered quickly, though, professional that he was.

"Sir! The forward pickets have chased the enemy skirmishers back to their lines. They have re-formed with the advance companies and are awaiting your orders."

Granz nodded. "Very well, Major. You may advance."

"Yes, sir." The officer pulled out his comm unit. "All forward companies . . . advance."

Granz nodded, and then he looked out into the dense woods. His people had crushed the rebels once before, and there was no reason for things to be different now.

But as he watched the forward line disappear into the thick brush, he couldn't force the worry from his mind.

The fire was heavy all across the line. The federals were serious about this attack, and they were coming on hard, their strike units leap-frogging forward as heavy weapons teams provided supporting fire through carefully designated fire lanes. It was a perfectly planned attack, absolutely textbook. But it was also what Luci Morgan had expected, and her people were ready for it. They weren't the same troops they had been six months before. The federals would encounter more than they'd bargained for, even before they faced Captain Grant and his people.

"Watch your cover, and keep up the fire. They're attacking. They've got to come to us." She shouted facing east, and then turned and repeated herself to the west. Her soldiers were a match for the federals now, or close to it, but the enemy still had the technological edge, and they'd jammed her comm hard.

They have the technological edge until Grant and his people get here. Then we'll see . . .

She crouched down behind the berm her troopers had hurriedly thrown up. It wasn't exactly a trench, but it was decent cover, and she had a surprise or two ready for the feds, even before the armored troopers entered the battle.

"Get ready, Cliff." She turned and looked back at Cliff Halken.

The engineer and his team had spent the night leaving care packages on all the trees.

"We're all set, Colonel."

Ideally Morgan would have waited longer, but the federal jamming capability meant her people had been forced to rely on hardwiring, and while Halken's techs had tried to hide the cords, she didn't trust a pile of leaves as cover.

"Do it," she said calmly.

"Yes, Colonel." Halken held a small controller in his hand, a wire extending from the device over the berm and out toward the federal line. He hesitated, just for a second. Then he pressed a small red button.

The explosions were loud, the closest ones almost deafening. The battlefield erupted in smoke and flying shards of wood as fifty explosives went off at the same time, turning fifty massive trees into matchsticks in seconds.

Morgan looked out over the field, trying to get a view of the forward enemy positions, but the smoke was too thick. Seconds passed, and still she could see nothing. The enemy fire had trickled down, almost to nothing. She hoped the explosions had taken down some feds, but she doubted it was many. That wasn't the purpose.

She stared ahead, as the smoke finally began to dissipate a bit. The trees were gone, and the underbrush, replaced by an open plain covered with shattered chunks of wood.

A perfect killing field.

The smoke began to stir, and she saw the federals pushing forward, now out into the open. They moved with confidence, almost certainly expecting to find the same green troops they'd faced in the fall, but they were in for a surprise.

"Autocannons, open fire."

Her heavy weapons were carefully placed, with interlocking fields of fire all across the open area. She watched as almost the entire front line of federals fell, and the troops behind dove to the ground, grabbing whatever meager cover they could.

"Mortars, fire." Her force only had three mortars, and they were positioned right behind her. Barely a second after she barked the command, she heard the distinctive sound of the weapons, and then the explosions as the shells landed in the middle of the field. The federals were stalled, and then they began moving back, crawling toward the edge of the remaining woods. Her mortars kept firing, several of them scoring direct hits, taking out as many as three or four enemies at a time.

"Cease fire," she shouted. "All weapons, cease fire."

The federals had pulled back to their lines. They were in cover, leaving what had to be eighty to one hundred of their number on the field.

She'd have kept up the barrage, but she couldn't waste the ammunition. The army still had plenty of small arms reloads, but the mortars and autocannons were almost out. Damian had given her all he could spare, yet the battle could last all day, and no matter how cautious she was, her people were going to lose their heavy weapon support at some point.

Morgan stared out at the field with mixed feelings, pride in her people's performance, in the disciplined manner in which they repelled the federal assault . . . and sorrow for the men and women she had killed, that she had once called comrades.

And fear, too. Her troopers had given the feds a bloody nose, taught them a lesson for arrogance, for underestimating them, but she knew they'd be back, and they wouldn't make the same mistake again.

That was war, and her people would be ready.

The battle had just begun.

CHAPTER 32

The Third Battle of Dover—The Federal Attack

"General, Colonel Morgan's forces are being pushed back. She just sent a runner to report she was going to try to make a stand at Carver Ridge."

Damian shook his head. "No, no . . . send the messenger back. Carver Ridge is a wrinkle in the ground. It's not even close to a strong enough position. Tell her to pull back to the prepared line behind Gullen Creek."

"Yes, sir." Katia Rand turned and walked back out of the tent.

Damian wasn't surprised. Luci Morgan didn't like to give up ground. Her people had held on their initial line for far longer than he'd thought they would. He'd almost sent orders for them to retire before Katia made her report.

Morgan's people had done their jobs, and then some. He could only guess at the casualties they'd inflicted on the feds. It had to be in the hundreds. The federals had lost more soldiers here in two hours than they had in the entire battle the year before. If they hadn't realized before that the soldiers they were facing were different, they knew it now.

And things were just getting started.

Damian turned abruptly and followed Katia out of the tent. He'd been in headquarters all morning, but he couldn't stay there all day, no matter how much his people seemed to want to protect him. It made sense, of course. He was the army commander, and aside from whatever actual ability he possessed, the persona that had developed around him had a utility all its own, whether it was deserved or not. He didn't understand much of it. After a year of waiting and preparation, all he'd managed to do was lose a battle and then drive the few of his soldiers that remained into the ground with merciless drilling. He knew they'd called him names behind his back, cursed him for rousing them at the frigid crack of dawn to march kilometers through waist-deep snow, and yet they also loved him. It made no sense, none that he could comprehend, but he had become, in every way that mattered, the father of his army. He knew his death would be catastrophic to the cause, and though the thought made him uncomfortable, he realized it was true nonetheless.

Yet worrying about his own safety while sending his people into battle sickened him. He'd always shared the dangers with his soldiers before, and now he realized just how much that had played into his ability to live with it all. He'd been behind the lines for too long now, and he'd had about as much of it as he could take.

"Sir . . ." Katia turned, even as she was walking back toward the messenger.

"You have your orders, Lieutenant," Damian snapped, more harshly than he'd intended. It was the stress, the tension. His people were doing well, better than he'd had any right to expect, but they were still being driven back. Even though that was the plan, it was unsettling, and it only drove home the point that if Grant's attack didn't swing the battle, they were as good as lost. The feds just had too much of a numerical advantage, too much superiority in logistics.

Damian had high hopes for his new weapon system, but now

that the fight was raging, doubts started to plague him. Holcomb's invention was amazing, beyond anything he'd ever imagined, but the suits his people wore had been hastily assembled in tiny make-shift factories, using whatever raw materials John Danforth had been able to find. They were a poor copy of the systems Holcomb had envisioned, like some version of a gourmet meal cooked from half-spoiled leftovers.

Then there was the other issue. He couldn't forget that nearly three hundred of his soldiers were carrying rough and poorly shielded fission plants around on their backs. He had images of troopers dropping in the battle, weakening from fatigue, choking on their own vomit as radiation sickness ravaged their bodies.

The troopers knew the risks, though, and knew what was at stake. The federals were just too strong for his army to defeat without the armor.

Maybe even with it.

His people were too outnumbered. Perhaps he'd been wrong. Perhaps he should have been harder on deserters, lined them up against firing squads in front of the rest of the troops. The thought disgusted him, but now he wondered if his mercy had condemned the rest of his soldiers, the loyal ones who'd remained, who'd endured the bitter cold and grueling training and now had to face an enemy more numerous because of those who had fled.

Damian walked out into the woods. He could hear the distant sounds of gunfire, Morgan's troops about three kilometers forward and to his left, and Devlin Kerr's wing extending to his right. And beyond, about five kilometers farther, outside the extent of the federal line, Jamie Grant and his three hundred waited. They waited for the word to advance, a message Damian knew he'd likely have to send by runner due to the federal jamming.

The timing of that message would be vital. If he sent it too soon, the federals would have time to react. And if he waited too long, his army would be destroyed. However effective those three hundred armored soldiers proved to be, he couldn't win the victory he needed without the other units of the army counterattacking. He had to send Grant's people in before the rest of his forces were completely spent.

He started moving deeper into the woods. He could hear the scuffling behind him, the sounds of orders being yelled, and then leaves and branches rustling, the inevitable guards Ben Withers had sent after him.

Damian knew Withers himself would have come, save for the express orders he'd given his aide to remain in HQ, to act as his chief of staff and stay on top of the reports coming in from all around the field. Damian's purposes were deeper than mere organization, of course. If he was killed or wounded, Luci Morgan would take command, but Ben Withers was the only one who knew the plan as well as Damian, and the new CO would need him. As much as Damian valued Withers's presence with him, he wasn't going to allow a random enemy shell to take them both in one moment.

He almost laughed as he realized how that sounded. *Only* I *have permission to get killed.*

He could feel his pace quickening, even as the guards were following him. It was juvenile, and he was also very aware that the troopers sent to protect him would follow at a dead run if he forced them to. He just . . .

No. Let them do their job.

He slowed down, slightly, and he could hear them moving up behind him, with two slipping around to the front.

"Let us screen the path, sir," the apparent leader, a sergeant, said. Damian knew the man, but he was having trouble coming up with a name. *He's probably ready to die to protect you, and you can't even remember his name . . .*

"Very well, Sergeant." Damian sighed softly, but he tried to keep it quiet. Truth was, it didn't hurt to have some protection. He *was* being a bit foolhardy. And at least they hadn't come to try to bring him back. He watched as the men took their positions around him, then said, "I'm going up to Colonel Morgan's line, Sergeant."

He could see the noncom stiffen, clearly nervous about the general going so far forward. But he said simply, "Yes, sir," and continued forward.

Damian had to go to the front. He had to do it for himself . . . and he had to see the federal attack, had to gauge just when to send in Jamie and his people. There was no room for error. The fate of the entire rebellion quite possibly rested on the timing of that single order.

"You are to keep moving forward, Major. No halt, no respite. However exhausted your soldiers are, the rebels must be as well. Worse, even. I'm sending you reserves, but I expect you to maintain the pressure without pause."

Granz cut the comm line. He wasn't in the mood to listen to a perfunctory acknowledgment, and less even to arguments why his orders could not be obeyed.

The rebels had fought hard. More than hard. Though it wasn't in him to admit the citizen soldiers were the equals of his own troopers, he couldn't avoid the conclusion that they were damned close. And dug in as they were, the burden of the attack on his people, casualties had been horrific.

His mind raced to understand what had happened. How had the force he'd faced just over six months earlier become so much stronger? Their numbers had dwindled, perhaps to no more than a quarter of what they'd fielded before, but those who remained were grim and well drilled. They stood in unshakable lines, mowing down his attacking troopers, and then retiring to prepared fallback positions.

Perhaps worst of all were the constant messages from Semmes, demanding to know when he would sweep the rebels from the field. The frontal assaults he'd sent in hoping to break the rebels had been far too costly, and now he was moving his forces to the flanks, trying to find a less well-defended approach. He still didn't doubt his forces would win the battle, but now his mind was burdened with thoughts of horrendous casualties.

He heard a sound from above, one of his airships. The damned raiders who'd been operating in Landfall for so long had devastated his already meager air forces, and now he had a total of three craft ready for service. They were all deployed now, but the rebels remained in the woods, avoiding any areas that presented a target to the aircraft.

There was nothing to do but fight it out on the ground, one bloody meter after another.

He reached down and grabbed his comm unit. "Captain, I want fifth and sixth battalions committed at once. They are to reinforce the right and left center, respectively."

"Yes, sir."

More force. It wasn't elegant. It wasn't tactical brilliance. But it was what he had. The rebels were outnumbered, and he was going to make that count.

Yet even as the troops moved forward, he couldn't help but be nervous about how many of his reserves he'd already committed. He couldn't leave his troops pushing forward through the meat grinder they'd been in all morning, but it was a risk. After a moment's hesitation, he committed to his own plan, and the worry changed to determination.

It was time to push, time for the final attack.

Time to break through, to destroy the rebel army.

He reached down again, his hand gripping the comm. *They'll break*, he thought. *If I throw in the rest of the reserves . . . one massive attack.*

They'll break.

"Get going. Pull back two kilometers and get headquarters set up again." Damian was standing in the middle of what had been army headquarters. The federals were less than a kilometer away, and Devlin Kerr's forces were dug in no more than five hundred meters forward.

"Get going? You're not coming?" Ben Withers managed to sound both horrified and totally unsurprised at the same time.

"No." Damian was staring off in the direction of the enemy.

"No? Would you care to explain why not?"

"No. I didn't think that was one of the army commander's obligations." He smiled. "Seriously, I just need to wait. I had gone to the line to send in Jamie's armor, but it hadn't been time then. We need the right moment."

"But you still need to wait? Don't you think it's time now?"

"Not yet." He was still looking off into the woods as he spoke to his aide. "Our people are holding out too well." The words sounded strange to him even as they came out of his mouth. "I mean, I want the feds a little farther forward. We need to maximize the shock of this attack. You know how good those troops are, how tough it will be to rout them, to send that whole army pulling back in disorder. We need a few more minutes, and I need to stay here and make that call. Leave me two runners, and make sure the HQ gets set up as quickly as possible." He turned back, exchanging glances with Withers for the first time in the conversation. "I'll be right behind you, Ben. I just want to make the right call on this. I won't grab my pistol and dive into a pack of feds, I promise."

Withers looked back, nodding, but clearly not entirely convinced Damian *wouldn't* throw himself into the middle of the fight. "Yes, sir." Withers turned, but stopped midway. "Be careful, Damian."

"I will, Ben."

He moved forward, toward the hasty works Kerr's troopers had erected. It wasn't much, but any cover was worth its weight in gold when the shooting started. Which it already had.

Damian ducked down as he heard a bullet whip by him. The

feds were still forming up for their attack, but that didn't mean there was no fire coming in. Even as he looked around for Colonel Kerr, he saw a trooper hit. She'd been semiprone behind a mound of dirt, but then she'd popped up over her cover to peer out toward the enemy line and caught a round in the shoulder. Damian didn't think it was all that serious a wound, but it looked as if it hurt like crazy.

"General, you should fall back. The feds will be coming in a few minutes." Damian hadn't found Kerr, but the colonel had found him.

"I can see that, Dev, but I'm here to get a feel for the enemy strength. I need to know they've committed at least most of their reserves before I send Captain Grant's people in."

"They have to have most of their reserves in, General. We've hurt them. Bad. I can't even guess at their casualties so far, but they just keep coming."

"I need to be sure, Dev. We've got one shot at this. We . . ."

The ground in front of Kerr's line erupted suddenly, what sounded like at least twenty autocannons opening up and raking the rebel position.

Damian dropped to the ground instinctively, as did Kerr and his two runners. But one of the officers had been too slow, and Damian could see him lying motionless, his still-open eyes staring up from his dead face.

He looked over at Kerr to check on him, and he saw the colonel was doing the same with him. The two exchanged glances, and then Kerr crawled forward, snapping out orders to the troopers within earshot.

Damian stayed where he was, watching. The autocannon barrage continued, perhaps for three or four minutes, and despite their cover and their caution, at least a dozen of Kerr's people had been hit.

Then the fire diminished, perhaps six guns still shooting, now on carefully constructed fields of fire. Damian knew exactly what was happening. He couldn't see the advancing federals, not through the dense woods, but he knew they were coming.

He could hear them now, the fire of their assault rifles as they surged forward, leapfrogging, blasting Kerr's line with covering fire. It was a big attack, strong. Strong enough that Kerr's people couldn't hold, and when they pulled back, Morgan's line would have to retreat as well. The feds had pushed hard all morning, throwing more and more forces into taking each of his fortified positions. They had to have most of their forces deployed.

They *had* to.

CHAPTER 33

The Third Battle of Dover—The Ambush

Jamie Grant stood silently, staring out into the trees, waiting. Waiting for the word to advance.

He was scared, of course, as any sane person would be before going into battle. More than that, though, he was nervous, fully aware of the fact that three hundred lives, not to mention, possibly, the fate of the entire army and rebellion, depended on how well he executed his orders.

But most of all, he was uncomfortable.

The suits were amazing pieces of technology, and their potential as weapons was unmistakable. But the damned things were a nightmare to be trapped inside of, especially for hours on end. Holcomb had told Jamie that his initial plan called for heavy conditioning as part of the training program, and a cocktail of drugs to help troopers endure the experience. But there hadn't been time for such training, and the army's dwindling drug supply didn't include the kind of mind-affecting pharmaceuticals Holcomb had specified. So his people had no choice except to endure, to ignore the claustrophobia, to try their best to ignore the itches, the urges to scratch or wipe away droplets of sweat. He almost craved the messenger who would give him the order to lead his command forward, to finish this one way or another.

"Captain, do you think we should move forward? It sounds like the enemy is pushing our people back." The voice was a bit staticky over the comm, but clear enough.

Grant turned to face the officer, though as he did it, he realized it was fairly pointless. All his people looked exactly the same when armored up, and notions like eye contact were irrelevant. Plus, his people had the advantage of active comm, at least at short ranges, courtesy of their nuclear-powered backpacks' ability to burn through the federal jamming. He couldn't reach HQ, or any of the units on the line, but his own troopers could communicate. That was another advantage, one he expected would be a surprise to the feds.

"No," he said, though he felt the same way. It was surprisingly difficult to stand there, waiting, while the enhanced audio built into his suit picked up the sounds of fighting kilometers away. But he trusted Damian with his life, and he was going to wait until he got the order to move forward. "We are to remain here until the runner arrives."

"Sir, what if the runner never gets here? The army's in trouble, Captain. You can hear that much."

"You hear the sounds of combat, Lieutenant, and that is all. Don't pretend you know what is actually happening up there." *And don't forget, the whole plan is to lure the enemy in, to feign a retreat.*

"Yes, sir."

Lieutenant Ferris didn't sound satisfied, but he didn't argue further, either, and Jamie was willing to accept that. Soon enough, his people would have plenty to occupy themselves. The combat power of the suits was unquestionable, but there were other factors on his mind. They were barely tested, and they were built under terrible conditions. He considered it a mathematical certainty that some of his people would die today from malfunctions. A power failure or servo malfunction would render any of his soldiers motionless. Human muscles were inadequate to move the ten-ton suits so much as a millimeter, and a failure anywhere in the system was a death sentence on the field. Weapons system breakdowns, radiation leaks, not to mention human error by troops with a laughably small amount of training and practice time—it all made the operation staggeringly dangerous, beyond even the combat itself.

Jamie stared out into the woods, cranking up the vision mag system, trying to detect any movement at all. Despite what he'd said to Ferris, he *was* worried that perhaps the runner hadn't gotten through, that something had gone wrong. What if the army was in trouble, if Damian needed his people *now*?

He was still arguing with himself when he saw something. Movement? Or his imagination.

He turned his head sharply, fixed his eyes on the position. Yes, it was motion. Someone was coming.

He felt tension all through his body, his stomach clenching hard. Was it time?

A few seconds later, a figure emerged completely from the dense forest, an officer, waving his hands and shouting. "Captain Grant . . . the general orders you to begin your attack. You are to hit the enemy directly to your front, which will be their rear flank."

"Very well, Captain," Grant responded, turning down the volume on his outside speakers when he realized how loud they were. "Go back and tell General Ward that we are on our way."

"Yes, Captain." The messenger turned and dashed back into the woods.

"All right, let's move out." Jamie waved his arm, gesturing toward the woods. "It's time to give these fed bastards a surprise they won't soon forget."

He stood, his massive arm pointing in the direction of the advance, as his soldiers stepped off into the woods. The armored figures were huge, cumbersome, and his soldiers swung their arms in front of them to clear away anything but the largest trees.

Jamie watched, feeling a sense of satisfaction at the relative order his hastily organized unit displayed. His excitement was tempered by the sight of four or five of his troopers motionless, their suits clearly malfunctioning in one way or another.

"If your suit's not responding, activate the diagnostics right away." A pause. "And if you can't get the thing working, pop yourself out, and get back to HQ. And don't forget, activate the destruct sequence before you abandon your suit." The last thing the Haven army needed was for their new secret weapons to fall into federal hands. It was their one advantage, and giving the enemy a few of them to analyze would be a disaster.

Jamie turned, watching as his column continued off into the woods. He took one glance back at the malfunctioning units—seven now—and he took a deep breath and followed his troopers into the woods.

Toward the federals.

"They're breaking, Colonel. We've taken their abandoned headquarters, and their forces are pulling back all along the line."

Colonel Granz stood stone-faced, deep in thought, even as he listened to the third messenger in ten minutes, all of them delivering optimistic reports about the enemy withdrawing.

Withdrawing. Retreating. Pulling back.

He thought of the words in these reports, and he compared them to those from the year before. *Running, fleeing, routing.*

There was no question, his people were driving the rebels from the field. But there was no panic, no disorder. Each time his forces took one of their lines, they fell back in good order and formed another defensive position. They were taking losses, of course, but nothing like the horrendous casualties his forces were enduring in the sustained attacks. And they were giving as good as they were getting.

Still, his army was winning the day, and despite their vastly improved performance, he couldn't imagine the rebel cause could sustain another defeat. His troops were exhausted, and they'd suffered badly, but when the rebels finally broke, he was going to drive his people forward. This time there would be no retreat, no further withdrawal. He wasn't going to allow Damian Ward to regroup his defeated forces. Whatever it took, however costly in casualties and misery for his soldiers, it would almost certainly be a better option than allowing this conflict to continue.

He hesitated. He knew what he needed to do, but there was still a seed of uncertainty. He'd already committed most of his reserves, meaning he had only two fresh battalions left. If he deployed them now . . .

But if he didn't, his exhausted soldiers might not have enough left to destroy the rebels, and he wasn't about to let them escape again.

"Captain," he yelled toward one of his aides. "The eleventh and sixteenth battalions are to advance and support the center assault."

"Yes, sir." The officer pulled out his comm unit and relayed the order. A moment later: "Colonel, we're getting reports from the left flank, some kind of enemy force advancing."

Granz spun around, an intense glare falling on the officer. "Cancel that last order. Both battalions are to intercept the new enemy force."

"Colonel, we're just getting scattered reports. We don't even know . . ."

"Do it!" Granz's caution was hardening into tension. *So this is your plan, Ward?* He'd expected something from the rebels, some kind of ploy. A flanking force? It made sense, a way to take advantage of the rebels' superior knowledge of the ground. But two fresh battalions should be enough to handle it. More than enough.

Jamie stopped for a moment, leaning slightly forward and digging his armor's feet into the ground as Holcomb had taught him. He extended his arm, aiming the rail gun carefully. Holcomb had told him a dozen times, the hypervelocity weapon wasn't technically a rail gun, but every other name he'd given was just too big a mouthful. And it didn't matter what it was called anyway. The thing was a beast.

He fired again, feeling the massive kickback, even in his powerful armor. The projectile, really just a piece of depleted uranium, streaked through the sky at 5,000 meters per second, far too fast to follow with the eye. All that was visible was the glow of ionized air behind it, and the wild tumult of obliterated trees and shards of pulverized wood flying through the air.

He moved his arm, snapping the weapon back into its holding place, and began moving forward again, firing the dual autocannons as he did. The firepower of the suit was immense, even more astonishing in actual combat than it had been in training. His strike force had virtually annihilated the federal troops they'd encountered first, driving the few survivors off in unrestrained flight.

Then they'd encountered two fresh battalions. The federals were still moving up, so they hadn't had time to deploy or dig in. But there were over twelve hundred of them, and they were ready to fight.

Jamie's people opened up on them, the withering fire from their suits chopping their forward companies to bits before the rest of the troopers dropped to the ground and grabbed what cover they could. Then they began returning fire, and within another minute, their own heavy weapons began to tell.

The suits were tough, proof against most assault rifle rounds, unless a lucky shot hit a weak spot. But the autocannons were a different matter, and Jamie's force began to take casualties. He'd already lost more than twenty of his people to malfunctions and mechanical failures, and now the federal fire began to take a toll. He glanced down at the small screen in his helmet. It was hard to read, and even harder to manipulate, but Holcomb had gotten it functioning, at least to an extent. Jamie had a partial unit as the commander, and six of his officers did, as well, but the rest of his troopers had only basic computer enhancement and comm units.

A more sustained glance suggested only half of those were actual casualties, that the rest were troopers whose suits were damaged. Yet another reason this was a fight to the end. If the rebel forces retreated, they'd leave at least some suits behind—particularly those with dead operators who couldn't self-destruct—a gift to the federals. If the rebels had managed to build three hundred suits over the winter under nearly impossible conditions, he shuddered to think of what the federals could do with the technology.

But as much as that worried him, he felt like they had the upper hand. The federals had powerful weapons, but even the autocannons required a well-placed shot to really take out an armored trooper, and the volume of fire was lopsided, the federals losing dozens of their number for every rebel they took out.

The calculus was beyond Jamie at the moment, but it seemed like they might actually come out of this thing with the upper hand.

"Team Blue, around the left. Team Green around the right." He knew his people could beat the federals in a straight-up face-to-face battle, but he didn't want to pay the price for that. His troopers were faster, far more mobile, and he intended to take advantage of that.

"Red, Yellow, and White teams, maintain fire, and continue advancing."

He maintained his fire, switching both cannons to full auto. He'd been conserving ammunition so far, because the army had no real battlefield logistics capability, and when his troopers ran out of what they had . . . well, they'd better have won the victory by then. But these soldiers weren't exhausted, battered troops who'd been attacking all morning. And so it was going to take more than targeted fire to dislodge them.

He meant to show them a maelstrom of bullets.

Because it was clear the federals were outgunned. The lumbering suits of powered armor seemed unstoppable, and their nuclear-powered arsenals devastating. Half the federals, at least, were down, and now the others were falling back.

Jamie continued forward, redirecting his fire to the retreating troopers. He knew Damian and the other veterans had mixed feelings about gunning down their former comrades, especially when they were running. But Jamie shared no such hesitation. The federals had stolen a decade of his life, stripped him away from the mother he barely remembered now. He had endured horrors that still tormented his sleep, and he didn't care to differentiate between one group of feds and another. Those soldiers were here to crush his new home, to kill his comrades and allies. And that was all that mattered.

The federal retreat was quickly turning into a rout as soldiers began to turn and run, their discipline finally failing them.

"Target those fleeing feds," he shouted into his comm. "None of them get away, do you hear me? Keep after them. This is our time! Time to repay these bastards for years of misery and death and oppression." Damian had discouraged Jamie from choosing too many former prisoners for the new corps, but he'd still put about fifty of them in. Some of them were problem types, but nothing he couldn't handle. And nobody hated the damned feds worse than men who'd been imprisoned in that mine.

"After them," he yelled. "Nobody escapes." He fired his auto-cannons, taking down a whole row of troopers who were in wholesale flight. "Nobody!"

CHAPTER 34

The Third Battle of Dover—The Pursuit

"The entire line is to fall back two kilometers."

"Yes, Colonel." The aide repeated the order into the comm unit, the edginess in his voice clear. Granz wasn't surprised. He felt it himself, though he dared to guess that he hid it better than the young lieutenant manning the communications board. He didn't like depending on an officer's academy grad still wet behind the ears as the conduit for his orders, but he'd sent all his more experienced aides off to the army's left, to try to halt the collapse of the line before this still mysterious rebel assault.

"And I want every third company to pull back and re-form. Their parent battalions are to thin their ranks to cover the gaps."

"Yes, sir."

It was one thing not to have any reserves when pushing forward, finishing off an almost broken army, and quite another not to have any when retreating. Which was what Granz knew his army was doing, even though he hadn't overtly acknowledged that to himself.

He'd imagined a tough fight, and as things progressed, he'd come to realize just how costly the victory here would be. But he'd never really seriously believed the rebels could beat his army. He'd blamed many of the problems encountered so far in the war on Semmes and his interference, but he was an honest enough man to realize he'd lost this fight himself.

If it is lost, a stubborn thought shouted from within. *Reorder the line, redeploy troops from the right.*

But even as the voices echoed in his mind, he shook his head. There wasn't time. Too much of his army was spent. If he issued the retreat order now, he could withdraw in good order, rest and re-supply. They still held Landfall, and from there the war could continue. The rebels were as exhausted as his troops, and they would have a much harder time replacing the vast amount of ordnance they'd used.

And you will have time to find out just what is attacking your left flank, what kind of rebel trick or deception it is . . .

"Lieutenant, I want all supply transports to begin moving south. We're going to disengage. As soon as the army has pulled back to the new position, we're going to start taking units off the line and getting them on the road."

"You mean we're running? That the rebels beat us?"

Granz felt a burst of anger at what he could take as insubordination. But he knew it was just the pride and spirit of a freshly minted officer talking.

"No, Lieutenant, we're not running. It's a strategic decision, a redeployment preparatory to reengaging at a more advantageous time." He shook his head. He'd always despised that kind of bull-shit, the attempt to disguise failure as something else. "Yes, Lieutenant, we're retreating. The rebels got the best of us here, but we'll make sure that doesn't happen again. But we're not running. We're withdrawing in good order. Have I fully explained myself enough for your satisfaction?"

"Yes, sir."

"Then give the order."

And let's hope whatever the hell Ward has out there doesn't destroy us before we make our escape.

The runner came bursting out of the woods, heading right for Damian. The guards snapped their rifles out, alarmed at the potential threat to their commander.

"Hold," he yelled, afraid one of the overzealous sentries would shoot the messenger. "Report," he said to the new arrival as he skidded to a stop right in front of him.

"Sir . . ." The runner was gasping for air, and he was soaked in sweat, despite the definite chill in the air. "Captain . . ."

"Take a breath, soldier. Another few seconds isn't going to matter."

The trooper nodded and sucked in a deep breath, exhaling loudly. Then another.

"General," he said, still out of breath, but far better than he had been. "Captain Grant sent me to report. His assault is under way. His people encountered light resistance at first and swept all federals they encountered before them. Then they met up with what he believes were two fresh battalions. The fight went on for about fifteen minutes, sir . . . and the federals broke. Captain Grant and his people pursued, and he believes they virtually destroyed the two formations."

Damian felt a wave of relief. Things were far from over, and a hundred things could still go wrong, but it was good news no matter how he looked at it. Especially if Jamie was right about two whole federal units breaking.

"That's good news, Corporal." He turned toward one of the guards standing behind him. "Take Corporal . . ."

"Koogan, sir."

"Take Corporal Koogan and get him some water, and a place to rest for a few minutes."

"Thank you, sir."

Damian nodded. Then, turning toward Withers. "Get me a fresh runner, Ben. I want to send a message to Jamie."

"Yes, General."

Damian allowed himself a moment of satisfaction. Perhaps his people could get their victory after all. That would be a great success, but his excitement was tempered. It was far from decisive, at least in terms of the rebellion as a whole. Even if Kutusov had been honest, if he would lobby his government to intervene, he still had to figure a way to get him back to Earth, and those there had to listen to him. Winning here at Dover would be only the first of seven or eight things that all had to work if Haven was going to win its independence.

But you can't get to seven or eight without getting past one.

"General!" The runner was a captain, and from the looks of him, he was at least a veteran of the last year's fighting. Ben Withers clearly understood as well as Damian what a crucial juncture they'd reached.

"Find Captain Grant, and tell him to keep up his advance no matter what, in spite of resistance, casualties, anything. He is to angle his direction toward the enemy rear, attempting to get behind the federal army."

"Yes, sir."

"Go," Damian said. Then, as the officer turned and started to run, "And, Captain . . ."

The runner stopped and looked back.

"Tell him not to let anybody by. We need to bag as much of the federal army as we can."

"Yes, General."

Damian waved, and the officer took off again, disappearing into the dense woods.

"Ben," he yelled, and then turned, realizing his aide was right behind him. "Ben, army-wide order. All units are to advance. The feds are pulling back. Now let's see what we can do to turn that retreat into a good old-fashioned rout, shall we?"

"Yes, sir," Withers said, with about as much enthusiasm as Damian had ever heard in the grizzled veteran's voice.

"Keep firing. If you're getting low on autocannon rounds, concentrate on the closest targets. Those lasers you've got'll turn these guys into Landing Day dinner at a hundred meters or less." Jamie was moving forward, firing aimed shots now, dropping one federal after another. It was easier, and a lot more fun, when the bastards were running instead of shooting back. A few thoughts tried to drift out of the recesses of his mind—guilt, pity—but then another recollection of the mine came bursting out of his memory and he gleefully shot another fed.

He kept firing, and then, when the warning light flicked on, advising him he was down to his last 10 percent of heavy rounds, he took his own advice, and activated the lasers built into each arm of his suit.

He extended his right arm and tapped his finger inside the suit, firing the weapons. The lasers made a high-pitched whine inside the armor, vaguely annoying, but nothing he couldn't ignore. His first shot missed. The lasers had a different aiming dynamic than the autocannons, and he had to adjust. It took three more shots, but the fourth practically sliced a federal trooper in half.

He kept moving, and then he froze. There was something up ahead. It was the Sanderson Road, with a whole line of transports just sitting there.

"Take those transports," he yelled into the comm. "That's the federal supply column. We're behind the army! Get over there, take out those transports before they can withdraw, and cover that road. My bet is we'll have retreating feds coming right into us."

Jamie swung around to the side, avoiding the small remaining cluster of federal troops in front of him. There were plenty of his people still there to finish them off. He wanted to get to the road.

Another ten or twelve steps and he was there, standing out in the open, looking at a confused mob of feds, on the verge of panic. A few started shooting at him, but most of them were too busy trying to get away.

He swung his arm around, clicking the control to activate his right autocannon. He didn't have much ammo left, but this was a good use of it. He opened up on the crowd, just as three of his people burst out of the woods and did the same. It was a nightmare, a massacre like none he'd ever seen before. There had been perhaps four hundred federals stacked up on the road. Maybe one fourth of those escaped into the woods . . . and the rest were sprawled out on the blood-soaked road, dead or dying. Even Jamie's rage and hatred was satiated, and he turned his attention to the trucks.

"Careful with these transports. They may have supplies the army needs. Just make sure none of them get away." As he spoke he saw a small column of vehicles among the supply transports. They were different, bigger, with large dish antennas on top. They were some kind of communication vehicles, he could guess that much. But what?

The jamming?

He had no idea. He couldn't tell a jamming transmitter from a telephone, but it seemed like a good guess. And he was damned sure Damian would appreciate some clear comm for a change.

"Take out those vehicles over there," he shouted, pointing toward the trucks. "The ones with the dishes on top. Take them out now."

He stood where he was, staring at the forward vehicle, as he brought the rail gun up to bear.

"General, the federals are breaking! We're getting reports from all across the field. They're breaking." Katia came rushing toward Damian from the small tent where his people had set up the main comm station. The federal jamming had left her without much of a job, save to answer repeated requests for updates from the Haven Congress, in session back at the army's old camp, but then, suddenly, the interference was gone, and almost as one, every unit on the field reported in, all with the same message. The federal army was running!

Damian felt a rush of excitement. He'd hoped the pressure would push the federals back, but the disappearance of the federal jamming was something he'd never thought about. He didn't know what had happened, and he didn't care, but he intended to get the most out of his clear communications while he had them.

"Let's go," he said, waving toward the comm tent. "Send messages to all units. Attack. My orders to all commanders are attack."

"Yes, sir." Katia was excited, as well, because the battle appeared to be swinging their way, of course, but also because the success indicated that Jamie's armored troopers were doing well. Damian was enough of a veteran to know that victory didn't mean Grant's people hadn't suffered losses, or that his friend couldn't easily die in the triumph, but he didn't want to darken her hope. It would serve no purpose.

The two of them slipped inside the tent. Katia sat at her station. Damian listened for a few seconds as she repeated his order to the various commanders along the front.

The whole thing still seemed unreal, almost like a dream. He tried to restrain his thoughts, to remember that even a crushing win here—and he was far from sure his people would achieve that—was no guarantee of winning Haven's freedom. But the discipline he'd demanded of himself since the day he'd accepted command of the army had its limits, and he let out a deep breath and gave himself a few seconds to smile, a moment of pride for his soldiers. No one, at least no one with any military experience, had given his people a chance, any chance at all, he was sure of that, and he counted himself in that group. They'd had an assist here from Holcomb's amazing armor, but he reminded himself to give credit to the men and women as well as the tech. His troopers had fought doggedly all across the line, inflicting massive casualties on the attacking federals, even before Grant's armored troopers attacked.

He took a few steps—three were enough to reach the other side of the tent—and he picked up the headset for the second comm unit. He reached down and turned the channel controls. He had to report this to John Danforth, now. It wasn't out of any sense of obligation to the congress, but Danforth was the father of the rebellion, probably the man most responsible for all that had happened. And he was Damian's friend.

Damian didn't like jumping the gun, reporting things before they were fully in hand, but he knew Danforth would be waiting, his gut twisted with tension. He deserved to know, as soon as possible.

"This is General Ward," he said softly. "Get me President Danforth. Now."

CHAPTER 35

The Federal Retreat

"Stay on them. They're still disorganized, even if they've rallied some. Pick a spot, sneak up on their line of march, take out a few, and slip away before they can do anything. Then do the same damned thing again." Patrick Killian was standing in front of a dozen rebel soldiers, gesturing to the west, toward the road that was clogged with the retreating federal army. He'd gotten Damian's permission to take a force in pursuit of the feds, to harass them and inflict as many additional casualties as possible. His efforts had borne fruit, but less than he'd hoped. His rangers had been almost annihilated in the protracted fighting around Landfall through the winter, and now he had mostly line troops—not quite up to the guerilla tactics he employed.

He turned toward Des Black. "Des, I want you to take half this group. Slip down that ravine"—he pointed to the south—"you re-member it, right? It should give you a great route to sneak up and grab some high ground with a good field of fire to the road."

"Yes, Colonel. I remember it."

"I'll take the rest, and we'll backtrack. These units closer to the rear are still pretty shaken up. If we can hit them a few times, maybe we can slow them down, give us the chance to hit them a few more times."

"I agree, sir."

"Good. Get on that ridge and hit them as hard as you can. But pull back before they can come at you. You're better off repositioning and hitting them again than getting into a firefight."

"Yes, Colonel." Black turned and started barking out orders to the troopers standing in front of him. A few seconds later, they slipped off into the woods.

Killian pulled up his rifle and moved toward the remaining troopers. "Okay, you've done well so far, but the job's not done, not yet." He paused, looking off through the woods for a few seconds before continuing. "Let's go. We've still got work to do."

"Colonel Granz, I will see that you pay for this. Our plan was flawless, the enemy on the verge of total collapse, and yet somehow you managed to turn certain victory into a unmitigated disaster." Robert Semmes was more than angry.

He was completely unhinged.

Granz stood and silently endured Semmes's tirade. He was too miserable himself to even care about the general's abuse. The whole thing still seemed surreal. In a single day, he'd gone from the expectation of victory to the officer who had led federal forces to the worst defeat in their history. It was a nightmare, a living one, and part of him wished a bullet had found him, that he was one of the nearly fifteen hundred of his soldiers dead on the field.

He'd come close to total despair, but just for a moment. His life had been one of duty, and he refused to fail that now. He had thousands of wounded soldiers, and the rest of the army retreating. They needed him. They had to re-form, reorganize, prepare for the next fight. Granz was no expert on revolutions, but it was clear even to him that news of Damian Ward's victory would spread like wildfire. Recruits would pour into the rebel camp, thousands of volunteers, and the general had already shown his ability to turn those unseasoned colonists into hardened warriors.

Granz hadn't wanted to come to Alpha-2. The idea of fighting colonists who were his countrymen had been unsettling to say the least. But the last thing he'd expected was a real war, one his army could lose. Now, for the first time, he contemplated just such an outcome.

Damian Ward had proven himself, and he'd won Granz's respect. And this new weapon the rebels possessed was worrisome. He'd finally had a chance to piece together the reports, and in the closing moments of the battle, he'd witnessed the things himself. He knew the federal authorities had been working on powered armor for a long time, but had never figured out workable prototypes. He had no idea how the rebels had managed to develop such weapons, let alone produce what seemed like hundreds of the suits.

There was one bright spot, at least. He had multiple reports of the suits breaking down, of the enemy losing strength as they pressed forward. It made sense. Whatever miraculous effort had allowed the rebels to build those suits, they clearly hadn't had the time or resources to test them and work out any problems. That meant—probably—it would be some time before they'd be able to put more of the weapons into the field, so the quicker Granz could get his army reorganized and ready for action, the better.

If only this madman would shut up and let me do my job.

"It is unforgivable, Colonel. Your incompetence is . . ."

Semmes was still ranting. It wasn't like Granz to zone out completely on a superior officer, but the other option was to pull out his pistol and silence the bastard for good. On the scale of mutinous activity, tuning the general out was clearly the lesser offense.

Granz did draw one shred of satisfaction, a spark of joy in his sea of misery. He tried to imagine Semmes having to tell his father about the defeat, about how, despite the astonishing flow of troops and supplies, the rebels were still not only in the field, they *held* the field. Granz was disgraced, but he took comfort in the fact that, however much Semmes would try to blame him solely, the mud would splatter across the general, too.

There was another shred of pride, one he knew was misplaced. Damian Ward was his enemy, the commander of the rebel army. His triumph was nothing for a loyal federal officer to celebrate. And yet, Damian Ward had once been an officer of Federal America, too. His skill, the man he clearly was, had been forged in the same furnace as Granz himself. Unlike Semmes, whose earlier service had been the result a politically obtained commission that was wholly undeserved, Ward was a man he could respect.

But could he defeat him?

Jacob North sat in the damp, cold cellar, the refuge that had kept him alive, if barely, all the months he'd been trapped in Landfall. He was a scrawny remnant of what he'd been half a year before, when he'd first staggered into the run-down streets of Landfall's oldest neighborhood, in search of a place to hide from the federal patrols on his tail.

He'd found that place, and he'd managed to avoid the incessant Peacekeeper patrols for more than six months, though at times, he'd almost wished a federal's gun had taken him down. His refuge had no heat, and he'd shivered through winter nights, too cold to fall asleep, counting the passing minutes until morning's light brought at least some scant warmth to the air. He'd scavenged for food, but the gaunt stick figure that replaced his once muscular frame testified to the fact that what he'd found had been enough to keep him alive, but not much more than that.

He would never speak about some of the things he had to eat.

He'd spent the first months in hiding planning to escape the city, to head north and find Colonel Killian or the army. But as cold, sickness, and hunger drained his strength, that had become less and less of a possibility. His aspirations had dwindled from escaping and returning to the fight to simply surviving. Even that had been a tremendous struggle, one that had taken all the will he could muster. But today he felt something that had been long absent, a warmth that filled him with hope.

He'd managed to make a few contacts, citizens who'd snuck him what food they could spare, as well as blankets and medicines. They didn't have much—Landfall was on strict rationing, and there was little to go around—but North knew he'd never have survived without their help. They were a small group. The Peacekeepers were everywhere, and he dared not trust anyone he wasn't completely sure about. But today they had given him something new, something he wouldn't have traded for a gourmet feast or a fancy hotel suite.

News of a victory.

He hadn't believed it at first. But then he heard it again, and again. He still had trouble convincing himself it could be true. The Haven army had won a battle. Not just a victory, but a full-scale triumph that had sent the federal forces racing down the Old North Road back to Landfall.

It was more than he'd dared to dream about those frozen nights, more than his wildest dreams when he'd torn scraps of meat off the bones he'd pulled from garbage bins. It renewed his faith, his determination. It filled him with a strength no food could match.

The fight wasn't over, not for Haven, and not for him. He'd been spent, ready to give up, to die in his hidden cellar, weak and defeated. But not now. There was a rebellion to finish, freedom to win.

North didn't know what he'd be able to do, how he could help his comrades. But he knew he had a part left to play.

He was still hungry and cold, but that didn't matter. His hope was back. He was determined again, ready to do whatever he had to do.

CHAPTER 36

Damian Ward had led his army to an unexpected victory, a historic and unprecedented win over a veteran army that outnumbered his forces nearly two to one. Even his grim outlook on the rebellion and its prospects for success couldn't hold back the satisfaction, the joy he felt. For a few brief, shining moments, it had seemed like nothing could stop that, drain away the pride and good feelings.

But it turned out, all it took was Cal Jacen.

"We barely have enough provisions to feed the army. We've got the congress, the civilian government staff, the families of the soldiers. There is no room for captives." The politician stood in the room, interjecting his views into a discussion Danforth and Damian had been having with several other officers and senators. Damian had not invited Jacen, but he'd come anyway, and now he was shouting the others down.

Damian felt the acid in his stomach, and he wondered how one man's presence could so easily simulate the feeling of overindulgence in a poorly chosen meal.

The topic was prisoners. Against all expectation, and all probability, Damian's army had captured over five hundred federal soldiers. He'd seen with his own eyes proud veterans putting their arms down and surrendering.

There had been incidents, of course, and he had no idea how many federal soldiers were killed trying to give up. He disapproved, and he'd hold any soldier accountable if he could, but he was realistic, too. Some of his people had had family members in Robert Semmes's camps the year before. Many had already lost loved ones to the rebellion. There was a limit to what men and women could endure, and pain brought out the worst of human nature. But that wasn't the issue with Jacen. He hadn't lost any loved ones. As far as Damian knew, he didn't have any.

He was just a fucking lunatic.

"Cal, we can't resort to such tactics. We're going to have to negotiate with the federals at some point, and prisoners could be valuable . . ."

Damian had listened to Danforth debating Jacen, giving his old ally all kinds of reasons why it didn't make sense to line up a bunch of POWs and just shoot them, but now his patience was gone.

"Listen to me, you slimy piece of shit," he said. "I've put up with you as much as I'm going to. We are *not* going to shoot helpless prisoners. I don't care what kind of twisted shit goes on in that excuse for a brain you have, but so help me God, if one of those prisoners dies, and I don't care if he's shot by a firing squad or if he chokes on his dinner, I'm going to blame you. And if that happens, there is no place on this planet you'll be able to hide from me."

He stared at Jacen, his eyes glistening, his rage pushing against his own usual stern control. He reached down to his side and pulled the pistol from his holster.

"Do we understand each other?" He raised the gun and held it centimeters from Jacen's face.

"Damian . . ."

"No, John . . . no more. You're my friend and I respect you, but I'm done with you making excuses for the pile of filth." He stared back at Jacen, unhappy with himself for the sheer joy the man's unmasked fear gave him. He didn't consider himself sadistic, but he was enjoying Jacen's discomfort.

"Damian, please . . ." Danforth took a step forward. "Don't do this, not now."

"I'm not doing anything now. I *should*." God knew he wanted to. He could feel the urge, part of his mind pushing at him, images of squeezing his finger, finishing this once and for all. It would take only an instant, a mere fraction of a second. "He's a schemer, an untrustworthy, worthless worm."

"Damian, please don't." There was real fear in Danforth's voice. Clearly he was afraid Damian was going to do it.

Jacen just stood against the wall, unmoving, clearly too afraid to even speak.

"It's up to him, John. Do we understand each other, Jacen?" Damian stared at the terrified man with cold intensity.

Jacen tried to answer, but no words came out. He managed a small nod.

"That's not good enough. Do . . . we . . . understand . . . each . . . other?"

"Yes," Jacen managed to croak out. "I understand."

Damian's arm relaxed and dropped to his side. He shoved Jacen away from the wall. "Then get the hell out of here, and out of my sight!"

Jacen turned back, flashing a quick glance toward Danforth, as if looking for support. Then he walked out of the room.

Damian stared at the others present, then toward Withers, who'd been standing against the far wall, watching the entire time.

"Ben, go find Colonel Morgan and tell her I want her to take over responsibility for the prisoners."

"Yes, General."

"And, Ben, tell her if Cal Jacen or any of his Society thugs so much as come within ten meters of the holding areas, she is to have them shot on sight. Understood?"

Withers snapped to attention and saluted. "Yes, sir. Understood." He turned and walked out, leaving Damian behind with the others, and a stunned silence in the room.

"I appreciate your willingness to take such a risk, Sasha, but do you really think Ambassador Kutusov is going to agree to jump on board *Vagabond* and make a desperate run past the federal fleet? He may be stuck here, but even if we lose the war, he can always surrender to the feds and ask for repatriation. They'd never let him go, of course, while the rebellion is still going on, but even Semmes wouldn't dare harm a Union diplomat."

Damian was in his quarters, with a group that included Sasha Nerov, John Danforth, and Luci Morgan. They were at a small table, enjoying the first hot food any of them had eaten in days.

Damian's billet was a small but comfortable house Withers had somehow found for him among the remains of the badly damaged village. Dover had seen no less than three battles over the past two years, and whole sections of it were in ruins. If he'd been paying more attention, Damian would have refused the accommodations, slept in a tent, but Withers had taken him by surprise, and the wall of overdue fatigue that had hit him as soon as the stress of battle was gone had been too much to endure. The thought of an actual bed . . . it had been more than he could resist.

"I'm afraid that Damian is correct, Sasha." Damian had asked for first names and no military formality for the evening, and Danforth was complying with his friend's request. "I've come to know the ambassador rather well, and while he is—much to his surprise, I believe, as well as my own—made of somewhat sterner stuff than many of his profession, I do not believe he has in him what it takes to endure such a risk. What do you think your chances are? Fifty-fifty?"

"I'm sorry you think so little of my piloting skills, John. How many loads of weapons and ammo did I get to Haven? Where would you all be now without those stockpiles?"

"I meant no disrespect, Sasha, nor any lack of gratitude, but there'd never been a full fleet surrounding our planet before. And," he said with a kind smile, "I will note that prior to your spiritual awakening as a true rebel, you were very well paid for those guns."

"I can get past the federals, John, Damian. I *know* I can."

"I appreciate that, Sasha, but there is still a tremendous risk, even to someone as capable as you. Would your crew be willing to take such a chance? And even if they are, again, I don't see how we could possibly get the ambassador to go along with it."

Nerov sat across the table from Damian. She reached out, grabbing her glass and draining the final drops of wine, a luxury the diners had enjoyed courtesy of the last bottles John Danforth had managed to spirit away from his estate before he'd abandoned it. Then she smiled, the mischievous grin she'd worn so often in the past, but that they'd rarely seen in recent months.

"I've thought about this, Damian, and I know just how we can get him to do it."

Damian looked back, a bemused expression on his face. He had no idea what Nerov had in mind. "You think you have some way to persuade him?" He knew Kutusov was attracted to Nerov, but he couldn't imagine the veteran smuggler thought she could flirt with him enough to overcome fear *and* self-preservation.

"I wouldn't say persuade, exactly . . ."

"Then what?"

"We lie to him, my good General Ward. We tell him one wild, flashing whopper of a lie."

CHAPTER 37

"Steady, Griff. They'll challenge us before they do anything hostile." *I hope.*

"Whatever you say, Sasha." Nerov's first officer, and best friend, sounded edgy, which, considering the insanity of what they were attempting, could have been worse.

"We'll be fine." Nerov was impressed with the certainty in her tone. It had been deliberate, of course, but she'd expected at least some of the fear in her gut to slip out.

"The engines are ready." Daniels was staring at the small screen at his workstation. *Vagabond* was an old ship, but Nerov had reinvested a large chunk of her smuggling profits into her beloved vessel, and the free trader had a lot more lurking under her battered hull than appeared at first glance.

"System status?"

"All systems at 100 percent functionality."

Nerov nodded and sighed softly. She'd been a little worried about the effects of the months her ship had spent submerged in the salty water of Haven's sea. It had been an ingenious plan, if she did say so herself, to hide the vessel in the water, and a ship designed for the vacuum and rigors of space should have been up to the hazards of the environment. But the water pressure *had* been significant, and despite her maintenance and upgrades, it *was* an old ship. It wouldn't have taken much of a hull failure for some leakage to cause damage to some of her systems.

"Sasha, we've got a federal frigate engaging its thrusters. My guess is they're moving to intercept."

Damn. Nerov had hoped the federals would send a communiqué first, demand that *Vagabond* cut her thrust and await boarding. If a ship was already heading toward her, she'd have to play her gambit earlier than she'd hoped. It would still be a surprise, at least she was pretty sure of that, but the farther *Vagabond* was from the jump point, the less chance she had of getting there before the blockading ships closed to firing range.

"Make sure everybody's strapped in, Griff. We may have to hit the thrusters sooner than we thought." *And hope like hell they work. Vagabond's* engines had always been reliable, and she'd always treated them with care. But now she was going to abuse the hell out of them, one wild gamble to get out of the system before the federal navy blasted *Vagabond* to scrap. She'd made most of the mods herself, but Jonas Holcomb had added a few details, and when she hit the switch newly installed on her workstation, *Vagabond* would—should, at least—have roughly double the thrust capacity she did before.

It was risky, of course, and she couldn't maintain it for long. But the trick was just to make it out of the system. Once they were clear of the federal fleet, Nerov's smuggler's instincts would take over, and she would plot a course around any other likely areas of interference.

Or, I'll flip the switch and the engines will blow, and we'll be nothing but a cloud of dust and hard radiation. Unless they just burn out, and then we'll get the pleasure of a federal trial for treason before they execute us. Assuming they don't just space us on the spot . . .

"Griff . . ." She was distracted by a sound behind her, the bridge door sliding open. She turned abruptly to see Andrei Kutusov standing there, a smile on his face.

"Ambassador, what are you . . ."

"I just wanted to watch on the scanners as we slipped past the federal navy. Truly, if you are willing to allow us to study and replicate the system, I can almost guarantee the Council will grant your request for intervention in the rebellion." A brief pause, then: "And how many times have I told you, it is Andrei."

Nerov felt her stomach tighten. The plan had seemed perfect when it had popped into her head, and despite some initial reservations, General Ward and the others had all agreed it was the only option. But now, with the Union ambassador standing two meters away, about to find out just how blatantly she'd lied to him, it didn't seem quite as clever as it had.

"Andrei, there is something I have to tell you . . ."

"Sasha, we're getting a transmission. Putting it on speaker."

She felt the urge to tell Griff to keep the communiqué off the main channel, but it was too late.

"Unidentified freight vessel, this is the Federal America frigate *California*. You are in prohibited space, in violation of the Alpha-2 Blockade Resolution, and you are not transmitting an identification beacon in compliance with the Standards of Space Mercantile Operations. You are ordered to cut all thrust immediately and prepare to be boarded."

Nerov was staring at Kutusov as the voice continued, watching his expression morph from pleasant to confused. To scared.

"This is a war zone, and failure to comply will result in the immediate destruction of your vessel. There will be no further warnings before action is taken."

"What is happening?" the ambassador asked, the fear heavy in his voice. "Has the stealth device failed? Did someone betray us?"

"Ambassador . . . Andrei . . ." She had to tell him, but the words didn't come.

"Sasha, we're picking up energy readings. I think they're arming their weapons systems."

"Sasha—"

She held up her hand, gesturing to Kutusov to wait. He glared back, but he also remained quiet.

Nerov flipped on her comm unit. "Federal vessel *California*, this is the free trader *Gazelle*. We are carrying a small group of loyalists who escaped from rebel captivity. We have injured aboard, and we request aid and assistance." She amazed herself sometimes, how well she could lie, even with the might of the federal navy bearing down on her and a terrified—and soon to be enraged—Union diplomat breathing down her neck.

"We read you, *Gazelle*. Cut thrust as ordered and reduce energy output to minimal levels. We will send a shuttle to dock and retrieve your wounded and passengers." It sounded like the federal officer had bought her story. *Why wouldn't he? Who would be insane enough to try to run the federal blockade?*

"Acknowledged, *California*. Cutting thrust now." She gestured toward Griff, slicing her hand through the air. Her second understood immediately, and a few seconds later, free fall replaced the almost 2g of pressure on the bridge. "Be ready, Griff. Their approach angle works for us. They'll have a significant amount of vector modification to match us." Nerov had plotted her course carefully. Her ship's current vector was close to directly toward the jump point. It would be an advantage when *Vagabond* finally made its desperate run.

"I insist you explain to me exactly what is going on."

"Andrei, I will be happy to explain, but since you did not listen to me and remain in your cabin, I have to insist you sit in that seat over there and strap in. We're going to have one hell of a rough ride in about a minute."

"I don't . . ." Kutusov looked like he was going to argue, but then he just turned and did as Nerov had told him. The look of fear had transitioned to one of terror. That was good, Nerov figured. It would hold back the anger, at least for a while. Long enough to get out of the system.

Or long enough for it not to matter. If there was an advantage to getting blasted to oblivion by a federal frigate, it was the fact that it would get her off the hook for having to explain to the Union ambassador how she'd lied to him and tricked him into running the federal blockade.

And, as Damian had noted to her after the group meeting, if a Union ambassador was killed by a Federal American ship, it could only help the cause.

So . . . silver lining?

"I'm still picking up energy readings. My guess is they've got their weapons on standby. I'm also reading some positional change, probably that shuttle launching."

"Okay, get ready, Griff. We've only got one chance at this." It seemed the federal officer was still buying her story, at least somewhat. She'd have preferred if he'd shut his weapons down completely, but that was too much to ask for. She'd fenced for years with the federal navy, and as much resentment as she'd built up from that time, she'd never have said they were anything but sharp and professional.

"All systems check, Sasha. We're as ready as we're going to get." A few seconds later, "That shuttle launch is confirmed. Estimate eight minutes to docking range."

"Andrei, are you strapped in?"

"Yes . . ." The ambassador was definitely too scared to exchange lengthy comments, and certainly to vent his rage on her. But he did manage to add, "Perhaps we should surrender . . ."

Sure, odds are they'd just hold you until the rebellion was over and then send you home. But even if I was okay with sacrificing myself so you could enjoy a plush captivity and eventual return home, I'm not sacrificing my crew. And no fed is stepping onto my ship.

So . . . sorry, my good ambassador, but you're stuck in this one with us.

She took a deep breath, her eyes fixed on the screen. The shuttle was heading toward *Vagabond*, the frigate not far behind. The closer she let *California* get, the more thrust it would take for the frigate to offset its vector and pursue *Vagabond*. But it also let the federal ship into firing range.

She was counting down in her head, trying to hold off the fear closing in on her. A miscalculation, even a bit of bad luck, could finish them all. Even letting her worries delay her actions a moment could be fatal.

"Now, Griff." The words burst out of her mouth, almost surprising her. She braced herself in her chair, knowing what was coming.

Daniels's hands moved over his controls, and a few seconds later, every surface in *Vagabond* rattled as the ship's engines fired with a ferocity they had never achieved before, pouring out a volume of thrust far in excess of their highest-rated maximums.

The g-forces slammed into Nerov, pushing her deep into the cushioning of her chair. There was pain, a feeling like every bone in her body was about to break under the terrible strain. But the breathing was the worst. For a few seconds, she felt as though she would suffocate, unable to force even the smallest gasps of air into her tormented lungs. But then she focused, pushing with all the strength she could muster, and slowly, the feeling of cool, fresh air infiltrated the primal fear caused by the lack of oxygen.

She turned her head so she could see the main display, not an easy task by any means. She could hear Griff grunting as he struggled to breathe, and Kutusov, as well. The ambassador had howled when the pressure first hit him, but one effect of barely being able to breathe was the inability to complain.

She could see flashes of light on the screen. The federal ship was reacting already, firing its lasers at *Vagabond*. She was concerned, but not overly so—at this point, a hit would be a true stroke of luck for her attacker. *Vagabond*'s move had been a surprise, and she'd included some evasive maneuvers into the thrust pattern when she'd programmed it into the AI. With any luck, her ship would be out of range in a few more seconds. Then she'd see how quickly the feds could react.

She tried to ignore the pain, but she was sure she'd at least dislocated her shoulder. An advantage of multiple sources of misery was the inability to focus solely on one. She could see from the dispositions on the display that her plan would work. *Vagabond* would get away. Jubilation was mitigated by an important condition: if, and this was a big *if*, the old ship could endure the insane thrust for another seven minutes. It was a long time, longer even than she'd ever run *Vagabond* at its normal full blast capability. It wasn't only the engines that could fail, but also the reactor, or even the structural frame of the ship. Some of those failures would be merciful, instantaneous destruction with no warning. Others, like a systems burnout that didn't destroy the ship, would lead to a longer and more agonizing end at the hands of the federal authorities.

But *Vagabond* endured, the engines blasting away, the reactor continuing to operate on a massive overload. The old vessel shook hard, and a few bits and pieces broke free and slammed into the walls. But the minutes went by, explosive decompression failed to appear, and the jump on the federals grew larger.

The frigate had now started its pursuit, blasting its own engines and aligning its vector to match *Vagabond*'s, but the smaller ship had gained a huge lead, not just on *California*, but the other federal ships now firing their engines to join the pursuit.

She watched, trying to keep her mind off the pain, the terrible feeling of near-asphyxiation. The jump point was getting closer. *California* had matched her course, and the faster warship was closing now. But they weren't going to get back into weapons range, not in time. Not unless *Vagabond*'s abused systems gave out.

"Griff . . ." She barely managed to get the sound out of her mouth.

"Here . . ." Her friend didn't sound any better than she did, but she believed in him. He had one job to do, one detail that would greatly increase the chances of escape. And she trusted him to see it done.

"Now," she managed to say, putting all the strength she had into the soft yell.

Daniels didn't answer, but he somehow moved his hand enough to the small button, and he pressed it. The display flashed brightly, and an instant later, *Vagabond* slipped into the strange alternate reality of intersystem travel. Then the ship emerged again into regular space, and the AI cut the thrust.

Nerov sucked in a deep breath, then another. Her lungs burned and her diaphragm was like electric fire each time oxygen went in and out, but at least her vision was clearing. She moved slowly to the side, and then she slammed herself back, shoving the dislocated shoulder back into place. The pain was astonishing, and despite her best efforts, she let out a loud grunt.

Then she unlatched her harness and stood up. Her legs were shaky, and to the best of her knowledge, there wasn't a square centimeter of her body that didn't hurt. But she was alive, and *Vagabond* was no longer in the Epsilon Eridani system. She'd left Haven, and the federal fleet, nine light-years behind.

"I demand to know just what is going on." Kutusov was fumbling to unlatch his own harness, without much success. To her surprise, he seemed to have come through the ordeal more or less unscathed.

She walked across the bridge, leaned down, and put her hands on the buckle, and unhooked it gently. "You are a true spacer, Andrei," she said, as sweetly as she could manage in the situation. "I am impressed." She paused for a moment, hovering close over him. She'd worn the pants he'd so liked, and a low-cut top she'd managed to find among her things. She didn't think she could flirt her way out of the fact that she'd lied to an ambassador, tricked him into taking a terrible risk . . . but she didn't think it would hurt, either. Especially since Kutusov had been pursuing her every chance he got for almost ten months now.

"Thank you, Sash . . ." The diplomat was taken in for a second, but then he glared at her. "You lied to me, didn't you? There is no stealth device? You tricked me so I would come on board while you made a desperate run past the federal blockade. We could have been killed!"

"I am sorry, Andrei. I had no choice. We need you so desperately." A pause. "I need you. You are the only chance we have." She was laying it on thick, and she could see it was having an effect. On some level she was amused that a man whose career was negotiating could be so easily manipulated, but that was a more complex line of thinking than her battered mind and body could manage at the moment.

"I understand your needs, but that does not excuse what you did. And what if the federals pursue us here?"

"I don't think that is very likely, Andrei. First, we dropped an explosive right before we jumped. Not much of a weapon, I'm afraid, but laced with some heavy elements. It will have left quite a dirty cloud of hard radiation, one sufficient to block the last-second vector change we made on the jump. It is very unlikely the federals will be able to determine where we went, Andrei, and even if they do, I doubt they would dare to follow us."

"And why is that?" His anger was still there, but she could see the intrigue and curiosity pushing it aside, at least somewhat.

"Because it would be an act of war, that is why. The heavy acceleration across the system wasn't the only chance we took, Andrei. We tried a very precise jump angle as well, and a long trip.

Welcome to the Algol system, Ambassador Kutusov. I'm sure the Union's largest colony will be able to welcome an official of your stature far more appropriately than we managed."

She leaned forward, pausing for a moment when she realized he was staring at her. Nerov knew she was an attractive woman, but she'd always been more comfortable utilizing a cold pistol in her hand rather than her well-placed and displayed curves. But she was a pragmatist, and she figured holding a gun to Kutusov's head probably wasn't the way to get him to forgive her. And without his goodwill, the entire operation was pointless.

"You can flirt with me all you want, but it doesn't change what you did. We could have been killed."

"I know, Andrei," she said, leaning closer to him and putting her hand on his cheek. "But I also knew you were a courageous man. What other ambassador of your rank would willingly put himself in the middle of a revolution?" She was working it hard. But Kutusov knew he was safe now, and that would go a long way toward defusing his anger. And she was giving him the chance to return home and present himself in just the way she'd described. A hero back from a war zone. At the very least, it was the stuff of years of stories to tell the other diplomats at their exclusive clubs. *He'll even get to bed me in the retellings, no doubt,* she thought with a grin.

"I hope we can still count on your support. After all, you saw yourself that the rebellion is credible, that General Ward and the army are perfectly capable of defeating the federal forces."

"We will see, Sasha." But she could tell from his tone his support was still there. "First, let's contact system control and make sure no Union ships come swarming up after us. I've had quite enough of *that* for one day."

CHAPTER 38

"Thank you, Minister Karenski. It has been a pleasure meeting you and your esteemed colleagues." Nerov smiled at the official she knew was the third or fourth most powerful individual in the Union. The last weeks had been a whirlwind of introductions and functions, ones that had her head spinning. She'd seen herself as Ambassador Kutusov's transportation, but she hadn't even considered her role as the representative of Haven's new government, not until the Union leadership started treating her as exactly that.

"It was my pleasure, Ambassador Nerov. Your stories of your people's exploits against the American federals have been wondrous to hear. I only wish I could have accompanied Ambassador Kutusov and witnessed such glory for myself."

"You would love Haven, Minister, and if we do become allies, I would urge you to visit one day. I can assure you a planetwide welcome of epic proportions." *That's the fourth time you've mentioned alliances or military intervention. Andrei told you not to push too hard.* "Of course, for now, I will settle for the chance to see this lovely city. I never realized so much of the original architecture of Moscow was re-created in the rebuilding. It is truly magnificent."

"Thank you, Ambassador. I am happy that our fair city pleases you."

There he goes again with the "ambassador." Nerov was uncomfortable. She wasn't an ambassador—at least, she had no kinds of credentials, not even the type a government hiding in the woods could bestow. Not that she cared about any of that. Such things were of little interest to her and generated even less respect. She rated people on their abilities, not on what documents and government pronouncements said. But the title still made her quiver a little. And the full-length dress she wore, which Karenski had given her and which she suspected had cost more than she'd grossed on some smuggling runs, was driving her crazy. She missed her leathers and the holstered pistol that had come to feel like part of her leg. And she didn't want to get started on the bewildering collection of undergarments the dress required to . . . have the desired effect.

She had been uneasy, edgy, virtually every second since she'd arrived. She wasn't a diplomat. Her past was . . . unsavory, and her profession in recent years had seen her spend far more time in run-down spacer's districts than upper-class salons. Hell—in the first part of the rebellion, she'd spent a good deal of time in a sewer. She wondered if Karenski had ever seen a *picture* of a sewer.

She was, quite decidedly, out of her element.

Sure, she was good in a fight, but the halls of government and international relations made her skin crawl. For one thing, she wasn't allowed to punch a single person she saw. She'd found herself longing for another honest flight past the federal blockade, but she knew this was where Haven needed her. And despite her well-practiced image as a cold-blooded mercenary, she'd had to admit to herself, she'd found a home on that far-flung planet, complete with a roster of friends she'd hate to see on the gallows . . . and one or two dirtbags she just might like to watch gasping for their last breaths. Whatever she could do to save Haven, she had to do. Even if that was becoming a diplomat.

"So, Minister, I was told there was a special function this evening, but I'm afraid no one gave me any details."

"That was an oversight, I assure you. This is a reception to welcome the diplomatic delegation from the Hegemony." Karenski looked around the room and then continued, his voice hushed. "I will tell you, Ambassador, that the victory in the field of your arms has been very persuasive. A majority of the Council is prepared to vote in favor of recognition . . ." He paused for a few seconds. ". . . with one proviso. We can only risk such provocation if the Hegemony is willing to join us in a simultaneous declaration, and a plan to support your republic and guarantee your independence."

Nerov tried to hide her surprise. It had seemed daunting enough to convince one government to intervene, but two? She'd made enough effort to bring Kutusov back to her side, and she'd gone through a lifetime of charm dealing with Union functionaries. The idea of starting all over with a new batch was about the worst thing she could imagine.

Just as she was about to protest, a voice called out, "Introducing His Excellency, Chancellor Deng Wu, and the esteemed delegation from the Asian Hegemony."

Her head snapped around toward the massive double doors as the announcer continued, reciting a seemingly endless series of designations and titles.

A small group stepped into the room, four men and three women. They were all Asian in heritage, as were most of the people in the Hegemony, and although they clearly had different ethnic ancestry, they all wore the colorful silk attire that dominated the formal wear of that massive nation. All except one, a woman, who wore a western-style suit. Nerov's eyes focused on the woman, who'd been in the rear rank at first. Now she could see the woman wasn't Asian like the others.

That's strange. She almost looks like . . .

Her mind froze. *No, that's not funny.* For an instant, she'd thought the woman was Asha Stanton, the former federal observer. The woman who'd been in charge of the federal forces during the

initial months of the rebellion. The woman who'd allowed Robert
Semmes to build concentration camps, to punish rebel soldiers by
arresting their families and locking them up in deplorable conditions where many of them died. But that wasn't possible. There was
no way Stanton would be with a Hegemony delegation.

"Captain Nerov," the woman said, stepping away from the Hegemony group and walking toward her. "I was told you were here,
but I couldn't really believe it until I saw it with my own eyes. You
are to be commended for getting through the federal blockade.
That couldn't have been easy."

Nerov felt her stomach heave, and she barely held back the bile
that threatened to empty from her stomach. It *was* Stanton. She
didn't know how or why, but her thought went immediately to federal treachery. Had the feds gotten to the Hegemony? Was her mission already hopeless?

Her hand moved down to her side, to the place her pistol usually
stayed. But there was nothing but the soft material of her dress. *Not
that I could kill her here anyway*—there were guards everywhere,
and shooting a guest of the Hegemony diplomats was not the best
way to achieve a desirable outcome. Still, she figured it would have
been about fifty-fifty if the gun had been there. And she didn't have
a doubt she could have put a nice wide hole in Stanton's head before the guards took her down.

Okay, starting over wasn't the worst thing she could imagine.
This was.

"You? It's not possible. Life has its twists and turns, but this is ridiculous." Nerov looked over at Stanton, feeling as stunned as she had
earlier, in the reception hall. She'd been speechless when she'd
first seen the former federal observer, typical fedspeak for military
governor, and then the dam broke and she asked a stream of questions in rapid succession. Stanton had stopped her and suggested
the two of them find someplace more out of the way to talk, and

as unwelcome as anything from the federal official's mouth might have been, she had to agree on that count. "Next thing, Everett Wells is going to walk through the door, and we can all have a reunion."

"Everett is dead, Captain Nerov." Stanton's tone was sorrowful. "He was caught by the federal authorities trying to help me enlist Hegemony aid for your rebellion."

Nerov tried to maintain her poker face as her thoughts reeled. "Dead?" She felt a wave of regret. She didn't think much of *any* feds, but she had to admit, Wells had been a decent man. A bit of a fool, perhaps, but someone she believed actually tried to do what he thought was right. That was something that could be said about an infinitesimal minority of people in Nerov's worldview.

"Yes, unfortunately. He killed himself in captivity . . . to avoid torture. And the likelihood that he would break and alert the federal authorities about our efforts."

Nerov shook her head. "I am sorry to hear that." The news of Wells's death was distracting, and it blunted some of the initial hostility she'd felt toward Stanton.

Then, her mind just registering what Stanton had said: "Trying to get the Hegemony to aid Haven?"

"Yes, Captain, though I know that may be difficult for you to accept. But that's exactly why I'm here at all. We were in the process of attempting to secure the Hegemony's acknowledgment of the declared republic and its intervention in the conflict. As I still am doing now. Everett and I both realized Alpha-2 . . . Haven . . . had no real chance to win, not without foreign recognition and support. So we utilized my family's connections to gain access to the Hegemony government. We have long had business dealings there, except, of course, during the years of the war."

Nerov's head was spinning again. "Correct me if I'm wrong, but a year ago you were trying to defeat that very rebellion, were you not?" Her anger and dislike for Stanton were returning. "You are a federal official, a cog in that horrible machine. You expect me to believe we are somehow allies now?"

"Captain, let me be blunt. We are not friends. We do not share political philosophies. As far as I'm concerned, your little planet, whether you call it Alpha-2, Haven, or paradise itself, is utterly irrelevant. I did not choose my assignment there, and I did not wish to be there. The relative success of your rebellion cost me dearly in career prospects, not to mention the risks I've been compelled to take to redeem my position. But we share an enemy. Robert Semmes is evil to the core, and he is as well connected politically as it is possible to be. He will crush your rebellion if he can, and he will exact a terrible toll on the people of your world. After that, he will return to Earth a hero and come after me for his personal revenge. So you don't have to like me, and I don't have to like you, but fate's twisted ways have put us on the same side, in a manner of speaking."

Nerov wanted to argue . . . except everything Stanton said made sense. She'd come to Earth ready to do whatever she could to save Haven, but in all her wildest, most nightmarish imaginings, this eventuality had never occurred to her. "So, what do you propose we do?"

"Well, I have made excellent progress with the Hegemony Inner Circle, and from what I have heard, you have the Union officials intrigued. As I see it, both powers are leaning toward recognition, but neither will move without the other. I am not surprised that Damian Ward was able to secure a victory against Semmes. It is not taking much of a stretch to say the better man won there. But we both know that triumph will be short-lived unless we can cut off the flow of reinforcements and supplies to the planet. And to do that, we will need not only recognition, but full-scale military operations. A game of chicken, Captain Nerov, if you are familiar with the concept. If we can get the combined Union and Hegemony fleets to Epsilon Eridani—perhaps under the guise of a trade convoy—they will outnumber the federal forces there by a considerable margin, and if we can maintain some level of secrecy, we can prevent the federals from transferring more naval units. The forces on site will be compelled to withdraw, and the senate will have to face a choice of letting Alpha-2 go or fighting an all-out battle with both opposing superpowers."

"What will they do? You know better than I would."

"Indeed, that is true, but I'm afraid I don't honestly know—it's a bit of a gamble. Alistair Semmes may try to force a confrontation to save his son from another humiliating defeat, but even a man of his ability and influence has limits to his power. The cost of fighting on Alpha-2 has become critical. The economy was just beginning to improve since the end of the last interstellar war, but now it has fallen into a deep recession. A renewal of hostilities with the Union and the Hegemony would almost certainly cause a full-scale panic and depression."

"So you're saying we'll either get the federals to back down . . . or we'll start another full-scale war?"

"I never said the stakes were low, Captain. But it's the only bet that offers your world a real chance at independence." A pause. "So, are you with me?"

Nerov nodded, almost without thinking about it. Actually, thinking too much about the current situation was about the last thing she wanted to do. "Yes, but we still have to get the Union and Hegemony to commit. I know they are interested, but it's a gamble for them, too. What's in it for them? Yes, if the federals back down, they will be able to weaken and humiliate their enemy, but it would be at a significant cost in mobilization and deployment expenses. I can't imagine the outlook for their own economies is any better than Federal America's."

"You understand the situation better than you think, Captain." Another pause. "There is something else we can do, a way to sweeten things for our potential benefactors."

Nerov stared at Stanton, just knowing she wasn't going to like what she was about to hear. "Go on . . ."

"If you were to offer certain concessions—rights to imports and exports of various types—it just might be enough to tilt things in favor of action. I wasn't kidding about the Union and Hegemony fleets coming in the form of a trade convoy. Money is truly the universal diplomatic language. Of course, any deals would be secret, withheld from the federal authorities until after they've withdrawn from the planet, but there'd be ships ready to take advantage of that partnership right off the bat. If anything, it would be a further benefit to Haven—supplies and such at hand to start the rebuild and all that."

Nerov didn't quite like how she seemed to hand-wave away the idea of "the rebuild and all that," but she caught the basic gist of the plan. There was still one problem, though.

"I don't know what you think I can do about that. I'm not a member of the Provisional Congress, and I have no authority to conduct trade negotiations."

"You are Haven's representative to the Union, are you not?"

"No . . . I mean, I guess. I have no official mandate. My purpose was to get Ambassador Kutusov back here, that's all."

"But the Union has treated you as an ambassador, haven't they?"

"Yes."

"So why are you making this more complicated than it has to be? Make whatever deal you have to. You can sell it to the Havenites later."

Nerov was going to argue again, but she stopped herself. She didn't know if it was being around so many people who lied constantly for a living, but telling the truth, about her authority, about trade deals, about anything, just didn't seem so important. Not compared to gaining the aid her people needed.

She laughed. "You're a pretty good diplomat yourself. Very well,

I will do it. Think of what would be the most attractive to offer, and we will see if we can get this done. Every day and week that goes by is that much longer for the feds to recover from their defeat and resume the offensive."

"Excellent." Stanton hesitated, an uncomfortable look on her face. "I have one other thing to ask of you, Captain Nerov. A personal favor."

Nerov felt a wave of anger. She was already hating herself for working with Stanton, and she wasn't of a mind for doing favors. "What?" she asked curtly.

"There is someone I'd like to find on Haven. She may be lost, or she may be in trouble. I really don't know. But I would like to help her."

Nerov looked at Stanton. Whatever she'd expected the federal to ask of her, this was definitely not it. "Who?"

"Violetta Wells."

Nerov was shocked again. "Governor Wells's daughter?"

"Yes, I . . . I promised Everett I would do all I could to make sure she was safe. Robert Semmes would . . . well, it would be bad if he found her. He is a vengeful man, and he blames Everett and me for what happened last year."

"Why do you care? Wells is dead. What does it matter what happens to his daughter?"

"It just does . . . to me. Everett Wells killed himself to keep from telling the federal investigators about me. In return, I promised to do what I could to find his daughter. Do you know where she is? I will give you some currency for her, and if she wishes to return to Earth, I will arrange transport as soon as the blockade is over."

Nerov almost laughed. She considered lying, not telling Stanton anything, but her normally suspicious instinct told her Stanton was genuinely concerned. "She is fine, or at least she was when I left. She is part of the rebel army. Rather, she is part of General Ward's staff. My guess is, she is as safe as anyone on Haven can be now, unless, of course, the army is defeated and destroyed before we are able to arrange aid."

Stanton sighed with relief, and Nerov's impression confirmed what she'd thought. Stanton's interest in the girl was real.

"You think I'm a monster, that it's not possible for me to be concerned about someone for selfless reasons. But Everett Wells did what he promised, and I intend to do the same." She hesitated, and then she added, "Thank you. For telling me. We don't like each other, that much is clear, but that doesn't mean we can't work together, and treat each other with some level of respect."

Nerov had the urge to argue, to tell Stanton eight different ways to reproduce with herself, but she realized her new ally was correct.

She extended her hand. "You're right. It seems fate has thrust us together, on the same side this time."

Stanton reached out and grabbed Nerov's hand, shaking it firmly. "Shall we go back and see to our respective contacts? The Hegemony is inclined to do as I ask, but they will not act alone . . . and I'd be surprised if you didn't find yourself in a similar situation with the Union. Why don't we see what we can do about that?"

CHAPTER 39

Andrei Kutusov stood on the flag bridge of the battlecruiser *Kirov*, Sasha Nerov right at his side, both staring at the main display. *Vagabond* was docked with *Kirov*, Nerov's vessel a small bump off the side of the Union's massive flagship. She'd intended to fly back into the system in her own ship, but the Union authorities had insisted their sole link to Haven's government, and their new ally, travel in something better protected than a rickety old free trader. Nerov had a faith in her vessel she knew was hard for others to understand, but she'd adapted well enough to her new role as a diplomat to know when she had to humor her new friends.

"We'll soon know if negotiation or conflict will resolve this situation, Ambassador."

She had been on a first-name basis with Kutusov for some time, but she'd gotten the impression that the Russian enjoyed calling her "ambassador," even though he knew full well she had no such official designation. Still, she'd negotiated the entire treaty between the powers, agreed to a wide array of trade deals with both the Union and the Hegemony, and signed the documents on behalf of the Haven Republic. She was astonished at just how far she'd overstepped her authority, but then she figured those who'd sent her were just rebels. *If Cal Jacen can call himself a senator, then I can call myself an ambassador.*

"Yes, Andrei." That's what had her concerned this entire trip. She didn't know what had happened in Haven in the weeks she'd been gone, or what would happen in the space around the planet. The combined Union and Hegemony fleets should be enough to overwhelm the federal forces in the system. But even if the blockading ships withdrew, that didn't mean the feds wouldn't be back. If the senate decided to fight to the end for Haven, they could assemble a fleet capable of matching the forces of their enemies. Haven's rebellion had cast a shadow across the entirety of human-occupied space. Federal America had a choice now: let its wayward colony go . . . or cast all of mankind into another full-scale war.

The potential scope of what she'd helped to bring into being was just coming into focus, and she wondered if Haven's victory was worth the risk of millions of deaths in a war that could quickly spread out of control.

"Ambassador Kutusov, I have Admiral Taggart on the main comm line." Admiral Bellakov's voice was tight, hard. It was clear the officer was ready for battle, if that was how the situation developed.

Kutusov glanced at Nerov and nodded. "It's time." He'd been placed in charge of negotiating with the federal forces in the system. Nerov knew the ambassador had a difficult choice himself to make. If he let the federals go without a fight and they reneged on any agreements, he would have sacrificed the chance to inflict enough damage to affect the outcome of a new war. But if he refused, if he sent Bellakov's forces into battle, he would lose any chance to end the conflict without galactic bloodshed.

"Put him on the main channel, Admiral." There was no point in secrecy, not now. The spacers of the fleet would know soon enough if his diplomacy succeeded or not.

"Admiral Taggart, I am Andrei Kutusov, representative of the

Eurasian Union. I am authorized to treat with you on the current situation in an effort to avoid conflict between our respective nations."

"Ambassador Kutusov, there is no need to treat on any matters. Your forces have entered the space of Federal America without permission or authorization. You have violated the terms of the recent treaty between our nations, and you have committed an act of war. I insist that your forces withdraw at once. If you do, I will make every effort to encourage the senate to overlook the violation and maintain the peace we have enjoyed for the last five years."

"Well spoken, Admiral, but I'm afraid we disagree on the details of the situation. This space belongs to the Republic of Haven, which, per official proclamations being delivered even now to the senate on Earth, is now officially allied to both the Union and the Hegemony. This combined expeditionary force under the command of Admiral Bellakov has been dispatched to provide aid and support to the Republic."

The line was silent. Nerov exchanged glances with Kutusov. She knew the response that was taking so long would be the first hint as to how the situation would progress. Taggart's forces were at a disadvantage, but from what she'd heard of Federal America's admiral, that wouldn't stop him from fighting.

"I must categorically dispute your assertions, Ambassador. The planet Alpha-2 and the Epsilon Eridani system belong to Federal America, and the purely internal disturbance now in effect is of no concern to the Union or the Hegemony. I repeat my demand that you withdraw from the system at once."

Nerov considered herself a good negotiator, hardened by years of bargaining with some of the lowest elements of human society. But Taggart's tone was unreadable, at least over the comm. Her mind bounced back and forth between expectations that the federal officer was ready to fight, and that he would negotiate a settlement of some kind. She hoped Kutusov's experience would give him a better read, but a quick look at the diplomat's face told her he had no idea, either.

Kutusov walked over to the communications panel, gesturing for the officer there to cut the line. "Admiral, bring the fleet to battle stations."

Nerov stood and stared, impressed at the coolness in his voice. She'd grown to like the ambassador, his constant flirtation and his ultimate delivery of the support she'd sought combining to create some level of true affection. But she'd considered him a little effete, too focused on societal niceties for her tastes. Now she saw an iron firmness that had been hidden before, and her respect for the Russian grew. She didn't know if he'd be able to stare down Taggart, but he seemed ready to push things as far as he had to.

The bridge was quiet, the tension heavy in the air. Kutusov stood there, waiting.

"Admiral, the federal fleet has gone to full alert. We're picking up thrust readings. It appears they are shaking into a battle formation."

"Very well," Bellakov replied. Then he turned toward Kutusov. "Do we engage, Ambassador?"

Kutusov paused for a moment. Then he answered, "Arm all weapons. Prepare for battle. But you are not to open fire without my permission."

Nerov could see Kutusov was still banking on Taggart giving in. She didn't know what she expected, but she'd never seen time pass more slowly.

"All ships ready for battle, Ambassador."

"Very well, Admiral." Kutusov stood where he was, staring at the comm unit.

Darryl Taggart sat in his command chair, his eyes moving from one of his people to the next. The images he saw were all the same, the tension almost visible in the air around them.

Taggart felt trapped. The military situation was hopeless. The Union and Hegemony forces had too large an advantage, in both numbers and position. He could try to withdraw, but the newly arrived fleet was between his ships and the main transit point. If they decided to attack while his task force was preparing to jump, he could lose half his ships. *Hell, I could lose them all . . .*

Better to fight in that case, and at least cause some damage to the enemy. There was little doubt a major battle at Epsilon Eridani would be the start of a new war, and the loss of his task force would severely weaken the federal fleet. Whatever damage he could inflict on the enemy here would be crucial.

Fighting here would be foolish, but he wasn't sure he had a choice. He considered the struggle for Alpha-2 to be pointless, the total cost of crushing the rebellion almost certain to exceed the economic value of a valuable, but sure to be devastated, colony. He would have yielded, given the colonists the freedom they so desperately seemed to desire, but he didn't have the authority to negotiate. Neither did he have permission to engage Union and Hegemony vessels, to risk starting a full-scale war.

Slowly, reluctantly, he realized he was going to have to do just one of those things, that yielding or fighting and risking the start of a new war were his only choices. And that either of them could effectively be the opening line in his court-martial.

He hated the idea of backing down, of retreating and leaving the ground troops stranded on the planet. It could be months before the federal high command managed to get enough forces to the system to challenge the combined Union and Hegemony fleet, and the army down there would be cut off from supplies and support that whole time. And if that allied fleet included ground troops, there were greater concerns. Losing Alpha-2 was bad enough, but allowing it to fall into enemy hands . . . that was inconceivable.

Perhaps there was room for a settlement here. The Union and

Hegemony had the advantage at the moment, but he could imagine they wanted total war no more than Federal America.

"Get me Ambassador Kutusov again." Taggart didn't like blinking, calling back the man who'd cut the line, but he wasn't going to let his pride kill hundreds of his spacers and the troops on the ground. And he had a deal to cut.

"I have the ambassador, Admiral." The communications officer was trying to hide the tension in her voice, but not very well.

"Ambassador . . ."

"Yes, Admiral?"

Taggart didn't think much of diplomats in general, but he was impressed with Kutusov. He had tried to read the ambassador's earlier words, to determine where serious threats ended and clever bluffing began, but he couldn't get a feel.

"Any agreement to withdraw would be contingent upon two stipulations. First, your fleet must take position at the perimeter of the system, and must not approach the planet, nor take any actions toward landing any troops. Second, once your forces have complied with condition one, my fleet will be given time to withdraw the ground forces on Alpha-2." Taggart hoped he'd convinced Kutusov that he'd just drawn the line he wouldn't cross, because he was ready to live or die with his conditions. He *could not* allow enemy forces to land on the planet, and he *would not* leave the troops down there behind, cut off and ultimately at the mercy of victorious rebels.

"That is not possible, Admiral. You overstate your position. It would take too long to evacuate, and while I appreciate your efforts to stall and buy time until more federal forces can arrive, I cannot allow it. Your forces must withdraw at once."

Taggart stood up, looking around the bridge before he answered. Kutusov had conducted himself brilliantly, but the admiral finally thought he'd caught a hint of weakness in the diplomat's voice. Kutusov was trying to sound tough, but there was something else there. At least some of what he'd just said was bluff. It was time to match bluff with bluff.

"Prepare to engage the enemy," he said, turning toward his comm officer. "All ships are to open fire as soon as the approaching ships come into range." It *was* a bluff. *Maybe.* He honestly wasn't sure if he'd really allow his vessels to start shooting, but he'd left the comm to Kutusov open intentionally.

He said nothing further to the Union diplomat, nodding to the comm officer as he stood in the center of the bridge. He wondered if Kutusov would give in, and if not, he tried to decide whether he would back down or follow through. The tension was tight throughout his body, and he walked across the bridge, too wired to sit.

"Very well, Admiral." Taggart felt relief, as he realized his opponent was now the one to blink, at least to an extent. "You may load your ground forces, but you must conduct your operation in a mutually agreed-upon manner, and you must complete it in no more than three Earth days' time. Once you have loaded your ground forces, your ships will withdraw to the transit point, and our forces will leave the system together—minus our trade delegation, of course."

"Three days isn't enough, Ambassador. I will need at least a week to finish the withdrawal operations, perhaps ten days."

"Well, you have three, Admiral Taggart. You pushed hard, and I have yielded to your requests, but I have now gone as far as I will. As far as I can. Three days, Admiral."

Taggart was far from sure he could complete the withdrawal in such a short time. But now his gut was telling him Kutusov was not lying about the line he'd just drawn in the sand. Perhaps more important, he knew if he had been in the Russian's position, he would draw the same line. Allowing a longer time simply left too much room for trickery, too much time for federal reserves to arrive . . . or for that monster Semmes to do something truly stupid.

"Very well, Ambassador. I cannot guarantee that the senate will

ratify Alpha-2's secession from Federal America, but I will withdraw the military forces currently engaged."

"Then we have a deal, Admiral Taggart. As I noted, our ambassador to Federal America is about to deliver a proposal to your
senate, one that will ensure continued peace between our powers."

"If you'll excuse me, Ambassador, our parameters give me little
time to waste. May I suggest that we both cancel the red alerts in
effect in our fleets?"

"By all means, Admiral." Kutusov could hear Taggart speaking
to someone else. A few minutes later, he could see the scanners
confirming that the Union and Hegemony ships had powered
down their weapons systems. "There, Admiral, an act of good faith
on our part that I trust you will emulate."

Taggart turned toward the comm station. "All ships are to move
to status yellow. All weapons system are to disengage."

There was a moment of silence. Then Kutusov's voice resumed
on the comm. "Very good, Admiral. We have done humankind a
service here today, both of us. Avoiding war is always a worthy goal.
I feel we have saved the lives of many thousands, perhaps millions.
I thank you for your reason and your wisdom."

"And yours, Ambassador." Taggart was glad at the prospect—
far from certain yet—of avoiding war, but he couldn't be quite as
positive about it as his Union counterpart. The enemy had scored
a great victory, a humiliation and weakening of their adversary. He
could feel good about saving the troops on the ground, about side-
stepping the destructive conflict that could so easily have occurred,
but he was still presiding over a defeat. Alpha-2 would be the first
Earth colony to break away from its parent government, and the
loss of the valuable world would weaken Federal America's edge in
the space race.

Too, while Kutusov had scored a great victory, Taggart knew
he'd be lucky to avoid a quick and involuntary retirement himself, if
not outright court-martial. Robert Semmes was a miserable son of a

bitch, but the maggot knew all about self-preservation, and Taggart was sure his colleague would do everything to push the blame for failure onto anyone else. He might even get away with it.

He shook his head, wondering what foul fortune had put him in command of this cursed expedition. But it didn't matter. He was where he was, and he knew what he had to do.

"Get me General Semmes, Lieutenant." He suspected dealing with the military governor would be far more unpleasant than his words with Kutusov.

CHAPTER 40

"No, Admiral Taggart. Need I remind you that you are subject to *my* command while in this system? This army will not withdraw from Alpha-2, and you will not suffer the presence of enemy warships, much less acquiesce to their demands. Prepare your fleet for battle, Admiral, and take position to defend the planet."

Robert Semmes's heart was pounding so hard he could feel it in his pain-wracked head. He was furious, at Taggart, at his father for not providing more troops and support, at Colonel Granz for falling into the rebels' trap and getting the army badly chopped up. But mostly, though he wouldn't admit it to himself, he was scared. He was afraid of losing the war, of his father giving up on him, casting him from the family. Alistair Semmes was a hard man, one who believed in a level of family loyalty, but also one who lacked the emotional weaknesses that would lead a man to risk everything for the love of a son. The senator would cut him loose at some point, there was no question in his mind about that. And sitting in the capital with the rebel forces camped outside, growing every day as hundreds of volunteers streamed in to join the colors, had to push things close to that mark. Especially with the Union and Hegemony involved now. Semmes didn't understand politics like his father and brothers, but he knew enough to realize the family would lose support for continuing the fight against the rebels if the cost threatened to be full-scale conflict with the other powers.

He felt another wave of fury, this time at Taggart for allowing the rebels to get messengers back to Earth. *Can't I rely on that fool for anything?*

Taggart hadn't responded. Semmes put his hand on his headset. "Admiral, do you hear me?"

"I hear you, General. What you order is hopeless. If I renege on the agreement with the Union ambassador, their fleet will attack mine, and destroy it. They will then use the opportunity to land an expeditionary force." A pause. "If we allow the enemy to get boots on the ground, we will never get them off of Alpha-2. At least if we withdraw, the prospect is less dire, a single independent planet, one with no off-world military capability."

"You make surrender seem so appealing, Admiral. But it is out of the question."

"General, I will not renege on the agreement with the Union and Hegemony forces."

"You will do as I command, Admiral."

"No, sir. I will not."

Semmes's hands balled up into fists, and he glared across the room. "You are relieved of command, Admiral Taggart. You will turn control of the fleet to Captain Eurace."

"Negative, General. I will not. Captain Eurace is with me. All the senior captains are with me. If you insist on ordering us to violate the agreement and engage the enemy fleet, there can only be one result, the destruction of all federal forces in the system, and the occupation of Alpha-2 by Union and Hegemony forces. Such a course of action would be disastrous for Federal America, and as such, I will refuse to follow it, as will the other senior officers of the fleet."

Semmes's anger was hot like a raging sun, but he just stood silent, not knowing what to say. He wanted Taggart dead, and he swore he'd see the mutinous officer—*officers*—stand before a firing squad. But he didn't know what to do now. Without the fleet, his forces were cut off from resupply. Worse, if the traitorous admiral pulled his forces away from the planet, he'd be exposed to enemy invasion. He'd watched as Ward's rebel army had grown, but he'd been well aware that, even after the defeat at Dover, the federal forces, once resupplied and reorganized, could still defeat their enemies. Most of the new strength that had flocked to Ward's colors was untrained and raw. And they had to be running low on weapons themselves. But without the fleet . . .

"General Semmes, I have agreed to have all ground forces evacuated within seventy-two Earth hours. That leaves little time to waste. We must begin as soon as possible."

"There will be no evacuation."

"General . . ."

"No, Admiral. You may be a coward, too afraid of the enemy to do his duty, but this army will not withdraw. We will not shirk our duty as you have done."

"General, if you don't withdraw, you're inviting the enemy to land ground forces. You will be facing Union and Hegemony troops as well as the rebels. There is no chance to prevail, and your action will provide the pretext for the Union and Hegemony to land."

"You are a gutless traitor, Admiral, who will face execution for your crimes. I understand my duty, and I will see it done. Whatever the cost."

"General . . ."

Semmes just stood there, silent.

"General, you have to order the evacuation. I have shuttles ready to launch in ten minutes."

Nothing.

"General . . ."

"Admiral, I will order the ground defenses to engage and shoot down any shuttles you launch. This army will not retreat. We are going to crush this rebellion and reconquer all of Alpha-2. And when we do, you will face cold accountability for your crimes."

Semmes cut the line. He had no time for traitors. He, at least, was loyal. He would do his duty.

He told himself it was courage driving his decision, loyalty. But deep down, some part of him knew it was fear, and in the background, a shadow looking over his thoughts, there was Alistair Semmes, driving a terror that outmatched even that caused by his enemies.

"Luci, get your people ready. We don't have a lot of time, and we've got to give this our best shot." Damian stood in his headquarters, an actual building for the first time since his forces had been driven from Landfall. The city was still in federal hands, but his army had occupied some of the outer suburbs and, along with some other advantages, that had brought with it the availability of actual permanent structures.

"We'll be ready, General. We'll have to go in at night. It's the only way we've got a chance to get past their defenses." Morgan's voice was grim, the same as Damian's. Somber tones for a wild gamble—he understood how she felt. The attack was hastily organized and, while not exactly hopeless, not too far from it, either.

It had all started less than six hours before, when Damian had received an unexpected communication from none other than Admiral Taggart, the commander of the federal fleet. Damian had suspected some kind of deceit at first, but as the admiral explained the situation, it all began to make sense. Sasha Nerov and Ambassador Kutusov had done it, somehow. They'd made it to Earth and returned with aid from both the Union *and* the Hegemony.

Damian had felt a surge of excitement at the news, but that soon faded as Taggart continued. The federal admiral had been clear. While he couldn't promise what the senate would do, he was ready to withdraw the federal land forces immediately and to leave the system along with the Union and Hegemony fleets. There was only one problem:

"I've been told in no uncertain terms by Kutusov," Taggart said, "that failure to remove troops would mean Union and Hegemony troops coming to the aid of their Havenite allies."

Which all translated to something Ward had always feared: trading one colonial master for another.

"We'll use night as much as we can, Luci, but remember how effective the federals' infrareds and scanner suites are. Don't over-estimate the cover you'll have, and don't forget, you'll have a lot of inexperienced troops with you."

"Sir, about that . . ."

"I know what you're going to say, Luci, but forget that right now. You know as well as I do how many of our veterans we lost in our *victory*. There just aren't enough of them. Jamie's barely got eighty of his armored troopers battle-ready, and you're at, what? Forty percent?"

"I know, but those colonists are going to get massacred, sir."

Damian nodded, an involuntary response that slipped out. His army had swelled to massive proportions, almost twenty thousand Havenites flocking to the colors in the weeks after the victory at Dover. He'd welcomed them all, despite a hint of disrespect for those who'd come only after the army had won a fight, but he hadn't expected to let any of them near a battle for weeks, if not months. Now there was no choice. If his people couldn't drive the federals out of the city and compel them to withdraw, his new "allies" would land. That would be useful in defeating the federals, but it was certainly trouble down the line. Not only would the other powers be reluctant to leave, there was no chance the senate would agree to Haven's independence if they believed it would fall under the control of its enemies.

"We need the numbers, Luci."

"General?" Patrick Killian stuck his head through the door.

"Yes, Pat . . . I called you to discuss the assault. I'd like you to command the force on . . ."

"Sir . . . excuse me, but I have something I want to say." He looked up at Morgan, then back to Damian, as if deciding the other colonel was trustworthy enough to remain in the room.

"What is it?"

"I think I have an option, one besides this attack. We all know we don't have much chance of taking Landfall in a frontal assault."

"What choice do we have, Pat? We can't allow the Union and Hegemony troops to land. That's a Trojan horse."

"I know, sir, but I don't think our problem in Landfall is the federal troops, nor even most of their officers. Taggart is well respected. I don't think most army officers would refuse his commands or his suggestions." He paused, and when he continued, his voice was darker, filled with anger. "It's Semmes, General. Semmes is the problem. That little shit doesn't want to go home in failure again, crawling before his daddy with his tail between his legs."

"That's probably true, Pat, but I don't see what it changes. Semmes has got Peacekeepers in there, and other security units. If you're expecting Colonel Granz to mount some kind of coup or something . . ."

"No, sir. Granz couldn't manage that. Not while Semmes is alive."

"What, exactly, is it you're proposing?"

"Making Semmes dead."

"That's a pleasant thought, but he's in there, surrounded by an army . . . which is why we're about to attack that army."

"It doesn't take an army to kill a man, General."

"It does when a man's got an army all around him."

"No, sir. There's another way."

Damian looked over at Killian, suddenly understanding what the ranger was proposing. "Patrick, there's no way. You'd have to get into the city, past their pickets, and then you'd have to make your way to headquarters. There's no way," he said again. "It's a million-to-one chance."

"I figured you thought better of me, General. I know my way around Landfall, and I'm not just talking about the main streets, sir."

"It's no lack of confidence, Patrick. But there's a good chance I'd be sending you to your death. Even if you managed to pull it off, how would you escape? Colonel Granz might secretly thank you for ridding him of Semmes, but he couldn't exactly let an assassin walk out the door now, could he?"

"First off, you wouldn't be sending me—I'm volunteering. And besides, I'm willing to take the risk, sir. If I succeed, how many soldiers will I save? Two thousand? Five thousand? You know what's going to happen if you send these green troopers into the city. The streets will flow with blood, and there's a damned good chance you'll just end up back where you started, Semmes still asleep in his bed in *our* city and those Union and Hegemony troops coming onto *our* planet."

"But, Patrick . . ."

"Damian . . . you know my past. You know I owe this to Semmes. I'd do this no matter what. I'd take any chance, even die if I have to, but at least now I also have the chance to save thousands of our soldiers." He stared at Damian, fingering the knife hanging from his belt. "You know I can pull this off, Damian."

Damian was far from sure his friend could "pull it off," but he also knew there were few men he thought had a better chance. And friend or no, he couldn't argue with the rationale of risking one man instead of thousands. If it failed, he could always then lead the assault tomorrow.

"Okay, Patrick. Do it. Take whatever you need, but you've got to go right after nightfall . . . because if you don't get it done by, say, two hours before dawn, I have to send the attack in."

"I understand, sir."

"Do you want to take some troopers with you? At least a hand-picked squad, I'm thinking."

"No, sir. I'd rather do this alone."

"Patrick, alone? You're going to need some support."

"Since when?" the ranger asked with a tight grin. "I work well by myself, sir. You know that."

Damian nodded somberly. "It's your call." It felt as though he was saying goodbye to his friend.

"I can do this, Damian."

Damian nodded, but he was far from convinced. He reached his hand out, but then he just leaned forward and hugged Killian.

"Good luck, Patrick."

"Thank you, sir." He walked out.

"Jesus," Luci said.

"Yeah."

CHAPTER 41

Killian trudged forward, through the almost waist-deep water in the tunnel. The conduit had been part of the early flood control system of Landfall, but its use had been supplanted twenty years before by a new, far more extensive system. The old pipes, two meters in diameter, had been all but forgotten, until Killian pored over every record he could find in the civic archives before the federals returned, looking for every space that might be useful for defending—or attacking—the city.

The water was cold and covered with a brown, oily muck. The pipes were no longer in active use, but that didn't stop them from filling up with water, and whatever other fluids flowed down into the old access points and the sections where the cement had collapsed, leaving large holes.

Killian came to a spot where two other pipes combined with the one he was in. The conduit ahead was larger, perhaps two and a half meters in diameter. It was the one that led to his destination, a spot near the Federal Complex. But first he had a detour to make, one he thought of as a waste of time, but he had promised Damian. He knew his chances of seeing his friend again were not good, and he didn't want the last thing he left the general to be a broken promise.

He turned and slipped down the other pipe, heading toward a spot he knew well from the weeks his forces had held out in Landfall. It was the designated rally point, a place all rebel operatives in the capital were supposed to come when called. Damian had insisted on sending out the encoded message. Killian was certain there were none of his people left in Landfall, not after so long. Those who could escape had done so, whether they'd returned to the army or not, and those who couldn't were dead. But a promise was a promise, and it would take him only a few minutes out of his way.

He reached the point and looked up. There was a small access above, a metal hatch he knew led to a mostly abandoned side street. He climbed up the small ladder and reached to the lever, pulling as hard as he could. It was stubborn, but then it slipped free and moved quickly to the open position. He had reached up to push the hatch open when it swung up by itself.

He jumped back, his hand reaching to the gun at his side. In a flash, it was in his hand, his eyes focused on the shadowy figure above. His finger was tight on the trigger, but something stopped him from firing. He'd come to see if any of his people were still there, and while he hadn't expected to find any, he couldn't just shoot, not without being sure.

"Colonel?" The voice was weak, soft. But it was familiar.

His hand loosened a bit on the gun, and he turned his head, focusing on the dark, gaunt figure above him. It was a man, rail thin, haggard-looking, with a long, stringy beard. He had no idea who it was . . . at first.

"Jacob?" His voice was heavy with shock. He'd been sure Jacob North was dead, and could that stout warrior really have wasted away to the figure looking down at him?

"Yes, sir. I got the rally signal." He held up a small comm device, and as Killian looked up, he could see the man had a large rifle in his other hand.

"Jacob, I thought you were dead." Killian climbed farther up the ladder, his body popping about halfway into the street.

"I nearly was, sir." Killian hoisted himself up and reached out to his ranger, embracing him.

North winced as Killian closed his embrace, and he lurched back. "Sorry, sir. My shoulder's a little . . . sore."

Killian's eyes focused on North's shoulder, twisted and disfigured by a wound that had not healed properly . . . or at all. "Jacob . . ."

"It's okay, sir. I tried to get the bullet out, but I'm afraid all I managed was to get it worse infected."

Killian tried to imagine the pain from the wound, and just how his injured soldier had managed to survive the winter. Clearly, North had been short of food. The man had lost at least twenty-five kilos since Killian had seen him last.

"Jacob, we've got to get you to the field hospital."

"After, sir. After the mission. I assume that's why you sent out the signal."

"No, Jacob. I mean, yes, there is a mission, but I can handle it. You just wait here . . ." Killian shook his head. He wasn't really expecting to come back. "Jacob, I need you to follow this tunnel back the way I came. It will take you to a small building near the edge of the city. There's a monorail cut just across the street from there. If you're careful, you can follow it out of Landfall. Our lines are about four kilometers past the city limits."

"No, Colonel . . . I'll go when you go. I'll help you with whatever you're doing first."

"No, Jacob." His voice was firm, almost angry. He felt guilty almost at once, but he didn't have time to argue. "Follow my orders. Let's go." He reached out his hand and helped North climb down the ladder.

"Sir . . ."

"No arguments." He gestured down the way he had come.

"That way, Jacob. Just be careful once you come aboveground. It should be pretty deserted, but there could always be a guard."

"Colonel, I . . ."

"Now, Ranger. You have your orders." Killian stood for a moment, watching North pause and then turn and start down the conduit. He watched for perhaps thirty seconds, and then he continued on his way. He felt good that North had survived, against all his expectations, and he hoped the soldier would make it out. But he had more important things to think about now. Killing Semmes could save thousands of lives, and he told himself that was why he was there. But there was more, and the vengeance he'd so long craved drove him just as much. He didn't want to admit it was even more of a motivation . . . so he tried not to think about it at all.

"Look what Ward's machinations have brought upon us. Union and Hegemony soldiers? On Landfall? Now we have some desperate plan to prevent this disaster, the one he created by reaching out to Federal America's foul brethren?" Cal Jacen was furious. Zig Welch had urged his comrade to hold his tongue until they were clear of army headquarters. Welch understood Jacen's anger toward Damian Ward, but since the victory at Dover, the rebel general was even more revered by his soldiers, and most of the population, as well.

"The general is handling it, Cal. I know he is a potential problem, but for now . . ."

"Potential? It is bad enough that our forces are compelled to assault Landfall on almost no notice, but now even that plan seems to be on hold."

Welch knew Jacen was also mad because Damian hadn't given him any notice of what was going on. If it hadn't been for Violetta Wells, neither of them would even have known there were Union and Hegemony forces in the system. Even getting the information from Violetta had been difficult. She had also fallen under the spell of the great General Ward, and she'd continued to feed information to Jacen only out of her loyalties to the Society and her naïve notion that they were all allies and that their differences were minor.

"Cal, there is nothing we can do now. Whatever differences we have with General Ward, he is no fool. All we can do is wait. The time will come for action."

Jacen stared back, his face twisted with rage. "Oh no, my friend. The time will not come. It is already here. We will allow General Ward to execute whatever scheme he is hatching, and we will hope he is successful. But if our forces do take Landfall, if the federals are broken or withdraw, the good general has outlived his usefulness."

"Violetta will never do it. You know that, right? She worships him just like the rest of the soldiers." Jacen and Welch had once planned to use Violetta as their instrument to assassinate Damian, but Welch knew that plan was as good as dead.

"Yes, I know. She has been useful for information, but ultimately a disappointment. Her commitment to the revolution, the true revolution, has been a disappointment."

"Perhaps, but it leaves us with few opportunities, at least in the immediate future. Violetta was expendable, but if we are to move on the general ourselves, we must be cautious. Nothing can lead to us, Cal. Apart from our Society members, the soldiers would tear us to pieces."

"We will be careful, Zig, but we cannot wait, not if Landfall is taken or if the federals withdraw." Jacen paused, looking at his long-time colleague. "If either of those things happen, Damian Ward must die. Immediately."

Killian slipped back into the alley. He'd heard something, footsteps, he thought. He leaned against the cold stone wall, his fingers gripped tightly around his blade. He had no idea who was coming, but he knew what he had to do. It was likely a fed of some sort . . . the curfew kept civilians in their homes at this hour. That wasn't a guarantee, however, and he couldn't keep his mind free of images of helpless civilians, their throats cut by his own hand.

Any kill, one of a federal soldier, even a Peacekeeper, richly deserving death, was a complication now, and he'd resolved to wait, only to strike if he had no choice. Better to hold for a moment, to see if whoever it was just left. He didn't have much time—he figured maybe ninety minutes before Damian would order the attack—but a fight now had risk, even a quick, clean kill. He didn't have time to hide a body, and if anyone found a dead sentry, all hell would break loose.

He held his breath as he heard the sounds coming closer, and then he felt a wave of relief as they moved off into the distance. He waited, giving an extra moment, and then he looked into the street.

All clear.

He moved across the street, not quite a jog, but as quickly as he could while staying almost silent. He'd had multiple ways to get into Landfall itself, but only one he knew of that led into the Federal Complex. He had to get as far as he could without setting off any alarms. Then he had to find Semmes . . . and when he did, he would shed a burden that had plagued him for years.

He reached a small door, about a meter high, a hatch to an electrical maintenance room. He knew about the room's access to the main federal structure from several former city electricians, all closet rebels who had supported his people when they'd been in Landfall. He moved his hands over the panel, fingers sliding across the touchpad. He knew he could hack the thing. The only question was, could he do it quickly enough and without setting off any alarms?

With another sigh of relief, he felt a small click, and the door popped open. He took one last look out at the street, and then he ducked over and slipped inside.

The tunnel was cramped, the low ceiling barely high enough

for him to crawl. There were conduits and cables all along the walls and ceilings. He knew they should be insulated, but he also suspected maintenance had been spotty since the regular electricians had gone over to the rebellion. One live wire could end his mission in an instant.

He crawled forward cautiously. He had some idea of the layout, and three or four reasonable guesses where he might find Semmes. The building had a few apartments that were plusher than the others, including the one Everett Wells had occupied. If he'd had to bet—which, in essence, he did—he'd have gone with that suite. But this wasn't a normal night, not by a long shot. Killian didn't think much of Semmes, but the man wasn't a complete fool. He had to know he was in danger, and Killian figured he could still be up, in the situation room or somewhere else, directing operations. That would be bad. He might catch Semmes alone in his bedroom, or at most, with a guard at the door. But if he was in the control center, there was no telling how many others might be there. Killian was ready to die to complete his mission, if he had to, but too many officers and soldiers would make it hard to pull off even such a suicide attack.

He came to a hatch, not unlike the one he'd used to get into the tunnel. It was locked as well with the same small touchpad next to it as the first one. He ran his fingers along the pad, entering the same code he'd used before. The hatch popped open, and Killian peered out, his pistol in his hand.

It was a hallway, with unfinished concrete walls, some kind of cellar or subbasement. He climbed down, setting his feet quietly on the floor. Then he turned and looked again each way.

He crept down the corridor, continuing for about ten minutes, every fifty meters or so coming to a turn. There was no one around. He suspected the lower level was empty except when maintenance crews were dispatched. That was unlikely in the middle of the night, not without a real emergency.

He turned his head abruptly. He'd heard something in the hall behind him. At least he thought he had. But when he turned back to look, there was nothing there.

He continued, finally coming to a staircase leading up. He checked behind him again … still nothing. His mind playing tricks on him? If he'd been discovered, no federal would just follow him. He waited a tick, but saw nothing else, and kept moving deeper into the compound.

He made his way through the building, slipping by five or six federals in the hallways, until he came to Wells's old apartment. There was a guard, but he wasn't in front of the door. He was sitting on a small bench at the end of the hall. Killian wasn't sure what that meant, but he knew there was no sneaking past this one. He reached under his shirt and pulled a small throwing knife from its hidden sheath. He gripped it carefully. He'd have one chance, and even if he was able to kill his enemy, the noise could give him away.

No choice.

He swung around the corner, whipping the knife as he did. It felt like the blade took forever to cross the six meters or so to the target, but then it hit its mark, cutting deeply into the soldier's throat. Killian was right behind the blade, his much larger combat knife in his hand now. He reached out and put his left hand over the victim's mouth, muffling his attempted scream, as he plunged the blade deep under the man's rib cage. The soldier fought for a few seconds, and then his body went limp. Killian held on to it, lowering it slowly.

The clock was really racing now. He didn't know if there were surveillance monitors in the hallway, but all it would take was for someone to pass by and see the dead sentry, and it was game over. He searched the man and grabbed the key card on his belt. He turned and pressed it against the touchpad next to the entry, slipping inside as soon as the door slid open. He pulled the man inside with him and raced around the apartment, from one room to the next. He was ready, his pistol in hand. He found a stack of documents, and a quick scan all but assured him this was his intended victim's quarters. But Semmes was nowhere to be found.

Damn.

Killian turned and ran back into the corridor. The situation room was his next bet. If Semmes wasn't asleep at 3:00 A.M., he was dealing with the current crisis.

He made his way through the mostly deserted corridors of the Federal Complex. It was a fair walk from Semmes's quarters to the main tactical area, but he ran into only three federals, and he managed to slip into empty rooms to avoid two of them. The third had come out of one of the rooms, right in front of him. As with the guard outside Semmes's room, he hadn't had any choice there, and he'd left the man dead in the room he'd come from.

He crept up toward the door he knew led to the main control center. Most likely, Semmes was in there. The federal commander would almost certainly not be alone, and that complicated things.

It would have been easier if the bastard had been in his bed . . .

Killian took a deep breath. He knew he'd only have one chance . . . and he also knew his chances of escaping from that room were poor. *Damned poor.*

He'd ached for revenge, for the chance to make the man who'd destroyed his career pay for his offense. Robert Semmes had turned Killian into the monster he knew he'd become, twisted by bitterness and hatred. It was time to repay him for that gift.

Still, it was one thing to crave revenge, to whisper silent prayers for it in the night, vowing again and again your willingness to die to achieve it, and quite another to stand outside the door, knowing you were on the edge of attaining that long sought-after goal, and also staring into the face of almost certain death.

Killian felt his heart pounding, and his mind began to race, images of a free Haven, one he knew he was unlikely to see. He dared to imagine a life on that planet, one where he could shed the demons that had plagued him. As he stood on the cusp of the goal he'd sought for so long, he felt the urge to slip away, to let go of the rage, to look toward the future and not the past.

But that was impossible. If he didn't kill Semmes, thousands of Haven soldiers would die. Worse, they would likely die in a failed attempt to take the city. And if they did fail, Union and Hegemony soldiers would land and engage the federals. Landfall and much of Haven would be reduced to ruins, and in the end his adopted home world would never rid itself of the foreign troopers, no matter which side won.

He couldn't let that happen. He had to kill Semmes. Life, freedom, home . . . that wasn't for him, but just maybe, his death could make it happen for his comrades and friends.

He steeled himself to do what he knew had to be done, but then he heard something. He swung around, looking down the corridor. Then he thought he saw something, a flash of a figure ducking around the corner. But then he wasn't sure. It didn't make sense. If it was a federal, there'd already be alarms sounding, if not gunfire blasting his way.

You're hearing things, Killian. You thought you were more ready for death than you are. Your mind wants more time, a few precious moments of life, but that would come at the cost of risking the mission. Time to go. Now.

He moved toward the door, putting his hand over the small pad next to it. He was ready to pick it if he had to, but then it slid open, revealing a large room full of workstations, not unlike a ship's bridge. There were about half a dozen figures inside, a pair of guards against one wall, a cluster of officers gathered near a center console.

No, more than half a dozen. Seven . . . eight . . .

Killian sprang into action, but it took him perhaps a second to identify Semmes. His target was standing, looking down and pointing at a screen, yelling at one of the other officers.

He whipped up his gun, his eyes locking on his target. But it had taken too long to find Semmes, and he knew it, even as he fired.

The federal commander saw the threat, and he ducked to the side, grabbing the officer next to him and using him as a shield. Killian saw one of his shots hit the officer in the shoulder, even as Semmes slipped completely behind the man.

Dammit!

He tried to take aim, to get another shot at Semmes, but even as he did, he knew he'd been too slow. He could hear orders being shouted, and even as his finger started to tighten on his weapon, a wave of energy hit him. A stun gun. His body went limp and his mind began to slip into darkness.

No . . .

He'd been ready for death, more or less, but fate had devised a worse torment for him. Being captured by the federals.

Being captured by *Semmes*.

CHAPTER 42

"I shouldn't have sent him. I let myself believe in nonsense, that it was possible to get to Semmes. I might just as well have shot him here myself." Damian sat at his makeshift desk, ignoring a small shiver that passed through his body, despite the coat he wore and the small portable heater in the corner.

"That's wrong, sir, and you know it. It was a long shot—one we can't be sure hasn't paid off—but Killian wanted to go. He *had* to go. You know that." Ben Withers was sitting on the other side of the desk, on a small wood-and-cloth folding chair. He managed to look content despite the fact that Damian was well aware of just how uncomfortable that chair was.

Damian nodded. "I know. But I could have ordered him to stay. It wasn't worth throwing his life away. I even let myself believe he had a chance of getting out of there. It's amazing what the mind will do to ward off guilt and self-loathing."

"You've got no call for either, sir," Killian volunteered. "Patrick knew what he was doing. He wasn't just chasing after revenge, though we all know he would have gone just for that. He is trying to save soldiers, perhaps thousands of them." A pause. "You understand how ugly this is going to be if we have to go in. We'll be sending thousands of untrained recruits against federal regulars, entrenched and defending. If there was even a chance of avoiding that . . . Pat Killian is a hero, Damian, but he's not a victim. He knew exactly what he would face."

Damian sighed, looking down at the small chronometer on his desk. "Well, it looks like sending those recruits to their deaths is the next nightmare we've got to face." *There's no "we" here. You're going to send them to hell.*

Damian knew just what was going to happen when his soldiers hit the Landfall defenses. The sudden wave of new recruits had exhausted the supply of weapons built up before the rebellion. Many of his new soldiers had their own guns, weapons vastly inferior to the military-grade assault rifles his veterans carried. Some didn't have rifles at all. He shook his head at the absurdity of sending soldiers into modern combat armed with only knives and household tools. He might as well kill them himself and save the trouble. Worse, he would knowingly use them as cannon fodder, casualties that would allow his veterans, the ones with a chance to win the fight, to get through.

He realized he'd let himself believe Killian could succeed. He'd done it because he considered the ranger a friend, and also because it would have spared him from the nightmare bearing down on him.

"We might as well get ready, Ben. Patrick's likely as not dead already, and we've only got two and a half hours of dark left."

Withers nodded. "I wouldn't give up on Killian just yet, Damian, but you're right. We need to get the troops ready. In case they have to go in."

"Let's get moving." Damian stood, looking across the room at his aide. *There is no "in case," my friend. That's just wishful thinking, a way to try to escape a hell you're already in . . .*

"Violetta, it is good to see you." Cal Jacen walked into the headquarters tent, and he nodded. "I was hoping to catch the general before he left." That was a lie. Jacen had spent the last half hour standing around the perimeter of the camp, waiting for Damian to leave.

"I'm sorry, Mr. Jacen, but you just missed him. He left for the lines. The troops are about to go into Landfall." Her voice was somber. Everybody in camp knew what kind of fight the army had ahead of it.

"Damn. I rushed over, but I was afraid I'd be late."

"You might be able to catch him. He just left."

Jacen turned and looked toward the tent flap. "No, that's okay. I don't want to distract him, not right before the attack. I'll just wait here if that's okay. I was hoping to have a private word with him."

Violetta looked up. "Of course, Mr. Jacen, but he may be quite some time. I think he's planning on leading the attack himself, and there's no way to know how long the fighting will go on."

Maybe a federal bullet will do the job for me. That would make things a lot easier. The fallen hero . . . we could use that very well.

"I think I'll wait. I really do need to see him."

"Okay, Mr. Jacen. I'm sure the general will want to see you as soon as he gets back."

He nodded, and he walked across the tent, sitting on one of the portable chairs. His plan was clear. Violetta was alone in the tent. With any luck he could be waiting when Damian returned. He'd kill the general . . . and then Violetta. Her service to the Society would take a different turn than she'd expected, but one far more useful. She would take the blame, the former governor's daughter, a closet fed, murdering the victorious general at the moment of his triumph. Better still, the assassin killed by his own hand as he walked in on the horror. He would be a hero, and he'd already written the somber address he would give at Damian's funeral, the words that would propel him to control of the senate, to become the firm hand Haven needed to see the revolution to its ultimate fruition.

Killion was on the floor. He was confused, disoriented. For an instant, he didn't know where he was. Then it came together. The stunner.

It had hit him hard, but somehow, he'd managed to remain conscious. Barely.

"I believe we have Patrick Killian here. He served under me during the war, before his cowardice and treachery cost the lives of dozens of my people. I had heard you were crawling like a worm through the bowels of the rebel army, Killian. Now you are here, and no doubt full of useful information about the rebel forces."

Killian's confusion vanished as the unmistakable sound of Semmes's voice cut through his head. He felt a burst of rage, and he tried to lunge forward toward his hated enemy. But his muscles were still spasming, his control over his body only slowly returning.

"You are a piece of shit, Semmes. I might have failed, but someone's going to put a bullet through that head of yours. You'll never leave Haven." It was hard to speak, and he knew his words were soft and a little slurred. But he could see from the rage on Semmes's face, his nemesis had understood every word.

"We will see, Killian. Clearly your pathetic effort has failed. Perhaps there is someone else in that motley army of yours with more ability, but I'm inclined to doubt your idle threats. No doubt you're trying to convince yourself, so you don't die wallowing in hopelessness and failure. Well, I can alleviate your concerns, to an extent. I have no intention of killing you, not for quite some time. We will get every bit of information you possess that is of any value, and then we will make an example of you. You will die, but not before you beg me to let you."

"You will rot in hell before I beg anything from you." Killian's speech was clearer, louder. His anger was helping him overcome the effects of the stunner.

"We shall see." Semmes turned toward an officer standing next to two guards. "Shackle him, Major Brendel. We wouldn't want the infamous Patrick Killian loose in here when the stunner's effects wear off, would we?"

The officer gestured to the two guards—Peacekeepers, Killian recognized from the uniforms—and they moved toward him and grabbed his hands, pulling them behind his back. He resisted. His motor control was returning, but he was still weak, and the troopers wrenched his arms back hard, painfully.

Killian was trying to fight off the hopelessness threatening to take him. His mind was racing, trying to find a way to get loose of his captors. His eye dropped to the major, to the sidearm she wore on her waist. One quick move, a single shot, and Semmes would be dead. And the guards would shoot him, not an ideal result, but far better than weeks of torture at the hands of the Peacekeepers.

But he was too weak. He could shoot the weapon, he was pretty sure of that. Getting it from Brendel would be the problem. She was sharp, attentive. He'd get no jump on her. And his chances of overpowering her in his current state were nil.

Still . . . he had to try.

He pulled his arms back, putting all the strength he could muster into the move. He surprised the two guards, and they reached for him, grabbing at him. He lunged toward Brendel, but before he'd gotten halfway to her, she stepped back, drawing her weapon, and the guards pulled him back, hard.

"A noble attempt, Killian, but not enough, I'm afr—"

The door slid open suddenly, and gunfire erupted. One of the guards fell back, and Killian could feel the man's warm blood splattered across the back of his neck.

He saw Brendel raise her weapon and fire, but even as she did, he saw the expression on her face, and he knew she'd been hit. An instant later, he saw the widening circle of blood, dead center on her chest as she fell back.

He shoved his arm back, smashing his elbow into the face of the remaining guard. The man had been moving to face the door, and Killian caught him by surprise. He spun around, as quickly as he could manage with his still recovering nerves and muscles, and hit the trooper as hard as he could. The man fell to his knees and then backward to the ground, clutching at his crushed larynx as he struggled to breathe.

Killian still didn't know what had happened, but he dove toward Brendel's body, grabbing for the pistol she'd dropped. His eyes shot a quick glance toward the door, and he saw a lone figure, gaunt, slim.

Jacob North.

He followed me. That was what I kept hearing . . .

He felt a rush of excitement, and then he saw his savior drop to his knees, blood pouring from a hideous wound on his neck. *Brendel got off a shot . . .*

He shook his mind free for an instant. His hand felt the cold plastic grip of Brendel's gun. He looked up. Semmes was rushing toward a door on the far side of the room. He had a second, perhaps two. Then his enemy would escape. There was another officer on the far side of the room, and two guards behind him, regulars. The guards were bringing their weapons to bear even as Killian took aim.

He pulled the trigger, his eyes focused on his target as the top of Semmes's head exploded in a grotesque cloud of red mist and chunks of bone. The federal commander dropped hard, his momentum carrying him into the far wall.

Killian knew he was dead. The guards would fire any second. But he was ready. He'd done what he'd come to do. Perhaps now Damian could negotiate with the new federal commander. And the man who had destroyed his life was dead by his hand. There were worse ways to die.

"Hold!"

The voice was loud, commanding. Killian wasn't sure what was happening, but he was still alive. He looked up and saw that the other officer had issued the order. The two guards had their weapons trained on him, but they hadn't fired.

"Drop the weapon, Colonel Killian."

Killian paused for an instant, but then he did as the officer commanded. He stayed where he was for a moment, but then he turned to the side, crawled toward North.

"Jacob," he said, still not knowing what was happening, why the federals had not killed him yet.

"Did we do it, sir? Did we get him?"

"Yes, Jacob." Killian felt his emotions rising up. He'd given North up for dead months before, and he still hadn't reconciled with the shock of finding his ranger alive. Now, as he looked down at the stricken soldier, the guilt began to come on him. He'd abandoned one of his most loyal troopers, left him to fend for garbage in the streets and to hide from roving patrols through the coldest winter since Haven had been colonized. North had hidden, hour after hour, day after day, enduring the pain of his infected wound. And yet he'd answered the call, come to Killian's aid.

And now he was dying, the price he'd paid to save Killian.

"For freedom, Colonel. For the rebellion." North looked at Killian for another second, and then he let out a final deep breath, and it was over.

Killian stared at North's face, his hands moving slowly, closing the dead man's eyes. He knew the federals were still there, that he would likely follow North to the grave, now or after weeks of hell at the hands of the inquisitors. But he didn't care, not right now.

"General Semmes was assassinated by a rogue colonist, Sergeant. The assassin also killed Major Brendel and her two guards . . ." the federal officer was saying. He walked across the room, and Killian watched as he stood over the wounded Peacekeeper, pulling out his own pistol and firing a single shot. "The major killed the assassin as well, with her final shot."

Killian looked up at the officer, utterly confused as to what was going on. Then he recognized the man. Colonel Granz. He remembered Granz from the first war, though the officer had been a major then.

"Colonel Killian, I think it's time for you to leave the way you came."

Killian had gotten back to his feet. "Colonel Granz?"

"I see you remember me." He looked over at Semmes's body. "The general would have gotten thousands of soldiers needlessly killed, and still lost Alpha-2 in the end." He looked over at North's body. "This assassin did us a service, of a sort. Perhaps we can end this pointless conflict now, before more men and women die to no purpose."

"Yes, sir . . . Colonel. I, ah . . ." Killian didn't know what to say. Of all the scenarios he'd imagined, this wasn't one of them.

"I would love to sit and talk about old times, Colonel Killian, but for a man who wasn't here you are awfully . . . present. Perhaps you should be going, as I suggested before. And use those skills we've seen so much of in the field to make sure no one sees you." He turned to face the two guards standing behind him. "The sergeant and the corporal here didn't see anything except General Semmes's assassin, isn't that right, Sergeant?"

"Yes, sir," the noncom snapped, not a hint of emotion in his voice. It was clear Granz had chosen his most loyal troopers for duty in the army's headquarters.

"Yes, Colonel . . ." Killian nodded. "I believe you are right." He took a last look at North, and then he turned toward the door. He stopped, pausing a moment. He didn't turn around. He just said simply, "Thank you, Colonel." Then he slipped out into the hall and headed back toward the tunnels.

CHAPTER 43

"I have spoken with both Admiral Bellakov and Ambassador Kutusov, and they have agreed to extend the withdrawal deadline by forty-eight hours."

Damian sighed softly as he adjusted the portable headset he wore. The communiqué had been a bit more involved than that. The Union officials had pushed hard to land forces, stating that the federals' failure to meet the deadline gave them every cause to do so. Just to ensure against any treachery by the federal forces, of course. Damian had come close to stating that his army would consider *any* Earth troops that landed to be invaders and respond accordingly. He'd never considered himself a diplomat, but he had to admit, he'd trod a masterful line between threatening hostilities and enthusiastically thanking allies.

"Thank you, General Ward. Admiral Taggart has mobilized every shuttle in the fleet. We will make the revised deadline." A short pause. "You understand, General, that neither I nor the admiral have any authority to grant cease-fires or peace treaties, and certainly none to recognize your independence. All I can do is evacuate my forces, and that is all the admiral can do, as well. There's a good chance we will both face considerable disciplinary action when we return."

"I understand, Colonel. Ambassador Nerov will be returning to Earth with the Union forces to negotiate with the senate." John Danforth had corrected the earlier oversight. Sasha Nerov would conduct her affairs this time as a fully authorized and credentialed ambassador, for whatever that was worth negotiating with a body that didn't yet recognize Haven's authority to grant such titles.

"I wish you well, General. You were one of us once, and it showed. The Havenites would never have prevailed without your leadership."

"Thank you, Colonel. That means a lot. For what it is worth, Colonel, I believe things would have been quite different if you had been in command. Semmes's . . . shortcomings . . . contributed to the final outcome."

"Your forces can occupy Landfall in three days' time. Is that satisfactory?" Granz didn't respond to Damian's roundabout tribute, but his expression softened. Slightly.

"It is, Colonel. I wish you the best as well. I hope that you are not unjustly treated. You deserve better." *You deserve a better nation to serve.* He found himself wanting to invite Granz to stay, but he knew it was pointless. Granz would never leave his troops now, and the officer had served Federal America for far too long. He would see defecting as an act of disloyalty. *Too bad. We will need men like Granz if we're to build a viable nation.*

Damian walked back to the small tent he was still using as an office. He'd just returned from the front when he'd been called to the communications shed to take Nerov's transmission. He'd been moments from sending the army in, launching the attack he knew would be a horrendous bloodbath, when Granz's communiqué had come in. He'd been stunned at what the federal officer had said. Jacob North had killed Semmes? None of it made much sense, at least not until several hours later, when Killian walked back into camp and told him everything that had happened. He'd known the regulars didn't like Semmes, but he was still stunned at what had transpired.

Granz was right, of course. Any deals he made were subject to the senate's approval or rejection. But the rebellion was over, Damian was sure of that. There would be negotiations, and no doubt the new republic would have to make various concessions to its former government, quotas of raw materials, for example. Damian had already spoken to Nerov, and he'd told her she could agree to anything she thought made sense, but not any provisions that interfered with what she had already promised the Union and Hegemony—or anything that would ultimately put the planet in the sphere of influence of another nation ever again. He knew he'd overstepped his bounds, issued directives that should have come from President Danforth, but he did it anyway. He had no interest in becoming a politician, but he would not allow the republic's new allies to be betrayed, even though he knew full well they would have taken any chance to try to seize control for themselves. He'd fought for a free Haven, and he'd be damned if he'd see it become another version of the foul governments that ruled Earth. He'd lead another rebellion before he'd allow that.

He walked through the tent flap and saw Violetta. He'd come to like Everett Wells's daughter. He respected the strength it must have taken for her to stand up to her father, to give up all she had to remain on Haven. She'd been a good aide, and he intended to make sure she was well set up in some kind of civilian career. She deserved nothing less.

"It looks like the rebellion is over, Violetta." He smiled, but he could see from her expression they were not alone. He turned, and the instant he did, the pleasant feelings of victory slipped away.

"What do you want, Jacen?" His voice was coarse, and he made no effort to hide his distaste for his visitor.

"I wanted to congratulate you, General, on our great victory. We have much to celebrate. And much to discuss."

"I do agree the end of the rebellion is cause for celebration, but I might suggest that we wait until the federals are off-world and all the Earth fleets in the system have departed." He paused, turning away from Jacen. "As far as us having much to discuss, I suggest you seek out President Danforth. My responsibility is ensuring the withdrawal of the federals, nothing more. And frankly, I don't much care to have protracted discussions with you. I suspect we agree on very little."

Damian started to walk toward the flap that separated the anteroom from his office. He stopped suddenly. It was something, a feeling, a quick glimpse of movement that didn't look right. Perhaps just combat reflexes?

He spun around, his hand dropping to his pistol, even as he saw the weapon in Jacen's hand. He was going to be too late, he could see that in an instant. He felt his muscles react, trying to dodge the shot he knew was coming. They did the job, in part at least, and the bullet that was aimed at his heart hit his arm.

He fell to the ground, his balance lost as much by his wild evasive maneuver as by the wound itself, and he hit the dirt hard. He rolled to the side, trying to avoid the second shot he knew was coming. But it didn't. Not right away.

He could hear Violetta scream, and then a crashing sound. His eyes barely caught the image of her throwing her tablet at Jacen . . . and then he saw the Society leader turn and shoot her.

Damian saw red. He cursed himself for not taking care of Jacen sooner. He was trying to move, to pick up the pistol he'd dropped, but he wasn't going to get it in time. Violetta's sacrifice would be for naught. Jacen would succeed in his assassination, and he had no doubt the liar had a perfect story concocted already.

Damian's hand gripped the pistol, even as he tensed, waiting for the bullet he was sure was coming. Then he heard a loud crack . . . but he didn't feel the impact. He swung around, bringing his pistol to bear. But the man standing in his field of view wasn't Jacen. His would-be assassin was on the ground, dead.

"We caught Zig Welch hanging around the perimeter, Damian.

Evidently he was the backup if Jacen failed. He didn't want to talk at first, but it's amazing how much you can incentivize someone by putting a gun to their head." John Danforth stepped forward, reaching out to Damian, the guards behind him moving quickly into the tent. "How badly are you hurt?"

"It's nothing. But Violetta . . ."

Damian was very afraid his aide was dead, so he was pleasantly shocked when he saw that she was breathing as he limped across the room. "Get the medics in here," he screamed to the troopers standing around the room.

He looked down at her, pulling open her jacket. He was scared at what he might find, but then he saw the wound. It was bad enough, yet he was pretty sure it wasn't mortal. She'd spend some time in the hospital, but her heroism wouldn't claim her life. Damian was relieved. Violetta didn't deserve to die, and enough people had fallen already in the rebellion. It was time for peace, for rebuilding. For creating a nation that was worth the price so many had paid to make it a reality.

Damian stood up, stepping aside as the medics came into the tent. As they started working on Violetta, he looked at Danforth. "Thanks, John. I know he was your friend, once."

"I don't know what he was, Damian. Was he always a monster, insane, so radical he would do anything to see his twisted ideas become reality? Or did the rebellion do this to him? I don't think we'll ever know."

"And I don't care. I never saw the good in him you did. We're better off without him." He paused for a few seconds. "Anyway, John, my work is almost done. Once the federals are gone, we'll know we've won. There's no way the senate could fund another expedition, especially one likely to trigger reactions from the Union and the Hegemony."

"I am inclined to agree with you, Damian—to a degree. Yes, we are as good as free. But the work is just beginning. If Cal Jacen has taught us one thing, it's that we must be vigilant. There are always those who would steal freedom, even in the guise of saving it."

"That's true, John, but *your* work is just starting. I'm no politician. I told you that when I took my commission, and I'm telling you now. I'll see that the federals are gone, and I'll stay through disbanding the army. But then I'm a farmer again, and this time I'm going to stay one."

He paused and smiled at his friend. "You're a good man, John, one I'm honored to call my friend, and my president. Do what I know you can do now: prove to us all that political leaders can be something other than the self-serving, power-mad vermin they've been throughout human history. Show us the Haven we've dreamed of, fought for, is actually possible. I think my work will pale in comparison to what we all hope and pray you are able to do."

Danforth nodded. "I will try, Damian. I will give it all I have to give."

"That is all we can ask of any man." Damian smiled, and then he saluted the president. "To the Haven Republic. To freedom and prosperity."

EPILOGUE

Jamie Grant climbed slowly from the transport, wincing as he did, more at the fatigue than any real pain he felt. The suits had been a massive success, but not without cost. He had been battered and bruised more in the last few days than he'd experienced in the prison mine, but the worst had been the radiation poisoning. Almost all of his surviving troopers had endured trying rehab periods, his own among the most arduous. He was through it now, all but the crushing exhaustion, and the doctors had assured him that would pass relatively quickly.

All things considered, though he knew he'd have some sustained side effects, he was among the fortunate ones. The rebellion had been good to him, seeing his transition from a slave-prisoner sent to the mines to die to a man with a future . . . and someone to share that with.

Katia ran around the transport, rushing over to his side, slipping her arm under his, helping to steady him as he walked toward the house. They'd had a few months there before the federals returned to Haven, but now he dared to hope their lives together could truly begin.

Jamie had become a more successful soldier than he'd dared to dream, but he'd had enough of war. More than enough war—he'd gotten his fill of revenge against the federals who had so unjustly im-

prisoned him all those years ago. The blood he'd let in the woods . . .
he never needed that experience again. He craved little more than
hard and satisfying days in the fields, helping Damian get the farm
back in shape . . . and quiet evenings with Katia. Perhaps even children one day.

Haven was free, and so was Jamie . . . and he intended to grate-
fully embrace all that offered him.

Jonas Holcomb sat quietly in his lab, staring at the piles of data chips
and bits and pieces of circuitry. His suits had played a vital role in
the battle that had led to Haven's independence, something he'd
hoped for, but still surprised him. The whole operation had been
so shoestring, so much of the tech specified on his original plans
jury-rigged and half-assed. *But it worked.*

It actually worked.

He looked down at the schematics on the table, drawing after drawing, his original designs re-created in their entirety, and much more.
He'd been dedicated to his work for most of his life, and he'd thought
he had lost that forever. There was no way he would ever design more
weapons for Federal America's political masters. But he would finish
the designs of the suits, and he would see them produced, properly
this time and not thrown together in a bunch of sheds. His disillusion-
ment was gone now, his disgust at serving Federal America replaced
by loyalty to a new home, and a determination to do all he could to
ensure Haven's independence and its ability to defend itself.

If Federal America tried to come back in a few years to retake
their lost colony or if any of Haven's new "allies" decided to try anything, they would have a rude awakening.

His creations would be waiting for them.

Asha Stanton sat in front of the fireplace, staring into the flames, her
thoughts drifting over the events of the past few months. Haven was
free, Robert Semmes was dead . . . and Alistair Semmes had been

hard-pressed to hold his senate seat when the word came out about the true scope of the resources he'd funneled to his son's failed attempt to crush the rebellion. The old power broker had survived, barely, but his influence was greatly diminished. She had nothing to fear from him, not with her family's money behind her.

She thought of Everett Wells, of his death in prison. She'd never considered him a man of particular courage, but now she reconsidered that assessment. He'd done what she'd asked, sacrificed himself to keep alive the effort to defeat Semmes and ensure Violetta's safety. She found herself grateful . . . and guilty, too. She wondered if there had been any way to rescue him instead of getting him to commit suicide. There hadn't been, not really, but that didn't keep some doubt from plaguing her.

She'd kept her word at least, reaching out to Violetta on Haven and offering to help her return to Earth and establish herself, but the girl had refused. She was a Havenite now, through and through, and with her father gone, she had nothing left on Earth. Asha had offered her currency, which she'd also refused, so then Asha had set up a trust—as much of one as she could in Haven's new financial system. Violetta wouldn't even know about the money, not for five years or until the executor determined that she needed it. Asha told herself she was just keeping a promise, but the extended effort to look out for Wells's daughter was also her way of dealing with the guilt over all that had happened.

She let herself dream that when the senate shakeup was complete, her own disgrace would be washed away, that her dream of becoming a member of the august body could be reincarnated. She wasn't sure if such thoughts were realistic or just wishful thinking. But there was no question, her situation had improved. Only time would tell how much.

John Danforth stood on the hillside, looking out over the workers moving all around, pulling out charred chunks of what had once been his home. Danforth Hall would be rebuilt. That was the easy part. Dealing with all those lost in the war and their dependents, and forging a new nation worthy of such sacrifice, that would be the truly difficult task. So many Havenites had lost loved ones, himself included. His brother had worked with him in the years leading up to the rebellion, but he'd been fated not to survive long after the outbreak of open hostilities.

He felt pressure now, pressure to make good on so many promises and expectations. He'd prepared for revolution for so long, and then the battle had been so terrible. He'd come to doubt what he had done, wondered if anything could be worth such horrendous losses. He wanted to say yes, to thrust his arm into the sky and declare that Haven would be a model for the future of mankind. But he knew history better than that, enough to realize the odds were against the fledgling republic. Corruption and oppression in government were so endemic—almost the default in human society—constantly encroaching on freedom. He would try to prevent that from happening to Haven, but there were a thousand ways even he could become the seed of liberty's downfall. Cal Jacen had been only a warning. How many others were out there, waiting for their chance to grasp at power, to mold Haven in the image they wanted?

He'd asked Damian to take control of the army, to find a way to win Haven's independence. Somehow, despite every difficulty, every challenge, his friend had done just that. Now it was his turn. He couldn't let Damian down, nor all the soldiers who'd fought so bravely for independence.

I won't fail you, brother. I won't fail you, Damian.
I won't fail you, Haven.

Damian walked in the cool drizzle. The chill of autumn was in the air, and he buttoned up his coat, suppressing a small shiver. The spring and summer had been crazy, exciting, one hectic negotiation after another. But now everything was done. The senate of

Federal America had approved the Treaty of Beijing, and all three of Earth's superpowers had recognized Haven's freedom. The republic, so long a dream, was now a reality. Whether it would live up to the hopes of so many remained to be seen, but Damian had chosen to be optimistic.

He'd taken on his own mission, even as he gradually disbanded the army. His people had hunted down Society members, rooting out those responsible for various crimes, including the murder of loyalists in Landfall. Those atrocities had been unforgivable in Damian's view, and they had served only to energize the loyalists' hatred of the rebels and send them flocking to the new battalions Semmes had organized. The bitterness had been too great to overcome, the dozens of incidents of rebels and loyalists conducting savage reprisals against each other, making the idea of rapprochement inconceivable.

John Danforth had handled the situation with considerable wisdom, allowing the loyalists to emigrate to Earth, and ensuring that they were able to receive fair value for all their possessions, despite the fact that rapacious profit-seekers had sought to virtually steal the properties of those they considered traitors. When Federal America had refused to pay the transport costs for the repatriated loyalists, Danforth had stepped in and committed the government to fund the emigration. With that act, Haven's president had proved himself an honorable man, and he'd given the new republic something else that seemed to be a rite of passage for a nation.

Its first national debt.

Damian continued down the stone path, sighing softly as he did. He'd just come from his last meeting with his officers, a meal with the men and women who had fought and bled and struggled to help him achieve Haven's independence. Many of them were fellow farmers from around Landfall, and he knew he'd see them on a fairly regular basis, but the hours they'd spent together talking had made him realize just how much he'd changed. He'd told himself all he wanted was to return to the farm, and to an extent that was true. But now he realized how much he would miss the camaraderie of his fellow soldiers. He was glad the killing was behind them, but memories flooded through his mind, nights around the fires, talks that ran well into the night. He'd been thrust against his will into the role of Haven's first general, and that experience would always be with him.

He stopped abruptly, looking down at the well-tended gravestone. "Hello, Alex. I know it's been a long time. The rebellion is over. Haven is free. I know you were on the other side, that you never really had a chance. I'm so sorry. I think you would have been happy with us, and I know you would have looked forward to a life of true freedom. You never really had the opportunity to imagine a future like that. You adhered to your duty, did what you believed you had to do. I understand that, and I respect you immensely for it. I know you wanted more from me than friendship and respect, and I'm sorry for any pain I caused you."

He took a deep breath, and he looked down at the grave, the grass covering it just beginning to turn brown. "You will always be with us, Alex, and you will be remembered fondly and respected as a good and honorable soldier. I miss you, and for whatever meager consolation that might have given you, I will endure it, and I will remember all that you were, and the wondrous array of all you could have been had fate been kinder."

Damian realized that all he'd done, whatever role he'd played in the rebellion . . . none of it would have been possible if Alex Thornton hadn't saved his life. Though she'd served the other side, he was sure, if she'd lived, she would have rallied to the rebellion. And he would make sure everyone else believed that as well. He would make sure she was listed among the heroes of the rebellion, with all the others who had fallen.

It was a miserable bit of recognition, but it was all he had to give her, all he had to offer to a friend.

He looked at her grave a little while longer, and in a flash, the two years passed through him like a bolt of lightning. He shivered, then frowned, but then he smiled.

He turned around, and headed back to the whole reason he had fought in the first place.

He headed back to his home.

ABOUT THE AUTHOR

Jay Allan currently lives in New York City, and has been reading science fiction and fantasy for just about as long as he's been reading. His tastes are fairly varied and eclectic, but favorites include military and dystopian science fiction, space opera, and epic fantasy—all usually a little bit gritty.

He writes a lot of science fiction with military themes, but also other SF and some fantasy as well. He likes complex characters and lots of backstory and action, but in the end believes world-building is the heart of science fiction and fantasy.

Before becoming a professional writer, Jay has been an investor and real estate developer. When not writing, he enjoys traveling, running, hiking, and—of course—reading. He also loves hearing from readers and always answers emails. You can reach him at jay@jayallanbooks.com, and join his mailing list at http://www.crimson worlds.com for updates on new releases.

Among other things, he is the author of the bestselling Crimson Worlds series.